POLL HAVEN

By C. Locke Marshall

**FriesenPress**

Suite 300 - 990 Fort St
Victoria, BC, Canada, V8V 3K2
www.friesenpress.com

Copyright © 2014 by C. Locke Marshall
First Edition — 2014

All rights reserved.

No part of this publication may be reproduced in any form, or by any means, electronic or mechanical, including photocopying, recording, or any information browsing, storage, or retrieval system, without permission in writing from the publisher.

ISBN
978-1-4602-5837-8 (Hardcover)
978-1-4602-5838-5 (Paperback)
978-1-4602-5839-2 (eBook)

1. Fiction, General

COVER DESIGN: SHELLY MERCER

Distributed to the trade by The Ingram Book Company

TABLE OF CONTENTS

Chapter 1 ✷ Late for 6:00	1
Chapter 2 ✷ Range Patrol	7
Chapter 3 ✷ Bogs	12
Chapter 4 ✷ Wait	20
Chapter 5 ✷ Spooked	24
Chapter 6 ✷ Recovery	32
Chapter 7 ✷ After Dark	37
Chapter 8 ✷ Home	41
Chapter 9 ✷ Kent	44
Chapter 10 ✷ Cat's Out	50
Chapter 11 ✷ Dear Diary	55
Chapter 12 ✷ Becky	61
Chapter 13 ✷ Puzzles	71
Chapter 14 ✷ Cackle Berries	79
Chapter 15 ✷ Explorers	85
Chapter 16 ✷ Fur	95
Chapter 17 ✷ The Service	101
Chapter 18 ✷ Declarations	109
Chapter 19 ✷ Intimidation	115
Chapter 20 ✷ Try Two	121
Chapter 21 ✷ Shoes	130
Chapter 22 ✷ Confessions	135

Chapter 23 ✷ A Night Out	143
Chapter 24 ✷ Admissions	153
Chapter 25 ✷ A Touch of Silver	156
Chapter 26 ✷ Phone Home	162
Chapter 27 ✷ Runoff	167
Chapter 28 ✷ Lost Histories	173
Chapter 29 ✷ The Den	183
Chapter 30 ✷ Have It Out	195
Chapter 31 ✷ Guidance	199
Chapter 32 ✷ Burn	208
Chapter 33 ✷ Interrogation	212
Chapter 34 ✷ Solitary Patrol	221
Chapter 35 ✷ Pick Up	227
Chapter 36 ✷ Way Out	231
Chapter 37 ✷ Homing	238
Chapter 38 ✷ Run	243
Chapter 39 ✷ Hemmed In	249
Chapter 40 ✷ An Offer	256
Chapter 41 ✷ The Slow Stampede	263
Chapter 42 ✷ Crash the Line!	266
Chapter 43 ✷ Corpse	273
Chapter 44 ✷ Surprise!	279
Chapter 45 ✷ Saving Saviours	283
Chapter 46 ✷ Haven to Haven	291

Chapter 47 ✳ Move	294
Chapter 48 ✳ Choice	298
Chapter 49 ✳ Breakdown	305
Chapter 50 ✳ Gone to the Dogs	307
Acknowledgements:	312

To my ranching friends and neighbours

Any similarity between the characters of this book and persons alive or dead is not coincidental. No one character is the exact likeness of any particular man, woman or child. However, to create the story I have liberally recombined the traits of many of the friends and neighbours I respect and love.

CHAPTER 1 ✷ LATE FOR 6:00

Bang! Rat-tat-tat, rat-tat-tat. The washboard road played an intermittent tattoo on the sixteen foot stock trailer that would have been the envy of the snare in any pipe band. It was already 6:10 and Mart was just passing the old one-room Seddon school house. The early morning half-light feebly illuminated the rubble inside the door of the derelict building through the bedsprings tacked across its open doorway to keep out the livestock.

Old Wendell would be chomping at the tbit. Even at the end of summer when the light was barely good enough to spot a Charolais bull in a mud hole, the old geezer insisted on a six o'clock start. In July the early departure beat the heat and the flies, but here at the end of August it was just plain stubbornness.

Mart had just about vibrated the rust-eaten doors right off the 1986 Wylee trailer after he left Alberta Highway 5. He was hoping Skip wouldn't be standing on his head when he opened those doors. Mart had taken the hairpin at the Beazer turnoff at such a rate of speed that he wasn't completely sure if light hadn't been showing beneath the passenger side trailer tires.

He took his battered hat off and threw it on the empty seat beside him. It landed on a lone glove that had no mate, two Mountain Dew cans and the brown bag from yesterday's lunch. There was a funky cloud of dust hanging above the ripped floor mat where his second best lariat was struggling to remain on top of a bouncing tow chain. He noticed that his lost hay hook had worked out from under the passenger side seat and was threatening to wear a hole in the heater vent.

Mart cursed himself as he slowed to take the crossing over a small tributary to Tough Creek. Why did he care that the crotchety octogenarian would be chafing? He wished he could just convince himself to let the old bugger wait. He rubbed the stubble on his face and reflected, with some self-loathing, on why he continued to dance to the old man's tune. Ever since Mart had spent that first summer at Uncle Seth and Aunt Emma's place he had been trying to measure up. You would have thought that his hometown, Medicine Hat, was New York City, or on Jupiter for that matter, the way some of the locals treated him like an absolute rookie. Most had never been mean about it, but he couldn't bear the, 'what can you expect from the city kid' look. He had tried to persuade himself that intolerant attitude was just something he perceived and that wasn't really there, but he had never quite been able to shake the insecurity. When he found out he would be sent to help at the ranch for yet another school break, he was determined that there would be no reason anyone could call him a greenhorn again.

He had done pretty well, too. By August of the second summer he could ride harder and longer than half the kids in all of Mountain View, Hill Spring and Leavitt. That was back when everyone worked stock from horseback. If things were then like they are now, that wouldn't have been hard to do. Many of the ranchers nowadays did the greater percentage of their stock work from the back of an ATV. Today some of the ranch kids could hardly saddle a horse let alone ride one for six hours straight.

Sticking to the old way of doing things had been easy enough given the circumstances. Seth Tidwell scoffed at the motorcycle cowboys and would not give in to Mart's yearning for a dirt bike. Then when his uncle had died, and he came to run the ranch for

Aunt Em, there hadn't been the money for much in the way of extra equipment.

The clock on the dash of the '91 Chevy said it was 5:14. That meant it was really quarter past six. Here it was the end of summer and he still hadn't remembered how to change the clock to match Daylight Savings Time. He dropped another gear to wind up the rutted hill leading into the shadowy deciduous forest at the edge of the community pasture. The quaking aspen leaves were twisting languidly back and forth on their stems. He hoped the breeze would last. It was odd that they were finally getting hot weather after a wet, cool summer. The pickup growled up the incline and Mart did another quick shift to avoid rolling back down the hill. The old half-ton and bumper hitch were hardly up to hauling stock on anything but flat ground. It was a good thing that only Skip was in the back. Mart couldn't help but envy the neighbours who had graduated to fifth-wheel trailers and three-quarter-ton trucks.

The deeply-rutted track led through the open wire gate and took a sharp right-hand turn. There, just east of the corrals, was Wendell's Ford and two-horse straight load. He was probably the only guy left in southern Alberta whose outfit was as outdated as Mart's. As could have been predicted, Wendell was leaning in the open door of the cab, a loose set of reins looping out the open door. The ends of the lines were attached to the bridle of a large grey mare standing hipshot and head down. She was looking as weary as if she'd been ridden a league or more before the ride had even started.

The old rancher did not look up when Mart pulled his trailer in a semicircle to point back toward the gate. The young rancher automatically turned down the radio. At least Wendell would have only criticized the infernal racket generally rather than abusing him for his choice of CJOC, the classic rock station, over Country 95. That was the typical censure he faced at the hands the rest of his ranching friends.

Mart turned off the ignition, let the truck roll until it stopped on its own, and then left it in first. He tossed the keys on the floor at the same time as he threw open the door and headed for the back of the trailer. He could hear Skip shift around while he rattled away at the lever that would allow the wide rear door to swing open. Even without considering the general lack of daylight and the shaded interior of the stock trailer, it would have been hard to see the horse two thirds of the way back. The dust from the gravel road had slipped under the doors and through the open slots along the sides of the vehicle. It was floating like smoke from a smouldering fire. Mart could just make out Skip's narrow white blaze through the haze. He walked in and took the halter off the horse and left it hanging by the braided rope shank from the metal tubing rail. He lifted the bridle from the saddle horn and slipped the bit into the willing animal's mouth. He noticed the horse's eyes were blinking out the road dirt and apologized softly for having driven so recklessly over the rocks and powdery ruts.

He accomplished all of this quickly, with an ease bred of habitude. Nevertheless, Wendell was already in the saddle and had walked the old mare up to the rear of the trailer as Mart and Skip stepped out.

"Rooster die?" was Wendell Jacobsen's greeting.

Mart opted for a good-humoured reply in the hope that the codger would lighten up. "Ate the bird last night."

Mart could not see Wendell's reaction because he had already turned his mount south to pick up the narrow track where their patrol would start. Mart still needed to retrieve his lunch from the cab and a battered plastic pop bottle full of ice he had almost forgotten in the deep freeze during this morning's rush. He watched the old-timer ride away while he pulled the latigo up a couple of notches to tighten the cinch. As much as he would have liked to please his riding partner by showing up on time, there was no longer any hurry. Wendell never pushed the grey mare.

The horse was unflappable, but she was also the slowest walker in the equine world. Her large head and wide hooves betrayed draught horse ancestry. Tom Wyslik had once noted that the only way to tell if Wendell and the grey were moving across the prairie was to stand where you could see a line of fence posts behind them.

Mart's anticipation of the slow pace is why he had selected Skip. Although the nine year old sorrel Quarter Horse could get out and walk pretty well when encouraged, he would dog along quite willingly with Wendell's mare. He seemed to enjoy the vacation.

Most of the quakers' leaves had ceased their fluttering. Only the edges of the clumps of trees were being worried intermittently by currents of air that were not easily detected by the horses or the humans making their way through the vertical latticework of greenish white trunks. Flies would be at the horses before long. Right now the air was cool, but Mart left his worn jean jacket on the seat of the pickup. His slicker was tied on behind the old Eamor saddle just in case. It had not paid to leave home without it this year.

The younger man caught up with the older one, but felt no need to converse immediately. He had pulled range patrol duty often with Wendell Jacobsen. Some of the other pasture riders were less enthusiastic about spending the day with the cantankerous fellow, or at least less reticent when it came to expressing their desire for more congenial companionship. At first Mart had just been too timid to make waves. Now he had to admit that he enjoyed the quiet rides punctuated now and then with the old-timer's repetitive history lessons. He sometimes worried he was becoming as reclusive as Wendell.

From the beginning of this morning's ride, it became apparent it would fit the mould. Wendell and his mare strolled along without looking at Mart, let alone striking up any type of friendly conversation. Mart took in the cool clean air and the green world that composed the backdrop.

CHAPTER 2 ✳ RANGE PATROL

THE CORRALS WERE located at the northeast corner of the grazing lease. From there the two ranchers had ridden southwest, picking up a trail that would eventually lead to the Tower Field up against the US boundary. To the border it was six kilometres, or the width of four sections as the crow flies. However, the pair were not birds and they definitely were not flying. Mart had come prepared to spend the day.

The area around the corrals and trails leading south or west from them was a complete morass from a mixture of wet weather and a multitude of rubber tires. The past two or three summers had certainly not been the normal hot dry months to which most locals had become accustomed.

The Poll Haven Grazing Association leased this provincial crown land. There were thirty-five members who held permits to graze anywhere from six to twenty-nine animal units during the four month grazing season. A cow-calf pair was considered 1.2 animal units and a yearling 0.75.

"These sixteen sections used to be part of the national park."

Mart rolled his eyes, but grinned. It hadn't taken the old boy long to start up. The Poll Haven Community Pasture was in the southwest portion of the province of Alberta, adjacent to Waterton Lakes National Park. East and north of the community grazing lease were mostly private lands and a few other provincial government leases.

"Used to be pretty much all one big chunk of brush and rangeland. Trees covered most of the landscape back then, but there were some open meadows and a few clearings have been made by logging. Now it's divided into several fields by cross-fences."

"It would have been nice if they'd divided it up more evenly," Mart attempted to redirect the lecture.

"Nonsense! Yeah, some fields are larger than others, but it all has to do with the terrain. You can't cut a mountain up like a pie!"

Mart smiled and shook his head. He was used to being corrected by Wendell. Other folks didn't take it so well. Wendell had a habit of pushing the buttons of just about everyone he knew. The old guy had never been too shy to chide anyone he found lacking.

Each of the members having stock in the pasture were obligated to participate in at least three days of fencing and some of the bi-weekly rides to check fences, make sure gates had not been left down and to push cattle around when necessary to make better use of the limited grass. At the end of the season all the members were required to participate in three days of round-up to take the cattle out.

For today's riders, a significant elevation gain was disguised by its gradual nature and the frequent ups and downs of the terrain. Before they were finished Mart and Wendell would have gained and lost most of 300 metres several times. Half an hour after mounting up, the sun popped out of the eastern prairie. Mart watched the clear alpine air against Chief Mountain transform into a late summer haze. With the haze came the warmth. By mid-morning the smell of horse sweat was noticeable in spite of the leisurely pace. Sunbeams had made a million silver coins of as many dewy aspen leaves. The darker pines and spruce on the highlands to the west made a breeching black whale of Mokowan Butte.

Two large spurs branched off of Mokowan and extended their toes eastward into the community pasture. First, to the north, was Poll Haven itself, and then the Hog's Back. Aspens gave way to conifers on those slopes and the rich odour of pine, fir and spruce floated down. Cooler bands of air snaked along the gullies and chilled the perspiration on Mart's face. The 1,500 metres of elevation tempered the late summer heat, but by afternoon the effect would be lost. The trees would block any breeze and they would wallow in the humidity rising from the waterlogged soil.

The pair of riders had crossed from the Corral Pasture into the Lake Field by passing through the Neilson Gate. From there they rode mostly westward along the partition fence separating that piece of the grazing lease from the New Field into which they would cross through the Stove Gate. The abandoned artefact from which the gate took its name continued to rust away not far off the trail.

Before they could arrive at the gate, Mart became aware of the sound of an engine approaching from behind. He swivelled to look back, noting that Wendell's worn out ears had yet to detect anything. The front wheels of a four-wheeler showed below a roughly built plywood box. Above the homemade carrier was the unshaven and grinning face of Jack Pruitt. Mart reined in his horse and turned to face the way he had come. Wendell felt his absence rather than actually seeing Mart stop and he pulled back on the grey mare's lines. He turned the horse slowly around instead of fighting his rigid neck.

Jack killed the engine and let it roll up under Skip's nose. "Hello, Mart."

"Morning, Jack. Hello Candace." Mart noted Jack's daughter pulling up behind on a brand new yellow quad. In spite of her continued interest in her family's ranch, Candace had benefitted from marrying outside the agricultural industry. Mart secretly wondered whether her husband, Phillip Cowan, resented cash from his successful accounting business swirling precariously above the Pruitt ranch drain. Jack had been struggling for years to keep afloat.

"You pulled the short straw again, I see."

Mart cringed. Jack was without a doubt referring less than subtly to his assignment to team up with Wendell Jacobsen. The young rancher tried to dodge the bullet by pretending he didn't get it. "Not at all, it's a beautiful day to do range patrol. A couple of rainy days this summer I'd have traded this saddle for the dentist's chair, but not today."

Jack pulled off a sweat-stained ball cap advertizing a Lethbridge feed supplier. He rubbed his shirtsleeve across a brow made more accessible by a drastically receding hairline. The wicked grin on his face made it apparent that he knew Mart had caught the true meaning of his jab.

Mart had occasion to wince once again as Wendell croaked from behind. "Not your turn to ride this week, Pruitt."

"Now, Wendell," Jack began with false cordiality, "Nothing stops me from doing a little more than my share if I can find the time."

"Humph!"

If the sour look that appeared on Jack Pruitt's face was not enough evidence that the artificial pleasantries were concluded, the next statement by Candace made it clear the longstanding feud would continue. "If we want to check on our stock, we can do it whenever we want, Wendell. We don't need the board's approval, do we?"

Wendell said nothing.

Jack added a jibe. "Don't need permission how we do it either."

Mart attempted to play peacemaker by deflecting the conflict. "Are you looking for anything in particular, Candace?"

The effort was wasted. Candace was a true product of the west. She was willing to wade into any tough or dirty job and she wasn't going to back down from Wendell Jacobsen's disapproval.

"Yes, we're looking to get past the old nag." It was somewhat uncertain whether she was talking about the horse or the rider. She wasn't glaring at the mare.

Wendell Jacobsen glowered back through his cloudy eyes. He blinked twice and then very slowly turned the old grey. The horse sauntered up the trail. Mart gave the father and daughter a sickly smile and reined Skip out of the way. The two engines chugged to life. Pruitt accelerated slowly past. Candace did the same. She did not look up at Mart. He wondered if her hostility was directed only at Wendell.

The ATVs were forced to roll slowly on the large heels of the grey. Jacobsen made no real effort to clear the path. Finally the trail widened and the machines gunned past with no backward glance from either rider. Mart pushed Skip up to ride behind Wendell.

"Some folks pull their weight and others just play at it," Wendell muttered. He kept his criticism general in spite of the clearly intended objects of his controlled anger.

"Jack's been trying hard to make up for the past. He never misses an assignment now. The Poll Haven board seems to have given up on booting him out."

Another humph. The ride continued in silence.

CHAPTER 3 ✳ BOGS

Poll Haven was an odd title for a place; strange enough that some locals even altered the name to call it Pole Heaven. Most were not sure how it got its name, but general speculation was that it made reference to the abundance of tall straight timber. Mart recalled another of Wendell Jacobsen's impromptu lectures. "There is a Pole Heaven in the Spanish Fork Ranger District of the Uinta National Forest of Utah. Some folks call it Pole Haven. Most of the early settlers of southern Alberta came from Utah, so it's a safe bet that the idea for the name came from there."

Mart stepped off Skip to open the gate, his second gateway of the morning. Wendell was a proud and independent man a year or two one side or the other of eighty. Nevertheless, he didn't complain when Mart got off to open all the gates in the crossfences along the way. The old man rationalized deference rather than any suggestion he may not be capable of the task. Mart didn't mind. He could do it much faster anyway.

Wendell rode through. Mart pulled the wires tight and slipped the loop over the chipped and cracked wood of the gate post. He walked around and ran a hand down Skip's off side back leg. The tractable gelding lifted the foot once he felt the pressure reach his fetlock. A frequent clicking noise had alerted Mart that the horseshoe was getting loose. It was the horse's only white pastern and the hoof didn't hold the nails like the three dark feet did. Mart would try to re-clinch the nails himself once he got home; if he ended up lucky enough to not pull the iron shoe off in a mud hole. Perhaps by tightening the nails himself he could postpone the eighty-five dollar farrier bill until next month when Skip and Slim would both need to have their shoes reset.

Mart walked unhurriedly around the horse and stepped into the stirrup. He was just hoisting himself up when he noticed Jacobsen's shaky voice. The old man was talking to Mart, assuming he was close behind. Skip was surprised to be kicked gently into a trot to catch up. Rather than admit to dawdling, Mart tried to catch the drift mid-statement.

"...we can meet up again there. Then I'll show you what I found. I've never seen anything quite like it. You'll see what I mean. It's the darnedest puzzle I've ever run into up here."

"So where did you want me to split off?" Mart attempted to appear to be simply asking for clarification.

Wendell twisted in the saddle to look at the young man. The older fellow did not seem able to turn his head on his neck anymore. Milky grey eyes squinted out from beneath a narrow-brimmed, grey felt western hat. Sweat stains rose up in fjord-like patterns from where the hat band should have been. He made an odd clucking noise and then faced the trail before continuing.

"At Glanders Flats, near the creek crossing. You know where to meet up again?" It was an accusation rather than a question. When Mart didn't immediately respond, Wendell continued in an exaggerated long-suffering tone. "Where Lee's Creek comes in from the States. From there we'll take down some wires and cross into the Glenwood Saw Set. We can go home by way of the Mackenzie cut line."

There had been quite a bit of logging and oil and gas exploration activity over the years. It had left the community pasture crisscrossed with old wagon roads and seismic lines that were often used as trails. The Mackenzie Cut intersected another seismic line below the Hog's Back. They formed a V, its two arms sweeping away from the international boundary; one northwest toward the top of the Hog's Back and then on to Poll Haven, and the other northeast, staying above several of the small tributaries to Lee Creek.

Riders often split up so that more fence line could be covered and more stock encountered. Now all Mart needed to do was to make sure Wendell got to the creek first. That way he'd take the trail the old man didn't, and avoid admitting he had not been listening. But there was a lot of ground to cover before the flats or Lee Creek and staying behind Wendell's plodding mare was a lot harder than taking the lead.

From the Stove they descended toward the shallow stream that was Tough Creek. The crossing was muddy and getting badly eroded. They traversed the New Field following a track that almost perfectly bisected it and pointed the riders directly at the thin nose of the Hog's Back. Mart climbed off and got Hog's Back Gate #1. Before they reached Hog's Back Gate #2 they turned southeast, taking the southernmost fork toward Glanders Flats rather than heading off toward the site of the old Lee Creek ranger station.

Glanders Flats was the location of a sad chapter in the history of the area. Old man Jacobsen began droning his history lesson about the name of that place – a story Mart had endured several times, along with repeated tutorials on most of the other local place names.

Wendell's wobbly voice echoed gently from the wall of tree trunks. "Glanders. At the turn of the century a lot of horses in the area contracted an infectious disease of the same name. The meadows were where the sick animals were taken to be shot rather than risk an expanding epidemic."

The riders paused occasionally to inspect small bands of cattle scattered here and there throughout the trees along the trail. The first was a cluster of red and yellow cows, all with white faces. They were Herefords and Herefords crossed with

Charolais. Almost all of them had black baldy calves, confirming the current trend to use Angus bulls.

"Those are Sam's animals," croaked the old man.

"The grass is good. They are wide as they are tall," commented the younger rancher.

"That skinny calf with them is Melvin's," continued Wendell. "He hasn't seen the momma in a month – figures she's dead in some bog."

"Was she that old Simmental-cross with the single bent horn?

"Yup."

"I'm surprised he sent her. She looked rough when he trailed them up here."

Wendell turned his mount and mumbled, "Wanted to avoid the cost of the rendering truck coming to haul her away, I suppose."

Several other small groups of cattle could be seen through the underbrush. Most were black baldy punctuated here and there with red and white brockle-faced animals. It was rare to see any cattle that weren't mixed or crossbreeds. Feed lot operators wanted the vigour produced by hybridization. Ranchers, like any other businessmen, bred their cattle to satisfy the biases of the buyers.

After more than an hour they reached the low hills above the flats. They descended into several gullies that made up small and chiefly ephemeral tributaries to Lee Creek. Most had water in them in spite of the late season. Wet weather all this summer and last had made a liar of explorer John Palliser. When he had led a government expedition into the Canadian west in the late 1850s, he had declared a huge area of southern Alberta and Saskatchewan completely unsuitable for agriculture. He claimed the prairie was semi-arid desert. The area defined by a line drawn vertically from the US boundary at the foot of the Rockies north almost to Edmonton and angling southeast through Saskatoon and Regina became known as Palliser's Triangle. It turned out to be good farmland in the end, especially when irrigated. But irrigation had hardly been necessary in the recent soggy summers.

When the horsemen slipped into the last gully before reaching the fence line, it became apparent that rather than deter the recreational vehicle crowd, the wet summer had been part of the draw. The banks of the creeks had always taken a pretty good beating from stock and truck traffic, especially at the crossings. However, this was a different problem. Mart had no desire to put his horse through the bog in front of them. Jacobsen appeared to have the same disinclination.

"We'll have to go up or downstream to find a decent crossing."

The ford had expanded the stream to at least triple its original width. Whereas ten years ago the ford had been simply a couple of gravelly tracks descending a steep bank and out again, it was now spreading up and down the creek. Each new set of tracks would be abandoned as the stream-bed was churned into a mucky array of ruts in various widths. When it became impassable, or nearly so, the next set of travellers would edge a bit downstream or up. The result was an ever-expanding mud hole that eroded even farther with each bout of spring runoff.

"Jackasses!"

That was pretty harsh language coming from the straight-laced fellow. Wendell Jacobsen was a devout member of the Church of Jesus Christ of Latter Day Saints. The Mormons, as they were more commonly known, discouraged cursing and Mart admired Wendell for living up to the standards professed by his religion. It wasn't just the general lack of strong language. Wendell didn't drink, smoke or gossip. Although he was well known as a grumpy old man, he was still the first to arrive to help a family move or shingle a neighbour's barn.

"This mess brings to mind a time back in the '40s when I was walking along and found a hat sitting on top of a muddy hole. When I picked it up, I was surprised to find a man's head under it. When I asked if he needed help, the head just said, 'Nah. I'm fine. I've got a good horse under me.'"

Mart snorted.

Pausing a moment to twist his age-welded neck to the left and then to the right, Wendell took a downstream tack, the old grey pushing at a determined but snail-like pace through the cracking twigs. Skip followed without any command from Mart. They had travelled for less than a minute before they encountered yet another mud hole in a hollow just off of the stream. This was not the braiding of a crossing, but an intentional obstacle used solely for fun by the four-wheeled enthusiasts.

Jacobsen emitted a second mild curse. "Idiots and their dang machines!" The pair of riders made another detour to avoid the thick black ridges forming sinuous, crenulated islands in the greyish liquid.

Recreational use was part of the shared management plan of the Poll Haven. Folks had used the pasture for hunting, fishing, camping and riding since before it was traded from Waterton Lakes National Park, and the federal government, to the province in 1947. It had been part of a land swap for a like-sized chunk to add a wood bison enclosure to Elk Island National Park east of Edmonton. There had been occasional conflicts between the cattlemen and the pleasure-seekers, especially during the late '70s when dirt bikes became the rage, but never had there been so much motorized recreational use as during the past decade.

All terrain vehicles had come within the economic grasp of a large percentage of the southern Alberta population and crown land was open for use. Wendell Jacobsen started in on his traditional tirade. "When is the government going to put an end to the abuse of public land!?"

Mart tried to cut the lecture short. "Wendell, you know that here, and in the Castle Wilderness, trying to keep ATV use to designated trails and roads has been a complete failure."

"It would have helped if the province and the county hadn't just handed the responsibility to enforce the restrictions over to the leaseholders. They had to know that associations like ours lack the manpower or any type of recognized authority to do anything but watch the four wheel drivers thumb their noses at us."

"No use grumbling about it. It's not just here. Through the whole province they seem to feel it is their right to go where they want to on public land." Mart would have liked to say that it was only a few bad apples who rode in the Poll Haven that caused the damage. Sadly, the majority of motorized users were unwilling to admit to the benefits of any management regime that would not permit them to go wherever they felt their machines could take them. The hardcore mud-boggers were the worst, but not the only offenders by any means.

"It's gotten crazy. We have to have men out here twice as often as we used to." The drastic increase in use had necessitated scheduling rides before and just after the weekends to put up gates that were inevitably left open.

The old rancher finally gave up on the topic. "This way," Wendell instructed as he found a narrow trail that led to a steep but useable crossing.

A trio of heifers with their first calves moved away from them, pushing through the underbrush and snapping twigs. Once the two horses had picked their way back to the main trail, Jacobsen cast a sideways glance at his young companion and pointed the mare's nose down a well-used cattle trail that would lead her off to the southwest just above Lee Creek. That left Mart the most directly southward-leading route and the most distance to cover. That suited him fine. Once Wendell had disappeared behind a patch of poplar, Mart urged Skip to pick up the pace slightly. Chances were good that he would make it to the rendezvous spot first in spite of the fact that Jacobsen had taken the shortcut to look for cattle. Mart would stay as close as he could to the partition fence that ran south to the borderline and then check the east-west fence running along the US boundary.

CHAPTER 4 ✷ WAIT

Mart crossed his reins and draped them over the saddle horn. He rolled up his sleeves. The bugs weren't as bad as they could have been. Several nights of early frost in late August had taken their toll on the insects. A tinge of gold could be seen on an occasional cluster of trembling aspen. Mart remembered his high school biology teacher's explanation of why one patch of these trees would leaf out earlier than others in the spring or turn into a scrap of yellow in a sea of green in early autumn.

"Aspens are seldom single entities, but rather part of a larger set of clones joined by the roots. These clones often spread out over almost half a hectare of land. Each genetically similar bunch has the potential to react slightly differently to the changing seasons."

Mart smiled. It was amazing he could remember that lesson almost verbatim. That Cardston teacher had been one of Mart's favourites. Overall his experience at Cardston High had been a good one. Mart had not moved here permanently from Medicine Hat until halfway through his first semester of grade ten. The school in Mountain View was only kindergarten to grade nine so Mart had immediately joined the rest of the local high school students in a twenty minute bus ride to Cardston every morning and back again in the afternoon.

Coming permanently to the ranch had been an unhappy but fortunate surprise for Mart. Uncle Seth had gone quickly from heart failure one Sunday morning in early October. Aunt Emma had been away at church and found him when she returned home. It had only been a few years before that she had started attending church services again. She and Mart's mom had been raised in a Mormon family, but each had strayed from the faith in their late teenage years. Emma, the senior of the two girls, had eventually married Seth Tidwell from Milk River country. He had been the youngest of several sons and had gratefully taken over the Mountain View ranch from Emma Gwynn's father. There was no chance of inheriting the small place where he grew up. There were too many claimants ahead of him.

Emma and Seth Tidwell had remained childless for several years and had eventually adopted a little girl. The child had been sickly from the start and all Aunt Emma's mothering could not put it right. The child had died a little more than a year later. Neither Seth nor Emma had been up to facing that kind of disappointment again and had lived as a quiet couple until Mart's summer indentures began. Any pent up mothering instinct had instantaneously bubbled to the surface in Emma. Seth had warmed slowly to the timid boy, but that slow boil formed a thick broth that glued them together permanently.

On leaving home, Mart's mom, Tina, had taken a job in Calgary where she met his father. William McKinnon was a geologist for an oil company. He had died in a head-on collision in a rental car in Texas when Mart was three. Tina had been offered a good clerical job at the same oil company office in Calgary. With that income, and the insurance money that had paid off the mortgage, they lived well enough until she met and married Mart's stepfather, Walter Taylor. Taylor also worked in the petroleum industry and took a position in Medicine Hat shortly thereafter. That is where Mart grew up.

Walter and Mart were fire and water; or perhaps fire and oil. Reflecting back on it now, Mart recognized that he had not made it easy for the man. Walter confessed freely that he had been ill prepared for parenthood. A long-time bachelor and a middle manager at work, his approach to children was too authoritarian. The summers on the ranch had been Tina's way of easing the tension. When she had suggested Mart move to Emma's, to help with the ranch on a permanent basis after Uncle Seth's death, neither Mart nor Walter objected. Mart had been fifteen. Now he was twenty-six. It had only been recently that Mart and Walter had admitted they both could have tried harder to make things work, especially for Tina's sake. For now the truce was holding. Distance made it easier.

Skip had to negotiate several more bogs and Mart's oaths were not as benign as Brother Jacobsen's had been. The fence along the east edge of the field was in relatively good shape. Access here was easier than for much of the fence elsewhere, so there was evidence of newer posts and deadfall had been thrown clear of the wires.

Ironically the slurping sound of Skips hind feet pulling free of a particularly eroded piece of the trail had just faded when the ears of both horse and rider caught the distant drone of a small engine. Mart pulled up and tried to determine the direction from which the sound came. He was almost to the southeast corner of the Tower Field. The US boundary was less than half a kilometre away. By pivoting his head back and forth to face the sound, he placed the vehicles just north and moving slowly westward. The varying pitches led the young rancher to believe there were at least two machines. It wasn't likely to be Jack or Candace revving around carelessly like that. He guessed that these were different riders who had come in from the Boundary Creek side, probably leaving a truck or trailer on the narrow gravel road and starting their ride just outside the community pasture. If they continued along their current trajectory, they would overtake Wendell before he reached his planned meeting place with Mart. The young man smiled to think of the unabashed tongue-lashing they would receive if they dared to approach the old man. Mart would be glad to miss the discomfort created by such a confrontation.

Mart rode for another half hour or more, crossing two more small branches of Lee Creek before he neared the upper stretches of the stream again. Lee Creek flowed into Canada from south of the border. Mart looked south toward its source near the base of Chief Mountain which was half in Glacier National Park and half on the Blackfeet Reservation. The mountain stood apart from its fellow peaks in the Front Ranges of the Rocky Mountains. It was of important spiritual significance to Blackfoot people who lived both sides of the border. The narrow ridge of crumbling sedimentary rock was among the oldest exposed in the Rockies. Large cracks were spaced along a slim summit that was barely the width of a city sidewalk. Mart and some friends had climbed it a few times. It required a permit from the Blackfeet and a long trudge around the back side where the debris of the eroding peak formed a talus slope angling from the valley floor almost to the summit. Walking through those loose rocks was more like tramping the mountain down than climbing it.

From the Canadian side, the mountain appeared as a solid block standing prominently out in front of the other peaks. As you skirted the east side of the Front Ranges and headed south into Montana it became apparent that it was a narrow crumbling ridge standing with its feet in the debris of a hundred thousand years of erosion.

CHAPTER 5 ✳ SPOOKED

Mart slid off his horse and sighted back along the creek bottom. Beyond the balsam poplars of the banks he could see the transition from wooded slope to open prairie and on to the ranches of Boundary Creek. The view northwest was restricted to about two kilometres by the Hog's Back. Lodgepole pine, white spruce and Douglas fir clung to the steep sides of the ridge. A couple of large clearings were a testament to the steepness of the slope in those spots. Frequent snow slides kept those inclines free of more brittle woody vegetation and favoured the springy stalks of mountain ash, Douglas maple and buffalo berry. A couple of bands of sedimentary rock sliced the ridge into sections.

Wendell had not yet arrived so Mart slipped his lunch and water from Uncle Seth's battered saddlebags. He felt a twinge of guilt for not waiting until Jacobsen could join him, but he knew it was just as likely the crabby old-timer had eaten in the saddle and would berate him for wasting time with an actual lunch break.

The ATVs were buzzing around somewhere to the northeast. The pitch of the small, inefficient engines alternated between low growls as they ascended steep sections or churned through muddy spots and brief bursts of high-pitched whining where the trail was dry. Mart listened to their progress while he finished both of his bologna and cheese sandwiches.

The rancher bit into his crisp Spartan apple and was just wiping the juicy spray from his lips when the ATVs below erupted into a torrent of activity. The reverberations of the two or three machines mixed in a frantic fugue of ebbs and crescendos. The commotion was centred on the same section of trail from which Jacobsen was due to emerge. Mart rubbed his eyes and contemplated the rebuke these citizens were bound to suffer. Wendell assumed every helmeted pleasure-seeker to be a slapdash ne'er-do-well. He grumbled about community grazing lease shareholders using motorcycles for patrols. It had been one of the points of contention between the Pruitts and the old man. He treated grey-haired retirees from Cardston out for a leisurely Saturday ramble to the same abuse as he did mud-flinging teenage hellions.

Mart recalled once reminding Wendell, "They have every right to ride here so long as they stay to the designated trails and don't hill climb and mud bog."

Jacobsen had simply stared at him and eventually emitted that odd cluck, shook his head and rode away in silence.

The frenzied activity did not let up through several more bites of the tart fruit, but it did migrate slightly uphill toward Mart's vantage point. He had almost made up his mind to climb onto his horse to investigate when the mechanized racket dropped to the uneven chug of idling.

"Wendell's got 'em," Mart said aloud with a grin.

Only a moment later the quads roared again into action. This time it was apparent they were retreating the way they had come. They were moving fast and it was not long before the sound of their motors was impeded by the slopes and forest of the Hog's Back.

Another fifteen minutes passed and still no Jacobsen. Mart began questioning his understanding of the location of the meeting. The old man couldn't be too far away. From the reaction of the motorcyclists, Wendell was just down slope from where Mart stood and the curmudgeon had successfully put the run on them. That was rare. Most four wheel enthusiasts would not stop to talk to a horseback rider. If they did, they seldom took any criticism of their activity very seriously. But why hadn't the old guy emerged from the overgrown trail?

Mart took up another notch in the saddle's latigo, decided to tighten the back cinch as well and swung onto Skip. He descended the brushy trail at a trot. After a few minutes the trees opened into a small meadow with scattered clumps of low scrub. He could see tracks where a couple of four wheelers had crisscrossed the opening and made a U-turn. A few wide hoof prints were visible among the tire tracks. Some of them were partially erased by the knobby tread marks. Mart spun Skip around to attempt to track the large grey, but stopped short when a small object pushed into the mud caught his eye. He stepped off the horse and dug up a ball of muck containing a pink and white plastic U. It was the lower plate of a set of false teeth.

Skip lifted his head and whinnied, looking back and to the left of the way they had come. Mart could not see over the bushes, but led his horse in that direction. Wendell's perspiration-stained hat adorned a buffalo berry bush at a jaunty angle. Mart dropped the reins and broke into a run. He retrieved the hat at the same time he spotted the rump of the grey. She was wedged between a small aspen and a dense patch of chokecherry and alder. Where the hell was Wendell? Mart scanned the clearing just as Skip walked past dragging his bridle reins.

The old mare managed to turn her head back to face the approaching horse. Her eyes were wide and she appeared to be having difficulty breathing. To avoid stepping on the dragging lines, Skip held his head to the side and continued to approach the frightened animal. Suddenly he shied away from something hidden in the brush and yanked his head back as he stepped on one of the reins, causing the metal bit to dig cruelly into his mouth.

Mart darted to the spot. Jacobsen was lying at the base of another buffalo berry. His face was against the springy stalks of the plant. His head was bent backward and to the side. The old man's torso was bent at an unnatural angle as well. Mart's first reaction was to shrink away. He had to force himself to kneel down alongside the grotesque spectacle.

"Wendell!" Mart resisted the urge to shake the man, even gently. Standard first aid from Scouts Canada had taught him to avoid moving a victim suspected of a spinal injury. He reached across to feel for a pulse at the old man's neck. Nothing! He fumbled around hoping he had yet to get to the right spot with his trembling digits. After several failed attempts, Mart threw caution to the wind and leaned over the old man to determine if he was breathing. Again there was no sign of life.

"Wendell!" Mart called again. "Answer damn it!"

After several minutes Mart took an even greater chance and rolled Wendell carefully onto his back, trying desperately to straighten him out gently. Jacobsen's head wobbled sickeningly. There was no doubt that his neck had snapped.

"No, Wendell, no!"

Mart sat back onto the moist ground. How long he remained immobile he was uncertain. At last he stood and shook his head. He had been trembling slightly. He cursed himself silently. He was in mild shock and had to shake it. It was too late to get help, but he needed to let someone know what had happened. He pulled out the archaic cell phone and turned it on. He had lots of battery, but no service. He cursed softly and muttered to himself, "Should I ride east to try to hit the Cardston tower or south and west to some high ground and hope for the one on the Birdseye Ranch?"

Skip had ambled over to the old mare. She had calmed considerably with the arrival of her comrade, but had not attempted to back out of the mess she was in. Mart owed it to Wendell and the old grey to get her out before he went for help. There was mud all up her back legs and nearly to her hindquarters. There were also some nasty abrasions on those legs. It was difficult to determine how bad they were because of the muck. She was jammed pretty tightly between the tree and the thick bushes, although that was not what was holding her in. She held one foot out in front of her. Mart looked under the mare and into the shadows. He could see just well enough to tell that the foot was held fast in a branched fork of the alder.

Mart spoke softly and pushed slowly past the wide rump, but could not get past the saddle and compressed branches of the shrubs. He hesitated, then hoped the confidence he felt in her good disposition was not misplaced.

"Whoa, girl," the cowboy crooned as he slid under the mare's belly and ran his hand slowly the length of her tangled limb. She instinctively pulled back. He uttered another gentle whoa and she relaxed.

He thought of using his knife, but didn't want to risk jabbing the horse. Instead, steady pressure forward pushed the hoof far enough into the wider section of the fork that the grey was able to pull it out and stand on it. Mart had to continually tell her to stand still in order to slide out from under the barrel-shaped belly and away from her hooves before she backed out from between the thick undergrowth and the tree. In the end she stomped on one of his feet anyway in her haste to get free. It hurt, but the soft soil yielded enough to avoid real injury.

Mart did not take time to do a thorough investigation of her injuries, being confident she was healthy enough she could wait. He tied her loosely to a low branch. Up on his own gelding, Mart headed east. He pushed Skip hard over the rough terrain, alternating between a fast trot and a slow canter. He checked the phone frequently and finally got one bar. He dialled 911 and was cut off before there was an answer. No service. It took another five minutes of riding to connect with the tower again. This time a very professional female voice came on the line.

"Please give me your name and state the nature of the emergency."

Mart tried to be calm and thorough in his response. "A man has been thrown from a horse. I am certain he is dead. We were riding in the Poll Haven Community Pasture and are just north of the US boundary."

"Is there a road nearby for ambulance service?"

"No, the trails to that spot would be almost impossible for even a four-wheel-drive truck."

"Do you have GPS coordinates?" she asked.

"My cell is way too old for that." Mart then described the location as best he could and indicated there were a couple of options to get a crew there.

"Sir, please stay on the line in case we need more details."

"I had to leave the scene to make this call. There was no cell service back there."

"Could you stay where you are until someone arrives?" she suggested.

Mart had macabre thoughts of crows and coyotes moving in to find Jacobsen. "I really don't feel comfortable being away for too long."

She began insisting. "I really need you to stay on the line, or at least where I can reach you on your cell, so we can continue to get information from you."

"The recovery team will not likely come past where I am now and will probably come from another direction altogether."

With that she acquiesced, "Please remain at the accident."

Mart disconnected and made a quick trip back. He dropped Skip's reins near the grey. She nickered her contentment at having company again. She had pulled the reins free of the branch and began browsing with Skip. Mart thought he detected a slight limp. It wasn't on the foreleg that had been pinched. She appeared stiff in the back legs instead.

Wendell lay undisturbed. Mart paced a while and then settled in to wait. Since he had made it clear that it was the recovery of a body and not a rescue, it could take a bit more time. The urgency was not there and whatever crew was mustered would not be taking any unnecessary risks to get there rapidly.

Thunderheads were accumulating over the mountains of the national park. So far they were not pushing out to where Mart sat leaning against the smooth green-white bark of a tree at the edge of the clearing. Tall dense cotton-ball cumulonimbus clouds stretched a kilometre or more high. The grey lower edges obscured the highest peaks. The bare trees of the 1998 Sofa Mountain fire were hairbrush bristles sloping up to meet the dark underbelly of the vaporous cloak. Mart thought he could hear rumbling.

Mart felt awkward sitting there and caught himself addressing an unhearing Wendell with wishes that the recovery team would soon arrive. The afternoon dragged on and Mart began speculating on what had happened. The idea of the old grey spooking at the approach of a couple of ATVs was almost completely out of the question under normal circumstances. She had encountered a couple of hundred such noisy vehicles, often standing calmly in their path as Jacobsen played his ineffectual enforcement role. It was obvious from Wendell's death pose that he had been thrown out the front. It appeared he had been pitched face-first into the shrub and that the impact had snapped his head back. It was likely that the weight of his legs coming up over his shoulders had broken his lower back as well.

Mart looked at the old mare and could not imagine her ever bucking. Perhaps she had stumbled? She would have had to be going quite fast to cast the old man to the ground with such force. Why would she have been running? Mart had hardly ever witnessed anything faster from her than a few steps of a reluctant jig. He rose and walked through the meadow, attempting to read the confusing jumble of tracks. It was hard to make any sense of them because the knobbed tires had obliterated most of the horse's prints.

Mart glanced down the trail from where both Wendell and the quads had come. He strode off in that direction. As he had suspected there were better tracks there because the four wheelers had straddled the grey's hoof prints. There was no doubt about it, she had been travelling at a rapid canter or perhaps even a gallop. He continued to backtrack and noticed some irregularities in the rubber tire tracks as well. At a couple of locations one of the machines had bounced off the trail; a set of its wheels actually leaving the ground to land pointed slightly off course. The tracks would then weave back onto the trail. Mart could see no obstacles that would cause the deflections, but he knew the tires were soft and bounced easily. He had limited experience actually riding the machines, so it was hard to speculate the cause.

Hopeful that the recovery crew would soon be arriving, Mart hustled back to the clearing. He recaptured the horses. They had wandered into the trees. Once again he did not bother to tie them, but dropped their reins near poor Jacobsen's inert form.

Why hadn't the operators of the ATVs stayed to help Wendell? They must have seen him fall. Maybe they got spooked because they thought they would get into trouble? Perhaps they had gone to call for help? No, that didn't make sense. One of them would have gone and the other stayed. Was it at all conceivable that they had not noticed the man and the horse ahead of them?

CHAPTER 6 ✳ RECOVERY

THE SOUND OF a vehicle approaching disturbed Mart's deliberations. The uneven rumblings came from the southwest. That surprised him. Although the rancher had indicated his proximity to the US boundary, he had assumed there would be a team arriving from the direction of Boundary Creek. He grabbed Skip's reins and swung into the saddle. The old mare whinnied, but only took a few steps to follow before she again stood still. Skip cantered up the hill and they reached the international boundary swath in time to meet a Royal Canadian Mounted Policeman and two Parks Canada employees. They arrived in a six wheeled ATV typically used by an initial attack fire crew and for rescues. A stretcher was lashed securely across the small shallow utility box at the rear. The Parks Canada driver killed the engine and stepped out from under the canopy of the vehicle. Mart had seen this one before. He was tall and slim with straight sandy hair poking from beneath a green cap.

He extended his hand and introduced himself in a quiet voice. "Mr. McKinnon, my name is Kim." He then turned and indicated his companion, a shorter powerfully built younger man. "This is Red." Why anyone would call him that Mart could not fathom as he had the darkest hair and the deepest brown eyes he had ever seen.

Kim then introduced the other member of the team. "This is Constable Boissoneau. He is in charge of the recovery, but requested park assistance."

That explained the arrival from the west. They must have driven through the park up the Chief Mountain International Highway and travelled most of the three kilometres to the spot along the cut swath of the US/Canada border.

The tall, dark constable shook Mart's hand and smiled. Without delay he asked, "Could you please direct us to the scene of the accident?"

"Follow me."

Back up on Skip, Mart led them down the narrow trail to the meadow. Kim killed the engine well back from the body. Red collected an emergency kit from the back and went immediately to Wendell's side. He made a quick assessment and then called Kim and the constable over. After a few words, the Resource Conservation duo retreated and Boissoneau began a narrow search of the area immediately around the body. He was meticulous and made every effort to avoid disturbing anything until he was certain it had little consequence. He took several pictures with a small pocket camera as he went. After more than an hour he nodded to Kim. The two park employees unlashed the stretcher and proceeded to move Jacobsen onto it. They handled the old man gently as if he were still alive.

"What is the name of the gentleman?" the constable startled Mart out of his preoccupation with the proceedings.

"Wendell Jacobsen."

"Could you spell the last name for me?"

Mart did so and then waited while the RCMP member wrote in his notebook.

"What is your relationship to Mr. Jacobsen?"

"We're not family. We ride together." Mart began babbling. He was having a hard time focusing. He stopped to collect his thoughts.

Constable Boissoneau showed no sign of impatience. Although he looked to be a young man, he had obviously learned to deal with distraught people.

"He is a neighbour and we are both members of the grazing association, so we ride patrol together sometimes."

"Please describe to me how this has happened." The constable had only a slight French-Canadian accent, but Mart noticed he sometimes phrased things a bit oddly.

"I didn't witness the fall, but I heard the noise of the quads," Mart began the explanation. "I can only guess that the ATVs were the cause of the wreck. I found Wendell and checked to see if he was still alive, but I guess I waited too long up the hill. In the end I moved him in a last ditch effort to see if he could be revived." He cautiously continued his recital regarding how he had interpreted the tracks leading to the meadow. He did not want to throw unwarranted accusations around. "It looks like they were right on his tail. They must have seen the old horse running ahead of them."

"Why do you think that?"

"They turned and left in a real hurry."

"I guess the horse would be scared of the noise."

Mart hesitated again and the constable looked up from his notes. "What is it?" he asked.

"That old horse never spooks from anything. I've seen ATVs practically drive over her front hooves and she hardly lifts her head. I can't, for the life of me, think why she or Wendell would run from a couple of four-wheelers."

"But animals aren't always predictable, eh?" offered Boissoneau.

"If one ever was, that's the one," Mart gestured toward the old grey nibbling on a tuft of herb.

"Any idea who was driving the motorcycles?"

"No, I am afraid not. The only riders we saw today were some locals that headed off another direction," Mart admitted.

"They couldn't have come this way, too?" Boissoneau asked.

"I suppose, but I doubt it. And Wendell knew them." Mart felt odd making the last statement. It wasn't like he could say they were friends.

"I'll have to speak to them, anyway."

Mart felt small giving the cop their names. Would Jack wonder if he had maliciously sent the police his way? "It was Jack Pruitt and his daughter Candace Cowan. Jack ranches near Mountain View and Candace lives in Cardston."

Boissoneau scribbled a few more details in his notepad. "Who would be Mr. Jacobsen's next-of-kin?"

"His wife passed away quite a few years back. I only know of one child, a daughter. She lives in Utah, but I don't know her married name. Your best bet would be to talk to the LDS bishop of the Leavitt Ward. He might know how to get hold of her."

Boissoneau walked back along the path with Mart. He made some notes and took a few more pictures. Beyond the stretch of trail Mart had already covered there was hard ground and distinct tracks became occasional. Then the pair returned to the clearing. The park guys were leaning patiently against the ATV upon which Wendell Jacobsen was covered and firmly attached.

Kim approached the constable and said in an apologetic tone, "I'm afraid you'll have to walk up the hill. It'll be too heavy."

Boissoneau nodded and replied, "You can start up." Kim walked back and climbed onto the seat. He alone rode on the machine as it crawled up the hill while Red steadied the inanimate load.

"I am sorry about your friend. I need to write up a report and will have to ask you to review it and sign. Can I meet with you sometime in the next couple days?"

Mart agreed and gave the man his telephone number. "Will the four wheelers be in trouble?"

"Leaving the scene is an offense. I hope they come forward when they hear what has happened. If they are from here they probably will. If they came from the city, it may be difficult to find them. We will ask around. Maybe someone saw their vehicle parked at the roads."

"Try the folks on the Boundary Creek side first. I'm pretty sure they rode in from over there."

Boissoneau thanked Mart and then started up the hill. He stopped and turned. "Are you coming up?"

Mart was unsure what was expected of him. He replied, "Would it be okay... Can I go out the other way? My trailer is there and I need to take out the horses."

"Of course. I was not thinking." Boissoneau offered a smile and walked energetically after the growling noise of the receding park ATV.

CHAPTER 7 ✷ AFTER DARK

The sloping shadows of the sun were extinguished early by the towering clouds. The thunderstorm had remained a captive of the mountain heights, never having advanced much farther than the purplish slopes of Sofa. Mart had collected the old mare, mounted Skip and followed Wendell's back trail to the creek where they had parted earlier. He followed the main trail back as far as the Hog's Back Gate #1. There he took a thickly overgrown single track through the forest that lead more directly back to the Neilson Gate and the corrals. The light was feeble, but had not faded to complete darkness until he was less than a half kilometre from the trucks.

The old grey was a nightmare to lead by the bridle reins. She kept to her plodding gait and would not budge from it. Mart had to occasionally stop to give his arm a rest. That appendage was continually stretched back until it almost rested on the muscular croup of his red gelding; the pale head and neck of the grey stretched to their limit. Mart fought the loss of his temper. Rage rarely improved matters when working with livestock. He reminded himself the old girl was injured. The stiffness in the mare's back legs worsened, especially after steep descents.

With the darkness came night sounds and smells. The soil offered up a dank odour reminiscent of mildly rotten vegetables. It was odd that it didn't seem unpleasant here where it would have in the old Frigidaire. A misguided snipe was winnowing;

climbing and diving to push the wind through its tail to create a strange whistling thrum. The bird obviously was not taking into account that the breeding season had fled a couple of months ago.

As Mart slopped through the last mud hole before reaching the corrals, a little brown bat banked past his battered hat. Jacobsen's white pickup was just visible against the quaking aspens across the fence. The grey must have made the connection to home because she actually let the bridle reins sag as she surged ahead into a slow walk. She balked again as Mart led her to the back of his own trailer. He tied her to one of the loops on the outside, took the bridle off of Skip and clucked. The tired horse stepped in and walked back to stand diagonally in front of his halter. In unaccustomed laziness Mart loaded the grey without bothering to tie his own horse. She climbed in without much of a fight. He tied her reins to the metal tubing and shut the door.

Mart felt spent. He had worked or ridden much harder in a day, but the stress and the waiting had been extremely taxing. He did take the time to collect Wendell's keys from the ignition. He locked the doors and went back to his own outfit. The Chev sputtered to life on the second attempt. For the sake of the horses he struggled against the urge to hurry as he bumped over the myriad of ruts and out of the gate.

Wendell's place was along Lee Creek. Like many of the locals the old man had called it "Lee's Creek." About three kilometres on the way back home, before reaching the Beazer junction, there was a cattle guard; beyond, a set of steep, gravelled ruts descended toward a neat old barn, several sheds, an aging but well cared for set of corrals, and a small, once-white house set just above the stream. Here, just off the headwaters, so-called hundred year floods occurred every eleven to twenty years. The flood years 1953, 1964, 1975 and 1995 had all been brought up in Mart's conversations with the old-timers – several recent near-flood events had happened since 2000. The fact that the house and barns were placed on the terrace higher than the current floodplain had been the salvation of the place.

Mart parked next to the barn and unloaded the grey. The bareheaded Skip was deterred from following by Mart's gentle whoa. The mare trudged contentedly behind Mart through the heavy sliding door that had been left half open. The light switch was just inside. He wished he had taken the time to retrieve the halter he assumed was still in the white Ford or in the straight-load trailer behind it, but found an ancient leather one hanging on a wooden peg. Its once oiled surface was caked with barn dust and he had to let it out to the very last hole to fit the long head of the big horse. He had been in Jacobsen's barn before so had no difficulty finding the oat bin and the heel of a bale of hay. He left the mare chomping on those treats and headed to the house on foot.

It was dark, but Mart could visualize the small overgrown lawn among the voluntary poplars. Wendell had never been much on yard work. Gardening had been his wife's passion. But the garden was gone now. The house had been white, but the paint had faded or fallen from the stucco. A couple of corners had been broken down to the wire beneath. Had there been light, the lathe and tatters of tar paper would have been visible at the edges of those cracks.

The screen door squealed a welcome. A single bare bulb illuminated the entry instantly when Mart closed the switch. There was a murky water dish and a few crumbles of kibble around a fairly new looking cottage cheese container. He made his way into the kitchen that he illuminated similarly. Mart was ashamed when he saw the fastidious nature of Jacobsen's housekeeping. His own place was never this tidy. Wendell had always referred to the building as 'Jane's house'. He had evidently felt some obligation to keep up the housework out of respect for his dead wife. The dishes were washed and neatly stacked on the drain board.

There was not a crumb on the floor or counters. The only items on the table were Wendell's bifocals and a Bic pen lying on the open pages of a large book; Jacobsen's journal. Another peculiar Mormon trait was the propensity to keep a personal history. Wendell's had come in handy from time to time when there had been discussions with other members of the grazing association regarding previous occurrences or decisions. Wendell's record-keeping was as meticulous as his housekeeping.

Mart was content that things were in order. He flipped off the switch in the kitchen. He made a quick reconnaissance of the entry and turned to exit when a somewhat matted long-haired tabby poured herself through a triangular flap cut in the screen. She blinked at the brightness and at the stranger in her house.

Feed the cat. Mart was able to retrieve the water dish and refilled it at the kitchen sink. The cat was seated patiently in a corner cleaning her paws. She paused mid-lick when Mart began opening and closing cabinet doors until he located the twenty kilogram bag in the closet. He should have known the frugal old man would buy in bulk.

The tabby walked cautiously over as Mart dropped two handfuls into the plastic container. She looked up at him once then began to purr as she crunched the first pellets. She was abandoned to finish her meal in the dark as Mart headed again for the barn. He almost shut the solid wooden door of the house as well as the screen, thought of the cat and left it open wide enough for her to squeeze through.

Mart turned the horse out into the pasture behind the barn. It was open to the creek so she would have water. He shut off the light, closed the barn door and headed for his truck.

CHAPTER 8 ✳ HOME

A DOZEN STREET lights were burning a white hole in the dark landscape as Mart coasted through the hamlet of Mountain View. He made the turn north onto his gravel road and drove the kilometre and a half to the Gwynn home place. The ranch had been home to the Tidwells for more than thirty years. Aunt Em had been gone, first to the nursing home, then to the hill south of Mountain View, for the past eight. Mart was a McKinnon. However, there was no convincing any of the neighbouring ranchers that it was anything but the Gwynn place. Maybe when the kids who had just started school this week were Mart's age they might start calling it the McKinnon place; if he hadn't gone bust before then.

The old barn with its loft and tall arched roof was still there. Nowadays it was only used to shelter an occasional cow and newborn calf in a storm. Uncle Seth had built a single story metal building with large sliding doors and enough space to squeeze a tractor down the aisle between the pens. It was the sole modern looking thing on the place. Seth had not been one to spend money unless it was necessary to keep the ranch running. Aunt Emma had frequently reminded her husband of the cost of that barn when he balked at small improvements to the modest three bedroom house. That humble edifice was a square structure with a hip roof and an odd flat addition to create a pantry and single bathroom.

When Mart had taken over he had converted one old shed near the new building into a simple stable with two tie-ups and a single box stall. Mart hung the old Eamor on a rope tied to a wire hung from a rafter. Initially the slick wire was the only way to keep the mice from climbing down the rope and chewing the saddle down to the rawhide covered tree. He had cut a hole in the wall high enough up to discourage skunks, but easily reached by an agile feline. He imagined quite a battle before the old black cat had finally subdued the rodent horde that had reigned there.

Skip had finished his oats and had drunk from the pail he was offered. Mart led him out and around the side of the building. Slim was leaning over the gate and Mart had to push him away to allow it to swing in to let Skip through. Skip pushed easily past the small, dark bay and immediately found a patch of damp dirt in which to roll. Slim dashed away across the narrow lane that formed the summer horse pasture. He disappeared into the darkness with only his thundering hoof beats betraying his progress. He was back again almost immediately, skidding to a halt just before hitting the gate. Mart shook his head.

"Thirteen years old and still acting like an unbroken colt!"

Instead of heading to the house, Mart took a well-worn path around the back and climbed the steps to the door of a battered fourteen foot-wide mobile home. He had bought it second hand from a dealer in Lethbridge in 2001. He could have moved into the house when Aunt Emma went to the home only three years later and certainly the following year when she had passed away. While she was alive he didn't like her thinking he was in a rush to take over. After she died he found he had no heart to have her prim furniture and tastefully scant trinkets constantly remind him she was gone.

Every November, when the winter winds would begin in earnest, he swore he would make the move the following spring. This was Chinook country – probably the windiest spot in North America. Gales of over 100 kilometres per hour were frequent.

Gusts reaching 130 were too. It was not unheard of to have the wind peak at 150 to 170 kilometres per hour at least once every couple of years. The mobile home was chained to cement pilings, but he had lain awake in bed far too many nights listening to the windows rattle like machinegun fire and waiting for the timber frame to collapse around him. Round hay bales weighing 300 kilograms were tumbleweeds this close to those brooding winter Rockies.

    It was already half-past eleven. He had been up since just before five. The fridge hummed in the hot kitchen. Inside was a container of left-over tomato soup. He tried it cold and gave up after two swallows. Two pieces of toast, a quick shower and a few strokes of a toothbrush later he flopped on the sagging double bed. One last thought of the twisted body of his long-time neighbour sent a shudder the length of his slight frame. He rolled onto his side and slipped into fitful slumber.

CHAPTER 9 ✷ KENT

"Hello," Kent's clear, cheerful voice came down the wire.

"You got time to give me a lift?"

"When are you going to trade in that scrap metal and get a vehicle, Mart?"

"Truck's fine. I need to get Wendell's outfit out of the Pasture."

"The old geezer sick?"

Mart hesitated. "Worse."

"No!" A short silence followed. "I'm sorry, Mart. Sure. Can you wait an hour?"

"Yeah, I should do some chores here first anyway. I'll need you to meet me at Wendell's house."

"About nine?"

"Make it 9:15."

"How did it happen?" Kent asked.

"Came off the old mare."

"You're kidding!"

"Afraid not. Quarter after, then?"

"Sure."

Kent Lindholm had been Mart's best friend ever since Mart slumped into the seat two rows over in English 10. Mart had ridden the bus from Mountain View to Cardston High School starting in November. It had not been all that hard to adjust to the school work. Mart had always been a good student and he had been able to get almost all the same classes as he had in Medicine Hat. Nevertheless, he had worried about being at a new school. He had never made solid friendships in the Hat.

The home room teacher had introduced him to the other students. After that first class a self-confident Kent had swaggered up to the new kid. Mart was sure he was in for trouble.

Kent was tall with straight very blond hair combed so that the forelock hung carelessly over his left eye. That eye and its mate were the pale blue of a hot summer sky. He wore a white tee shirt and Wrangler jeans with tennis shoes loosely laced. A couple of football stars played Gilligan to his Skipper. Girls giggled as he walked past with a lazy half-smile.

"All hell for a basement," Kent said.

"P-pardon me."

"Medicine Hat. All hell for a basement." Kent grinned.

"Kipling?"

Kent's smile broadened into a grin. "Now you've got it!"

Medicine Hat sat on a huge gas field. Rudyard Kipling had immortalized the town by making the statement alluding to the fires of the underworld.

Contrary to his cocky air and evident popularity, Mart found that Kent went out of his way to befriend his classmates. Mart had once watched Kent step up to greet the student body misfit like a cherished pal just in time to deflect the attentions of several class bullies.

Mart was quiet and a little backward. Nevertheless, looking back at high school it was surprising just how often he had associated with the most admired kids in town. Kent recognized his bashfulness and dragged him along to the best parties and to several reckless outings that were the talk of the entire student population. In contrast to Kent's Teutonic appearance, Mart was dark. His eyes were brown with thick black brows. His hair was curly and almost black. He was slim and not quite as tall as his blond friend. His features betrayed the Celtic origins of his Welsh and Scottish ancestors. With inclusion, Mart's shy nature faded slightly. He was never as outgoing as his comrade, but could fit in well enough with almost any crowd. By grade twelve he was even known for his quick dry wit evident in peculiar comments at the most unexpected times.

Under Kent's tutelage Mart had his first real interactions with girls. They were invariably drawn to Kent who seemed only casually aware that they practically stalked him. Mart benefitted by being nearby and many found his shyness endearing. It was rare that any of Kent's groupies developed more than a platonic interest in the dark, quiet sidekick. That was until Becky. She had changed everything.

Fuel costs were high enough that Mart chose Aunt Em's old Toyota rather than his gas-guzzling Chevy 4X4. He kept the car windows closed against the road dust until he reached Highway 5 and headed east. He got the small engine revved and made eighty kilometres per hour before he passed the sixty kilometres per hour speed zone sign at the turnoff to Mountain Meadow Trail Rides. Tourist season was drawing to a close and he wondered how the family-run business had fared through the cool wet summer.

To the west was the narrowest point in the Rockies. That meant the weather here was strongly influenced by the Pacific Ocean even though it was all the way across the province of British Columbia. Exceptionally hot dry years were often associated with warm El Niño ocean currents flowing up from Central America. In contrast, cold wet years like this one were often blamed on the cooling trend in the Pacific called La Niña. The mud and constant gloom had made for a dismal June and July, but what Mart really didn't relish about La Niña was the storm-ridden winters that tended to follow a wet summer.

Alberta Highway 5 formed the main thoroughfare of the small hamlet. Only about thirty people lived within the community itself, but more like 400 got their mail from the post office boxes at the Barn Store. Ranching communities were made up of neighbours who often lived just barely within sight of one or two other homes. Oddly they tended to have more to do with one another than those who lived on the same street in any city.

Mart slowed to thirty and watched the kids playing soccer while he crawled through the school zone. The players were of varied ages. Small country schools necessitated participation across several grades just to make up two teams for softball, touch football or today's choice. The local school had a good reputation. Parents from Hill Spring, Leavitt and even Waterton Park often chose to drive their students here rather than send them on convenient buses to schools in larger towns.

Mart pushed down on the accelerator and exceeded the sixty kilometres per hour maximum descending to Fish Creek. The hill out of the small valley and community robbed the aging compact car of much of what had been gained. It was only a five minute drive to the junction with Alberta Highway 501 where a brand new blue provincial sign advertised the hamlet of Beazer and the services of Police Outpost Provincial Park. The section of road as far as Beazer had recently been paved, abbreviating the dust and washboards of Mart's trips to the community pasture, and Wendell's place along the way.

As he took the sharp turn onto the gravel, away from Beazer and toward the now nonexistent hamlet of Seddon, Mart recalled his last fast predawn trip. It was hard to believe Jacobsen was not waiting impatiently at the end of today's jaunt. He had known the old man since his first summer here in '95. Uncle Seth had brought an excited boy to the Jacobsen ranch on the creek to introduce him to mountain stream fishing. Mart had caught his first trout upstream from the white stucco house on a bent safety pin tied to a mop handle – the best Aunt Emma could rig at the last minute.

Before he got to Wendell's, Mart spotted Kent's black extended cab GMC make the turn ahead of him. Another of Kent's near-perfect attributes – promptness. The small wheels of the Toyota thumped repeatedly over the cattle guard. Kent motioned Mart to his vehicle and then bent back to his Blackberry. He was still texting when Mart hopped into the passenger seat. The late-model pickup's interior was immaculate.

Kent's family had money. His lawyer father had kept their mixed farm south of Leavitt as a hobby. Mr. Lindholm had been disappointed when his son had dropped out of university a couple of years short of a business degree to make more than a weekend diversion of the place. The man had graciously admitted error when Kent had become one of the few thriving agriculturalists in the area. His investments in premier Red Angus breeding stock and good quality alfalfa hay had paid off quickly the no interest loans the lawyer had at first reluctantly extended to his son.

At times Mart envied his friend, but it was hard to begrudge his successes. Kent was generous to a fault and had never lorded his superior financial status over Mart or anyone else. He also had the good sense never to offer Mart anything that looked like charity. There was only one gripe Mart had concerning his friend and he would avoid that issue as long as possible.

The interior of the pickup seemed extremely quiet after the rattle of the old car.

"It's odd coming here and not expecting to get grilled by Wendell." Mart was awkward confiding his sense of loss related to the old man's death. "He's been such a fixture that I can't imagine the Poll Haven lease without him running the show."

Kent listened without interruption until he was sure Mart was through and then asked several questions about the circumstances of the accident. Mart explained what he had heard and how he found the old man. "He was all broken. His brittle bones couldn't take the fall."

"What kind of idiots would spook some old geezer's horse and then just ride away without checking to see if he was OK?"

Mart reluctantly voiced his suspicions, "The quad riders left knowing that Jacobsen was injured. I'm pretty sure of that."

"The cops'll get 'em," Kent offered.

Wendell's truck and trailer were undisturbed, but a couple of tall 4X4 pickups with trailers and an old crew cab with a deck for hauling ATVs were parked in a cluster around it. Mart had forgotten that today was Friday. The weekend warriors were getting a head start on their adrenalin-fuelled mayhem. Mart's blood began to boil. He tried to convince himself that yesterday's culprits would hardly be blatantly parked next to the dead man's outfit, but he regretted not having a fast saddle horse along to chase them down and remind them of proper etiquette. If nothing else, it would have been a fitting tribute to old man Jacobsen.

Mart thanked Kent for the ride.

"You okay?" was the blond man's reply.

"I will be," said Mart.

"You coming tonight?"

"Where?"

"The rodeo."

Mart had forgotten about the pro rodeo in Cardston tonight. He wasn't sure he was up to it. "Maybe."

"It might do you some good."

Mart smiled. Kent didn't want him to be alone. "Ah, shucks. You're worried about me."

Kent rolled his eyes. "Shut the door!"

Mart slammed it shut and Kent made a wide U-turn around the trailers. Kent Lindholm shook his fist in mock irritation as he exited the gate.

CHAPTER 10 ✷ CAT'S OUT

It took a bit of manoeuvring to get the trailer around the parked vehicles and headed out the gate. Mart cursed the recreationalists several times before he left the corrals and one more time on the road back to the Lee Creek Jacobsen ranch as yet another set of yahoos in jacked-up, mud-splattered four wheel drives going the opposite direction crowded him to the edge of the road.

The Toyota was parked at the barn. Mart drove past it and rolled the truck and trailer around the worn grass of an ill-defined turnaround. He climbed out of the truck and took out the keys. He started for the barn, but went back to the battered box of the vehicle for the halter. He would have to do something with the old mare eventually.

As he started back toward the barnyard a movement near the door of the house caught his eye. It was the cat. She was squatting beneath a shrub just outside and left of the doorway. She was not looking at Mart. Instead she crouched staring at the cut screen.

"I'll be right back to feed you," Mart reassured the feline fur ball and half turned toward the barn. Something made him slowly turn his attention back to the doorway. That was odd. The solid wooden door of the house was closed tightly. He was certain he had left it ajar so the cat could push through the screen and then around the door. Perhaps it hadn't been such a good idea. The wind must have pulled it shut and kept the poor creature out, though it was probably better locked out than in. He had not seen a litter box.

Once more Mart turned toward the barn. A third time he stopped. Wind? There hadn't been a breath at home last night or this morning. He doubted there had been much difference here. He looked at the cat one more time. Whatever was keeping her attention had to be pretty important to the scraggly puss. Or she must be very hungry.

"All right! All right! Here I come." Mart dropped the halter in the road and headed for the house.

The cat sat up on her haunches as Mart swung open the screen and placed his hand on the glass doorknob. It was one of those old-fashioned affairs formed to look like a huge cut diamond. The door dragged a bit on the worn linoleum and the hinges squeaked briefly. He stepped aside and looked at the cat.

"Coming in?" he asked her. In spite of his polite invitation all she did was to crook her neck sideways to peer around him and the edge of the open barrier. Her yellow eyes scanned the small room cautiously. "Well?" Mart insisted. Still the cat sat in her shady spot. She glanced up at him once then continued to scrutinize the interior of the old house suspiciously.

"Gees! Suit yourself!" Mart muttered and moved in through the entry. He left the wooden door wide open so the cat could push through the screen if she came to her senses.

He surveyed the interior of the kitchen. Nothing seemed amiss. The furniture was what you would expect. A metal-legged table covered with a laminate in a grey patchwork design was the main feature. Two chairs with a similar pattern in vinyl were pulled up to it. Another identical chair was beside a gas range minus a good fifth of its white enamel. The fourth chair had the same covering on the back, but its seat had been replaced with bright red Naugahyde. There was an old Bakelite radio on a fairly new Kenmore fridge. On the mottled green Arborite counter sat a microwave oven. The plastic cover still protected the glass door and finger pad. Had it been a present from the Utah daughter that old Wendell had never bothered to learn to use?

Mart turned slowly around. Should he really snoop further? That is when he noticed the cat food dish. It was overturned and water had been slopped to form small puddle around its own plastic container.

"Damn it! I probably let in a skunk." The cautious feline was still outside.

Mart carefully looked under the table and behind the stove. The refrigerator was pushed too far back to hide a stink-weasel. He poked his head around the wide painted doorjamb to scan the small living room. There were three doors off that chamber. Only one was open. That would be Wendell's bedroom. The others were probably vacant. He desperately hoped Wendell's was too.

Mart crouched warily in the centre of the living room and peeked under the two easy chairs and the chesterfield. There was no movement or observable striped fluffy tail. He stood and walked softly across the room to the open door. It was a cramped cell not more than three metres square. Gratefully the closet sliders were closed. The double bed was in one corner. It was going to be dangerous to look beneath it. He would be too close to the animal to escape a serious dousing if it were under there. Mart held his breath and dropped to his knees. No rustlings or malodorous emissions could be detected. So far so good. Another quick intake of air and Mart laid his head on the scarred hardwood. Nothing. Not even a dust bunny. The bureau was too low for anything but the smallest baby skunk. He would come back to it if he found nothing elsewhere.

Mart stood and re-entered the living room. He was out of ideas. Back to the kitchen he went. Then he noticed the bathroom. Its doorway had been hidden behind the open one that could be used to close off the entry from the kitchen. The bathroom's white painted door was slightly ajar.

"There you are you little bugger!"

Mart walked quietly, but with purpose, to the mostly-closed door. Through the hand-width crack he could see a small high window with faded yellow curtains. There were little blue ceramic fish on the wall above a vintage toilet straight out of a 1950s Alfred Hitchcock movie. By moving his head this way and that he determined there was no mustelid hidden behind that ancient piece of plumbing. Mart placed a hand on the middle of the three-paneled door. He began to tentatively swing it back. A bathrobe or some other piece of clothing was hanging from a hook on the back of the door. It blocked his vision so he stooped to look beneath it and through the slot between the hinges.

The wooden slab snapped back into the bathroom with a shocking velocity. Mart jumped back, startled. He looked up just in time to catch sight of a large black form and a white stubby bottle in a gloved hand being swung at his head.

Mart ducked and rolled away instinctively. The bottle glanced off his forehead just above his eye and bounced onto the floor without breaking. An odd thought crossed his mind at that moment; bottles do not really shatter like they do in the movies. There was a strong odour, but it was more pleasant by far than any skunk he had ever encountered. He tried to roll up onto his feet when a tall leather boot slammed into his ribs. Any air remaining in his lungs stagnated there as he gasped for breath. He continued to roll and took the next boot to the back before crashing into the chair and kitchen range. His head rebounded off the corner of the lower cabinets and vibrated the door open. He came face to face with Wendell's cast iron fry pan. He reached above his head and grasped the slotted handle of the heavy pan just as his assailant kicked again. His extended arm caught the blow intended for his skull. He was just able to keep the frying pan in his grasp. He spun around on the slick linoleum floor to watch the next swing of the black boot. The toe landed squarely in the centre of the iron pan. It jumped from Mart's grasp, but he picked it up again, rolled to a sitting position and swung it edgewise at the shin of a solidly built man dressed in black jeans and a dark blue T-shirt who was recovering for another kick. The tall boot spared the man a splintered tibia, but he dropped to one knee and cried out through a black and orange bandana covering his face below the eyes. He swung a fist at Mart, missed as the rancher slammed back again against the stove, then the masked man was up and out the door.

Mart tried get up in case the fellow came back, but he slipped on the wet, slick floor, went down and lay there gasping. His eyes were blurry and he felt like his kidneys had burst. Over the buzz inside his cranium he could barely make out the starting and revving of a motor outside. The mechanical sound augmented and then receded rapidly up the gravel road.

It took several minutes before Mart could finally breathe and see again. He noticed Wendell's cologne bottle spilled on the kitchen floor, the small red plastic stopper halfway across the room. He had nearly succumbed to death by Old Spice.

CHAPTER 11 ✻ DEAR DIARY

Mart sat up carefully and gently leaned his bruised lower back against the cabinets. He dabbed tentatively at his forehead with the ends of his fingers. There was blood from a cut, but not much. What there was a good deal of was swelling. A large bump was pushing its way from his left eyebrow. He took a couple of small breaths, then larger ones, trying to determine if any ribs were broken.

Mart had been in few fights. None had been very serious. He had typically talked his way out of the usual type of confrontations one has in high school and in bars. He had not always done so without giving the impression he was a bit of a coward. Perhaps he was one. Mostly he had not wanted to have to admit to Aunt Em that he had been fighting. But today his regret was related more to the physical rather than to the emotional repercussions. The dark-clad guy had been pretty serious. Mart glanced at the cast iron implement overturned on the floor and cringed. He wondered what would have happened if he had not been able to put up some kind of opposition.

Mart winced at the needles of pain in his side and back while pulling himself up using the edge of the kitchen counter. He slid his hand into the pocket of his shirt to attempt to reach his telephone. His forearm felt like it had been driven over by a small truck. He fished out the big black device and pulled up its short antenna while it went through the lengthy process of turning on.

He dialled 911 and placed the device next to his left ear, flinched and transferred to his right. No service. He would have to go to the top of the hill. The slopes of the Lee Creek Valley were blocking his transmission. He took two steps toward the door.

"What am I thinking?!" Mart exclaimed. He was completely muddled. He turned back to the kitchen, picked up the receiver of Wendell's old black telephone, almost placed it against his sore ear, transferred it to his other hand and dialled. The land line worked fine.

To a man with a raspy voice Mart gave his name and explained briefly that he had been attacked. "I guess you better send the police."

The fellow immediately asked, "Are you injured, Mr. McKinnon? Should I dispatch an ambulance?"

Without hesitation Mart said, "No," but could tell that one was going to be sent anyway.

"Constable Boissoneau from the Cardston detachment may want to be contacted. There might be some connection with the death of the owner of the house only yesterday." Mart ignored the man's urging to stay on the line and disconnected.

Turning again to the centre of the room, Mart began to wonder why on earth there had been a man in Wendell's house. A burglar? Unless the old man had hundred dollar bills stuffed in his Posturepedic there were relatively few treasures in the modest home. It would hardly be worth even the small risk of being caught. What is more, why would the fellow choose to be there when there was a car parked in the yard?

Mart was starting to feel a bit queasy. He sat gingerly on the mismatched kitchen chair and laid his head in his hands with the same type of care. After several minutes the unsettled feeling passed and he looked around the kitchen. As far as he could tell, the spilled cologne, upturned skillet and a slight rearrangement of the furniture resulting from the brief scuffle were the only changes the room had seen in twenty years. The table was a bit askew. Wendell's eyeglasses were on the floor, but the pen had miraculously remained on the table top.

The man had emerged from the bathroom. It was the only room Mart had yet to check in his search for the other skunk. Another fifteen minutes passed until he stood carefully, waited to make sure he was not going to feel sick again, and shuffled to the now wide-open door.

The medicine cabinet was closed and the toilet lid was even down. There was an empty spot on a low glass shelf where a slightly worn ring indicated several years of residency by the white bottle now lying spilled in the kitchen. The clay fish scrutinized Mart with pursed lips. Apparently they saw nothing amiss either.

Mart opened, scanned and closed the triple-mirrored vanity. He embarrassed himself by opening and closing the lid on the obsolete porcelain throne. "What did I think I'd find in there?" he wondered to himself.

The sound of crunching gravel and the hiss of a switched off air conditioner compressor caught his attention through the single glaze of the small window. He stepped into the kitchen and turned toward the front door. He fought the urge to straighten the table. As he stepped around it he remembered the journal. He was on his hands and knees looking for the book when a stentorian voice came through the screen door.

"Mr. McKinnon?"

"I'm in here," answered Mart. He winced. Talking hurt his ribs and his head was really beginning to ache.

Constable Boissoneau stepped into the room. His weapon was not drawn, but his hand was near the black rubber-cushioned handle. He found Mart in a humble kneeling position. Mart stared up at him and said, "He took the book."

Boissoneau scanned the room, gave Mart a pitying look and called over his shoulder, "It looks clear." A medium-sized woman with short blond hair sticking out from beneath the shiny black beak of her cap stepped in next. She ignored the constable and Mart. The stripes on her greyish-blue shirt announced she was Boissoneau's superior. She inspected the place efficiently without disturbing anything but the previously closed doors and then returned to give the constable a nod.

By this time the young French-Canadian had crouched to look Mart in the eye. Once again he called to someone outside. Two Cardston emergency medical technicians dressed all in navy blue came into the room, the first carrying an oversized duffle bag which he folded out on the floor. The second man crouched next to the constable. "Where are you injured?"

The young rancher tried to make a comprehensive list. "He hit me with the bottle." Mart pointed to the bump over his eye. "He booted me pretty hard in the ribs and again on my back. I blocked a kick with my arm." It was starting to sound like the laundry list from a cage fight, so he gave up the inventory.

The EMTs made a quick exam using several tools that they unclipped from their well-stocked belts and a few things from their large kit. After a few minutes one of them offered the proclamation Mart feared. "You'll need a trip to the hospital to determine if you have suffered a severe or a minor concussion."

Mart's odd objection only served to convince them of the need. "He took the book," he declared again to the two RCMP members. They stared back. Mart realized it sounded like babbling. He tried again. "I searched the whole house. Everything is here except Wendell's journal. Why would he take that?"

Boissoneau replied, "Mr. McKinnon. I think we better wait until after you have seen the doctor before we take your statement."

"I'd rather talk about it now," countered Mart.

The constable looked at the medics and one gave him a shrug and a nod.

"This is Sergeant Dietrich. Just give us a small account."

Mart relaxed somewhat at the man's use of term "small" instead of "short". He found the constable's slight accent and professional demeanour quite reassuring. He went over the details of his arrival. He even gave credit to the cat. "She tried to warn me that something was wrong." He finished by reiterating that the old man's diary was missing.

"How do you know the book is gone?" Sergeant Dietrich asked.

"I saw it when I was here last night. The glasses and pen are still here, but not the brown notebook that was lying open on the table."

"You're sure nothing else is gone?" asked Dietrich.

"I guess I'm not completely certain. Nothing else seems disturbed."

"No TV or DVD?" Boissoneau queried, looking into the small living room.

"No reception." Mart had to elaborate when both RCMP looked at him in mild disbelief. "The creek valley blocks it. You can't just use an antenna. Wendell wouldn't bother with satellite dish." He hesitated and then asked them a question. "How would the guy know Wendell wouldn't be here?"

The sergeant shrugged. Her green eyes were striking and she flashed a pleasant smile aimed at reassuring him. "There are people who make their living breaking into the properties of deceased persons. They check obituaries and listen to town gossip. It's more common in the city, but could happen here. Mr. Jacobsen's death made the Lethbridge radio news this morning. It seems a long way out of the way, but perhaps the seclusion is what made it attractive. We will try for some prints on doors and on the bottle," she pointed at the cologne container and the constable immediately retrieved and bagged it.

"Gloves. The guy was wearing gloves."

Sergeant Dietrich shrugged again.

The EMTs moved restlessly and the sergeant stepped aside. Mart had the length of the trip to Cardston to ponder the missing chronicle.

CHAPTER 12 ✽ BECKY

Mart was released by mid afternoon. He had to call Kent for a ride. For the second time that day the pair parted company at the Jacobsen ranch.

"For heaven's sake Mart, let me drive you the rest of the way." Kent had voiced his concerns over Mart's state of health for the greater part of the drive out.

"I'm fine – just a bit of a headache."

"You sure as hell are!"

Mart rolled his eyes at this bit of habitual amicable abuse and had to catch himself by grabbing the edge of the pickup's box to keep from losing his balance. He hid the dizziness from Kent by shutting the door quickly. Kent drove away shaking his blond head.

The cat was back and seemed less apprehensive about the house, but was more wary of Mart. He left food and water and risked leaving the door open one more night. He would check with Mrs. Lorne. Mattie had been begging for a cat and Mart was certain Wendell would be happy to know his only house companion would be taken care of. And nine-year-old girls ought to have a pet.

The halter had been run over at least once, but was not severely damaged. He took it to the barn and checked on the old grey. The wounds on her hocks and rear cannons were puzzling. Some of the muck had fallen off and one scrape on the left gaskin was particularly bad. Mart bent stiffly to scrutinize the abrasion. There was a black stripe above and below the injury. Mart tried to rub it off, even licking his less than clean fingers to wash it off. It wasn't mud. It looked like the rubber left on cement driveways when someone turned their wheels sharply. Mart recalled the evidence that the ATV tires had bounced off of something before the mare had gone berserk and thrown Wendell. Now he had something more to add to his statement to Boissoneau. After the attack in Jacobsen's house the constable would have two for him to sign.

He let three black bulls out of the corral and into the same pasture as the grey. He would probably separate them again when he came for the cat.

Mart had been instructed not to drive, but took the Toyota home anyway. Kent had given up playing mother hen after the first ten minutes of the argument on the drive out from Cardston. Now Mart regretted it. The glare of the sun seemed worse than usual, but his mild concussion felt no worse than a bad headache.

At home Mart took care of a few chores. He turned out the horses. No riding today. He had scheduled some time to gather a few more of the large round hay bales Peterson had baled for him on the eighty acres along the road to Hill Spring. He decided to spare his concussion the bouncing along in the tractor. The bales were almost too heavy for the twenty-year-old Ford tractor and any pocket gopher mound set it to dancing like a marriageable Masai.

Mart went inside and sat in the old recliner that Kent had claimed no longer fit in the Lindholm house. Mart had been warned about going to sleep, but was sure he could resist. Two hours later he awoke with a start. He was sweating profusely. Late summer sunshine was angling through the west windows. Typically he closed the blinds when he came in for lunch. He was off his routine. Happy to discover he had not died in his sleep, he threw forward the lever that lowered the leg rest, grabbed the arms of the chair and pulled himself upright. He then attempted to sit back down before he fell. He had arisen too rapidly. Unfortunately his lightheaded state resulted in his missing the seat of the chair and plunking down on the arm. Nevertheless he was able to retain the narrow perch long enough to regain his sea legs. He finally stood up slowly and added a bruised tail bone and damaged pride to the list of injuries.

Mart plodded through his evening chores and went back in. There was a message on the scratchy tape of the answering machine from the LDS bishop in Leavitt. Mart was too cheap to pay the phone company for voice mail. The bishop said Wendell's funeral was set for Monday. Mart was surprised to hear that the family had requested he be a pallbearer. He sat at the kitchen table for a few minutes and began contemplating that request and his Friday evening. Kent had suggested the rodeo. That was before the beating. He didn't feel much like sitting his bruised butt on bleachers, but wasn't too keen on spending the evening trying to stay awake until bedtime. He left the table, started a can of beans warming on the stove and went to look at himself in the bathroom mirror. The goose egg had diminished in size and was barely noticeable. There was a nasty gash above his eye and he could just detect a purplish bruise beginning to form around that orb. If he wore his good hat low it might not be too obvious.

A meagre meal, careful shower and his best old clothes later, Mart was back in the Toyota. April Wine was pounding out Oowatanite and he regretted having to keep the volume low for his head's sake. It had been one of his mom's favourite songs. It was due to her influence that he listened to rock from the sixties and seventies.

He drove through Mountain View, ignoring the thirty kilometres per hour zone because school was out. Some tourists were lined up at the Barn Store market to get the cheaper gas before hitting Waterton Lakes National Park. A couple of old guys were sitting in the shade of the building licking ice cream. The place was well known for its generous cones and heaps of fries.

Once he was rolling freely out on the highway, Mart made note of the lack of heavy traffic. The busiest part of the summer season was definitely over. Just past the Beazer turn-off he instinctively raised a hand to a white Chevy. The driver was either blinded by the evening glow in the western sky, or she had decided to snub him. Candace Cowan grimaced and held the steering wheel with both hands as she flew past at a rate Mart guessed was well beyond the speed limit.

A few minutes later he was passing the hamlet of Leavitt. The Latter Day Saint church building was just off the highway. Old Wendell's life would be celebrated there before they took him west of town to the cemetery. It was still hard to imagine the old grouch was gone.

It was getting late. The rodeo would have already started. Twilight had settled on the Town of Cardston as Mart crested the rise east of Leavitt. The Mormon Temple was all lit up. It was the first thing motorists noticed as they approached town from the west, like Mart was doing, or from the direction of Lethbridge. It was an impressive blocky structure of white granite quarried from a site near the Kootenai Lakes and Nelson, British Columbia. It had taken the Mormons ten years to complete its construction. It had been the first Latter Day Saint temple built outside the USA.

The members of the church had a strange affinity for the United States of America. This was in spite of the fact that the first Mormons to arrive in Canada had done so in order to escape persecution and imprisonment in the States for their practice of polygamy during the mid to late 1800s. The continuing connection with the US was no doubt due to the fact that the church's headquarters remained in Utah.

The rites carried out in the spectacular white building were held in reverence and not discussed outside of it. Regardless of its use or origins, there was no doubt that it was a beautiful structure. It was no wonder that the federal government had designated it as a national historic site.

Mart rolled over the last two hills before descending into the town. The Agridome was located west of the community and just a few blocks south of the highway. He made the turn just before the UFA fuel outlet and the John Deere dealership. The Agridome parking area was lit by scattered sodium vapour lights on power poles. It was full! Mart had to turn around and park out along the street. The long walk to the doors allowed him to hobble out some of the stiffness. By the time he arrived at the table and folding chairs that made up the ticket booth, his gait appeared to belong to a man only twice his age.

He paid his fee to a pleasant pair of senior citizens and stumped up the few steps leading to the bottom of the grandstand. The public address system was turned up too loud and the announcer's voice was a knife through Mart's ears. His nose twitched in reaction to the arena dust and an aroma that was an odd fusion of manure, sweat and boiled hot dogs. The young rancher waited until there was a break between barrel racers and walked across the front of the stands, trying not to stumble while scanning the crowd for someone he knew. He almost trampled two small kids on their way to the concession stand located below and at the back of the bleachers.

The crowd was made up of a mixture of townspeople, County residents, out of town supporters of one contestant or another, and residents of the Blood Reserve that was located adjacent to the town. Mart had counted on spotting Kent. The tall blond fellow was usually easy to notice and often at the centre of some lively activity. Instead he spied another blond head that made his heart leap a little.

Becky Sorenson half-stood and waved exuberantly. Her smile was dazzling in the harsh lights of the stadium. Her greenish-blue eyes always squinted when she smiled or laughed. She had been cute in high school. She was a beautiful woman now. Her presence was welcome and at the same time unsettling. She scooted her two female friends over to create a spot for Mart and patted the seat beside her. Mart sat, but just grinned through her greeting until she cuddled up to him warmly. Then the grin faded beneath a solid blush.

"Mart, I am so happy you came. I was hoping to see you. I talked the girls into a night out. I promised it wouldn't all be dust and manure. I knew there'd be somebody to visit with. Do you know Pam and Martina? There was just nothing else to do in town. We almost drove to Lethbridge, but what are chances of catching up with anyone we know there?"

Mart grinned into her barrage. It was after she had bubbled along through several more rather meaningless explanations of what had brought her there that she noticed his bruised face. Unabashedly she yanked off his slightly dusty tan Biltmore and inspected the cut and purplish skin.

"What did you do to yourself, Mart?"

Because the announcer had begun to banter with the clown-clad bull fighter, he was forced to shout some basic details into her ear in order to bring her up to speed. "I was riding with Wendell. Wendell Jacobsen. Some four wheeler riders spooked his old horse somehow. I said, the old mare spooked and Wendell came off."

He had only been seated for five minutes, but Becky stood and dragged him into the aisle, down the steps and through the crowded portal leading to the concessions. They were salmon swimming upstream as a couple of dozen spectators rushed back to catch the bull riding. It was always the most popular event.

Becky pulled Mart past the washroom doors and to the far end of the hallway under the stands. "Okay, I got that Mr. Jacobsen had an accident, but what happened to you?"

Becky listened intently as he described his discovery of Wendell Jacobsen in a bit more detail. He left out some of the more graphic details and omitted his suspicions about the lack of ethics exhibited by the drivers of the quads.

"There was a guy at the Jacobsen house when I went back there this morning. I am completely puzzled by the attack on me. The cops think it was a thief who keeps an eye out to rob old folk's places when they die." The explanation seemed to deflect some of her concern. Mart gasped when Becky stood on her toes, wrapped her arms around him and maintained the embrace. It was not just the bruised muscles that made him catch his breath.

"I'm so sorry, Marty," she reverted to the high school nickname she had often used to pester him. Although he didn't like the appellation as a rule, coming from her it was an endearment.

Becky had been at least in the top ten as far as popularity went. She hadn't been homecoming queen, but she had been courted by every jock and town councillor's son throughout her school career. She had dated all the most popular guys and had received at least a dozen offers to go to the graduation ball. Mart had not been one of them, although he thought she had hinted at it. He didn't know if the insinuation had really been there or if he had simply been flattering himself. Kent had gracefully avoided the issue. In the end she showed up with some doctor's son who had graduated from Raymond High School two years previously. He had been a rival football star and a few of the Cardston Cougar grads had commented bitterly on her choice of companions. Mart had wished he had shown the same gumption that Kent had when he had rapidly defended her.

Becky had followed the handsome young Raymond man to the University of Alberta and eventually married him a year before he finished his studies to become an orthodontist. Although Mart had secretly pined for the vivacious girl, her departure had quelled the tension that had been brewing between Kent and him for the last year and a half of school.

Mart had heard nothing of the trouble in that marriage until the end of last year when Becky had reappeared sans wedding band. She had stayed with her folks for a couple of months and then moved in to replace the renters in her grandmother's old house. The familiar butterflies were back, but so was the subconscious strain on the relationship between the two friends.

Becky held Mart close for a long time. The butterflies had metamorphosed into fireflies and were well on their way to becoming meteorites as she drew away and looked directly into Mart's eyes. A moth to her flame, he was just about to kiss her when he froze in place. Just down the hallway, and with his hand already on the swinging door to the washroom, Kent had paused to gaze at the intimate scene taking place in the corner.

Mart stepped back, embarrassed. Becky looked at him quizzically. Kent looked uncomfortable, but pushed his way into the washroom. When he came back out Becky and Mart were talking quietly a few steps away from the doorway.

Mart stumbled through his excuses. "I was just telling Becky about Wendell." It felt a little like lying even though it was the truth. He glanced at Becky who seemed oblivious to the strained circumstances.

She expressed her shock in the usual rapid fire style. She even reached up and brushed her hand across Mart's damaged forehead as she conveyed her outrage at the brazen attempted robbery and assault at the old rancher's house. "Look what they did to our poor Marty!" Mart almost jerked his head away. "Why would anyone attack him? We shouldn't be making him stand here. Are you all right, Mart?" She grabbed his hand and dragged him back up the steps to the seating area of the stadium.

The three returned to Becky's seat. The first round of bull riders had taken their scores and the second steer wrestler was backing an excited horse into the space beside the chute. His hazer was already in place. Again Becky's girlfriends reluctantly shifted, displacing a young couple and their small child one seat over as well.

The spirited young woman chatted to Mart and Kent collectively, but occasionally placed a hand on the knee or arm of one or the other to share a private remark. Mart was as confused now as he had been as an adolescent. There was no doubt that he was attracted to her, but he just couldn't figure out whether she was really interested in him or in Kent. He couldn't help but resent his friend's good looks and easy manner. How could anyone compete with that? Yet he thought he detected an unusual nervousness in his comrade as well.

The tension had eased slightly by the time the last round of saddle broncs finished with a spectacular and unintentional dismount by the rider. He had gone over the big piebald's head, flipped over casually and landed on his rear in the soft churned up dirt. The crowd gasped in unison as the big Clydesdale cross had leapt right over the cowboy seated in the centre of the arena.

As the audience rose to swarm toward the doors, the clown provided one last thrill as he raced through the thick dirt just in advance of a strategically released Brangus bull.

Kent led the way into the human gridlock. Mart hobbled down the aisle, the slow flow of the crowd concealing his painful shuffling. Becky was between them and her girlfriends followed the trio.

Negotiating the parking lot was another challenge. Headlights were beaming in every direction as vehicles nudged their way into the queue toward the two narrow drives. More than half of them were pickups and another good proportion were minivans. The predominance of pickups was more a statement about North American culture than it was about the rural nature of the area. The minivans attested to the inclination in LDS communities toward larger families.

The small group stood next to Kent's truck and chatted. There was no hurry until the majority of spectators had cleared the parking lot. One of Becky's friends was an old classmate who was from around town. She was married, but had somehow ditched her family for a girls' night out. The second was oddly enough her former sister-in-law from Raymond. The five of them tarried until Mart was feeling exhausted. The banter had been light. They were all having fun, but he was relieved when the married lady excused herself.

Pam, a short lady with curly brown hair spoke up, "Perhaps we better go check to make sure we still have live spouses and standing houses."

Jan, the sister-in-law, headed out next driving a small Volvo that seemed quite out of place amid the Fords and Dodges.

Becky babbled on for a time. She finished with a declaration. "It's great to have some of the old gang back together."

Mart hardly heard her. Fatigue mixed with uneasiness made it difficult to concentrate. He was torn between the desire to flee a situation that may soon become more uncomfortable and jealous apprehension at leaving Becky and Kent alone.

The ringing in his battered skull finally won. Mart stated his excuses. "I need to get my sore head home. I'll see you guys soon." He suffered an uncomfortable hug from the slim beauty and blurted another awkward farewell to his best friend. "Thanks for being chauffer today, Kent."

The old Toyota stuttered to a reluctant start and Mart rolled away without daring to look back.

CHAPTER 13 ✷ PUZZLES

Saturday dawned cool and overcast. Mart gazed off to the northeast. There was little wind, but the hint of a breeze could be felt from that direction. The high ground north of Mountain View, locally known as the Watson Ridge, was barely visible through the low cloud. Uncle Seth had once remarked about the upslope weather in relation to those hills. He had indicated the ridge and asked, "You see those hills?" Mart had nodded naively. "When you can see those hills it's gonna rain." Seth continued – ignoring the young man's confused gape. "If you can't see them, it is raining."

Mart plodded through his morning chores. His head felt much better, but his ribs ached terribly. If the rain held off he just had to get in the rest of the hay. Peterson had done him the favour of getting it baled up early in spite of some challenging wet weather and he wanted to get the yearling heifers onto that piece to eat up some of what was left along the fences and irrigation ditches.

It was still not raining by 10:30, so he hooked his rickety flatbed trailer onto the hitch of the pickup and headed to the Hill Spring road. The tractor was already there. He would have to get a neighbour to ferry him back to get either the pickup or the tractor once he was done. Running the ranch alone had several drawbacks and getting his equipment from place to place was one of them. Aunt Emma used to jibe her husband about having to drop whatever job she was involved in just to play cab driver for him. That ended the first summer when Seth allowed an unlicensed Mart to drive between the scattered parcels of land that made up the ranch. The traffic authorities turned a blind eye to underage ranch kids driving in those days. It was considered a necessity of agricultural life. Emma Tidwell's taxi service began again when Mart took over after Uncle Seth's passing.

The whole process of bringing in the hay was slowed by the fact that he had to tow each load home with the tractor. He needed its frontend loader to load in the field and then to unload back at the home place. That meant he had to unhitch it at home and again in the field when he brought the empty wagon back and started to collect more bales.

Mart had pulled home two loads when the mist began to moisten his crack-streaked windshield. He hurried and loaded one more batch, hooked the tractor to the wagon and headed out for the slow ride home. It would have to be the last trip of the day. The big round bales being a bit damp when stacked wasn't as big a deal as the little rectangular ones had been, but he didn't like to place them one on top of another after a good dousing nor did he want to cut up the rain-wet turf around the stack yard with his tractor tires.

Mart had pondered over two important problems while bouncing around the field. Some tasks lent themselves well to reflection. Rounding up large spheres of spun prairie grass was one of those. The first issue was what to do about Becky. He just could not read her intentions. Did she want him or Kent? Perhaps she did not know herself. His brow became deeply furrowed when he considered that she might be playing them both. She had always been a flirt.

On his eighteenth birthday he had worked up enough courage to ask her to celebrate with him the following weekend. Her reaction had made his heart leap like a month-old calf. She had beamed her pure white smile at him, said she'd be delighted and had given him a big hug on the spot. He had been certain at that moment that she had simply been waiting for him to make a move.

The Saturday evening dinner had been one of the most memorable events of his school years. Becky had appeared on her parent's stairs while Mart fidgeted under the amused scrutiny of her mother and father. He had vaulted off the sofa to watch her slim form descend to grab his arm and squeeze it intimately. She had seemed so at ease that he was actually able to eat a few mouthfuls at the restaurant. As usual, she dominated the conversation, but he relaxed enough to make several very witty remarks. She sat so close to him in Uncle Seth's old pickup that he felt as if his thigh would spontaneously combust where hers made contact with his. The goodnight kiss turned into kisses and he was pulling up to Aunt Emma's flowerbed before he realized he was driving home.

Unfortunately the real reason the night was so memorable was that it was their last together. The following Friday Mart had gone to town searching tentatively for some excitement. The Tidwell ranch truck had rattled off Main Street to drive up the hill toward Cardston High. The dusty headlights reflected briefly off the shiny fenders of Mrs. Lindholm's new Buick as it turned into the Lions' Park drive and rolled slowly past the baseball diamond. Kent had to be the driver. His mom would hardly have been cruising town that late in the evening.

Mart roared in after the car in the hope of joining whatever crowd of boisterous town kids Kent had accumulated for the night's merrymaking. He skidded to a halt when Kent nosed the car up to a tree across the driveway from Lee Creek. The vision of Becky's bright yellow bouncing ponytail was still imprinted in Mart's memory. It spun away from him and her face glowed white in the pickup lights. Kent's eyes were squinting directly behind her. She was practically in his lap.

Mart had tried to back the vehicle away nonchalantly, hoping the bright lights would be taken for those of just some other joy rider, but he knew he had hesitated too long to be dismissed so easily. The blond couple had stared after him until he was certain the dusty two-toned GMC had been identified passing beneath one of the sparingly scattered street lamps. He had not answered when Aunt Em questioned him on the early arrival home. He had gone straight to his room and shut the door.

Mart and Kent had hardly spoken for almost a month after that night. The healing had only started after Becky had shunned the hometown crowd to choose her Raymond alumnus date. Her absence from their circle of friends did not go unnoticed, but out of kindness was never mentioned.

The second riddle troubling Mart was about Wendell. Mart stared off toward the dark bulk of Poll Haven. Just what had happened up there with the quad riders? He went over all the events of that day. It just did not add up. Why had the old mare spooked? Who were the riders of the all terrain vehicles? He felt a stab of remorse when his mind turned to the Pruitts. But maybe Jack and Candace had seen something. Then Mart remembered that Wendell had been talking about something just before they had separated. He had spoken of something he had seen recently that was strange to him. He claimed he had never seen it before. Could that have anything at all to do with the accident?

It was bucketing down when Mart darted from where he parked the tractor and hay wagon next to the barn and skipped up the slippery wooden steps of the mobile home. He dropped all his wet clothes except his boxers at the door; one of the advantages to living alone. He took a very quick shower and found some dry jeans and tee-shirt. He gobbled down two slices of toast and a handful of grapes that tasted slightly musty. He had left them too long and they had begun to wrinkle. On his way back out he almost kicked the wet garments aside, but went back to hang them over the shower curtain rod.

The Toyota's wipers could hardly clear the water enough for Mart to see the road. He had to keep under eighty kilometres per hour to avoid skidding the bald tires in the linear puddles forming on the asphalt. Once he touched the waterlogged gravel of the Seddon turnoff the drag of the mud was the new deterrent.

The rain had corralled the cat. She stretched and yawned from the kitchen doorway as Mart ducked into the entry. She had an odd expression when he grabbed her makeshift dishes and the bag of food from the closet. After loading those in the car he returned for the tabby. She was content enough when he picked her up, but became less so when he dashed through the rain and deposited her on the passenger seat. She became downright agitated when he fired up the engine and made the turn back toward the barn. He checked on the grey mare and the bulls the lazy man's way through the blur of his inundated windshield. What would Jacobsen's family decide to do with the stock? Selling the place would take some time, but could wait. They couldn't very well leave the cattle unattended. The ancient grey was the only horse Wendell had left. She was old enough that she only had value by weight. Maybe Wendell would have been okay with her going to the canner, but Mart would try to persuade the daughter to give the horse to some family with small kids.

When Mart pulled away again the cat was nowhere to be seen. He guessed she had never before been in a car. When he pulled into the Lorne residence the rain had let up enough that he opened the car door and scanned under the seats. The frightened feline glared back from behind an empty juice bottle. Mart had to fish her out from under the passenger seat. She growled, but did not scratch.

Young Mattie Lorne was already standing on the wet gravel drive in her stocking feet. Her mother was on the porch. Mart could tell she was amused by the little girl's eagerness, but not relishing the Tide challenge of getting her neat white socks sparkling clean.

The Lorne family had purchased a five acre piece of land from one of the local ranchers. Mattie's father was a surgeon from Calgary. They only came to their place near Mountain View in the summer and on nice weekends the remainder of the year.

Subdivision of ranch land was a bit of a contentious issue. The independent character of southern Alberta ranchers was typical of rural folks and perhaps native Albertans in general. They did not like government meddling in how they chose to manage their lives and business. Cardston County had chosen to adopt a liberal attitude toward applications to convert agricultural land into country residential lots. The result was that numerous parcels had been carved up and the demand for lots had made land prices edge up beyond what ranchers could pay and realistically recover the cost through agriculture. They could not compete with wealthy urbanites looking to share little pieces of heaven. Sons and daughters of ranchers who could not afford to just give the ranch to their children had little hope of acquiring land and continuing a ranching tradition. In the words of the Eagles' Don Henley and Glenn Frey, "You call someplace paradise, kiss it goodbye."

Low cattle prices and bad weather years had forced many ranchers to consider selling small parcels and land speculators abounded, hoping to turn an easy profit by subdividing larger pieces. The County Council had persisted in the belief that more houses on smaller parcels meant more tax income. They ignored the fact that every county in western Canada and the USA had found the new subdivisions a financial drain, sucking up more funds to provide services than they yielded in their tax assessment. That left struggling agriculturalists to subsidize the services provided to the second homes of the rich.

"It's so soft!" cooed the freckle-faced youngster.

"She is used to being outside or in," Mart explained. "She may be nervous and want to wander a bit at first, so you may have to keep her inside for a few days. I have no idea if she knows how to use a litter box."

The cat cuddled up to the little girl. It would learn to be happy here and at the family's primary residence. The Lorne's had another acreage near High River. Agricultural land was disappearing at an even more alarming rate anywhere near enough to Calgary to allow upper class professionals to commute to the city.

In spite of being philosophically opposed to allowing farm land to be forever lost to secondary homes, Mart could not hold a grudge against the cash-strapped ranchers who sold it nor the pleasant folks who bought it. They generally purchased the land innocent of any harm it did to the agricultural industry. The Lorne family was a prime example. Mart had met them at a community function three or four years ago and had immediately been adopted by their little girl. She was unabashedly enamoured with cowboys in general and Mart specifically. The furry gift he had just delivered had probably kicked the crush up several notches. He thought about the old horse, but decided not to risk further alienating Mattie's mother. The idea of the cat had been hard enough to sell.

It was late afternoon when Mart pulled back through Mountain View. He automatically glanced at his speedometer when he spotted the white RCMP cruiser in the LDS church parking lot. The police were frequently there encouraging citizens to observe the thirty kilometres per hour school zone. It was odd they were there outside of school hours. He was not speeding, so was surprised when the car pulled out behind him and flashed the light bar on briefly. His first thought was that some overzealous constable had decided the aged automobile could use an inspection to make sure lights and buzzers were working. His spirits lifted and he quit rifling the glove box for registration and insurance when he recognized Boissoneau's wide shoulders and pleasant smile emerge from the sedan.

Seeing that Mart was confused over the delay, the constable explained. "I had stopped at the Barn Store to enquire after having discovered that you were not at home. They described your only two vehicles and I decided to wait a few minutes rather than drive all the way back to the Cardston detachment."

Mart and the constable agreed to meet back at the convenience store for coffee so Mart could read and sign his two reports. The owner of the place was seated behind the counter watching golf on a small television. He chuckled and addressed Mart as he walked in just behind the policeman, "I squealed on you to the cops."

"Thanks a bunch."

"I'd have caught him eventually anyway," countered the constable. "You know, Mounties always get their man and all that."

They squeezed into one of the two small booths after Boissoneau collected his coffee and Mart pulled a Mountain Dew from the cooler. The report was pretty accurate. He asked the constable to add a line about the injuries to the mare. "I suspect they are from being hit from behind by the tire of one of the quads."

Boissoneau added the observation at the end in very neat handwriting and passed the documents to Mart. While Mart scratched his messy signature on the line provided, Boissoneau stated, "If those were tire marks, I guess we can rule out the idea that the motorcyclists didn't know they had scared the horse."

Mart bit back a sarcastic remark. Boissoneau was being cautious. You could not very well expect the police to throw around accusations based solely on observations made by untrained eyes.

CHAPTER 14 ✽ CACKLE BERRIES

Instead of heading straight for home, Mart turned south on the road leading toward Payne Lake. Two dusty travel trailers were pulling out onto Highway 5 as he turned in. Each truck towing the trailers was occupied by an elderly couple. No doubt they were folks who lived in the region and who were frequent campers there. They tended to vacate the provincial recreation area at the lake whenever the weather crapped out or when it got too crowded for their tranquil fishing trips.

Two or three minutes of washboards offered access to a narrow drive between patches of diamond willow. Another five minutes of dirt road revealed a single-storey clapboard house with odd bluish and curling shingles. Several squat outbuildings created a fortress-like ring around an overgrown yard.

Mart negotiated a tight turn around a couple of rabbit hutches and drove slowly over a frayed rope attached to a fencepost at one end and to a cream-coloured nanny goat on the other. The goat stood up from her weed-encircled nest, but Mart was relieved she did not bolt while the Toyota was straddling the tether. He parked the car alongside an enclosure of rusty chicken wire that bellied out into the yard and sagged precariously from the boards of varying widths and lengths that endeavoured to hold the metal netting up. It was patched here and there with pieces of window screen and lengths of baling twine.

The door of the dilapidated cottage was wide open. Two or three accidentally free-range pullets could be seen against the wide blue skirt and rubber boots that seemed to be standing idly in the doorway with no upper torso to give them further direction. Mart's slamming car door elicited the resurrection of the back and head from below the ample backside. The head turned to reveal a reddened plump face and wispy white curls beneath a man's red plaid winter cap. The earflaps were engaged, but the cap was pulled up high to allow the ears to poke out below. Mrs. Anna Parascak was home.

The elderly lady grinned broadly as Mart walked toward her. Mart smiled back, "Hello, Mrs. Parascak. How are you getting along today?"

"Mart! Mart, I can't get my door to close. It has flapped in the wind all night."

There had not been much wind for a week or more, so Mart suspected her two or three dogs and half-dozen cats had been the perceived breeze pushing at the unlatched door. He scanned the yard at the thought. Where were the mutts that made up her pack? They habitually swarmed him at each regular visit. At that moment he heard a muffled bark from the small pasture at the back of the house. At least one of them was out there digging at pocket gopher mounds or pouncing on deer mice. A couple of the cats had emerged to lean against his pant legs and purr.

Mart stepped forward slowly. Mrs. Parascak shuffled stiffly backward out of the way on arthritic knees. He swung the door closed. Before it could latch, the bottom of the rickety wooden slab scraped at the trampled soil in front of it. Years of traffic by the household pets, and perhaps a few chickens and goats, had completely covered the cracked cement of the stoop. Pushing the door over this obstacle had dragged a bit of dirt back to the sill each time. The dust had been compacted there when the panel was forced to close and the build-up would no longer allow the latch to slide past the strike plate and into the hole.

"Where's your shovel, Mrs. Parascak?"

The old girl chuckled, "Now Mart, Mr. Parascak would never try to fix a door with a shovel."

Mart smiled back. "Let me give it a try. I promise not to break anything."

The elderly lady grinned, shrugged and pointed to the shed nearest the house. Mart walked over, pulled a rusty bolt out of the staple and swung the hasp aside. The hinges squawked and Mart ducked into the dim interior. He had scanned the disarray in the entire shed before he found the spade leaning next to him against the jamb.

Back at the doorway Mart scraped the dirt off the cement. There was a crack in the blade of the shovel and the handle was badly splintered, so he was careful to live up to his promise to avoid damaging anything. Once the cement was bare, he pulled the folding knife from his belt and began carefully prying the compressed soil from the sill and lower jambs.

"Helen phoned yesterday and told me about poor Mr. Jacobsen," Mrs. Parascak exclaimed over Mart's shoulder. "How did it happen?"

Mart paused and looked at the concerned woman. Her hearing was bad and he tried to remember to face her when he spoke. "Wendell came off his horse. I found him, but it was too late."

"And him such a good rider all these years."

"It was a bit of a surprise, but maybe it was the best way for him to go," Mart offered. "He seemed happiest when he was on horseback."

"I suppose." She hesitated, shuffled to a spot against the house where sat a weathered wooden chair without its back. She plopped down and gazed pensively at her hands folded across her abundant lap.

Mart felt a pang of regret, both for old man Jacobsen and for this kind old lady. It was easy for him to speak philosophically about leaving this world when that time seemed so far off for him. He could not quite imagine how he would feel fifty years from now. Would he still be able to speak of a friend's passing in any detached fashion?

Mart tilted back from his knees and remained squatting on the stoop. Mrs. Parascak looked up and he met her gaze. He spoke softly, but clearly. "I'll miss him. He was a bit of a grump sometimes and I thought he was kind of hard on me, but I see now how much I relied on him. He was my encyclopaedia when it came to running cattle and riding the rough country up there." Mart tilted his head southward, toward the dark slopes of Mokowan.

The declaration seemed to comfort the woman. She smiled and offered this insight, "A sculptor wouldn't bother chipping away at a rock if he couldn't see the potential for a beautiful statue somewhere locked up inside."

Mart smiled back. He hoped that was the case. He finished chiselling away the grime and tried the door. It shut easily.

"Ah! Mr. Parascak couldn't have done any better," the widow exclaimed. She pushed herself up with her hands on her knees. "Come in for some milk and cookies."

Mart grinned. She still treated him like he was eleven.

"I was hoping to buy a few eggs."

From halfway through the doorway she replied, "You can get the fresh ones from the nests on your way out. Come in! Come in!"

Mart relished the oatmeal cookies and struggled through the goat's milk while wedged between the cook stove and the kitchen cabinets. He could handle it when the nanny had been on grass, but the weedy pasture lent the liquid a flavour comparable to spoiled Brussels sprouts.

"Mrs. Parascak, you keep a diary, don't you?"

"Yes. I try to keep up with it. Sometimes I wonder why I do. Nothing very interesting happens to me anymore. It was different when Vern was here."

"What kind of things do you write? I mean, is it just personal stuff or do you keep important papers or financial information in it?"

The old lady looked a little puzzled. "Well, it's mostly an account of what happens to me and how I feel about it. I really don't have any important finances, but I don't think I'd keep any of that in there. Why do you ask?"

"It's Wendell. His journal went missing from his house." Mart chose not to offer the details. So far she had not noticed his bruises.

"His folks probably have it."

"They have not arrived yet. Anyway, there was a break in at Wendell's house."

"Oh, my!"

Mart couldn't help but be amused at her stereotypical exclamations. He sometimes felt he was talking to a storybook character when he was with Mrs. Parascak.

"Can you think of any reason why someone would take his journal?"

She pondered that. "Maybe the thief picked it up with some other valuables."

"I couldn't see that anything else was gone."

"Strange, very strange indeed."

"That's what I thought. Could it be that they mistook it for bank records or something like that? It was a big book kind of like a ledger an accountant would use."

"That must be it, dear." She stood and began clearing away a few crumbs from her small kitchen table.

Mart saw an opportunity to move on. He felt guilty at having to find an excuse to escape. Mrs. Parascak had no family nearby and relished visits from any of her neighbours or the ladies from the church.

"I should be heading home, Mrs. Parascak. I could use a couple dozen eggs. Would you like me to bring in the others?" He dug out some cash while he made his way to the door. He deposited it where he habitually did on the counter.

"Just take any you find, Mart. It will save me the trip out. Do you need something to put them in?"

"I brought a bucket, but thanks anyway."

Mart stopped at the car for his ice-cream pail. The widow smiled from the doorway as he entered the coop. There were probably thirty hens inside. Most were a white leghorn cross, but a few were reddish-brown Rhode Island Reds. Mart wondered how the semi-crippled elderly lady managed to care for this flock and the rest of her menagerie.

Most of the nests had eggs in them, but were vacated. However, he endured the pecking of one old hen that would not leave the nest. He got four eggs from under her and about fifteen others. That meant he got short-changed almost half a dozen. The hens were getting old and their caretaker probably overestimated their productivity. Mart did not begrudge the cash. Mrs. Parascak did not have much of an income. Selling a few eggs to neighbours and goat's milk to some folks who were lactose intolerant helped a bit.

Mart held up his bucket and waved to his elderly friend. He would come back in a few days, but his recent loss gave him a strange sense of loneliness. The old folks he had always looked up to were going. It had only been recently that he began to understand what that was going to mean to him.

CHAPTER 15 ✳ EXPLORERS

When Mart walked into his trailer the red light on the dusty answering machine was blinking. He pushed the button while he ran the faucet to get cold water. The goat's milk still clung to his oesophagus and pop always made his mouth dry. He should quit drinking soft drinks. He believed the recent reports that the stuff was a considerable health risk.

A scratchy version of Tom Wyslik's voice came from the speaker. The man had no patience with answering machines and just said, "Call me, Mart." He didn't even say his name.

Mart dialled the number from memory. Tom was on the Community Pasture board.

"Tom, Mart here."

"Thanks for calling. I am contacting all the members. The seismic crew figures it's dried out enough they can start up again. I guess they started last week. The damn fools called and left a message with Reg. It took until now for him to say something about it."

Reg was Tom's teenage son. He had a learning disability and, although he was likeable enough, he had trouble sorting out what was important from trivial matters that he dwelled on sometimes for hours. It didn't help that some of the school kids were less than kind. The teachers had done a good job of getting most of Reg's classmates to accept the boy, but one or two bad apples kept at him. The result was that he often withdrew, even around his own family.

"So, are they blasting already?"

"No, they said they'd call again when they started shooting. Right now they are just laying out the lines and clearing brush. "

Mart thanked Tom and disconnected. He leaned back against the sink and finished his glass of tap water. He admitted to himself that he was a bit of a hypocrite. His business relied on fossil fuels, but he hated the thought of any extraction in his back yard. He was particularly unhappy about the proximity of several sour gas wells. It seemed impossible that with so many health problems being experienced by the neighbours of operating sour wells and their livestock that the industry and the provincial government, who had become rich off of the associated taxes, had yet to admit to a link.

Then there was the exploration itself. The blasting required to discover new resources had been implicated in spoiling dozens of wells throughout the province. He looked at his empty glass. If you let the explorers onto your land, they agreed to compensate you for any damage to water quality and paid for the testing prior to the charges being set off. But how could they ever compensate for having no potable water? Hauling it in trucks to use in the house would be bad enough, but for a couple of hundred thirsty cattle? If you refused to let them onto your place you avoided that risk to a degree, but if any of your neighbours decided to take the money and the guarantee, the blasting on their place could fracture rocks and contaminate your well. Then you would suffer the damage, but have no agreement to fall back on and no easy legal recourse.

You could refuse the seismic work, but not the drilling. Nobody around here had mineral rights. They were owned by petroleum companies who had the legal entitlement to drill. The mineral rights to crown land like the Poll Haven had been gobbled up years ago. There had been some exploration in the

1940s and again a few times since then. Nothing had come of it, but the industry had since sucked out all the easy gas in other locations. Technology had improved enough that tackling difficult geology and tapping into sour gas reserves laden with poisonous hydrogen sulphide were both becoming more attractive.

Mart suddenly stood upright. If the seismic crews had been working for more than a week, there may have been a crew somewhere around when the quads had gone in or come back out. Perhaps the workers had seen something. He checked his watch. It was after ten. He would try to contact Boissoneau sometime tomorrow morning.

By six o'clock the next morning Mart was pulling on his boots. The leather across both toes was cracked and they had already been to the Hutterite shoemakers twice for new soles. A week ago he had pulled his finger right through one of the leather loops at the top of the left one of the pair. Since then pulling it on had been more difficult.

The air outside was cool. He pulled up the collar on his faded jean jacket and tugged the bandana from his pocket. He wrapped the limp cloth around his neck with the knot in the back and the edge up over his chin. He was glad for the old wool sweater he wore over his T-shirt.

It was light enough to get around, but three quarters of an hour before sunup. The mountains to the south and west were a dusty blue shadow. Soon they would have fuzzy tinges of pink and grey as the rays of the late summer sun kissed their summits. The familiar block that was Chief Mountain stood out boldly almost straight south of where Mart hesitated at the rusted metal gate to the horse pasture.

Skip and Slim were at the far end as usual. Mart walked over to the shed that was his modest stable and grabbed Skip's halter. He was halfway up the narrow lane when the sorrel and the bay lifted their heads simultaneously as if by some unseen signal. Skip played coy and trotted a few paces north, feigning panic. Slim lifted his head and tail and walked straight toward Mart. He had always been a pet. It was annoying when he was constantly looking over the rancher's shoulder when the man was trying to work at something or another in the barnyard, but it made the small horse a joy to catch. No matter how hard Mart worked him the day before, Slim always walked right into the halter.

Skip was hardly wild, but the big Quarter Horse never gave up hoping that playing hard to get would actually allow him to escape a day's work. Mart stroked the fine head of the bay and whispered some nonsense before Slim nudged him gently with a velvety nose. Skip was showing a degree of repentance and had walked to within an arm's length. Mart shifted to slip the lead rope over the red muscular neck, but was met by a round rump. Mart clucked his disapproval and the big horse stood still with his neck bent around to allow the halter first over his nose, up over his ears and then snapped beneath his strong jaw. Mart led them back toward the shed, Skip nearly walking on his scuffed heals. Slim followed halfway then raced past them and ahead to the barn.

Mart led Skip in to the stable and tied him into his habitual stall. Slim walked in and stood in his until Mart fetched his faded blue nylon halter. They each got a sniff of grain as a treat, then Mart busied himself with a few other chores. The barn cat remained underfoot until Mart scooped a few kibbles from the bag he kept in the corner of the oat bin.

Mart missed the old dog. It had been almost two years since he had come back from town to find the black and white collie curled up and still in the grass at the feet of the horses. Mart had been dreading putting the old girl down and she had obligingly gone to sleep in a sunny patch with her equine partners holding a silent vigil.

Mart hopped into the Toyota and drove to get the pickup he had abandoned in the hayfield. When he drove back into the yard, he swung the Chevy around and backed it unerringly up to the stock trailer. He got out and spun the hitch down onto the ball, hooked up the safety chains and the light cable. He looked at his watch. It was almost nine.

Back in the mobile home, he looked up the detachment number, dialled and asked for Constable Boissoneau. He was told that the constable was out, but Constable Lynch would take a message.

"My name is Mart McKinnon. I was riding with Wendell Jacobsen the day of the accident. I just found out that a seismic crew was working in the grazing lease that day. I wondered if anyone had talked to the workers."

Lynch excused himself, but was back on the phone in a couple of minutes asking for Mart's patience to the sound of shuffling papers. Before long the constable confirmed that there was a note on the file. "Constable Boissoneau spoke to a Mr. Stimatz. He indicated the crew was working well away from the scene that day."

Mart thanked him and disconnected. That had been a dead end.

Mart had spent a good portion of the night before, while he was trying to get to sleep, mulling over old Wendell's failed revelation. It probably had nothing at all to do with the accident, but Mart couldn't get it out of his mind. For the past ten years the two of them had ridden patrols together in one of the Poll Haven fields or another. Jacobsen had been riding there for forty years before that. What could have caught the old man's attention to the extent that he would actually bother taking Mart to investigate? Wendell was not easily distracted from the job at hand. Well, it was Sunday morning and most of the rest of the world didn't work seven days a week. Mart was going to take his first vacation of the summer and ride up there to find out.

Skip was leaning over the fence whinnying when Mart loaded Slim and pulled away. "Fickle beast!" exclaimed the rancher. "You'd be sulking if I had thrown the saddle on you."

The choice of Slim was not solely based on the fact he had ridden Skip the Friday of Wendell's death. While the big Quarter Horse was undeniably the best cow horse of the two, Slim was the traveller. Mart recalled the reaction of several of his neighbours when he had bid on and purchased the animal at a Lethbridge horse sale. Aside from the low price, Mart wondered just what it had been about the bony green-broke four-year old that had called out to him. It was obvious from his dished face and short croup that his ancestry was all or mostly Arabian. Many ranchers had little good to say about the breed in spite of the fact that just about every modern equine race had been improved through breeding to Middle-Eastern stallions. Even their beloved Quarter Horses had benefitted from Arabian and Barb blood by way of the Thoroughbred and before that through the Spanish ancestry of American mustangs.

Aunt Em had simply said, "Where's the new horse? It looks like you brought home a mouse."

Kent had christened the little bay "Scrawny" and called him that still. Mart decided "Slim" was a little less derogatory. After all the criticism, he approached the horse's training with some scepticism of his own. That was soon laid to rest. He had never encountered a more willing beast. If Mart put him at one, the bay would attempt to climb a tree. Slim followed Mart around and would even seek him out if he escaped through a carelessly closed gate or due to a poorly tied halter. The dark bay walked extremely rapidly which worked well with other fast-travelling horses or when alone. It was downright annoying when accompanying slower animals as he would simply walk away from them without any concern about staying with the herd. The stamina of the little horse was also a big benefit. He could work all day with lather from his flanks to his ears without his response to any command lagging in any way.

Mart's outfit rattled through the hamlet and past the Latter Day Saint church house. The parking lot was almost full ten minutes before the services were scheduled to start. He recalled Wendell bragging that an article in the church news back in the '80s had commended the Mountain View Ward for having the best attendance records in the entire Mormon Church worldwide. Mart believed it. You could hardly find a soul home on a Sunday morning. Mountain View also had the reputation for one of the best church choirs anywhere. Mart had attended several special performances over the years, usually around Easter or Christmas. The choir members ranged in age from teenagers to grandmothers pushing ninety. They could lift the brown tiles off the roof.

There was a lot of traffic heading west. Late June to Labour Day was the main tourist season, but nice weekends through Thanksgiving brought regional traffic in droves to Waterton Lakes National Park. Poor weather in the off-season pretty much made a ghost town of the village in the centre of the park. Today the oncoming traffic all but disappeared after Mart took the Beazer turnoff.

Mart was careful to close the doors at the back of the trailer after unloading the eager bay. The area around the corrals was congested. Flatbed trailers and pickups were parked willy-nilly around the clearing. They ranged from homemade outfits using old tent trailer frames or simple Canadian Tire ramps, to hydraulic decks that would hoist your machine onto the pickup for you.

Mart had just begun adjusting his cinch when a brand new blue Dodge crew cab pickup pulled slowly through the gate. He looked up to see a company logo for Southwest Seismic stencilled onto the back window. It was pulling an empty flat deck trailer that was only slightly older.

Mart put a foot into the stirrup and then pulled it back out. He led Slim over to the two men who were still sitting inside the cab, the Cummins engine rumbling noisily. It was hard to see through the tinted windows, but Mart saw the driver gesture to the passenger who then turned to find the rancher and his horse waiting outside his door. The electric window buzzed down. A large man with a red face and perfectly combed and lightly greased steel-grey hair looked out from under dark brows. His expression was hard to read. It was not particularly malevolent, but neither was it friendly.

"Hello. I'm Mart McKinnon. I am one of the members of the grazing association."

"We have the contract from the petroleum company to do the seismic work," the man growled.

Mart decided to try to put him more at ease. "Yup, I know. The Association Board told us you'd be working here. I guess you are working weekends to catch up after all the rain."

The big man relaxed only slightly. "So what can I do for you?" The driver was also a large man, but not as tall as the passenger. He kept his sunglasses on and faced straight ahead, only glancing in Mart's direction occasionally and then only briefly. His skin was quite dark, but his features were unlike any Mart had seen from the Blood or Peigan communities nearby. Perhaps he was from one of the bands up north?

"I suppose you heard about the accident involving one of our members on a patrol?"

The two reacted strangely. The driver immediately looked out his half-opened window. The man with whom Mart was speaking just stared at him without offering a yes or no. Mart felt uncomfortable in the silence and continued to explain. "I was the dead man's companion and wondered if you or your crew had seen any quad riders or parked vehicles that morning."

"We told the cop where our crew was." That was all that the fellow offered.

"I was just hoping that maybe you saw something out of the ..."

"We're just waiting for some of our crew to get back and have some paperwork to finish. Have a good ride."

The window buzzed back up, leaving Mart to gaze at his own reflection and the hazy silhouettes inside.

Mart was no diplomat. He was somewhat asocial and sometimes came across as unfriendly. He was also used to dealing with folks like Wendell who were sullen at best. But these guys were just plain rude. The interview had been terminated. There was nothing much to do but get on the horse and ride. Mart's inquisitive mood had been spoiled by the encounter. He muttered to himself for several minutes, questioning just what the unpleasant topping had been on the man's breakfast cornflakes. Finally he made the effort to shake it off and began to focus on the nebulous nature of his mission.

Whatever Jacobsen had wanted Mart to see was near or beyond the location of their missed rendezvous. Mart selected what he considered an easier route to the spot since he was under no obligation to check fences today. Avoiding the worst mud holes as best he could, he pointed Slim westward. He would cross into the Lake Field and then south to the Tower Field. He would follow the same paths as before until he reached the Mackenzie cut line. From there he intended to follow the cut until it intersected with the other prominent cut line in the Glenwood Saw Set Field and then to follow that one up to the US border. Failing any type of discovery there he would take the steep trail that led up the Hog's Back. He could only assume that Wendell's puzzle was somewhere close to those locations.

The hills were definitely alive, but no nuns were singing. Mart could hear the noise of small engines in almost every direction. As he passed through the Neilson gate into the Lake Field, he stepped aside and held the gate for a couple on a shared quad. A slim middle-aged woman was perched comfortably behind and just above her male driver. The seat and armrests formed a pillowy easy chair. The couple waved as they passed and Mart hid an amused smirk by turning to close the gate. He couldn't help but think of Granny perched in her rocking chair in the back of the pickup during the theme song to Beverly Hillbillies reruns.

When Mart had reached the intersection of the two cut lines, he increased his vigilance. Wendell's mystery could be anywhere in the Glenwood Saw Set Field. He decided he would follow the overgrown seismic swath until he found the small opening that was the beginning of the trail back up over the Hog's Back. The forest was at times open with little understory, but other spots were thick with alder or buffalo berry. Mart started down every passable cattle trail that crossed his path. After more than an hour of poking around, discouragement settled in again. Although there was a good chunk of daylight left, he chose to turn his mount toward the steep slope to the northwest.

Bands of greyish-brown sedimentary rock were just visible through the tops of the coniferous trees at the base of the Hog's Back. Mart decided he would not make the climb, but head for home if nothing turned up in the next half hour.

CHAPTER 16 ✵ FUR

Much of the motorized activity had died away as Mart approached the international boundary. A few zealous riders were testing their machines in the distant bowl at the back of the Poll Haven. It was a popular location for snowmobilers in winter, too. Slim steamed along in the hot, humid air. Mart had given him no rest, but he showed no sign of tiring.

Before Mart could make the ascent to a ridge slightly west of where he had terminated his disappointing wait for Wendell just three days before, he was surprised to catch a glimpse of two ATVs cruising slowly down an opposite low crest. They were only occasionally visible through the open lodgepole pine forest. It would have been relatively unremarkable given the intensity of use on a Sunday morning, but a few interesting things about the pair stood out.

First, the pair appeared to be young men with all the most current clothing and protective gear. They wore full helmets that wrapped around their heads and protected their faces with transparent tinted plastic. And they were travelling very slowly. Usually such a duo would have been riding hard and fast, vying to outdo one another.

The second oddity was that Mart could hear them occasionally shouting back and forth over the sound of their engines – and they weren't speaking English. It was not that peculiar to hear French being spoken occasionally, even here in Western

Canada. Many Québécois found their way west to Alberta where the economy stayed strong and jobs were more plentiful. But this was not French. It was hard to tell exactly what it was, but he thought it was reminiscent of the language spoken by banditos in old westerns he liked to watch. Spanish? Maybe Portuguese?

Mart sat and let Slim blow. He pondered the implications while he watched the two quads rumble slowly along an open section of trail. They appeared to be scanning ahead and behind them with some interest or concern.

Something in Mart's head started to click. That was it! The fellow driving the Southwest pickup had looked Hispanic, not from some tribal band that he had ever encountered in Alberta. He had come across Mexican-Americans on a couple of trips south. Many had lived all or most of their lives there. Some had recently arrived. The influx of illegal aliens into the southern United States to find jobs was an issue there and had been for decades. Mart had heard news reports of several instances lately where some of those workers had been discovered subsequently illegally entering Canada. When the economy in the US was floundering, the building booms of Calgary and Edmonton had only slowed. Mexican nationals had found even the low paying labour jobs in California, Texas and Utah disappearing. Some had continued north hoping for better. It may have been illegal, but it was hard not to sympathise. They were being exploited; paid less than minimum wage in most cases. But it was still better than what they had left behind. If this was the case for Southwest Seismic, Mart could understand their reluctance to get involved in any type of investigation or to even discuss their crews' activities.

The third noticeable discrepancy was the large black rug that appeared to be covering something on the carrying rack on the back of the first quad. The second machine was encumbered by a huge toolbox. If this was the seismic crew's outfit, the toolbox is what you'd expect. The furry black object was a mystery. Had the pair shot a bear? Mart considered taking out the battered Tasco binoculars he often carried, but realized the intermittent screen of brush and the distance would make it difficult to determine just what was going on.

Impetuously, Mart clucked to the relaxed Arabian. The small horse hopped easily into a slow canter. By following the narrow trail another half kilometre at a relatively fast pace and then finding a cow trail across to the wider track the two ATVs were following, Mart hoped to get a closer look. Given they were travelling generally back to the northeast, Slim was happy to be hurrying toward the stock trailer and his ride home. He hesitated slightly when Mart pulled him up and pointed him southeast into a narrow slot. It had been created by deer and cattle through the thick brush in the low gully between the two ridges.

Mart had to practically lie down on Slim's neck. Cattle were much shorter than a mounted rider and the branches almost joined to form a ceiling of foliage just lower than the withers of the horse. Mart closed his eyes and bent his head to let the battered black hat take the brunt of the cracking twigs. Sometimes the saddle horn would catch the thin limbs and Mart would have to flip them up and over to continue. He was leaning off the side at one point and simply let himself slide out of the saddle to duck under a fallen tree lying across the trail at a low angle. He had just manoeuvred Slim under the same obstacle when he heard the sound of the slow moving vehicles just ahead of him. Mart swung into the saddle and pushed the pony a little harder. They emerged into the road in time to see the huge toolbox vanish around a tight turn.

Again the small horse swung easily into a canter and Mart leaned forward. Slim took the cue and flattened out to run the short section of clear trail before the bend. Rounding the corner, Mart again caught a glimpse of the quads as they mounted a small rise and descended into another hollow. In the brief moment while the first machine was above the second, Mart was startled to see a portion of the black rug lift and stare back toward him with yellow-brown eyes.

Slim galloped up the slope. Mart achieved the small summit at the same moment the quads reached the top of the next knoll. This time both the rug and the second rider were looking back at him. Mart slowed his mount. The four wheelers did the opposite. The second rider shouted a warning to the rider preceding him that was undecipherable to Mart. "¡Apúrate!" Then both machines accelerated.

Mart pulled back gently on the reins. Slim slowed to a walk. It had not been the rancher's intention to initiate a race. It was obvious the riders had no desire to stop and chat with anyone. Mart was not confident he could keep up with them on the uneven terrain, but even if he could catch up, how would he explain his pursuit?

Mart let the horse stand to rest. This diversion had sent him in the opposite direction from his objective. It was approaching noon and he was feeling guilty about work he had yet to do at home. He looked back toward the south. He would have to return another day.

Mart followed the tracks of the two ATVs back out of the pasture. For the first kilometre they were the only fresh traces and it was easy to see they had retreated with some haste. There were skid marks around corners and the leaves and grasses around mud holes showed significant splash zones. After that first distance the tracks blended with several others and Mart had been overtaken by a few parties, one a line of seven quads, their riders ranging in age from early teens to what must have been grandpa. Two large jacked up 4X4 trucks going in the opposite direction pretty much put an end to his ability to make any distinction between the traces of numerous vehicles that had used the narrow road.

When Mart arrived back at his outfit, the Southwest Seismic pickup was gone, as were several other vehicles. Slim hopped into the trailer just as another long fifth wheel stock trailer and Ford diesel pulled in. It rumbled up and Mart leaned against the dusty box of his truck to wait. First out was young Bobby Renfrew. The slim six-year-old skipped to the back of the trailer and bent sideways to peer back impatiently to where his dad, Bob Sr. was sliding out of the driver's seat. Bobby's two older sisters exited the back seat dragging a couple of bridles. They were evidently heading out for a Sunday afternoon trail ride. Mart walked over to exchange greetings with the stocky thirty-something rancher from Boundary Creek.

After the obligatory comments on the weather finally showing signs of improving and the wet, cool summer, they jumped to the topic of the recent spate of oil and gas exploration. Mart decided not to comment on his earlier disappointing conversation with one of the supervisors. He did mention that they had been there that morning when he left for his own ride.

"They have been parked over on our side of the Pasture every day for at least a week," offered Renfrew.

Mart did not try to hide his surprise. "All except Friday, right?"

Renfrew rubbed the day-old stubble on his fleshy chin. "Well, I was pretty sure they were here Friday, too. I think that was the morning I was moving heifers and they passed me. It was two guys with truck and trailer. They had a couple of quads. They seemed impatient to get past and parked where they had the two or three days before. I noticed when I finally got to my gate. They had almost blocked it with the end of their trailer. Why do you ask?"

"That was the morning Wendell got thrown." Mart hesitated. He wasn't quite sure how to explain the rest. "Somebody from the seismic company told the RCMP they were working over on the other side of the Poll Haven that day."

Bob Renfrew turned his blue-grey eyes on Mart and stated without hesitation, "I thought they were here Friday, too. It would have been between 10:00 and 10:30 when they went in. I guess I could be mistaken."

Mart thanked Bob, called to the kids to have a good ride and headed for his own pickup. His wild theory about the illegal alien workers was suddenly looking more plausible.

CHAPTER 17 ✳ THE SERVICE

IF THERE HAD ever been a perfect morning in south-western Alberta, Monday started that way. The sky was a dark cerulean bowl that evolved into a paler shade as the sun crept upward from the Watson Hills. There was a slight breeze gently stirring the long grass at the edges of the hayfields. It was from the northeast. Gentle upslope weather was often the best there was, especially in the late summer and fall. Mart spent an hour moving some cow-calf pairs from the eighty acre home place to a half section north of the hamlet of Mountain View and just above the Fish Creek valley. The stream wound its way in tight curves northwest from there to join up with the meandering Belly River on the boundary of the Blood Reserve.

Mart had to push Skip a bit to make it back in time to treat himself to eggs and toast before dressing for the funeral. While the butter sizzled on the old cast-iron griddle, he went through his collection of six ties to determine which one would be the only colour in his black suit and white shirt ensemble. He had replaced the shirt once since his high school graduation, but the suit was the same. He dashed back to drop the eggs onto the hot surface and watched as the thin edges curled and crisped. This breakfast combination and oatmeal were the only dishes he could conjure that had any resemblance to Aunt Emma's country cooking. He could barbecue a mean steak, but rarely did.

What was missing when he did was the rest of the traditional Tidwell meal.

Glancing at the cracked face of his Timex, Mart wolfed the eggs and settled for plain toast. He dropped the dishes in the sink and headed for the shower. Half an hour later he was dressed, combed and climbing into the Chevy. He had yet to retrieve the Toyota.

The parking lot in front of the tan brick Latter Day Saint church house in Leavitt was still quite empty. With some satisfaction Mart spotted the Utah plates on a SUV. He had hoped to talk to Jacobsen's daughter before the family greeting line-up began. That would be at 10:00. The service itself would start an hour later.

Mart slipped out of the truck and dusted off his pants and then noticed that his shoes were no better. He walked up to the main doors and was greeted by a pleasant gentleman he recognized as one of the representatives of the funeral home in Cardston. Mart introduced himself and told the fellow he was one of the pallbearers and would like a chance to talk to Wendell's daughter. A glance at his own cheap suit stirred Mart's envy – this man looked very sharp in his grey pants and blue blazer.

The funeral home attendant recognized that Mart may not have known the daughter's married name and instinctively came to Mart's aid. "That would be Janet Lewis." He then turned to lead Mart toward a door at the rear of the church house. Here the family would gather to greet those who came early to pass along their condolences.

Janet Lewis turned with a smile from her conversation with another of the funeral service staff. She was a pleasantly plump woman in her fifties. She had beautiful white teeth and laughing eyes. Mart liked her even before she opened her mouth to speak. The first words she uttered after a quick introduction were expressions of gratitude. Mart was taken completely off guard.

"I am so very glad to meet you Mart. Dad had so many nice things to say about you. Thank you so much for looking after him and for being here today."

Wendell had said nice things about him? Mart was flabbergasted. The old guy had been pretty rough on him sometimes. Mart had considered himself tolerated at best.

"Wendell...your dad and I rode together a lot. There's probably nobody around who knows the country like he did." It was a lame response to a very generous statement and Mart felt ashamed he could not do any better.

Mrs. Lewis did not seem to be put off by Mart's reply and continued by introducing her husband and three grown children. The youngest was just starting university at Brigham Young in Salt Lake City.

Mart broached the subject for which he had come early. "Mrs. Lewis."

"Janet, please."

Mart shifted uncomfortably, "Janet, I was wondering what I should do about your father's stock. He has twenty-one head in the community pasture, another fifty or so on the home place along with an old horse that I fear is not going to fetch much of a price, but would be great for kids if you'll let me find a family for her."

Janet Lewis paused long enough to process Mart's blurted and lengthy declaration of goods. "I had considered the cattle, but not really thought of the old mare. Please try to find a home for her. She was the last of the foals Dad raised himself. I was hoping to impose on one of his neighbours to ship the other animals to a sale."

"Burt Greenfield is your father's nearest neighbour. Burt often uses your dad's corrals to truck his own animals. I could ask if he'd mind adding Wendell's herd to his when he sells his calves. It would mean waiting another three weeks to a month, but it'd probably be worth it to put that much more grass in them before you sell."

"Thank you, Mart. That would be fine. How do we get the twenty out of the hills?"

"Twenty-one. I'll bring them out with mine and have them here before Burt ships."

"Dad was right, you are a wonderful neighbour."

Mart dropped his gaze to the floor and Mrs. Lewis diffused his embarrassment by hurrying on to another topic. "Will you join the family for dinner after the service?"

It was customary for the Relief Society, the women's organization of each Latter Day Saint Ward, to organize a meal for family and close friends who had travelled far. This simple bit of Christian service often took a huge load off of the surviving spouse or distant relatives.

"I'd be honoured ma'am."

Janet's ample smile expanded at Mart's response. She placed a gentle arm on his sleeve and whispered, "I've missed the courteousness and neighbourliness of this place. I really have."

Perhaps she missed it, but she hadn't forgotten how to extend it. Wendell Jacobsen's daughter was a truly gracious lady.

Unlike the funerals for more prominent citizens, Wendell's was a quiet affair. Nearby neighbours, a few Cardston businessmen and one or two representatives of many of the Mormon families in the Leavitt and Mountain View area filed through the back of the chapel to where Jacobsen's coffin stood open. The Lewis family was present to greet them. Wendell's only siblings had predeceased him, but an occasional cousin drifted in with the well-wishers and took a seat in the room to support the family. The others continued out to the chapel and large recreation hall to whisper among themselves and enjoy the muted organ music provided by another good sister of the Relief Society.

Whoever had prepared Jacobsen for his last rites was an artist. There was no trace of any of the injuries he had sustained.

He lay in white clothing in a relatively simple casket of natural wood. The only thing that seemed out of place was perhaps the hint of a smile, but the dead are always remembered at their best.

As a pallbearer, Mart remained in the room with the family. Jacobsen's two grandsons and a couple of favoured nephews made up the remainder of the complement of those who would symbolically accompany the coffin.

Kent came through with his parents and his married sister. He nodded to Mart, but saved his kindest words for the Lewis'. Mart envied his ease with strangers.

Mart could not hide his reaction to the arrival of Becky Sorenson several minutes later. As inappropriate as it may have been at a funeral to grin and to follow a lady appreciatively with one's eyes, it was exactly what Mart did anyway. He was not alone in this. She wore a modest dark blue dress with a subtle ruffle around the skirt that swept up to a shallow inverted V at the knee. Her flaxen shoulder-length hair was gathered into a queue and tied low on her tanned neck with a plain yellow ribbon. The ends of the golden mass curled randomly. If she was wearing makeup it was minimal. She flashed an intimate smile at Mart as she edged into the doorway in the row of supporters. She discretely turned her attention to the family in front of the casket. It took several minutes for Mart's heartbeat to return to normal after she left through the door at the other side of the chapel.

After a short family prayer, the accordion doors at the back of the chapel were opened to the recreation hall where the funeral attendees sat patiently. The crowd was not large, but hardly disappointing for a man who had mainly kept to himself and whose acquaintances had mostly preceded him to the windblown cemetery west of the hamlet.

Mart scanned the attendees. Someone from outside these communities would have wondered from where the mourners had come. Here in cattle country they would have expected nothing but Stetsons and bolo ties. But these folks were not drugstore counterfeits. They were real ranchers. They wore utilitarian clothing to work their stock and machinery. Ball caps were as common as felt hats. When they went to church, funerals and weddings many wore suits and oxfords. When they went on holiday, their pale arms and legs protruded from cargo shorts and flowered shirts just like every other tourist's.

As usual, the eulogy revealed a lot about a man who Mart thought he knew well. Also surprising were the feelings of loss and, to a degree, loneliness that Mart experienced as the finality of the parting became clear. As often as he had griped about the man, Mart confessed to himself how the grumpy codger had helped to shape his life. Friendship has many forms and not all of them are hugs and kisses.

There was the traditional Latter Day Saint talk about God's plan for frail humans before birth, on this earth and ending with assurances that we could be reunited with those we love if we lived worthy of such. Mart was uncertain how he felt about that common hope, but could hardly find fault with those who wished for it. His mind turned to Aunt Emma and Uncle Seth.

The bishop finished with a few thoughts about Wendell Jacobsen's contribution to the church and community. He was a middle-aged man about Mart's height and slightly huskier. He farmed nearby and volunteered his time to lead the congregation. This man would eventually be released from the responsibility and other faithful members would be called to serve in their turn. He thanked the attendees on behalf of the Jacobsen-Lewis family.

Mart and the family followed the bishop and the casket being rolled along on castors by the funeral directors. They exited the chapel to the solemn drone of the organ. Everyone rose as Jacobsen's last remains were trundled out in the now-closed coffin. The procession filed out behind the casket. Mart was ushered into a large white SUV with purple flashing lights.

Traffic on Highway 5 was delayed while the line of cars made its way the kilometre west before turning north on the gravel road to the cemetery.

The family and a few neighbours clustered around the fresh earth of the grave where another prayer was offered. Mart said a few words to the Lewis family, confirmed that he would be at the meal when pressed once again by Janet and turned to make certain the funeral home staff was not waiting on him to return to the church house. As he turned a familiar small hand slipped through the crook of his arm. He turned and immediately swam in the clear blue-green of Becky's eyes.

"Please bring your girlfriend to the family meal, too," urged Mrs. Lewis.

Becky and Mart exchanged glances. Becky's was more amused than Mart's uncomfortable grin.

The pair walked arm in arm past the white Suburban. Becky casually offered an excuse to the waiting driver, "I've got him, Sandy."

Sandy grinned and mumbled under his breath, "You sure do!"

Mart heard him, but did not dare acknowledge it. If Becky heard the wisecrack, she had the good grace to ignore it.

They rode back to the meeting house in Becky's sporty car. Much to Mart's mortification she again latched onto his arm on the way into the meeting house. It was his own fault. He had hurried around the car to hold the door for her. Mart was certain he was not imagining the inquisitive glances of the few neighbours who had remained behind to serve the lunch.

The meal was simple cold cuts, dinner rolls and the ubiquitous gelatine salads of Mormon gatherings. It still beat the dinner that would have waited at home. Macaroni and cheese, boiled frozen peas, and fish sticks had been on the menu. He raised beef, but couldn't afford to eat it very often. That particular macaroni meal was a staple at Mart's house. Kent had christened it 'cronies and shark farts'.

The company was certainly better at this meal as well. In spite of his discomfiture, Mart found himself relaxing under the barrage of Becky's cheerful repartee. Jacobsen's relatives ate her up. Even Janet's daughter-in-law confined her bitter stares to her husband rather than blame Becky for the way the eldest Lewis son fawned over the blond beauty.

Mart and Becky excused themselves after he had reaffirmed his commitment to take responsibility for Wendell's stock. He walked Becky to her car where she turned and casually reached up to loosen his striped tie and undo the top button of his shirt.

"What would you say to a drive to Waterton?" she asked, maintaining her casual demeanour.

Mart came out with an excuse. "I should check on Wendell's place." He regretted the statement immediately.

Becky pouted coyly.

"I guess it could wait until tomorrow morning," Mart blurted out almost too quickly.

Becky's eyes lit up and she slapped the keys into his hand. "You drive then, cowboy." She spun on her heel and walked swiftly to the passenger side before he could change his mind. She tried the door, but it was locked. She cocked her head sideways like an inquisitive kitten. Mart finally caught on and fumbled for the button that unlocked the car. She smiled and slid in. Mart looked up into a sky only slightly more blue than his companion's eyes, gave his head a quick shake and climbed in.

CHAPTER 18 ✸ DECLARATIONS

The small Mercedes was a joy to drive. It almost took his mind off the possible significance of the invitation for an outing. Becky watched Mart's excitement at driving the fine car with pleasure, but only tolerated it until they were through Mountain View and heading down the hill into the Belly River Valley. She then drew his attention abruptly back by placing her small hand nonchalantly on his thigh. Mart managed to put the car back into the centre of his own lane, exhibiting none of the same ease.

Becky's face displayed an amused smile. She attempted to calm the shy rancher with easy conversation.

"The Lewis's are sure pleasant folks."

"Yeah, Janet is probably one of the nicest ladies I have ever met."

Becky tapped his thigh lightly. "Really," she drawled in mock offense.

Mart was alarmed for only a moment. Her sly smile gave Becky away. "One of..." Mart reemphasized.

Becky continued. "I found it kind of strange that she was so friendly. You always painted her dad to be quite an ogre."

Mart squirmed uncomfortably. He felt both the need to defend his previous representation of Wendell and to express his true feelings about the man. "I griped more about Wendell than I should have."

"Feeling guilty at having slandered the dearly departed?"

"You could say that," Mart admitted. "He was kind of grouchy, but he taught me a lot. In spite of my ignorance, he kept at me and didn't give up. I guess that means he thought I was worth the bother."

"You might be," offered Becky with an intimate pat to his knee.

Mart could almost concentrate on the road again by the time they hit the national park boundary, which was fortunate. Two whitetail does with three young of the year were feeding contentedly in the barrow pit just south of Crooked Creek. One of the fawns darted across just ahead of the car and Mart had to brake hard to avoid it. A second young deer started across too, but turned back in time to avoid slamming into the side of the passing car.

Now Mart's heart was really pumping. Even Becky exhibited an anxious flush. They looked at one another and both burst out laughing at the same time. The tense atmosphere lifted its white-flag tail and fled with the deer. Mart told a story about a near miss during a high school era joy ride. Becky countered with another driving tale from back in the day. When they passed the turnoff to the Chief Mountain International Highway they were laughing comfortably.

"Do you remember the huge Christmas tree we had for our grade twelve dance?" Mart asked completely off-topic.

Becky did not seem alarmed by the change of subject. "I sure do. Mrs. Tomlinson actually cried when she saw it. She was so worried the student council wouldn't actually come up with one at all. It was only the day before the dance when it appeared. To have that perfect specimen arrive – it almost overwhelmed her. She couldn't speak for almost fifteen minutes. She just stood and sniffled."

"Do you know where it came from?" Mart asked.

"Well the council asked Burt, David and Mel to get one. They had snowmobiles and said they could cut one out of the Poll Haven."

"They cut it all right, but not from anywhere up in the hills. They took it straight off the mayor's lawn."

"No!" Becky exclaimed. Then she added, "I guess I shouldn't be surprised. They were a crazy bunch. I am just surprised you and Kent weren't involved in the shenanigans."

"Shenanigans? You sound like Mrs. Parascak." Mart responded to the archaic expression.

"High jinks, monkeyshines, tomfoolery. And who is this Mrs. Parascak? Something going on between you two?" Becky needled the shy cowboy.

Mart sputtered for a moment as his uneasiness returned. He recovered only after Becky burst into laughter. It trickled over the dashboard and gurgled in the hollow of Mart's chest.

They crossed the bridge over the Waterton River and turned to approach the entrance station. Becky rifled the glove box. "I have an annual pass in here somewhere," she exclaimed. She handed it to Mart just too late for him to choose the automated gate lane.

They waited behind an RV while the European tourists who had rented it finished their transaction at the gate. Mart flashed the pass to the pleasantly smiling lady at the counter, hung it on the rear-view mirror and accelerated smoothly until he was forced to slow to the pace of the rented camper. Its occupants were weaving gradually from left to right while they drank in the spectacular scenery of the Waterton Valley with its views of Middle Waterton Lake, Sofa and Vimy peaks and the odd prairie, forest and mountain mix that made up Canada's fourth national park.

In his youth Mart would have been impatient driving at sixty kph where the limit was twenty above that. But today, with Becky chuckling at his dry wit, punching him softly on the shoulder and recalling names of classmates at a machine-gun rate, the ride up over Knight's Hill and across Blakiston Creek Bridge could have been by team and wagon. Mart would have been completely content with a snail's pace.

The Europeans pulled into Pass Creek picnic area and Mart picked up the pace slightly. There was a long string of dude horses taking a group of tennis shoe cowpokes along the trail at Driftwood Beach. Mart just beat them to the crossing and avoided a wait while their patient guide shooed them across and stalled traffic.

On a whim, Mart made the left turn at the Parks Canada Visitor Centre and dropped the car into second for the climb up the hill to the Prince of Wales Hotel. The late afternoon sun trickled through the poplar leaves and the lacework of the evergreen boughs. The car emerged from the shadows onto the open gravelly kame terrace. In the middle of summer it was almost impossible to find a parking spot, but today the stalls farthest from the building were empty.

Mart parked, smiled at Becky. "How about we play rich tourist?"

Among strangers Mart experienced a new emotion when he walked his well-dressed friend up the stairs, into the shadows of the huge porch and toward the front doors. The feeling of Becky's arm on his blended pride and confidence into a heady cocktail. The kilted bellhop greeted them deferentially.

The lobby was dark and cool compared to the warm, brilliant sunshine outside. There was an odd shabby elegance to the early twentieth century furnishings. A heavy black iron chandelier hung down from the ceiling five floors above them and a handful of guests wandered the balconies encircling it. The building was another national historic site. Its role in the early development of tourism in southern Alberta along with its unique structural design had earned it the designation. Huge timbers with cables running through them allowed the building to yield to the

170 kilometres per hour winds of winter. The building actually swayed in the gusts.

For most visitors, the place could have been decorated in twelfth century Mongol for all the attention they paid to it. As interesting as the architecture was, the floor-to-ceiling windows were the source of the real attraction. Upper Waterton Lake stretched southward eleven kilometres, almost the last half of its length in Glacier National Park in the United States of America. It was the deepest lake in the Canadian Rockies and in the province of Alberta. Tall peaks lined the lake and Cleveland, tallest in Glacier National Park, was easily visible towering over the others south and east of the glistening waves. Persistent snow patches punctuated the blue-purple of the slopes.

Mart and Becky found themselves dodging politely around a wedding party posing before the great windows. They paused to take in the familiar view then moved aside to let others less accustomed to the sight ogle it in turn.

"Come on." Becky dragged Mart excitedly to the gift shop. Unlike other occasions when Mart had wandered in wearing jeans and T-shirt, a young salesclerk immediately came to wait on them. The clothes may not make the man, but they created the illusion.

Becky fondled several trinkets. She held up a daintily flowered teacup and whistled quietly at the price tag on the bottom. "I never liked tea that much anyway." She replaced the cup with mock care and tip-toed away from the display. Mart grinned and trailed along behind.

In the parking lot Mart surprised himself by unabashedly offering his arm to Becky. "Downtown?"

"Might as well," she shot back and squeezed his arm.

After leaving the hotel, their next stop was Waterton Avenue in the village. They sat on a bench, ate ice cream and drew appreciative stares from the dwindling shorts and polar fleece crowd. Mart was starting to feel quite comfortable with Becky cuddled up close beside him. They walked from there down to the marina to watch the tour boat return from Goat Haunt Ranger station on the US side. They stood in the shade of the large trees around the pavilion commemorating the Waterton-Glacier International Peace Park and its UNESCO World Heritage Site status.

This time with no interruption, Becky turned to Mart and kissed him. He held her close and she whispered, "I have wanted to do that for about ten years."

Mart felt awkward at leaving the first move to Becky. He experienced a twinge of guilt at never having had the courage to let her know how he felt during the whole time he had known her. But neither emotion could eclipse the feeling of elation at the realization that Becky Sorenson actually wanted him.

"Me, too." This time he took the initiative and kissed her long and passionately. The embrace would have endured had it not been for the tittering of a couple of elderly ladies walking arm-in-arm through the peace park exhibit panels.

CHAPTER 19 ✳ INTIMIDATION

THE RIDE BACK to Mart's old pickup was a quiet one with Becky resting her head on the young rancher's solid shoulder. There was another spate of passionate embraces as he leaned against his dusty pickup. The suit would need dry-cleaning, but Mart did not care. When he stumbled up the porch steps and into his stuffy trailer home he could hardly remember the drive from Leavitt. He poured a glass of water and sat in Kent's castoff recliner.

Mart stared at the black screen of the television and took turns grinning and puzzling over the day's events. Then he grabbed the leather of the chair with his free hand and panicked. Kent! He felt like he needed to confess to him. But of what was he guilty? Becky was not Kent's girlfriend. She had made a choice. Kent would understand. He just had to!

Mart tossed and turned for about an hour trying to find the peace of slumber, but awoke at the regular 5:30 time surprised that he had slept so soundly the remainder of the night. He lay there for another ten minutes reviewing the possible aftermath of the previous day's revelations. He was right to think of Kent. Somehow he knew it would not be fair to avoid explaining to his best friend what had happened. Mart wished desperately for a stoic response. After all, Kent could pretty much have his pick of any of the eligible females of the county from age eighteen to thirty. Nevertheless, Mart could not help dreading the confrontation. He suspected the consequences might be much different from those for which he hoped.

Skip and Slim wandered away from the barn after being ignored by their master. Only the purring barn cat got its habitual strokes from the distracted man while crunching at the dry kibbles. Mart hopped into the Chevy and was out of the yard and through Mountain View long before the school bus made its first pass.

Wendell's place was peaceful in the early morning light. The doors were closed and lights off. He could see signs of the Lewis family's visit. Pictures were gone from the wall and several gaps had appeared on the bookshelves. The small china cabinet was completely empty. He felt he had no right to look into Wendell's dresser drawers and night stand, but was confident any memento of family importance had departed with the daughter. He rifled the kitchen drawers and eventually found a key hanging on a coat hook on the back of the door. He locked up when he left. The lock stuck and was hard to turn. This was probably the first time in decades the portal had not been left unbarred for the convenience of neighbours needing a telephone in a snowstorm or a glass of water on a hot day.

The old mare looked up when Mart strode into the barnyard. She opted to stay with her Angus companions and went back to drawing longer stalks of grass from around a fencepost with her supple lips. Mart pushed down the barbed wire with both hands and stepped over the fence. The scrapes on her back legs were fading fast. When she sauntered away there was no trace of soreness. He walked over, ran his hand down her solid legs and lifted each of her back feet in turn. She showed no distress and went back to her grazing before he had returned the last foot to the ground. The small pasture descended the slope to the creek so water was not an issue, but he'd have to move the mare and the bulls before too long. The grass here would give out within the week.

Mart strode around the barn to survey the next field over. Wendell had cleared it of the tall grass with his ancient haying equipment. Since then the wet weather had revitalized the pasture sufficiently to allow another month's worth for the bulls. He hoped that soon the mare would be in someone else's barnyard. On his way back to the truck he noticed the deep grooves cut into the turf where his attacker had parked a vehicle out of site and had then escaped hurriedly. Mart wondered if Constable Boissoneau had made any progress in that investigation. Again he pondered the theft of the journal.

Mart made a sweep of the interior of the barn. He noticed with some satisfaction that Wendell's old saddle had left for Utah. There was something intimate about a real cattleman's saddle. Part of a man's soul got pressed through his jeans into the worn leather if he spent enough time perched there. Mart secretly hoped it had not been taken solely for its resale value. Someone had left the lid to the oat box open. A parting treat for the old mare? He closed it against the mice that would soon find their way in.

Mart slid the barn door shut and walked slowly back to the Chevy. He had yet to discover Jacobsen's secret. He probably never would, but he was going to give it another try. In fact he was pretty convinced he would never really give up looking for the old man's find. He chuckled at the thought of a decrepit old man McKinnon wandering the Poll Haven like a mad prospector searching for the Lost Lemon Mine. He would have to get a pick axe and a burro.

The old pickup was nearly out of fuel when he drove back through the hamlet, so Mart pulled into the Barn Store parking lot. He was feeling lazy and did not want to have to unlock the bulk tank at home. It was self-serve so he put in forty dollars worth of gas and slipped two twenties from his wallet before heading in to the counter. As he made his way from the pumps he noticed the box of a blue Dodge protruding from behind the store owner's van. Before he reached it, the store's glass door swung open and out stepped the man from Southwest Seismic who had cut short their last interview.

Mart was feeling bold so he said hello. The man vacantly mumbled hello back while reaching into his shirt pocket for a pack of cigarettes. Then his eyes narrowed at recognizing the young rancher. He averted his gaze and headed for the truck.

Mart was rankled. He paused and then took a step to follow the surly man. "Excuse me."

Mr. Southwest Seismic kept walking.

"Excuse me!"

This time he turned. His face was flushed and he was chewing the unlit cigarette.

Mart walked a couple of paces closer and saw the big man begin to bristle. Mart recognized he may have crossed some line with the man so he halted his approach and rejoined diplomatically. "I don't mean to cause you or any of your employees any trouble. I was just hoping you could tell me anything that might help us figure out what happened to my friend Mr. Jacobsen."

"I told you before. I talked to the French cop."

"I know, Mr...."

Mart got a malicious glower, but no name. This had to be the Stimatz to whom Boissoneau had already spoken.

Again Mart tried to reassure the man that he had no intention of turning in his crew. "I have no desire to make a problem for your men. I don't care where they come from or how they got here."

Mart had obviously struck a chord. Stimatz's eyes involuntarily grew larger and he almost let out a gasp that he stifled instantly. The man then took the offensive.

"Our crew has every right to be working on crown land. We have all the proper permits and won't be interfered with. We have cooperated with the grazing folks and the police. You quit your meddling in our business or I'll have another talk with that Frenchman."

Mart was taken aback. "I'm not meddling. I just wanted to…"

Stimatz stepped closer and lowered his voice. "You have no idea what kind of trouble you're getting into. Just back off now!"

As the man finished this warning, the driver's side door of the blue pickup swung open. The stocky dark-skinned man stepped out rolling up the sleeves of a plaid shirt worn open over a tank top that was stretched tightly over a barrel chest and an ample belly.

Stimatz glanced back to the pickup and Mart thought he detected a cringe. He tried to back away between Mart and his approaching colleague. Stimatz glanced at Mart and then back to the stocky man. The lines of authority re-established themselves in Mart's mind. Stimatz was frightened of the approaching man. Given that either of the two seismic foremen outweighed Mart by at least half again, he was beginning to experience a dose of fear himself.

Mart held up his hands. "No problem. I'll leave it to the RCMP."

The driver walked up to Stimatz's side, posturing the entire ten or twelve steps there. He did not remove his dark glasses, but turned to the sweating man with an inquisitive shrug.

Stimatz grimaced and looked back at Mart. "Are we done here?"

"I guess so," replied the rancher.

"We better be," stated the man. It seemed his new veneer of confidence was more to reassure his companion than it was to warn Mart, but both goals were accomplished.

The dark glasses turned toward Mart on a short stiff neck. They remained glued there for several seconds before both men turned and walked back to the Dodge.

Mart retreated to the doorway and listened as the Cummins motor chugged slowly out of the drive. As he paid his bill he was embarrassed to see that the twenties were crushed and damp in his hand. He could not help but feel the confrontation had been more menacing than even the simple terse dialogue had betrayed.

CHAPTER 20 ✳ TRY TWO

WEDNESDAY WAS ANOTHER glorious late summer day – at least until around noon. By that time Mart was already in the shelter of Poll Haven's patchwork forest. He had loaded Skip early and stopped at his south quarter section midway between the hamlet of Mountain View and Beaverdam Lake. There he had done a quick circuit of the fence. There was work to be done on the south line where a boggy area was finally drying out enough to slop over there with a few posts. Driving them into the wet ground with the heavy post maul would be easy enough. Perhaps that would offset the effort required to slog along through the muck several times carrying posts and tools. Mart had learned to be zealous about his fences even when many of his neighbours were not. According to Uncle Seth, "You will never be taken for a real cowboy if you actually approach fixing fence with anything resembling enthusiasm." Mart took the criticism for praise because Tidwell had been guilty of the same misguided fervour.

From his quarter section Mart had dragged the rattling stock trailer the rest of the way to Beaverdam, unloaded his horse one more time and ridden around the west end of the lake. He headed south from there. He skirted the east side of Archie's Beaver Dams, keeping to a track along higher ground to avoid most of the boggy patches. He passed through the wire gate into the Ski Cabin portion of the pasture.

Mart had strongly considered giving up the quest. Whether Jacobsen's discovery had anything to do with his death, Mart still had no idea. The threatening clash with the seismic foremen had definitely given him second thoughts about pursuing the matter any further. But there was no evidence to suggest their animosity had anything to do with Wendell's unsuccessful revelation. If Mart avoided pestering the crew he was unlikely to have anything to fear. He felt guilty for turning a blind eye to what was likely a case of exploitation. On the other hand he did not want to be the source of information that sent the workers back to a life with no job and few prospects. He hoped that Southwest Seismic was being a fair employer even if they were guilty of illegal hiring practices.

The sorrel gelding hiked rapidly along the winding route leading to the cabin. It was tucked into the evergreens at the edge of a long but narrow clearing dotted with a few trees and shrubs. Mart chuckled as he reread for the thousandth time the small sign above the door of that simple elevated shack that said Polecat Chateau. Someone had added that sign and unofficial appellation in the early snowmobile era thirty years after the cabin was constructed.

The presence of a cabin here for skiers, and later for snowmobile enthusiasts, dated back to when the area was part of Waterton Lakes National Park. Apparently some ambitious local folks had slapped together an unsanctioned shack they referred to as the Slab Castle. Park officials discovered its existence and rather than demand its removal, they had encouraged the unauthorized committee to improve the structure for recreational use using local lumber. The logs were skidded there with mules and the one-room shack had been used and maintained to a certain degree since then by local work parties and scout troops.

From the cabin Mart and Skip climbed over the small rise out of the basin where it was nestled among the tall spruce and fir. Mart resisted the urge to turn up the wide trail leading to the top of Poll Haven and the breathtaking view of the ranch land to the north and east. Instead, man and horse wound their way south and down into the steep valley between Poll Haven and the Hog's Back.

This valley was called Hell's Kitchen. It had been the source of firewood, logs and lumber for the residents of the southwest corner of Alberta since late in the 1890s. But the difficulty of getting logs from there to Wray Flats was legendary. With nothing but authentic horsepower to haul logs out of that steep drainage, it had been necessary to make several trips with small wagonloads or skid a few logs at a time to make the steep grade; thus the reference to the bowels of the underworld.

Wray Flats held their own legend, but the allusion was to a simple local family from which issued a famous Hollywood actress. Fay Wray of King Kong fame spent some of the first years of her life in a small house just north of the Community Pasture. A fountain in Ms. Wray's honour had been erected in the Town of Cardston, who claimed her as their own. But in reality, Mountain View, or the now defunct hamlet of Seddon, had superior entitlement.

Skip was blowing and his muscular neck was lathered as he climbed out of the south end of Hell's Kitchen and approached Hog's Back Gate #2 into the Tower Field. Alberta Sustainable Resource Development's southwest weather station tower was just visible on the highest point of the ridge above. Over that ridge a Chinook Arch was building.

Orographic lifting of moist air spiralling in from the Pacific was beginning to create a band of stratus cloud at the mountain peaks. There was a stiff breeze anywhere the forest opened to a meadow or where the trail lined up with the prevailing southwesterly flow. The wind was not necessarily cold, but it had a cooling effect on the horse and rider.

Chinooks in summer lacked much of the drama associated with the same weather in colder seasons. In winter the effect was augmented by how the Chinook interacted with cold continental air east of the Rockies. Most of the winter Waterton's mountains peaked from behind a Mordor sky. Air from the Pacific was protected from rapid cooling by its high moisture content as it came up the west slopes of the Rocky Mountains and billowed there as clouds. Because most of the moisture was lost when the moisture condensed as rain or snow at the mountain heights, the air was drier on the way down the east slopes. Without the vapour to slow the process, the air warmed up almost twice as fast coming down as it had cooled when it went up. The result was frequently a sharp rise in temperature, often twenty to thirty Celsius degrees, and above freezing temperatures during a violent midwinter blow. The gusty nature of the wind was the result of rotors created by the mountainous topography.

As Mart approached the Mackenzie cut line, the wind was tossing the tops of the larger Douglas firs. When Skip stepped out onto the old seismic slash it was whooping straight down the cut out of Glacier National Park and flowing toward the privately-owned portion of land from which the slash had gained its name. Mart pulled the old black felt down tight onto his brow. He pushed Skip directly into the gale knowing he had only a short distance to travel before he would encounter the cut that ran perpendicular to the prevailing wind. The wind speed would be reduced at least by half there.

Before he could gain the highest point on the Mackenzie line, Mart was startled by the first of two speeding machines hurtling directly at him from over the rise. Skip showed surprise as well and stopped abruptly, legs stiff and head low, ready to bolt should a real threat be confirmed. Mart pulled up the gelding's head and bumped him solidly with his right boot. The sorrel stepped sideways adeptly just in time to avoid collision with the first quad.

The rider yanked the handlebars violently to the left to swerve around the horse in his path. His steering was too sharp and the machine tilted up on two wheels. The mud-spattered driver then corrected once again too aggressively and almost succeeded in ramming Skip head-on. Without cue the agile Quarter Horse jumped left again, squashing a lodgepole pine seedling and planting his face in a tall alder.

The second ATV rider succeeded in avoiding the horse, but his front right wheel glanced off the left rear tire of his companion. The first rider entered the brush just behind Skip and the second shot between two mature evergreens on the opposite side of the trail. They both managed to halt before injuring themselves or damaging their machines.

Mart hauled Skip out of the shrubbery in reverse, being careful to bump his left boot slightly to guide the horse away from the chugging machine tilted precariously in the alders. He slipped from the saddle and inspected his cow horse for injury. Miraculously the big red equine was unharmed. Mart was just aware of the efforts of the quad operators to extract themselves from the bush and regain the trail. His attention was focused on the wellbeing of his mount.

Rider number one's engine was growling in reverse. He was off the machine and pushing it back by the handlebars while operating the throttle from the ground. Rider two had simply made a U-turn and was travelling aggressively back to the path that meandered from side to side within the straight line of the overgrown seismic cut.

Mart stood up from examining Skip. He wore an angry scowl that the first quad rider recognized immediately. The thin fellow hesitated only momentarily and swung back onto the seat. He had extracted the ATV in such a way that it sat perpendicular to the route, but he managed a tight turn and headed in the direction he had originally been travelling.

Mart hollered, "Hey! Hold on!" and reached to grab at the back of the retreating fellow.

Mart came to the end of the bridle reins before he achieved the object of his lunge. When he realized that the reckless rider had successfully escaped, he turned on the other approaching motorcyclist.

The second recreationalist had been lining up to follow the first, but his course was blocked by an angry rancher and a 500 kilogram animal. Instead of following his initial trajectory, he turned and raced back in the direction from which he had come.

Mart stood impotently in the pathway for several seconds. He then realized that the south-westward travelling man would either have to retrace his tracks or face a very long detour. He grasped the horn of his old Eamor and threw his leg over the smooth leather of the well-used seat. Skip sensed his haste and jumped into an easy lope. Although the thick vegetation either side of the worn rut practically intertwined along much of the way, Mart had been through this section of the cut line often enough to know where the occasional fallen log lay. He slowed his horse for those hazards and Skip hopped over them with ease. Even with his attention focused on the rough terrain passing by at a rapid rate, Mart could see where the four-wheelers had detoured around the obstacles, crushing plants and gouging into the soft soil.

It was only a matter of minutes before Mart once again encountered the rider of the second ATV. After his hasty escape that man had turned once again and was cautiously descending the trail trying to determine the location of the irate horseman. He stood on the footrests for the enhanced visibility the slight increase in elevation would afford. He was also scanning the forest on either side, looking for a possible route around the cowboy and one that would enable him to rejoin his comrade.

Blue plastic was just discernable through the smears of mire and globs of mountain turf clinging to the body of the machine. The cut and colour of rider's clothes were likewise mostly undetectable. He braked abruptly at the sight of the advancing equestrian. Through grubby goggles Mart could see the fellows gaze lift slightly to concentrate on something behind his horse. He slowed Skip to a cautious trot and turned his head to discover the red and white flamed helmet of the first rider coming up rapidly behind him. Mart slid his horse to a complete stop and turned crossway in the path. These gentlemen were going to get a Jacobsen-sized dressing down.

Almost too late Mart determined that Mr. Red Helmet was not slowing, but rather had gunned the small engine and bent low in the seat. He flew directly at the broadside of the large horse menacingly. Mart knew that the collision would seriously injure the ATV rider and damage his machine, but was going to sacrifice neither his fine mount nor his own safety simply for the sake of proving his moral high ground. He booted the sides of his horse and held on as Skip shot straight ahead through some brittle low-hanging limbs of spruce. They gave way and broke off, but their rough surfaces tore at Mart's shirt and pulled off his hat.

By the time Mart had cleared the broken branches with their lack of needles and festoons of witch's hair and wolf lichen, he began to grasp the import of this attack. If these two were willing to threaten a young man and a solid horse they could easily be the ones who had spooked a bag-o'-bones mare ridden by an elderly man.

Mart circumnavigated the spruce, leaned out of the saddle to snatch his hat from the ground and headed back for the Mackenzie cut line. When he emerged from the trees he could see the retreating quads bounce north-eastward. The sound of the engines was no longer discernable over the wind in the trees. Skip was urged into a fast canter in their wake.

On flat ground Mart's effort to catch the ATVs would have been sheer folly. But here he could rely on occasional rough terrain and the many detours around fallen timber and tight squeezes between saplings to slow his quarry. Skip could just go right over most such obstacles.

Mart could see over most of the vegetation on the line. He could keep track of his targets as their helmeted heads bobbed up and down through the green foliage. Skip kept the steady pace, remembering the needed steps over hazards even when Mart was unsure. They lost ground at first, but then two necessary diversions for the ATVs allowed the man and horse to draw closer.

As the leaves slapped his thighs and tore at his jeans, Mart contemplated his strategy. He had none. He was chasing a pair of steel and plastic machines with partially armoured riders. His own arsenal of weapons consisted of a lariat, a partially thawed water bottle and two cheese sandwiches. The lariat was a serious tool, but he was unlikely to be able to approach to within its reach to use it on the hindermost rider, and then what would he do with the other guy? Mart shook his head. The plan to actually capture these fellows was at least useless if not something a good deal more serious. If they were the men who had been responsible for Wendell's demise, they could be dangerous. If they were not, he would end up in trouble himself if he did something as careless as roping one off his speeding machine.

A relatively straight section of trail just before the quads turned to follow the fence line afforded a solution. Mart noticed a patch of white reflecting off the leading ATV. He then did something of which he was seldom guilty - he silently blessed the government of Alberta. They had made it mandatory to license and insure motorcycles and quads that used public roads or lands. The design of the first ATV had somehow spared the license plate from the coating of mud typically disguising the identification numbers on machines used for off-roading.

Mart risked diverting his attention from the rough terrain long enough to fish the battered Tasco binos from his saddlebags.

He slid his mount to a halt, lifted them to his eyes and saw nothing but leaves.

He gave Skip the boots again and they tore through the drag of the entwined plants. Again the horseman gained on the motorized prey. If he could just get a single good glimpse of that plate! Skip faltered through a muddy spot and when he emerged he surged forward once more, then he stumbled several times in a row. He kicked out with a back foot and then began running slightly askew. Mart could hear an occasional click and a strange double beat on the back end. He was forced to slow down and then to pull up entirely. He stayed in his seat and banged the field glasses painfully into his eye sockets.

CHAPTER 21 ✷ SHOES

"KSD 8?" Mart pronounced aloud. Mud and distance clouded the remaining digits.

Mart climbed from the saddle. Skip was blowing hard and kept lifting and setting down his hind off side hoof. Mart slid his hand down to the white pastern. When Skip lifted the foot, the iron U of the shoe swung loosely from the only remaining nail. Mart groaned and then grabbed the free end of the flopping horseshoe and levered it off. It took a couple of strong pulls at different angles to drag the partially clinched nail from the wall of the hoof. Fortunately it was already straightened enough that it seemed possible without tools. Skip attempted to pull his foot away, but a stern whoa effected a quick repentance.

A discouraged Mart slipped the horseshoe and the binoculars into opposite pouches of the saddlebags. There was no sense adding to the scratches and dings by allowing the glasses to rub and bump on the shoe all the way home.

Mart pulled his antiquated cell phone from his shirt pocket. There was no service once it booted up. Skip received some encouraging words and a few pats on a sweat-damp shoulder. The young rancher remounted and headed for home. Skip had had enough. Yet another failed attempt at Wendell's mystery, and his report to the RCMP would be delayed and incomplete.

It was not until he emerged from Hell's Kitchen and was again above the Ski Cabin that his cell showed limited reception. He got the dispatcher and reported the incident along with as much of a description beyond "muddy" as he could make of the offending riders. He dropped Constable Boissoneau's name again in the hope that dealing with that pleasant official would avoid long and repeated background explanations. For yet another time Mart had to explain why he could not wait on the line for the arrival of a member of the police. It was shocking to him how oriented to urban settings society had become. Most people just could not grasp not having a street address or the concept that perhaps fire trucks, ambulances and delivery vans could not just roll up to the scene and park on smooth asphalt.

It was late afternoon when Mart traversed Wynders' Flats west of Beaverdam Lake. He had been relieved that Skip had shown little soreness from the loss of the shoe. He had attempted to miss the rockiest ground and had constantly been on guard against any increased tenderness exhibited by the dependable creature. A man's horse became more than just a tool if he spent enough time relying on the animal. Working on horseback required a measure of teamwork that created a bond.

A few clouds had begun to scud along ahead of the strong west wind. Mart was certain the loons that typically haunted the lake would be tucked along some protected shore and that he would not be treated to their lonely, wavering calls. The bachelor flock of white pelicans was grounded on the muddy flats at the southwest beach. The waves were splashing a vigorous rhythmic tune on the scattered cobbles and muddy banks.

To Mart's surprise he spotted a white 4X4 sporting yellow, white, red and blue coloured stripes and a stencilled mounted policeman in silhouette. It was parked beside his truck and trailer. He climbed down to get the gate into the lane. He remounted and approached the trucks. There was nobody inside the vehicle or near it, but when Mart rode around the end of the trailer he saw a familiar form coming up from the lakeshore.

Constable Boissoneau smiled and called Mart by his first name, but the pleasantries ended there. He immediately took out his notebook and a silver pen.

"Please tell me exactly what happened up there."

Mart went into as much detail as he could remember starting from when he had first encountered the ATVs.

"You are certain that the letters and numbers you saw are correct?"

"Yes. But the others were covered by dirt. I couldn't get close. I threw a shoe."

Boissoneau's head shot up. He had a rather stern expression on his face.

"I am uncomfortable that you chased these guys. It was dangerous to confront them and you could be charged for assault."

Mart was shocked and a little offended. "Wait just a minute! How could I be charged? They ran me off the trail."

Boissoneau maintained his austere demeanour. "Running to catch them was not a good idea, but throwing anything could be viewed as assault."

Mart added confusion to his indignation. "I didn't . . . What do you mean?"

"A citizen can record and report an incident and even fight back if they are under some kind of threat, but you cannot use force to apprehend someone you suspect of a crime. You have not got the authority."

"All I did was to try to get them to stop. They took a run at my horse," Mart added.

"Yes. But did you throw it in self-defence or after, while you were chasing them?" the constable demanded.

"Throw what?" Mart was getting a bit angry.

"The shoe. You admitted you threw at them a shoe."

Mart opened his mouth to defend himself once again. Then he cut off his excuse and blinked at Boissoneau. "Shoe?"

"Yes. I see you got it back." Boissoneau pointed at Mart's feet.

Mart tried not to, but there was little help for it. He snorted out loud. Now it was the constable's turn to be offended.

"This matter is serious."

"You don't understand, Constable Boissoneau. My horse threw the shoe."

Boissoneau did not say a word, but his face became red and he appeared on the verge of losing his habitual cool. Blaming the horse? "That is a ridiculous accusation!" It was clear to him that the cowboy was mocking him. Mart recognized the building fury and the source of it dawned on him suddenly.

"Not like that!" interjected Mart before the policemen could voice his displeasure at being made fun of. "It's an expression. It means one of the horseshoes came off my horse's hoof." Mart pointed at Skip's hind foot.

"You didn't throw anything at the men on the motorcycles?"

"No. I had to quit chasing them before I got close enough to get a better look at the license plate. I had to stop my horse because his horseshoe came loose. He can't run with it half on and half off."

Boissoneau glared back at Mart. Then his eyebrows unfurled. His eyes opened up and a strange smirk spread across his face. Mart grinned back. Then they burst into laughter almost simultaneously. There were tears in their eyes before they were done.

Boissoneau wiped his eyes with the back of his hand.

"Eric," he said. "Please call me Eric. I thought my English was better than that."

Mart actually had to blow his nose before he could continue.

"Probably more a product of me using an expression that is common among horsemen, but not so much for everybody else. How long have you been stationed here?"

"Four months. This is my first assignment in a small town. I have been in Vancouver and Saskatoon. I grew up in the city, too. Montréal."

Mart smiled at the policeman.

Eric continued, "And me a Royal Canadian Mounted Policeman."

Again the two erupted into laughter, but they broke it off before any additional mirthful tears could be shed.

"I have run the plate and found three in the area south of Lethbridge that start like the one you reported. It was good that you got the first number too. If I had just used the letters it would have been more like forty. Same if I expand the search north to Calgary."

"I am pretty sure of those. After that it could have been another 8 or maybe a 3. The last number was completely covered."

"It's OK. I will go back to Cardston right away and start there. One of the plates is registered to a man there. The others are from farther away."

"Are you allowed to let me know what you find out?" asked Mart.

"Yes, to some degree. I can let you know if I find them."

Mart hesitated and then added, "I imagine that these are the guys who chased Wendell Jacobsen. I want them nailed for that!"

"We can't be certain it was them."

"I'm certain!" Mart stated. "They had no trouble taking a run at me. I imagine that an eighty-year-old man wouldn't have put them off much in spite of his bluster."

"I better get back to town and get started," Boissoneau cut off the conversation before Mart could get any more wound up. "I'll call you when I find out something."

Mart thanked the constable and loaded his horse. A lingering haze of dust was the only evidence remaining of the white SUV when the ancient Chevy's engine ground to life.

CHAPTER 22 ✹ CONFESSIONS

Mart awakened at 7:10 on Thursday. That was about an hour later than he had arisen for more than a year. He had stayed up watching some TV until quite late, hoping for a call from the Québécois policeman. During the commercials he had muted the sound and read a few pages of a biography of David Thompson that he had found in Cardston's Jim and Mary Kearl Library. The Hudson Bay Company's intrepid explorer and mapmaker had certainly led an intriguing life, but reading an exhaustive history that late at night was deadly. Mart was forced to abandon the effort or risk breaking his bobbing head from his stiffening neck.

It had been nearly a week since Wendell had been thrown from his horse. It still seemed unreal the old guy was gone. Mart's attempt at reading an account of Thompson's life, replete with quotes from his own journals, had set Mart to thinking about Jacobsen's diary. The mystery of Wendell's discovery nagged at the younger rancher, but the theft of the book was becoming equally unsettling. It made no sense that some thug from the city would drive all the way to Seddon to read an old widower's memoirs. Perhaps the thief had acquired some other booty that Mart and the cops had yet to discover – or perhaps never would. It was just as plausible that Mart had interrupted the burglary and the robber had fled before he had finished his clandestine exploration. But then why take the journal? Was it a last ditch attempt to get away with something of value?

A breakfast of cold cereal didn't seem to fill the void so Mart ate the last overripe banana and drank two glasses of milk. He slipped on his battered boots and headed outside. He didn't come in again until just after noon when he grabbed a quick jam sandwich and headed back outside to grab the spade he had left leaning against the wall to resume his irrigating. He had not had much of that to do this year given the wet weather, but he was going to make sure a couple of sloughs were full to provide fall and winter water for his stock.

Mart had taken the first two weathered steps down from the doorway of the mobile home when he was forced to do an about-face. The telephone was ringing. He shot back through the screen door and skidded on the kitchen linoleum. He picked up the receiver before the metal door had ceased its rattling.

"Hello," Mart croaked. He was always embarrassed when his seldom-used voice betrayed his lonely existence.

"Mart, this is Eric from the Cardston detachment."

"I was hoping you would call."

"I discovered something last night, but it was late. I did not call then and spent this morning getting more of the story straight."

"Did you get them?" Mart pressed the constable.

Boissoneau hesitated. "Yes and no. I have found the boys who you saw yesterday. "

Mart jumped in. "Well then, I imagine you've checked where they were last Friday?"

"Yes, but they weren't riding last Friday." Boissoneau heard nothing but silence on the other end of the line, so he continued. "The motorcycle riders from yesterday were two high school boys. One of the reasons they didn't want to get caught was because they did not go to school and took the four-wheeled motorcycles without their parents' permission."

Mart was dismayed to discover they were just kids out for a lark. "I guess they could have done the same thing last Friday."

"I checked this morning. Both kids were in class all day. I spoke with each teacher to be sure. Both ATVs belong to the same family. The boy's mother and father were away yesterday, but not last Friday. His mother was home then. She is certain the machines were not missing at all that day. She was working in the front yard and that is where the trailer sits. The ATVs were on the trailer the whole day."

Mart cursed under his breath. "It seems like quite a coincidence that both Wendell and I were attacked by four-wheelers less than a week apart."

"Not so much as you would think," countered Eric. "One of the boys had somehow heard that Mr. Jacobsen's horse had been scared by an ATV. Apparently one of his friends from Boundary Creek had overheard me questioning his mother. He heard it from his friend and said it kind of gave him the idea to chase your horse."

"I am disappointed you still haven't caught the guys responsible for Wendell's death, but I have to admit I'm glad it wasn't a couple of local kids."

"Now you have to decide if you're going to press charges, Mart. I know that I'd rather try to convince them and their parents to have them volunteer to do some community service rather than give them a record. I have spoken to them. They confessed to the confrontation they had with you yesterday. They seem to realize they made a very bad decision."

Mart thought for a moment. "That's what I'd prefer too."

"Since they are minors, I'd rather not give you their names, unless you want some sort of face-to-face apology."

Again Mart considered some of the pranks he had played as a teenager. Perhaps they had not been quite so irresponsible, but they were very nearly so.

"How about they agree to the service and each then write me a letter to apologize. I'd like something in the letters to indicate how they are going to ride those damn machines more responsibly. They don't have to sign the letters."

"That sounds like a good solution. Thank you, Mart."

"Have you made any progress at all on Wendell Jacobsen's accident, and how about the break in at his house?"

It was Eric's turn to hesitate. "Unfortunately we have made very little progress."

"What is 'very little'?" Mart had a hard time keeping the annoyed edge out of his voice.

"Aside from the information you have given us, we have nothing," the constable confessed. "There were no fingerprints but yours and Mr. Jacobsen's at his house. I called in an investigator from Lethbridge to look at the tire tracks at the barn. They were mostly unidentifiable in the soft ground because the wheels were spinning. Where they weren't rubbed out, they seemed to be a very common Korean light truck tire. We could never use them to identify a particular vehicle."

"You have my fingerprints?"

"Yes. We took them from where I saw you lean on the stove to get up. I needed them for comparison. Mr. Jacobsen's...well, we got them ..."

Mart spared the policeman the need to be delicate. "I imagine they were available at the funeral home."

"Yes, that's right." Boissoneau tried to reassure Mart. "I have done dozens of interviews with neighbours, the seismic crew and some local ATV enthusiasts. Mr. Pruitt and his daughter saw no other riders that day. We really are trying very hard to solve the case, but the trail is getting colder each day and soon other more current investigations will take precedence. I have to admit that I am not very hopeful. It is looking more and more like they were riders from far away who caused the trouble and then left. I am very sorry. My colleagues in Lethbridge have been trying to determine if there are any links to individuals or groups who are under investigation for robberies at deceased persons' homes. Nothing there yet either."

Mart swallowed hard. It was not easy to be understanding when a person you knew well had perished because of someone else's carelessness, or worse, maliciousness. Add to that a personal attack, and failure to achieve some resolution was a bitter pill. But in the short time he had known Constable Eric Boissoneau, Mart had been impressed by his professionalism and dedication. If the system had failed it was not likely because of the constable or officials like him. Mart fought back his frustration. "I understand you are doing what you can. I am impatient because it appears that nobody will be held accountable for any of this. Please let me know if you discover something new."

Eric replied, "I'll pass along any information that I can legally share with you." Then the constable continued in a cautious tone. "Do you know the Pruitts well?"

"I guess so. Jack has been one of the grazing lease members for at least as long as I have been here."

"I thought I detected some..., I thought he might not like Mr. Jacobsen very much. It was just a feeling I got when I asked him whether or not he had seen anyone else on motorcycles that day."

Now it was Mart's turn to speak carefully. "Wendell and Jack didn't see eye-to-eye on a few things. Wendell felt Jack didn't do his part when it came to fencing and patrols."

"Did they ever have fights – I mean arguments?"

Mart cleared his throat. "Please don't get me wrong. They never really had it out. It was usually just subtle words. It only recently came to a head during round-up a year or two ago. Jack and his daughter showed up late. Wendell made some remark and Jack called him a slow old man. It blew over when a few of us stepped in, but flared up again later in the day. Jack was just kind of cruising around on his ATV. I have to admit he wasn't being a lot of help. Most of the men there didn't have much use for quads on roundup day. Wendell grumbled about it and there were a few sharp words back and forth. Later that year Wendell tried to get the board to take away Jack's shares in the community pasture. They wouldn't do it, but Jack found out about it and the bad blood got worse."

"Did they argue the day of Mr. Jacobsen's accident?"

"No. There were just more snide comments and nasty glares." Mart risked being blunt. "You don't think Jack and Candace spooked Wendell's horse?"

"I think we'll just have to leave it there, Mart. I just wanted to get the whole story."

Mart got the hint. Boissoneau was not going to include him in the investigation in any way other than as a witness to the accident.

"I must go now, Mart."

Mart thanked the constable and disconnected.

Throughout the afternoon Mart plodded through his various tasks with Jacobsen's demise weighing heavily on his mind. Perhaps it was not really important how it happened. Was he just giving in to some misplaced desire for revenge? Maybe the culprits had no idea about the harm they had caused and were only guilty of negligence. Or, perhaps they knew very well what they had done and would be plagued by the guilt. Maybe that was punishment enough.

Mart was in late for supper. He resurrected the shark farts and cronies recipe, but switched it up by adding some fresh tomatoes Mrs. Sitter had dropped off with a note a couple of days ago. Mart had a habit of being adopted by empty nesters.

It was not until after supper that Mart noticed the red light blinking on the answering machine. He pressed the button and listened to a raspy reproduction of Kent Lindholm's mellow voice speak casually to the device. Another of Kent's annoyingly near-perfect traits, he always sounded completely normal while speaking to a machine. Mart frequently froze at the sound of the beep, like the proverbial deer in the headlights. He had once been guilty of slamming the receiver down after a long pause. The worst part of doing that had been that he could not phone back anytime soon afterward without the risk of being identified as the buffoon. He had opted to drive over a day later and speak to a neighbour about an eroded irrigation ditch flooding a corner of his land.

"Mart, let's get together tomorrow night if you have nothing going on. We could catch a flick and a burger. I wouldn't mind a chance to talk about a few things and catch up a bit. Give me a call."

Mart had always been glad to get an invitation from Kent. The most benign activities often turned into real blockbuster events whenever the handsome scoundrel started to cut loose. But this time he met the invitation with some apprehension. Kent had hinted he wanted to talk. That was a bit unusual – not that they should talk, but that Kent should mention it as part of the plan. Mart also realized that this could turn into his best opportunity to break the news to his best friend that Becky had made her intentions clear. It would test the relationship between them, but he could no longer keep it a secret. The few days of delay of which he was already guilty was stretching his integrity a bit thin.

Mart sat down with his David Thompson life story, but it remained open to the same page in his hand. He had to reread several paragraphs and in the end gave up. He brooded over his approach to telling Kent about Becky. He would watch the movie and eat his fast food, and then he would break the news. He hoped he could keep his cool until the right moment. He had a habit of ruminating on bad tidings and then vomiting them clumsily and often prematurely onto any clean surface.

Mart laid the book face down on the stained coffee table. He picked up the phone and got Kent's voicemail. He concentrated and attempted the same casual presentation as his friend's. The concentration spoiled the nonchalance. He muddled through a reply that was typical enough of his discomfort with leaving voice messages. Kent would never guess there was another reason for his impediment.

CHAPTER 23 ✳ A NIGHT OUT

On Friday morning Mart heard back from Craig Schofield. His kids would be glad for the old grey mare. So would the Shetland pony cross that had been so lonely since his stable mate had given up the ghost two years earlier. Perhaps the children were happy to receive the equine gift, but there was enough hesitation in the father's voice that Mart decided not to wait until Schofield had a chance to change his mind. He hitched the trailer to his pickup. Once he got to Schofield's house he would drop off the mare and then ask Craig to help him get the Toyota back to the ranch. Craig lived only a section and half over from Mart's hayfield.

The drive was uneventful so Mart had time to think. Perhaps he would not solve the source of Jacobsen's vague declaration today, but the dilemma of Becky Sorenson should have reached some type of conclusion by midnight. Would the result be the loss of his friendship to Kent? Mart sincerely hoped it would not. He tried to sort out how he would feel if it were Kent delivering a similar message. Would his loyalty to his high school saviour remain unchanged if Kent Lindholm pronounced his intention to pursue a relationship with Becky?

Mart thought so. He had prepared himself for that possibility since the young woman had returned to Cardston. But he had no way of knowing what Kent would do. Kent had never had to deal with rejection when it came to girlfriends. To Mart's knowledge

Kent had always been the one to break off any liaison with the opposite gender. And Kent had had many girlfriends. It seemed there had been at least one per year since high school. Only a couple of them had endured longer than a few months and Kent experienced long spells when he rejected any female who showed an interest. Mart had profited from those gaps. When Kent was single Mart's social life perked up considerably.

Mart pulled into Wendell's yard. He experienced a slight attack of apprehension as he climbed out of the vehicle and headed for the Jacobsen front door. He was reassured when the door was still locked and no sign of activity could be detected. He decided it was unnecessary to go inside so he turned and headed for the barn. He slid open the worn door and looked into the dark interior. The contrast between the mid-morning sunlight outside and the dim mouldering stalls inside necessitated flipping on the light. Mart selected the halter that the RCMP had run over last week. In spite of that abuse it was still the best one. After a quick scan to be sure all was as it should be, he reached for the light switch, but did not turn off the light. He went back to the hooks on the wall and took down the battered bridle. The old mare would be more comfortable with new riders if she was wearing the bit to which she was accustomed. He trusted Janet Lewis would not mind if the bridle went with the horse. He threw it in the cab on his way to the gate.

The old mare was standing quietly apart from the bulls. Mart had no trouble catching her. She followed him placidly, but he was forced to slow his normally energetic pace. He dropped the lead shank and slipped over to the wire gate that led to the adjacent pasture. He opened it and swung it back to lean against the fence. The bulls would find their way to the longer grass, but still be able to return to the small paddock for water.

Mart dragged the slothful grey out through the barn gate and to the rear of his trailer. He swung the door open. It complained with a loud metallic creak, but the mare did not protest at all.

Once loaded and tied, she stood with head drooping and eyelids half closed.

On the trip back to Mountain View, Mart resolved to abandon his worries. He turned up the classic hits and sang along to a couple of familiar tunes from the 1970s. His few friends always found it amusing that he knew so well the songs from a decade before his birth. They also joked about his poor singing, but in reality his voice and ear were quite good. He had taken up guitar, but the instrument spent a good deal more time in the closet than in his calloused hands.

Mart pulled into the Schofield yard. Like his experience with the cat, the kids were the first to greet him. Two preschoolers stood in anticipation as he unloaded the stolid grey horse. Craig listened quietly as Mart admonished the children to take good care of the old girl for Mr. Jacobsen. He tried not to make the speech too heavy, but wanted them to understand the responsibility of an older horse.

They led her away and immediately began to brush her beside the barn. They would probably wait until their older siblings returned from school to saddle her and catch the pesky Shetland cross that was leaning over the corral gate. The pair would make quite the Mutt and Jeff in the barnyard.

Craig said, "Sure, I could spare a few minutes to shuttle your truck around," and climbed into the driver's side of the Chev. He dropped Mart off at the gate to his hayfield. The car was just inside, unlocked and with the keys dangling from the ignition. Mart caught up with Schofield just as the older man swung the truck and trailer around in front of Aunt Emma's house. Schofield jumped out of the pickup and into the passenger side of the small car. Mart drove him back to his yard to complaints about the wet weather and speculation as to what the winter would bring.

"Thanks, Craig." Mart waved to the kids. They beamed back. The old mare was crunching away at a few oats from a battered pail.

Mart headed back home where he removed the plug from the oil pan of the tractor and left it draining into a pail while he went to find his coveralls and get a quick sandwich. The light was blinking again so Mart listened to Kent's suggested evening itinerary on the answering machine. He smiled when Kent insisted that he would drive from Leavitt if Mart would meet him there. Kent always pretended disgust at Mart's cluttered vehicles and fear that they would end up walking when the jalopies broke down. Mart suspected that it was a bit of a smokescreen to save him the expense of the gas. Kent would never consciously hint at the act of charity.

After the oil had been changed in the antiquated tractor, Mart checked his watch. He would have time to grease the points and clean up. If he had a few minutes after that he would change the front cinch on his saddle. The cotton cords on the forward edge were fraying. It could soon break under pressure. The last thing Mart wanted to do was dangle from the back cinch when Skip darted after an errant calf.

Mart skipped supper in order to prepare for his burger at the local drive-in. He shaved and showered, chose a clean pair of jeans and one of his two newest shirts. Shirts were something he rarely lacked since his mother tended to believe clothing was the only sensible birthday or Christmas gift. He made a mental note to call home soon. He had not talked to Tina Taylor since before Wendell's accident.

Mart hopped into the Toyota and headed for Kent's ranch in Leavitt. On his way through Mountain View he stopped at the store. He often picked up a soda pop there for his friend. Leavitt lacked a convenience store. When Mart walked in, the owner, Otto Tanner, was leaning over the counter chatting with a fellow decked out in the most recent style in cycling wear.

Mart had noticed the expensive touring bicycle leaning against the wall outside and a black late-model SUV with bicycle rack on the roof. He continued back to the cooler and grabbed two Mountain Dews. Before he reached the counter, Otto drew him into the conversation.

"Maybe Mart here could give you some advice. He rides quite a bit."

The cyclist turned expectantly and awaited some words of wisdom. Mart gazed in mild astonishment at Otto. That man had stepped back and was grinning broadly. Mart started to get the joke. He had not ridden a bicycle more than three times since he left Medicine Hat. Tanner obviously thought it would be amusing to set him up as someone who rides in spite of the fact that a horse and a bicycle were pretty different animals.

Mart started to chuckle, but then saw an opportunity if he could keep his composure. The cyclist leaned forward in anticipation.

"The best advice I can give you if you're riding around here is this: no matter how tempting it is to do so when cycling past stinky flyblown road-kill, never breathe through your mouth."

The cyclist kept his attitude of rapt attention for several seconds more. Just as that expression began to transform into one of mild confusion, Otto erupted into a fit of mirth. The owner of the bicycle turned to look at the red-faced proprietor, then back at Mart who was now grinning quietly. He then realized he had been had. He shook his head and joined in the laughter.

Mart silently blessed Tanner for his ability to read his audience. The cyclist was taking his ribbing very well.

"I don't know if Mart can even ride a bike. He would probably just get his spurs stuck in the spokes," Otto explained.

"Well it is good advice, nonetheless," admitted the cyclist trying to shake free of the unfortunate image of ingesting sticky, carrion-bloated flies.

The three exchanged a few more pleasantries while Mart scrounged for his cash and paid Otto. The jovial market owner treated the cyclist to a small ice cream cone on the house for his good-natured acceptance of the gentle mockery. Tanner was rewarded in return by a promise to stop by anytime the man was cycling this way from his home in Lethbridge.

Stepping out of the Barn Store door, Mart almost ran directly into Jack Pruitt. The man had been reaching for the door handle and stepped back politely. When he recognized Mart, his face immediately changed. "Just what in the hell are you thinking, McKinnon!?"

"Jack!" Mart sputtered.

"You got the cops all riled up about Jacobsen dropping dead off his horse. The old fool should've given up the rides ten years ago."

"Jack, I just told them you were up there, too. I didn't..."

"It's your fault!" Pruitt was nearly shouting now. "You should've stayed with him. Now you're trying to blame somebody else for your own carelessness."

"I didn't blame..."

"Piss off and get out of the way!" Jack pushed past and into the market.

Mart could see Otto and the cyclist craning their necks to discover the source of the commotion. He was too embarrassed to follow Jack in and confront him in front of an audience. He tried to decide whether or not to wait for Pruitt to come out, but Jack grabbed the sole small shopping cart and made for the back of the grocery section. "Damn it!" Mart hissed and stomped toward his truck. Once shut inside, Mart cursed several more times. He fired up the engine and jerked it into reverse, squawked the tires of the little car jamming it into forward gear and took a month's life off the motor pulling recklessly out of the parking lot. It took ten kilometres of muttering to calm down.

What was Jack bitching about? Only a fool wouldn't understand that the police were obligated to talk to anyone who might have information. You'd have to be an idiot to think anything else about it. Then Mart's face blanched. Stupid or guilty? It just couldn't be! Candace and Jack? They certainly had made no secret of their dislike for Wendell. But endangering the old codger's life and then covering up the result? That was playground bully behaviour. No responsible adult would stoop to a stunt like that. Again Mart grimaced. Irresponsibility was exactly what Wendell Jacobsen's charge against Pruitt had been.

Mart continued east to Leavitt and pulled off Highway 5. He turned left at the intersection near the LDS church and headed east again along a well-gravelled road, then south toward the hills above the Lee Creek Valley. In a couple of minutes he was paralleling Lindholm land.

The house was not new nor was it particularly assuming, but it was well kept. There was a semblance of landscaping to the yard and garden – something that was a bit rare on ranch land where a family's lawn and barnyard often melded into one another with little discernable division.

Kent's black pickup was inside the garage and the overhead door was open. Mart walked up to the step and his tall blue-eyed friend swung the screen door open to greet him with an easy smile. He had a cordless telephone pressed against one ear, but held the door open with his shoulder and gestured for Mart to enter.

The inside of the Lindholm place was immaculate and furnished in wood and leather. A housekeeper came once a week, but Kent had always been ready to pick up after himself. A modest fireplace faced the door on the opposite wall. Family pictures adorned the mantle along with an antique clock which signalled the hour and half hour with Normandy Chimes. A roll-top desk and leather swivel office chair partially blocked a wide hallway that lead to several bedrooms at the back of the house. It was the only item in the room that did not look like it came straight out of an episode of Bonanza and that showed any sign of un-Ponderosa-like clutter. The desk itself was more than a half-century old, but its open top revealed a laptop computer and the remainder of Kent's unfinished bookkeeping.

Mart kicked off his boots and walked across to the hearth. He enjoyed looking at the photos of the family that had accepted him as one of their own. Kent typically replaced them when nieces or nephews graduated or recent births prompted a new shot of one of his sisters' families. When Mart had frequented the house as a teenager there had been pictures of Kent in his football jersey or with his team accepting a trophy or a banner. These had been modestly packed away when Kent became the regular occupant of the home. The only relic remaining was one of Kent beaming into the lens and kneeling next to a half-grown Labrador puppy. Kent had been ten or twelve at the time of the photo. Toggs had been there to greet Mart throughout his Cardston High friendship with Kent. The lab was buried on the ridge above the Lee Creek swimming hole where Mart, Kent and Toggs had washed the hay dust from their dark skins late on summer evenings. The calming effect of the familiar surroundings took some of the sting out of his encounter with Jack Pruitt. He resolved to skip that topic tonight in favour of tackling the problem with Kent and Becky.

"How about we catch the early show and have a popcorn appetizer before we have supper?" Kent blurted out without any greeting or preamble as he placed the receiver on the charger.

"Yup, sounds like our regular plan."

"No sense messing with tradition," countered Kent, checking the platinum watch on his wrist. The European chronograph was indubitably a gift from his parents. Kent typically avoided any ostentatious display of the family's wealth.

Kent sat on a straight-backed wooden chair near the door and slipped on some freshly polished boots. Mart followed him and used the same chair to slip on his own once Kent had vacated the seat. They strolled down the steps and into the garage from outside to avoid tracking through the hallway with their boots. It was an old habit bred by a traditional respect for Mrs. Lindholm's requests that were now a decade old.

Kent struck up casual conversation as they backed out of the garage and swung around to point the vehicle toward the end of the driveway.

"I have my doubts about what's playing, but the Carriage House Theatre is the only option in Cardston," stated Kent wearily. "It may not be a one-horse town, but it is a one-theatre community." To broaden one's choices it was necessary to travel the extra eighty kilometres to Lethbridge.

Mart attempted optimism. "We might get lucky and the action will be good."

Excellent community theatre productions were regular fare at the Carriage House Theatre as well, so it was important to check out the nostalgic marquee or phone ahead to be sure what you were expecting to see was what was actually on the menu.

Mart and Kent arrived in plenty of time so they parked on the street directly in front of the theatre. It was a pleasant evening so they immediately left the truck and walked to the front doors. One of the adolescents often appearing in the live community productions greeted them at the door.

"There will be someone here shortly to sell you a ticket." She walked away carrying her broom and dust pan. The young actors were often employed at the concessions and to do other jobs to keep the place open and profitable.

The popcorn was excellent. The movie was less so. Hollywood's current preoccupation with vampires and werewolves had fortunately not infiltrated this particular film, but the movie industry had obviously allowed fantasy and magic to creep even into films touted as action thrillers. The effects were outstanding, but the plot was continually rescued by implausible whimsies and dream sequences.

The cowboy bachelors exited the movie house behind a batch of young teens noisily re-enacting the more violent sequences through realistic sound effects and bold gestures. Immediately following Mart was a young couple walking hand-in-hand and quietly discussing something that he was convinced was none of his business. Regardless of his discretion and their hushed voices, the conversation could not have gotten past the building anxiety Mart was experiencing. The intimate pair reminded him of Becky and of the pending revelation to Kent and possible confrontation.

CHAPTER 24 ✳ ADMISSIONS

The burger and fries were chased by a frosty ice-cream treat. It was over the desert that the conversation turned to the subject of Becky Sorenson. Mart was surprised when it was Kent who broached the subject.

"Mart, I need to talk to you about Becky."

The initial shock stunned Mart into silence.

"I know you have feelings for her. I don't suppose you'd be surprised that I do too," Kent continued, remaining the master of diplomacy.

Mart could not help but think that this was going to be easier than he had expected. Kent must have sensed that there was something going on between him and Becky. Mart faced a moment of guilt for having left it up to his best friend to tackle the problem. He imagined how Kent must be feeling. Yet here he was talking calmly about the relationship between a young lady, of whom he was clearly enamoured, and his own best friend. Kent had always been the bigger man and he was proving it again.

"Yes, I know you do," Mart blurted out. "I am truly sorry…"

Kent held up his hand to halt Mart's speech. "Please let me finish. This isn't the easiest thing I have ever had to do."

Although the two ranchers had been friends for more than a decade, their relationship was typical of those between males in general and southern Alberta men specifically. Giving voice to your feelings was not encouraged. Emotions tended to remain hidden and exhibiting them openly was almost always accompanied by a certain amount of discomfort. Mart decided the only fair thing to do was to allow Kent the dignity of bowing out gracefully so he shut his mouth and listened.

"I have never wanted to hurt you. We both know that Becky leaving after school was what allowed us to avoid the situation until now. I don't think we can continue to get around it any longer."

Kent hesitated, but Mart waited patiently.

"I know I don't want this to end our friendship. You have been good for me. You keep my feet on the ground and remind me what is important in life."

Mart couldn't believe his good fortune. Kent was doing all the work for him. He was expressing what he couldn't. Kent was surrendering something dear to him and yet making it clear that there would not be a grudge. Their companionship would continue. It would be awkward at first. He would feel some discomfort and perhaps even a little guilt anytime he, Kent and Becky were together. It would be the same or worse for his best friend. Mart was certain Becky would go through it, too. He hoped she would not force Mart to spend less time with Kent just to avoid the stress. He did not want to choose between them. These thoughts were ricocheting across Mart's mind and he nearly missed the import of the next statement.

"That is why I have to tell you that Becky and I have been spending quite a bit of time together."

Mart opened his mouth to reply, but the response he had been formulating in his mind now suddenly made no sense at all. He could think of nothing to say.

"It's clear to me that she feels the same way I do. I am sorry, Mart. I hope you can forgive me for not saying something sooner. I wasn't sure until this week. Please don't let this affect our friendship."

Becky and Kent were spending time together? When had this started? It had only been four days ago that Becky had snuggled up to him, kissed him repeatedly and given him every indication that she had chosen him over Kent. Mart babbled a poorly constructed question.

"How...when were you and Becky...How do you know?"

Kent maintained his even tone. "We spent the day riding last Sunday. She has been at the house twice this week. Mart, she made it clear..."

This time Mart raised his hand. Kent faltered and awaited his friend's reply. Mart remained mute and immobile. His eyes were on the table. Becky had gone riding with Kent on Sunday. She had spent most of Monday with Mart. She had been to Kent's house this week. Kent seemed convinced that she had chosen him otherwise this conversation would not be happening, at least not this way. Mart could only assume that Becky had responded to Kent's advances. Then Mart remembered that it had been she who had taken the initiative on their drive to Waterton. Had Becky done the same with Kent? Mart shook his head and shuddered slightly. This was too much for him to process. Without a word he stood up and walked out of the drive-in. Kent remained motionless on the cushioned plastic bench. He placed his head on his right hand and ran his fingers roughly through his perfect golden hair.

CHAPTER 25 ✵ A TOUCH OF SILVER

Mart maintained his normal daily routine on Saturday. He got up early, cared for the horses, fed and stroked the barn cat and loaded his pickup. He put in a couple of dozen posts, a roll of wire and his battered bucket of staples out of which protruded the handle of a hammer minus the rubber grip. He retrieved his fencing tool from a leather sheath made to be strapped to his saddle for emergency fence repair. Mart added the wooden stool he used to stand on while driving posts and the maul designed for that task. He headed for the quarter section north of Beaverdam Lake.

He was numb with fatigue even before he swung the heavy post maul for the first time. Lack of sleep from the night before had drained his normal nervous energy. After leaving the drive-in, Mart had walked up Main Street until he had reached the gas station at the intersection of that street with Alberta Highways 2 and 5. It was at that point that he realized he was in a bit of a predicament. His ride was back at the drive-in. Kent would probably be waiting there hoping Mart would come back to take up the conversation where he had so rudely broken it off. He would be anticipating giving Mart a ride home. Or perhaps he had left the restaurant by then and had begun searching for his friend. Mart had cursed Kent for his continual sense of responsibility and for his caring nature. It would be so much easier to hate the man if he had at least one damn fault!

Mart cursed again as he hit his fingers with the hammer for the second time that morning. The staples were always hard to hold in place, but today he was exhausted and distracted. It was fortunate he was not operating heavy machinery.

Mart had stood at that highway intersection last night in a bit of trance until he heard his name. He had turned to discover a silver SUV. Dr. Lorne's concerned face glowed with a greenish tint reflected from the dash lights. The surgeon was returning to Mountain View from his Calgary office. His family had come ahead of him while he finished up some work. Dr. Lorne had insisted on driving past his own house to take Mart all the way home. Mart did not think to ask to be dropped off at Kent's in Leavitt to get the Toyota. Perhaps it was just as well, in case Kent had beaten him home. Dr. Lorne had asked why he was on foot. Mart mumbled something that was less than convincing and perhaps not even coherent. The good doctor had been tactful enough not to pry further.

The answering machine had been blinking and the phone had rung twice after he kicked off his boots and threw himself on the bed. Kent would have been worrying about him, but last night Mart was not prepared to talk to him at all. He had listened to those messages this morning before his chores. Kent had asked him to call to let him know he was home. The last message lacked the tact of the first two. Kent had rebuked Mart for never turning on his cell phone and slammed down the receiver. Mart really owed it to Kent to let him know he was all right, but he left the house this morning spitefully ignoring his conscience.

Mart slogged away at the fencing task for the entire day. Oddly the work revitalized him somewhat. He found he had more energy by mid afternoon than he had that morning. The solitary task gave him time to think through the problem. He would talk to Kent about this soon. Kent had a right to know why he had reacted so miserably. Mart still had not worked out what to say to him about Becky. The fact that she had led each of them on several times and all within the same week was cause to question her intentions and did not speak all that well about her character. Like Mart, Kent probably had no idea she had been playing the both of them.

The sweating young rancher was so engrossed in his work and in his unpleasant thoughts that he only slowly became aware of the proximity of another animate being. He lifted his head gradually and looked across the fence and into the deep brown eyes of a sow grizzly. The wind tugged at the long silver hairs along her back and they rippled in waves like a ripened wheat field. She lifted her twitching nose high in the air and sampled Mart's scent. She shifted nervously from one front foot to the other. The huge muscles of her shoulder hump bulged left and right. Then she half-stood on her hind legs and focused on Mart's motionless form. She dropped down on her front feet again just as one, then a second, bear materialized from behind the same hill from which she had emerged.

'Great!' thought Mart. 'They are travelling in packs now.'

Mart had a hard time sorting out just how he felt about bears. There was no doubt that they, wolves and cougars, were a real liability in ranch country. Bears and wolves especially took livestock. Some years the depredations were occasional, other times almost epidemic. It all depended on what kind of year it was. Grizzlies ate mostly plants – about ninety percent of their diet was vegetation in the form of lily bulbs, wild legume roots, dandelions and berries later in the year. If any of those resources failed because of extremely wet, cold or dry weather, the bears altered their diet to include more ground squirrels, deer, insects and sometimes cattle. Occasionally one made the shift to beef for no apparent reason other than it was readily available.

It had taken thousands of years to breed the attributes of wild animals out of domestic stock in order to make them somewhat tractable and safer to be around. The same traits humans eliminated or minimized by selective breeding were those that natural selection would have favoured in order to make them more able to escape predators. The result was easy pickings for any predator that chose to concentrate on the docile animals.

Although the risks to livestock were real, Mart had to admit that one of the reasons he loved living here was that it was still wild. It is only true wilderness if it has all its natural parts. Bears and wolves were some of the components of that untamed beauty. Wilderness is not always convenient.

The mother grizzly glanced over her shoulder at the yearling siblings that would continue to rely on her until after they emerged from the den next spring. Grizzlies put a lot of effort into rearing their offspring and the cubs remained with their mother for two summers after birth.

East of the Rockies, near the Waterton-Glacier International Peace Park, was about the only place left in North America where you could still glimpse the large carnivores in their native prairie habitat. That had not always been the case. When Mart was young the bears rarely ventured out of the parks and remote sections of crown land. Recently sightings of grizzlies and wolves had increased out on private ranch land. Some people declared that a surplus of the animals was the reason for the increase. Researchers disagreed and Mart also guessed that wasn't completely the case. He suspected that the bears found life more tranquil amid the ranchers than among the ever-increasing buzz of ATVs and logging machinery on crown land.

The cost of disposing of dead livestock had also become an issue. With the Mad Cow Disease controversy, free dead stock disposal was a thing of the past. Many ranchers just left dead animals in the field rather than use limited financial resources for their removal. Bears and wolves scavenging on dead stock were more likely to loiter among the ranches and also more liable to turn to live cattle next.

Mart figured he was about thirty metres from the bears. That was too close. He turned his head slowly and guessed the pickup was only about ten metres away. That was too far. He doubted he could sprint the ten in the time it would take the bear to cover the thirty. Then he would have to get the door open, get in and shut it. A bear could run about as fast as a good racehorse. No, he had better stand his ground. He was relieved that the mother bear had not moved any closer. The two cubs had sauntered up to stand beside her. They were both almost as big as she was. Grizzlies here in the Rockies did not get as large as they did on the coasts of BC or Alaska. It was rare to see one that weighed much more than two hundred and fifty kilograms. This adult was not quite that large. But that was still about triple Mart's weight and he lacked the long claws and sharp canines.

Unlike laws regarding wolves and cougars, ranchers were not legally permitted to shoot grizzlies; not that it didn't still happen occasionally. Mart had mixed feelings about that, as did many of his neighbours. A livestock killer had to be dealt with. He knew that tolerance for bears and wolves among livestock operators would increase dramatically if the government compensation for predator-killed livestock were 100% of potential market value and more liberally awarded. As it presently stood they were only compensated if the kill could be confidently confirmed and only to the market value of the animal at its present age and weight rather than its probable value if sold in the fall. If society in general valued the grizzly population, the public should be more willing to foot the bill.

Mart grasped the fencing tool more firmly; squeezing the pliers' handles tightly after spinning them around to have the metal hook forward rather than the blunt face intended to pound fencing staples. He peeked quickly at the curved point. It was designed to remove staples and was no longer than his baby finger – no match for the sixty huge spikes shifting nervously in the grass and cinquefoil on the other side of the puny three-wire barrier.

Mart talked softly to the ursine trio. "Move on, old girl. I couldn't hurt those chubby kids of yours if I tried."

Mart gave an involuntary jump when mother bear uttered a short woof and hastily shuffled south and east toward a small rise and a half-dead patch of willows. One of the cubs immediately followed. Both mother and offspring glanced repeatedly over their shoulders as they retreated. The second cub did not move. It continued to stare at Mart who was doing his best to maintain his false composure.

"Off you go," continued the rancher in his most reassuring tone.

Again Mart twitched unintentionally as the big baby exploded into action and dashed after its sibling and parent.

Once the threesome had disappeared over the hill, Mart began to breathe more normally. He relaxed the grip on his frail weapon and shifted it to his left hand. He worked the cramp out of his right hand and forearm. Any lethargy remaining from the previous wakeful night had fled along with the grizzlies.

It was near dark before Mart loaded his tools and started for home. He was ravenous, but took the time to water the horses and the cat before heading for the mobile home. Seth had taught him to look after the animals before himself. He supplemented canned soup with several slices of bread and cheese. Canned peaches were a desert treat.

Realizing that he had avoided it long enough, Mart dialled Kent's number before he started the dishes. To his surprise he was actually relieved to get the machine and left a fairly coherent message. "Kent, I wanted to apologize for taking off and for not calling. I know our conversation isn't over. I need to talk to you some more about Becky. "

CHAPTER 26 ✳ PHONE HOME

Tina would not be working at all on Sunday, so it would be a good day to touch base with her. Mart's mom did not sleep late very often, but he waited until he came in from his regular morning chores before he sat down at the kitchen table to dial the Medicine Hat number. It was his stepfather who answered.

"Hello, Mart. How is the ranching business?"

Mart appreciated the attempt. His stepfather had been trying hard to repair the years of conflict. Taylor really had no knowledge of or interest in Mart's chosen profession. The man had grown up in the city, but was a reasonable outdoorsman from several years of field work for oil and gas companies. Nevertheless, with the exception of store-bought beef, horses and cattle were as foreign to him as were camels and elephants. In the few instances Mart had seen Taylor around neighbours' pets he had appeared awkward and perhaps even a bit apprehensive. For that reason Mart dwelt on the financial woes of the business rather than any detail about the work. Walter Taylor could understand that well enough.

After several minutes of polite chat, Walter offered the information Mart was really after.

"Your mom's not home right now. She has started walking a few times a week with a couple of ladies from work. They go down to Kin Coulee Park on the trails along Seven Persons Creek or on the path from the library over to Strathcona Island Park."

Mart was disappointed that his mother was away, but happy to hear she had started to get some exercise. She had never been slim, but when he had visited for Easter he noticed she had put on some extra weight. Heart disease was a feature of the Gwynn family and he had worried about her health.

"Can I have her call you when she gets in?"

"Thanks, but I'll probably be out. Maybe I'll call back around dinner time."

"We've been invited to the Chongs'."

Mart resisted the old joke about going out for Chinese food. The Chong family had been close friends since before Mart left home. It had been Dave Chong who had started the longstanding gag when he had called up the first time and asked the Taylor-McKinnon household if they felt like coming over for the Chong traditional Sunday meal. Dave and wife Leslie ran a successful Chinese diner downtown. Dave was the cook. It was all so stereotypical that Mart and his family had shown up expecting fare similar to that establishment's menu, or perhaps other exotic dishes from Asia. They had been served lobster bisque, pickerel that melted like warm butter and a soufflé that should have been a picture in an ad for Chez Louis'. Apparently the Chong tradition for Sunday dinner was for Dave to exercise his considerable culinary talents. The cheerful chef seemed to enjoy implying something different and observing the resulting surprise.

"Maybe I'll try tonight when I get in. Will you be late?"

"Hold on, Mart. Let me look. I think that is her car pulling in right now."

After a few moments of dead air, Tina Taylor came on the line with her typical out-of-breath bluster.

"Mart, I am so glad I didn't miss you."

"Hi, Mom."

Mart always relaxed when he could chat with his mother. She did a lot of the talking; sometimes about nothing much at all. She asked typical questions about his health and what he was getting to eat. When she got around to asking if anything was new in Mountain View, Mart told her about Wendell Jacobsen. He skipped the part about the attack on him personally and downplayed the incident with the high school truants and their run at him.

"I'm so sorry, Mart. That had to be an awful situation. I'm proud of how you're helping the family out with the cattle and things."

They talked for several more minutes before Tina Taylor touched on the topic Mart always tried to avoid, and about which he was even more reticent than usual.

"Are you dating anyone?"

"No."

"No prospects at all?"

"Not really."

Tina must have detected a slight hesitation. She swooped in like a gull to a thrashing ground squirrel on a long stretch of prairie asphalt.

"Come on, Mart. Spill."

This time Mart did hesitate. He gulped and measured his words.

"I thought there was someone, but it hasn't been working out."

Tina reconsidered her aggressive approach to ferreting out the declaration she longed to hear. She wanted so badly for Mart to find someone. She had never felt quite whole when she was alone. Walter had come along just in time to save her from a deep slump of depression. She had maintained her cheerful attitude at work, but returning to a home without a mate with whom to share the burden of raising an energetic boy was destroying her. Walter had come along just in time. But she had sensed Taylor's reluctance to become a family man. That he would have difficulty dealing with children was no surprise. She had not pressured him to have more.

"I just can't understand your comfort with bachelorhood, Mart. If there are no prospects there, sell out and move back to the city where there is some chance of a social life. You know, there is hope for an existence without the distractions of night checks on calving cows or long hours cutting and baling hay. I worry about you out in blizzards feeding cattle and knowing nobody is home to know if you're overdue."

Tina could ride, but the fact that Mart would stay in the saddle in rough country for hours at a time made her more than a little apprehensive. Who would miss him if he didn't come home for several days? Mountain View still functioned like a real old-time community. The neighbours looked out for each other. They had no qualms about poking into one another's lives if they thought they could be of service. At times it was annoying. Other times it saved homes, lives and even marriages. But all that didn't stop Tina from offering to rush to Mart's side anytime he admitted to a moderate bout of the flu.

"What happened, Mart?"

"I'm not sure exactly. Maybe she just turned out to be a different person from what I thought she was," Mart declared.

"Nobody is perfect, dear. Don't expect that."

"I know, Mom. It's a bit more complicated than that. I don't think I can explain."

Tina had the good sense to press no further.

"You know you can call any time." Then she added, "How about coming home for a visit?"

"I'd like to," Mart lied fairly convincingly. In spite of the improvement in his relationship with Walter, Medicine Hat didn't feel much like home anymore. Too much unpleasantness lurked in dusty corners and seeped from Mart's old basement bedroom. "Maybe after the calves are sold."

Again Tina didn't insist. She missed her son terribly, but knew the path he had chosen would continue to lead him straight into that violent Chinook gale and butt him up against those abrupt Rockies.

Mart sat staring at the silent telephone for several minutes after he had disconnected. The wall he had built around himself wasn't fair to his mother. He had a tendency to avoid human contact when he was troubled or hurting. He fit almost too well into the rugged independence of his adopted home. He had no trouble trading favours with his good neighbours, but the sharing did not extend into more intimate territory. He had no desire to inspect their dirty laundry and no urge to air his with them. Kent was the closest thing he had to a confidante. That was not an option this time.

CHAPTER 27 ✸ RUNOFF

The school bus rumbled past at 7:35. John must have had to wait for a tardy kid somewhere along the route. He was really moving, trying to make up some lost time. The dust lifted twice the height of the boxy yellow vehicle and drifted languidly eastward. Mart was busy dropping clods of mud dug from the narrow ditch in front of him into the notches he had cut from the banks late last week. He had not allowed any water to spread over the land like he did in drier years. The water he had released recently was solely to top up the sloughs he used to water stock through the fall and winter. Spring runoff and the wet summer had kept them nearly full, but he wanted to be sure. They were full now and he intended to avoid any wasted water that might trespass on the land of his nearest neighbours.

The morning was cool, perhaps even cold. The shorter days of late summer were beginning to show. The heat built up during the day dissipated through the longer nights. Aunt Em would have been gathering old blankets from off her beans in the old overgrown garden patch behind the hedge. She was always one step ahead of an early frost. Uncle Seth would pooh-pooh her effort and then dodge her I-told-you-so the next morning.

On the way back home Mart used the muddy spade to chop Canada thistle along the cattle trail. Invasive weeds were getting to be a big problem. New ones were showing up all the time. Non-native plants were seldom the target of wild or domesticated herbivores. Because of that they thrived and choked out the grasses and forbs cattle and deer would eat. The thistles were poorly named. They did not originate in Canada at all, but had come in seed from Europe.

The farrier was due at ten o'clock. Mart would have time to rotate the tires on the pickup. The front ones were beginning to show the typical wear of a four wheel drive. After that job was done, he finally went in for a bowl of cereal. A three-quarter ton with the catchy logo pulled into the yard and up to the barn just as Mart was brushing his teeth.

Horace Radner was a big, quiet man with a moustache reaching to the edges of his chin. Some of the ranchers could still set horseshoes themselves, but Mart confined himself to trimming hooves when the shoes were off. He just didn't trust himself not to lame an animal with the sharp nails. Horace had been his farrier for about ten years now. The familiar U-shaped lettering spelling out Horace's Shoes was stencilled on the rear window of yet another late model truck. This was probably the fourth spanking new vehicle Horace had possessed since Mart had first hired him. Either he was awfully hard on pickups or his business was thriving. Mart suspected that ranchers now made up the minority of his clientele. Acreage owners, recreational riders and racehorse stables probably created the bulk of his work.

Skip and Slim were in the barn. Horace knew the horses and went straight to work. The shed had no room so he moved Slim out into the sunlight and tied him to the corral rail. The lithe bay lifted his hooves obediently for a first inspection. Mart walked up just as the big farrier was removing the clinched ends of the nails so he could pull the first shoe.

Slim was allowed to put his foot back down while Mart and the big man exchanged a few words. Mart was surprised when Horace expressed his condolences for Mr. Jacobsen. Mart had forgotten that it was he who had referred Wendell to Horace once the old rancher had decided he could no longer hold the mare's feet up long enough to complete the job.

Horace asked, "What happened?"

Mart gave him the condensed version minus recriminations toward the ATV riders. Horace provided some of his own accusations without Mart's lead. He shook his head and berated the infernal machines. "Those damn things ought to be outlawed on public property! They at least should be kept out of grazing leases. You folks are trying to make a living here."

"Maybe we're dinosaurs, Horace. Folks are getting more mechanized. We're both stuck in the horse and buggy era and everyone else is using up rubber instead of iron." Mart gestured toward the farrier's box of tools and horseshoes.

"Don't say it, Mart. I've got a grandchild at home I got to get to college somehow. Anyway, we have to stand up to the trend. It's not a good one. I had this argument with Jack just a few days ago. He sure cursed Wendell."

"Jack Pruitt?"

"Yeah."

Horace really had Mart's attention now. "What brought that on?"

"I was in at the Co-op in Pincher Creek and ran into him. He was getting some oil. I asked if he had truck problems and he said it was for his four-wheeler. I must have squinted just the wrong way, 'cause he lit into me about being some kind of…let's see, I think he said purist. He crabbed about me lining my pockets catering to idiots who couldn't give up on some kind of wild-west dream. He said I was as bad as that old, well he used some language, and was talking about Wendell. But that was before the accident. I imagine he might be regretting his threats now."

"Threats?"

"He was just blowing off steam."

"What exactly did he say?" Mart asked cautiously.

"Just that the old bugger would get his. He mentioned Wendell trying to get him thrown out of the Pasture Association. He was griping about Wendell messing with his livelihood and tarnishing his reputation. Old Jack can be pretty eloquent when he gets going." Horace looked quizzically at Mart. "Jack's all bluster. You know that, don't you?"

Mart decided he'd better back off. "Yeah, I know. I was just wishing I could have gotten those two to bury the hatchet before Wendell...before the accident."

"You can't live other people's lives for them, Mart. They were big boys. They made their way without our help. They get to live with their choices."

Mart made a point of being obvious when he looked over at the stencilled logo on the shiny pick-up. Horace looked puzzled.

"I was just looking for the part that said Radner's Philosophy under the Horace's Shoes sign."

Horace let out a deep chortle and bent back to pick up a hoof. Mart left the farrier to his work and headed for the tractor. He started it up, filled it with diesel from the bulk fuel tank along the driveway and hooked up the flatbed trailer. He would get the rest of his hay in today.

When Mart returned from his last trip and finished stacking the big round bales he found the horses tied back in their stalls with brand new shoes. The bill was rolled and tucked neatly into the handle of the horse shed door. Mart slipped the invoice into his pocket and led Skip and Slim over to the hydrant where he ran some water into the battered tub. He threw the halter shanks over their necks and left them to drink. He went back to their stalls and dumped a few oats in each box. They walked directly back on their own to slick up the treat. He turned them out and headed in for an early supper.

Mart found himself tackling little housekeeping jobs that he typically avoided. When he grabbed the toilet cleaning supplies from under the bathroom sink he admitted to himself that he was procrastinating. He needed to call Kent. When he had flushed the sparkling clean bowl for the second time, he resolved to quit playing Mrs. Doubtfire and pick up the telephone. He was reaching for it when it rang. He pulled away his outstretched hand as if the device were bubbling acid. He paused for an instant and then grabbed at it hastily.

"Hello."

"Hi, Marty."

Crap! It was worse than what he had anticipated. If it had been Kent, he would have once again been caught forestalling his responsibility to face the conflict. Kent Lindholm would have yet again proved to be the better man. But this! What was he going to say to Becky Sorenson?

"Are you there, Mart?"

Mart stammered an affirmation.

"I was hoping I would catch you," Becky continued without commenting on Mart's strange lack of response. "I am heading to Kalispell for a couple of days."

Mart felt relief. That would get Becky safely out of the way while he dealt with Kent.

Mart pretended some normalcy. "Shopping trip?"

"Kind of, but mostly I just wanted to get one more trip over the Going to the Sun Highway before the first snows."

The Going to the Sun Highway over Logan Pass in Glacier National Park was a spectacular drive through the alpine beauty of that US national park. People from southern Alberta frequently took the drive one or more times every year.

"Do you have a passport, Marty?"

Mart confirmed he did before he realized what was coming. When he grasped where the conversation was headed he didn't know whether to do cartwheels or throw himself from Belly River Bridge.

"Why don't you come along?" Becky asked as nonchalantly as if she were asking him to share her ice cream cone.

After he hung up Mart knew he should have taken the opportunity to ask her just what the hell was going on. He should have demanded she tell him who she really wanted and in what way. Was he going to sleep on the hotel couch in Montana? If he had accepted the invitation was he going to find Kent already installed in the front seat of the car when she picked him up? Were they all just friends or was someone going to turn out to be more than that? Instead he had once again shown the backbone of an earthworm. He had given several excuses about the need to stay home and listed several obligations he had. Much of it was just plain lying.

What was worse is that he wanted so badly to say yes and go. Even if he later lost her to Kent, he would at least have had one last chance to capture Becky's heart. Damn Becky and damn Kent Lindholm! She was so beguiling his desire could have easily eclipsed his loyalty to Kent. But Kent was such a constant friend that Mart couldn't betray him, even though this probably meant the end of his prospects with the blond object of his ten-year long fantasy. It made him momentarily hate them both.

Mart had not run off with Becky, but now he really couldn't bear the thought of confronting Kent. How would Kent react to Becky's invitation to Mart? There was an even greater risk. What if he called the Lindholm ranch and Kent was not even there? What if he was gone for the next couple of days, too?

CHAPTER 28 ✳ LOST HISTORIES

While Mart was staring at the telephone and stewing over his approach to telling Kent about Becky, the thing rang and startled him again. Given the risk of it being Becky for a second time, or actually Kent this time, he almost ran from the room. He was not enamoured with modern technology and even less thrilled about paying through the nose for it to an impersonal phone company, but right then he could really have used call display.

He gave in and answered after three rings. His greeting must have sounded very tentative because Tom Wyslik was forced to ask if he was really there.

"Mart?"

"Yes, it's me Tom," Mart admitted with relief.

"You sound like you're down a sewer pipe."

Mart adjusted the receiver a little closer to his mouth. "Is this better?"

"Yeah, that will do." Tom continued in his normal straightforward manner. "You got any time tomorrow to help move my yearlings from Caldwell back home?"

"If we can do it early, I can be there."

"What's early?"

"If we started at 6:30 I would have time later to make it to town for a load of fence posts."

"The only problem I see with that is that if you buy posts you have to put them in."

Mart smiled. "I see your point. Maybe you could pound them in for me?"

"Got to go, Mart." Tom pretended a hasty avoidance of the question. "Meet me at home and I'll trailer your horse from there."

"OK. See you at 6:30," Mart replied, but Tom really had hurried off the other end of the line.

Another restless night made the five o'clock start a tough one. Mart found himself constantly backtracking to accomplish his preparations. He went back to the house three times to collect all his gear, extra clothes and lunch. It was only about a half-day outing, but there were clouds in the west over the mountains and it was hard to tell if the late summer heat would continue or if they were in for weather.

Mart loaded Skip and headed for Tom's. Wyslik lived east and north of Mountain View, on a gravel road about three kilometres off Highway 5. Mart sailed through the hamlet well ahead of any concern for the school zone. Some of the Parks Canada staff was already accumulating on the church parking lot to car pool to Waterton. He waved at one of the mechanics and an equipment operator who were also fellow ranchers with the second job to keep their ranches afloat.

Mart arrived right on time and thought of how proud Wendell would have been. Then he reconsidered. No, Jacobsen would not have been proud. He would have wondered why Mart was not ten minutes early so he would be ready to go precisely at half-past six. This time Mart smiled at the curmudgeon's hypothetical censure.

Tom, on the other hand, was just loading a couple of buckskins. They were a nice pair of Quarter Horses he had raised from his best brood mare. Tom's son Reg was throwing some coats in the cab. Tom was sometimes reluctant to handle a large group of stock with only Reg as his help, especially yearlings. Unlike older cattle the young animals often showed an odd disloyalty to the rest of the herd and ran off alone or in small clusters. Rounding them up was challenging and working with less experienced help in those circumstances was frustrating. Reg just never seemed to get the knack of working stock. Tom knew Mart was patient with Reg so he was often conscripted to help. The upside was that Tom went out if his way to return favours whenever Mart needed a hand.

Mart dropped his horse out of his own trailer and loaded the big red gelding into Tom's. He leaned against the pickup box while Tom shut some gates and stuck his head in the house to say a few words to Sheila. Mart could hear growling from behind him. He ignored the red-speckled heeler dog. The creature had seen Mart a thousand times and still would not be his friend.

As soon as Tom started for the truck, Mart climbed into the back seat. Reg was smiling shyly from the front of the crew cab. Mart greeted him warmly and the boy's face lit up. The drive back through Mountain View and onto the Hill Spring road was filled with the regular conversation and also some explanations for Mart. They were really not needed. Mart had moved young stock before for Tom from the half section along the Belly River north of the former settlement of Caldwell. Caldwell, like Seddon, was no longer a community, but was still referred to as a locale by the families who owned land there.

Tom, Mart and Reg climbed onto their horses and turned up their collars. The wind was coming up and it was not a warm one. Tom said, "I'll head down onto the river bottom along the north fence line. Why don't you ride diagonally through the field to collect that large cluster of yearlings we can see from here? Come on, Reg," Tom commanded gently.

"I'll go with Mart," was the boy's response.

Tom gave Mart a pleading look. Mart smiled and said, "Fine by me if your dad can handle things on his own down there."

Tom looked relieved and trotted away on the buckskin. The stock dog ranged out ahead of him, but was called back with a sharp command.

Mart and Reg took a curved trajectory around to the other side of the herd. It seemed to contain most of the sixty-odd animals Tom claimed should be there. Mart asked Reg a few questions about his family and school. "Do you like your classes? What subjects are you taking?"

"They're okay," the boy shrugged a response. He didn't talk much normally and shut right down once Mart asked these last questions. School was a struggle and Mart felt badly he had not left that topic alone.

The young cattle were hard to get straightened out. Many kept turning to face the horsemen and even came back toward them from time to time. Mart gave Reg some gentle instruction. "Reg, if you'll ride a short distance away from me it'll create a wider barrier for the cattle. They won't be able to get past us so easily." The boy half-heartedly directed his horse away a few times, but constantly allowed her to wander back next to Skip. It was not only the young horse that fancied companionship. Mart recognized that Reg lacked much in the way of self confidence.

Halfway to the gate and the highway outside of it, Mart caught a glimpse of Tom breaking brush down by the stream. The heeler dog was pushing a few animals out of the cottonwoods and Tom was cutting them off. Wyslik was one of the best cowboys Mart had ever seen. He could ride hard and was firm with stock, but seldom lost patience. Tom had worked hard to build on the modest legacy his immigrant parents had scraped out of the poverty they suffered in the late 1930s and the decade afterward. He was the only son after several daughters. They were all hard workers and those Mart had met were as decent and friendly as Tom and Sheila were.

The two herds met just west of the gate and Reg showed uncommon forethought by surging ahead past the cattle to get the gate. After he opened it he mounted and rode a short distance down the highway in the opposite direction to which the herd must travel. He had the right idea, but did not go far enough away from the gate so the yearlings stalled without exiting onto the road.

"Back up just a little, son," Tom directed as gently as he could and still be heard over the bawling, hoof beats and wind.

Reg looked a little dejected at the mild rebuke and moved his horse north another twenty paces.

"That's good, Reg." Tom tried to regain some ground.

Reg was extremely sensitive to criticism. It was hard for Tom to teach the boy without discouraging him to the point that he quit entirely. Coordinating ranch work called for a lot of yelling back and forth and taking orders from whomever was considered the most experienced hand. It was a hard profession to teach to a young man with such little confidence. Mart knew that Tom held slight hope that his son would form the next generation of Wyslik cattlemen. It was a bitter pill for the man. He had put his soul into the ranch.

The yearlings pushed and shoved each other through the narrow gateway and turned obediently away from Reg and south toward the junction with Highway 5. The three horsemen left the pickup and trailer there and pushed the yearlings ahead of them.

They tried to keep the animals out of the oncoming lane so that head-on vehicles could pass simply by reducing their speed. There was little traffic for the first hour, but after that occasional cars and trucks caught up with the herd. The cars that came up behind them were ushered through as Mart or Tom directed them in behind their mounts so they could trot along and push the cattle out of the way. Locals knew the drill and would stay in close to the horses' heels, but other drivers were reluctant to drive so close to the horsemen and cattle moved in behind the horse and in front of the car. Then the herdsman would be forced to stop, turn and open up the hole again so they could proceed.

At the junction with Highway 5, Reg rode ahead and turned the herd east. They were just descending the hill down into Mountain View when a vividly decorated motor home with Canadream logo pulled up behind them. When Mart attempted to get them to follow him through the cattle, the middle-aged lady driving the unit rolled down her window. The blustery wind tossed her short, straight, red-dyed hair into a loose eddy.

"Excuse me, sir." She beckoned him to ride up to the window.

"Will you let me take picture?" she asked politely. Her accent was strong. Mart would guess she was from Germany or the Netherlands. Her male companion was smiling and kept nodding.

This was not a new thing for Mart or any other local rancher who drove cattle along the highway. Being part of someone's holiday photo album was not high on Mart's list of ambitions. He didn't feel particularly photogenic, but understood that part of the attraction to the area was the cowboy way of life. Seeing an actual cattle drive, even if it were along a highway rather than on the open range, must be a treat for folks from the eastern parts of this continent and from Europe or Asia. It was hard to refuse the request from such an enthusiastic audience. Mart rationalized that nobody he knew would ever see the photograph anyway.

"Sure. Go ahead," Mart responded and stopped his horse in such a way that the cattle and the mountains would be his backdrop.

The smiling lady took a couple of shots and thanked Mart. "I will post on my blog."

The smile left Mart's face. He really was a Luddite. He had not thought of the internet. His friends could be seeing this picture two days after this nice couple arrived home in Frankfurt or Copenhagen. The pair continued to smile as Mart tipped his hat and rode on to lead them through the herd. He could not bring himself to attempt to dissuade them. They figured to be paying him a compliment by posting the shots.

The wind picked up slightly, but the late summer sun still packed a punch and Mart was able to remove his jacket. They made it through Mountain View well after the school buses had delivered the children, but before too much traffic was flowing. Reg kept looking at the school, hoping some of his friends would be enviously watching from the classroom he had escaped for the half-day cattle drive.

Tom and Mart engaged in sporadic bouts of dialogue. Reg listened, but did not seek to be included. The conversation turned to Wendell Jacobsen. Tom reminisced about the old man's idiosyncrasies. Wendell's habits had often been irritating, but the two ranchers spoke of them now with some degree of fondness. Tom mentioned Jacobsen's penchant for recording life's minute details in his diary. That prompted Mart to speak of the missing journal. He had not mentioned it to anyone else aside from Mrs. Parascak and the police.

Tom repeated the same seemingly logical explanation. "Did Wendell's family take it?"

"No. It went missing before they ever got here." Mart continued with an account of the kitchen battle and his discovery that the book was gone.

"Wendell wrote down everything he knew about the area in his scrapbooks, including stuff about the Poll Haven. He figured someday everybody who knew anything about the history of the area would be gone. I guess he was right. Not too many folks know the old names given to places up in the hills, let alone the origins of those odd names."

"Yeah. Glanders Flats, Barton Crossing, Glenwood Saw Set," Mart listed some.

"It was Wendell who told me about how some old-timer or another had built himself a whip out of a stick and some baling wire. He used it to drive his cattle to the pasture then left it hanging at one of the gates. He did it a couple of times and one whip stayed there for a couple of decades. That's how the Wire Whip Gate gets its name. Same idea goes for the Whiskey Bottle Gate at the US boundary – although I could have guessed that one myself. It was Wendell who showed me where the saw was set up in the Glenwood field. He wrote in that book where and when he saw bears, lynx or wolves – pretty much anything he noticed." Tom shook his head. "Interesting for us, but not much value to anyone else. Maybe the thief was writing a book."

Mart rode in silence while Tom shepherded another pair of cars through the yearlings. What was the significance of the journal? Maybe an account of the mystery Wendell had tried to reveal to Mart had been in there. Mart pushed his hat back slightly and rubbed his forehead. He was puzzled. A healthy gust of wind almost grabbed the battered black Smithbilt from his head. Mart clapped a hand over the mushy crown to keep it from lifting off. He then shifted his hand to the brim and tugged it down tight.

What extraordinary poor luck that the one place Mart could have possibly gone for information related to Wendell's puzzle had been snatched away from him. Poor luck? How could that simply be chance? Did the thief actually take the diary knowing there was something valuable in it? What had Wendell found, a vein of silver protruding from a game trail? How would the burglar have known there was anything of value in the book? Had he sat at the kitchen table to read Jacobsen's rambling descriptions and anecdotes? Perhaps the revelation had been on the open pages of the journal. The man could have spotted some reference that made taking the journal attractive.

Tom had arrived back at the rear of the herd.

Again Mart wondered at this line of thinking. "All this is just too coincidental, Tom. A man from some other town hears about a horseback riding accident and an old cowboy's death. He somehow finds out where the old man lived and travels from

Lethbridge or Magrath or perhaps Cardston. Cardston seems unlikely. I know most folks from the area and this guy didn't seem familiar. The thief then hides his pickup or SUV behind the barn and walks up to the house even though there is a yellow Toyota parked next to the barn. He knocks and discovers nobody home. How did he know Mrs. Jacobsen wouldn't be there?" Mart shuddered. "The fellow didn't seem to shrink from the use of force. Perhaps Mrs. Jacobsen would have received my beating if she hadn't already been gone."

"You're right, that sounds too odd to be true."

"Yeah. Then think of this, the thief checks out the house, maybe taking a bit of cash from some drawer or a trinket or two from the shelves – nothing anybody later noticed was missing. Then he stops to read a passage from the book on the table? Gutsy, but stupid!" Then Mart remembered the shape of the volume. "You know, that book was about the same size as a ledger. Maybe it did make sense that the robber hoped it contained financial records or bank account information." Mart became more optimistic. This made a little bit of sense. Perhaps the criminal grabbed it and ran hoping to commit some form of lucrative fraud in the future.

Tom shrugged. "The thief would have chucked the book in the nearest garbage bin once he discovered it merely contained Jacobsen's everyday ramblings – unless of course it did contain something of worth."

Mart became more sober. The book was gone forever. Chances were not good that the value had anything to do with some quirky discovery the old man had made at the south end of the Poll Haven Community Pasture.

"Maybe Wendell was keeping tabs on all our wicked deeds," Tom offered with a grin. "When word got out that he was gone, one of his neighbours sneaked in to destroy the evidence."

The blood drained from Mart's face. Tom saw it and looked away. He felt awkward at having made a jest when Mart was still so sensitive about the old man's death. He had no way of knowing that Mart had involuntarily shuddered as his thoughts shifted to Jack Pruitt and his volatile daughter.

Mart and Reg pushed the yearlings off Highway 5 and onto the long gravel road leading to the Wyslik ranch. Tom had remained in the lead the last half kilometre after guiding a couple of local pickups through.

Once the yearlings were locked into their new pasture Sheila invited Mart in for a quick lunch. She scurried around to make sure he had eaten too much and gathered some leftovers for the bachelor to take home with him in a grocery sack. She reminded him slightly of Aunt Emma. On the way out of the house the Australian cattle dog took a nip at Mart's boot. Mart growled at the heeler and it quickly backed down. Skip loaded easily. He was eager to get home. So was Mart, but he still had a trip to Cardston ahead of him to get some posts and maybe another bucket of fencing staples. The load would be heavy enough so he would have to return another day for ten or twelve blocks of stock salt that he knew he needed soon.

Mart only stopped at the house long enough to put the food in the old fridge and to unload his horse. He unsaddled and then left Skip in a stall munching some oats. After the trailer was unhooked, he headed back through the hamlet and to Cardston. The local hardware store was the only place selling posts anymore. He and the young yardman loaded sixty and Mart took a bucket of staples. He noticed the marquee had changed at the Carriage House Theatre. He thought of his ill-fated movie night with Kent and experienced another bout of guilt. He needed to call and explain himself to his friend – if they were indeed still friends.

CHAPTER 29 ✷ THE DEN

SLIM WAS PARTICULARLY spunky. Maybe it was the cooler weather. Mart had trotted the fine-boned equine for nearly two kilometres before he had settled down. They had again started the ride from the north side of Beaverdam Lake. Tattered wraiths were ascending from the tepid pools in Archie's Beaver Dams. Nights were getting cooler and the sharp odour of autumn vegetation was floating on an almost imperceptible breeze. As close as Fort Macleod and Lethbridge fall was still a month or more away, but at this elevation September had started to feel like summer was over.

A family of ruffed grouse rattled from the tangle of fallen trunks and cured grass to alight only a few metres away in the skeletal branches of a partially dead plains cottonwood. Slim gave only a slight start that created a trivial stutter in his normally smooth, fast walk.

Mart was feeling optimistic. He had telephoned Kent early this morning. He had missed talking to his friend, who was also an early riser, but had managed to leave a somewhat apologetic and fairly coherent message. Although he should have felt disappointed that they had not yet spoken, and perhaps apprehensive at how the conversation might turn, he was proud of himself for finally getting up enough courage to face the problem. He had rehearsed several approaches and had settled on what he thought was a good script. He needed Kent to understand his shock and to approach Becky's duplicity as tactfully as possible. He had no desire to besmirch her reputation or to have Kent perceive that he was just playing the Aesop's fox experiencing a sour grapes moment.

Mart picked his way along the cross fence from Atwood Gate to Four Corners. He stayed above the thick growth along Sand Creek. He always experienced a twinge of anxiety as he approached Barton Crossing. It had been shortly after his permanent arrival in Mountain View that Wendell had told him the story of the fellow who got bucked off his horse there. Old man Jacobsen had indicated in a very serious tone that all Mart needed to do was to die likewise in some spectacular accident up here to get his name forever stamped on some noteworthy nearby feature. Mart guessed it was the odd widower's attempt at humour.

It was barely nine o'clock when Mart reached the Mackenzie cut line. He spooked two whitetail bucks and a young doe from the open swath. The bucks were small and still in velvet so neither would be much of a trophy for this fall's hunters. They loped away, bounding gracefully over blow-downs and weaving in and out of the edge of the cut.

The image created by the threesome pulled Mart back to his musings about Kent, himself and Becky. He was angry with her, but found himself yearning for some solution that ended with the two of them together. He knew such wishes were madness. He tried to visualize the blond beauty greeting him at the trailer door with an apron around her slim waist and flour on her cheek. He rubbed his forehead and closed his eyes tightly. Although many women of the predominately LDS community still played that very traditional role, it was unlikely Becky would slip easily into it. He wasn't sure it would be what he wanted anyway. But the real disconnect there was Becky living in his fourteen-wide mobile home. Now that he really could not envision! He tried to conjure an image of her across the table from him in Aunt

Emma's tidy but cramped kitchen. That did not seem to fit either. He frowned as he trespassed mentally into the Lindholm dining room. She matched the polished wood and leather decor there perfectly; only it wasn't against his lithe frame which he imagined her supple body. Pangs of complete jealousy wracked his unsettled psyche.

He was jerked from these awkward deliberations by the sound of a starting chainsaw. Slim had detected the activity ahead, but Mart had been too distracted to read the cues the horse had given him. He pulled up his mount. The operator of the saw had not noticed his approach nor had the man's companion. They were clearing brush on a new line in preparation for the work of laying out a blasting grid for their seismic work. Two different quads from the ones he had encountered a few days earlier were parked a short distance away. Instinctively Mart directed Slim between a couple of young lodgepole pine trees. He then picked his way through the brush just below where the crew was working. He attempted to remain beneath their line of sight and used the din of the saw to cover the sounds of his detour. He did not return to the trail until he was fairly certain that the workers would not be able to see him. The saw was shut down about halfway through his bypass, but the noise from the activity of clearing away the cut brush reached his ears and he felt confident that the workers had not detected his presence.

After Mart had regained the trail and was close to where the Mackenzie cut intersected the other old seismic line, he began to feel cowardly and foolish. Why had he felt it necessary to circumnavigate the crew's activity? He was part of the grazing association and had every right to be there. How could they know he was actually looking for Wendell's treasure rather than simply checking gates? They probably could not care less anyway. What concern could they possibly have for an old man's discovery? Then he again remembered the unpleasant encounter at the Barn Store. Immediately he began thinking of paths that would allow him to miss being seen by Southwest Seismic on the way out. Perhaps he really was a coward.

Mart began his search in earnest when he reached the triangle created by the two old seismic cut lines and the US boundary. He used the trail that led down from the Hog's Back to get from one clump of brush to the next. He tried to approach the search systematically, creating a wobbly grid as he meandered around obstacles formed by the healthy vegetation and deadfall. But the rancher remained distracted. Mart muttered softly to himself to the point that Slim finally gave up twitching his ears to determine what was up.

The rancher was chastising himself for his lack of gumption in relation to Southwest Seismic as Slim poked out through a thick tangle to a point just north of the Whiskey Bottle Gate. Mart began to appreciate the fact that thoughts of Becky and of the seismic crew were compromising the objective of his mission. He resolved to pay more attention to the actual landscape and less to his convoluted psychological topography.

It was about thirty metres back from the small opening near the gate that Mart sensed rather than actually saw the irregularity. A horizontal edge vaguely visible among the host of vertical lines of the forest caused a momentary hiccup in Mart's Poll Haven paradigm. It was so subtle that the young man had looked right past it and away before the aberration in the regular pattern registered. By that time Slim had stepped over a log and through some alder shrubs. When Mart turned his head back to where he thought he had observed the anomaly, it was no longer visible. He put some pressure on the neck and ribs of the little horse and circumnavigated the shrubs. He scanned thoroughly for what he was not really sure was there.

There! A half hand taller than the majority of the bushes was the very top of a dome. It had a similar colour to the rest of the backdrop, but its texture was all wrong. Mart started to dismount, but thought better of it. This object, or mirage, was a good fifty metres away against a stand of white spruce, among buffalo berry and false huckleberry plants and a tangle of fallen trees. From the saddle it was noticeable, but he feared it would disappear completely once he lost this higher vantage. He pushed Slim through some gruelling shin tangle. He let the pony worry about his footing and kept his own eyes glued to the rounded shape. Slim shoved through the shrubs and at one point dropped into a narrow gully. Mart panicked as he lost sight of his goal. It took several seconds after Slim had scrambled out of the depression before Mart's watering eyes fixed on the odd object again. He breathed a sigh of relief and redirected the horse that was walking blind through saddle horn high vegetation.

It was not until Mart was within ten metres of the oddity that he began to determine what had differentiated it from the remainder of the thicket. Its apex was composed partially of a loose fabric disguised by fallen branches and nearby live plants. Mart climbed down and fought through the last several metres. Slim was content to stand and wait.

What came first to mind was a Blackfoot sweat lodge. An untidy frame of woven stems seemed to form the thing. They were springy sticks bent into a series of arches with their pointed ends dug into the ground. It would have been difficult to determine if the hump was manmade or natural if the next layer had not been of netting. The filaments were laced with dull green and brown tatters that resembled half-dead leaves. It was like the material Mart had seen on combat movies used to cover supply caches or mission command centres. The final layer was of native wood and leaves. Someone had gone to a good deal of trouble to hide the structure.

Mart wondered if someone was inside, but thought better of it when he noticed its size. It was slightly smaller than any typical backpacking tent Mart had ever seen. He thrashed around until he came to what was undoubtedly the front of the odd construction. It had a doorway, albeit the entrance was a smallish one.

It would have been adequate for him to enter only if he were to scramble in on hands and knees. He had little desire to do that. What if the rude edifice were occupied by something with fangs?

Mart cleared his throat. Nothing happened. He was about to say something when he thought better of his position. If something was in there it would run straight over him to get out. He stepped aside and leaned against the false huckleberry shrub next to the rude portal.

"Anyone home?" Mart was embarrassed by the ridiculous statement.

He humiliated himself a second time with a like greeting, received a similar lack of encouragement and then made up his mind to peer inside. He stooped slowly and jerked back as Slim snorted. He cursed the horse and then trained his eyes on the dark interior.

If there was something animate inside, Mart could not see or hear it. He reached a tentative hand into the shadowy interior. The vegetation had been trampled and lay flat in places. He poked his head farther in and could see a scrap of carpet along the very back wall of the shelter. Its fibres were also matted flat as if something had bedded down there. He crawled forward. He placed his right knee on something gritty and heard it crunch. He backed away one step and ran his hand along the floor until he sensed a gritty substance with his fingertips. He tried to pick it up, but it continued to fall apart at his touch. Finally Mart was able to extract a few specks of the grit and retreated into the sunlight. The crumbles were brown and coarse. When he rubbed them between his fingers gently they were slightly greasy and the crumbs threatened to disintegrate totally. Mart gave them a sniff. They did not have a distinctive smell. It slowly dawned on him that it was some type of animal feed. Back in he went, feeling ahead of him with his hands. He was rewarded when he encountered a spherical shape. When he again withdrew into the light he guessed the object he held was a piece of dog food.

Two or three more short expeditions into the small bower revealed nothing more of any interest. Mart stood and pondered the kibble in his hand and then the hut. Was this Wendell's discovery? It was truly odd to find the camouflaged structure here and even more perplexing to come across pet kibbles and a bed. Was someone using the shelter as some kind of blind from which to hunt? Or were they luring bears or wolves to it with cheap pet food? Baiting was illegal. Mart immediately placed the food pellet on his sleeve and rubbed his bare hand on his trousers. Was it poisoned? Or perhaps it was being used to attract animals to a trap or snare. The thought made him shudder. He looked inside again. Had he avoided placing his hand in a trap solely through dumb luck?

Mart went back to his saddle and used only his free hand to take his waxed-paper wrapped sandwiches out of the paper bag and dump them into the leather pouch. He rolled the kibble into the sack from his sleeve. He placed it into the saddlebag and returned to inspect the inside of the small enclosure again. There was no sign that a snare or trap had ever been present. He looked around and saw no dead birds or other animals. It was unlikely that there was poison, but he would definitely be washing his hands before he ate his lunch.

Mart began a circular search of the area around the camouflaged dome. There appeared to be a trail leading to its entrance that came from the southwest. It merged with another game trail not far from the hidden structure so following it would become futile. The network of paths created by deer and cattle would confound any attempt at backtracking. Approaching the dome again, Mart spied a piece of fluff caught on the thorn of a low gooseberry bush. He tugged it off and inspected a tuft of coarse dark fur. He instinctively scanned the area around him. Was it hair from a bear or a wolf?

The rancher made several more circuits of the area. He found nothing more that would help to explain the tiny hut. This had to be Wendell's find. It was strange enough to have puzzled the old cowboy. He definitely would have sought an opinion from other grazing lease partners.

Deciding that any more investigation was unlikely to bring any clarity to the enigma, Mart walked over to his horse. Slim had been trying his best to find a morsel of edible plant material from where he had been obediently waiting. He had taken a bite or two of leaves from the shrubs, but it appeared he had decided he was a grazing animal and not a browser.

Mounted again, Mart wondered what to do next. There was little to gain by continuing to ramble about in the dense shrubs. He decided to head back toward the spot where the cut line joined the narrow trail that lead off toward the Hog's Back. Then he would decide on the route home.

He was only a minute's ride from the Hog's Back trail when he encountered another irregularity that made him pause. Quad riders had pushed in off the trail, mashing shrubs and scuffing downed logs. That in itself was no discovery. Recreational riders were constantly creating new trails, or attempting to, and then abandoning the effort when the terrain got too tough. But this particular trail had been used many times in the past week or two. The crushed vegetation was still clinging to life, but was badly trampled.

Mart decided to follow this new trail as it led away from the cut line and Hog's Back path. It was most likely that the riders had pushed in from there. It was not long before he could tell he had made the right assumption. Most of the shrubs were laying in the direction he was travelling. They had been pushed down initially by tires rolling on that bearing, too. Mart found he was halfway back to the dome when the trail ended at a steep ravine cut by spring runoff. There was a small patch where the ATVs had jockeyed back and forth to retrace their tracks. Mart shrugged and turned Slim around, giving him time to do so without entangling his legs in the bent and broken alder and chokecherry stems. Slim had not yet completed his about face when Mart pulled him up sharply. Emerging from the southwest side of the tiny clearing made by the rotating quads was a narrow, tunnel-like passageway. Mart got off and looked down the channel through the thick underbrush. Something fluttered slightly about a metre back in the lacy pattern of light created by the foliage. Mart crouched and reached back for it. When he pulled it out in the better light of the turn-around he determined it was the same type of black fur he had found at the short, domed lodge.

"Must be a wolf," Mart declared to his horse, "not enough clearance in there for most bears."

To satiate his curiosity, Mart crawled back into the leafy tunnel. He had to crouch or scramble on hands and knees to get far. He watched the ground, but could see only fairly recently crushed forbs and grasses. The trail had only been used for a week or two. Then he saw what he had been looking for. A dusty patch of bare ground revealed about half of a distinct track. It was not quite as big as a full grown wolf's footprint, but it could have been made by a sub-adult.

Mart scurried back to the quad trail. There he looked around to find where the wolf trail would cross it and extend onward. Try as he might, he could see no continuation of the tracks. Perhaps the quads had frightened the animal into turning back. No. That didn't make sense. Both the quad trail and the wolf path showed signs of continual recent use. The ATVs could not have been here each time the wolf came this way. Mart searched again. There just had to be an exit path! After ten or more minutes, the rancher gave up. Odd, but he could draw no real conclusions. Just because he could not find the trail did not mean it did not exist. Perhaps the quad and wolf trails were one and the same from this point out to the main path. How the quad trail and the wolf tracks were connected, or if they were, was not something he could guess.

Again Mart and Slim struck out for home. He tried to persuade himself that he took the steep climb up the Hog's Back rather than the easier Mackenzie line simply because he wanted to see some different scenery. He could hear the saw droning from back the way he had come.

Mart climbed down once to wash his hands and let Slim drink at a narrow stream. Several red white-faced cattle were grazing slowly through the aspens and scattered pines. Before he returned to the saddle, lunch was pulled from the saddlebag. Mart ate in the saddle.

In the mid-afternoon sun Slim really worked up a lather as he carried Mart up through the open Douglas fir and spruce forest. The cool of the morning had been beaten down by the stark rays of the late summer sun. A couple of rocky bands made him scramble, but the wiry pony never faltered. Mart let him blow near the top. He gawked through the scattered treetops at the panorama of ranch land east and north of this wooded ridge. The huge wind turbines near Magrath seemed closer than they really were. They did not appear to be turning at all.

When the horse's breathing had slowed to near normal, Mart clucked and Slim walked out. He directed the willing equine along the ridge to meet up with the trail coming up from Hog's Back Gate #2. They had only travelled for two or three minutes when both rider and horse were startled by a loud cracking of dry branches. Just below them a cow moose shepherded her tall, gangly calf away from the human intruder. Their long legs stepped over shrubs and deadfall without hesitation as they travelled at a trot that would make Slim gallop to keep up. Mart thrilled to see them, but admitted he was glad they were running in the opposite direction. Moose were at least as unpredictable as bears and were less intimidated by horses.

Once the large ungulates were out of sight, Mart encouraged Slim toward the path that would lead them down into Hell's Kitchen. Again he could have taken the shorter route toward the Four Corners, but opted instead to head for the Boiler Gate and the Bear Pasture. That would mean another climb over the toe of Poll Haven. Several grey jays swooped from tree to tree paralleling, Mart's path. Their strange whispers could be heard occasionally over the sound of Slim's hoof beats.

Just as Mart turned his mount north to climb back down the ridge, a flash of brilliant light made him wince. Slim stopped abruptly as Mart pulled back firmly on the reins. He thought the flash had originated from a location south of his position, but he was not sure. The rancher pivoted in the saddle and scanned back toward the American side. All that was visible was a spiny carpet of trees of varying heights. He was about to chalk the interruption up to unexplained atmospheric phenomena when another brief reflection made him focus his attention southeastward. Again the source of the flicker had disappeared. Mart maintained a close scrutiny of the spot. The flash came again, and this time he got a good look at it.

Mart was pretty sure he understood what was happening. Someone was down there with binoculars. He was being glassed. It was at that same moment Mart realized that the saw had ceased its whining. The source of the reflection was only metres away from where the crew had been working. A mild panic seized the horseman. He froze and his tenseness set the little Arabian to fidgeting. It was not hard to get the animal headed down the hill and out of sight of whoever was holding the field glasses.

Slim was heading home and his walk was at its fastest. They crossed Hell's Kitchen in record time. Mart let him steam along while he ruminated. Perhaps there was no harm intended by the crew. He carried binoculars himself and enjoyed an occasional pause to glass for wildlife or to see if any of his neighbours were around. Maybe the young men used their coffee breaks to view the sights. Possibly it had been the pair of moose that had attracted their attention. In that case their interest in him would have been strictly incidental. There would be no particular reason the workers would mention his presence near their worksite to their grumpy foremen. Mart felt spineless because of his craven attitude toward Stimatz and his burly Hispanic companion. Their aggressive attitude had surprised and alarmed him.

Mart left the community pasture at its north-western corner and rode the short distance over to the clearing at the east end of Little Beaverdam Lake. There were no fishermen in sight. He opened the gate into the private land east of the lake and checked his cinch. Ranching neighbours seldom took exception to other locals crossing their land on foot or on horseback. As long as gates were closed and cattle were not disturbed it was generally not considered trespass. Mart swung up and let Slim trot and canter a good portion of the way along a wide trail leading north-eastward. He reached Wynders' Flats a short while later. Yellow grass punctuated here and there by large stones rose above him on tall, rounded hills. A clay scar gouged out of a hillside marked the rough road that would lead Mart back to Beaverdam and his truck and trailer.

CHAPTER 30 ✽ HAVE IT OUT

MART WAS TAKEN completely off guard when he saw Kent's black pickup beginning to pull out of the Gwynn place driveway just as his own rickety truck and trailer crested the hill on the gravel county road. Kent spotted the plume of dust created by Mart's outfit and put the shiny vehicle in reverse back up to the house, spun around and drove the short distance to the barnyard. He was leaning against the fender when Mart pulled in and stepped reluctantly out of the cab.

Mart's confidence had been rattled by the near encounter with the seismic workers. He had stewed about it all the way home. Although he had earlier felt somewhat confident in his approach to a conversation with Kent, that was no longer the case.

"Kent, I..."

"Take care of your horse," Kent responded.

Mart did as Kent bade him. His hands were all thumbs as he undid buckles and pulled saddle and sweaty blankets off Slim's solid back. He hung up his gear, grained and watered the animal. He stood briefly at the bay's head and looked into the large, dark eyes as if hoping for some kind of assistance. Mart did not stall for long.

Kent had dropped the jack on the front of Mart's trailer and lifted the hitch clear of the ball. The tall blond was now leaning against the old Chevy's end gate. "We have to sort this out, Mart," his friend began.

"I know."

"I understand that this has got to be eating away at you. I know you had feelings for Becky and her...well...her interest in me must be a bit of a disappointment."

"Disappointment!? For hell's sake, Kent, it was a complete shock!" Mart countered.

Kent's normal composure began to unravel slightly at the edges. "Now why would it be such a shock? You have eyes. You must certainly remember the problem it created between us in school. It's not like she hasn't shown some interest in me since she came back. You had to see it."

"Sure I saw it. Just the same as you should have seen that she was treating me pretty much the same way."

"I know she likes you, Mart. It's been the confusing thing all along. I could never make a move for fear of hurting you or risking that Becky would think I was a backstabbing S.O.B. But things have changed. She has made a choice."

Mart glared back at his long-time friend. It was hard not to make some awful declaration that would alienate Kent forever. The sheer arrogance, no, it wasn't that – the blindness Kent was exhibiting was beyond unusual. He was ignoring any of the signs that Becky and Mart might be involved in any way. He seemed to have completely ruled out the idea that Mart might be attractive to the girl. He had taken it for mere fondness. Mart took a deep breath and closed his eyes for a moment. When he began, he tried to speak coolly.

"Kent. I will admit that I'm disappointed." Again there was a momentary pause. "That is not really true. I am in fact hurt and frustrated. Sure, it's about losing all hope that Becky will choose me. As much as I have never wished to hurt you either, I still wanted her to take me over you. I never had much hope of that until recently. I was convinced that was the way it was going."

"Mart, I really am sorry." By Kent's tone of voice it was apparent that he was relieved that Mart was admitting defeat and that there was some optimism he would walk away with a best friend as well as Becky.

Mart stopped Kent's sympathetic soliloquy. "You still don't understand the real reason I am so upset by this. You don't seem to understand why I would be so harebrained as to think Becky might want me and not you."

Kent started to interject, but Mart cut him off. "It's been Becky who led me to believe she would be with me. She invited me..."

Kent began to bridle visibly. "Be careful what you say, Mart!"

Mart hesitated. Kent's posture was getting aggressive. He had seen his friend step in to defend Becky before. He would have to approach this more carefully.

"At the rodeo, she almost kissed me."

"You were hurt. She was concerned. Why shouldn't she try to make you feel better?"

"OK. After Wendell's funeral she invited me to go for a drive to Waterton."

Kent was getting agitated. "Why not? I've always known she was your friend, too."

"No, Kent. That is not how it ended up."

This time Kent practically growled. "If you finally made a move after all these years and she was kind enough not to reject you outright, that just proves she still wants to be your friend."

Mart lost some of the control he had up to that point. "She made the move. Can't you see? She moved on both of us the same week!"

Mart knew immediately he had crossed the line. Kent was not stupid. The declaration had been clear if it had not been direct – Mart was accusing Becky of romantic duplicity.

"What have you done, Mart!?" Kent was practically shouting. "Becky didn't mention a word of this to me. She must have hidden your advances from me. She knew it would tear us apart. Because you can't have her, you're trying to put the blame on her! Well, I am not listening to anymore of your bullshit!" He made a move as if to walk over and physically confront Mart, but veered off and headed for his truck before his outstretched hand actually grasped Mart's shirt. Mart shrunk back.

The tall blond cowboy yelled back over his shoulder as he went, "You can't drag Becky through your mud around me! I am through with you! I am fed up with your lousy, needy, poor-boy hang-ups. Go straight to hell!"

"Kent! I am not making this up," Mart pleaded, but the black door had slammed and Kent fired up the engine before Mart could make it across the yard. The 4X4 spun around in the driveway, scattering gravel. Kent did not slow when Mart tried to wave him down. Mart stood trembling with anger and frustration watching the plume of dust expand and dissipate. With it faded the faith that the friendship could weather any storm.

CHAPTER 31 ✷ GUIDANCE

"Almost two weeks," mumbled Mart. Skip and Slim were looking at him expectantly. Their interest was more about the oat bin in which Mart was fumbling rather than in anticipation of any clarification. Today was Thursday. Wendell had been gone for a while now and still Mart felt tangled up in the circumstances surrounding his death. He was beginning to understand why people talked about closure. He had had none. The unearthing of what he assumed was the man's mysterious discovery had produced less rather than more clarity. The seismic crew's perceived hostility clouded things even more. The reckless schoolboys' antics were puzzling. His disquiet about the Pruitts would not go away. Add to that Becky's deceit and Kent's animosity and Mart felt as though he had hit rock bottom.

The cat wound its sinuous frame around Mart's feet. In his foul mood, Mart almost resented the attention. He had a momentary and wicked desire to punt the poor feline across the barn. Instead he crouched down and stroked the dusty fur until some of the darkness faded. The cat purred loudly. Mart reflected that it had been quite some time since he had offered this type of affection to his only remaining pet. Depositing a few kibbles and topping up the water were instinct for him now, but he knew they didn't supplant meaningful attention. It was all too easy to take relationships for granted, especially with the humans in his life. He often kept more distant from them than he did his pets and livestock. It was about time he gave his mother another call. She needed to know he was all right and that he still cared about her. Heaven knew he could use the same reassurance. He would call tonight.

In a forlorn attempt at some companionship, Mart brushed down both horses until they gleamed through the dust suspended in the few rays of light coming through the grimy, cracked pane of the single small window. The saddle pad he had used on Slim the day before needed desperately to get rinsed off. He would do that later, but chose another and threw it over the broad back of the big red horse. Yesterday's cinch was as soiled, so he selected the old one he had just replaced and resolved to clean the new one along with the saddle pad. Today should be an easy ride so he strapped on the worn cinch with little concern.

Once Skip was saddled, Mart turned Slim out and mounted up. He headed straight north on the gravel road for about a kilometre and a half. There he slipped off, opened the wire gate, clucked Skip through and shut the gate again. He had wavered between deep depression and stolid determination several times in his ride so far.

Mart pointed Skip east toward the Watson Ridge. The landscape undulated with his mood. The bare hills bore tufts of long yellow grass interrupted here and there with patches of shorter greenery. The wet summer had provided fresh grazing for stock well into August and even now patches of moist pasture were keeping the cattle fat and contented.

Mart encountered a few scattered batches of black and black-baldy cows almost immediately after entering his most easterly quarter-section. They moved lazily out of his way as he pushed through them quietly to watch their movements and assess their general state of health. He repeated the exercise with other clusters of cattle several more times until he was certain none were lame or sick and that all were present. He sat his horse atop a low rise and watched the animals graze. He usually found solace out here with the stock that was his livelihood, but today it was hard not to reflect on the negative aspects of ranching. He was only solvent due to the operating loan from an impersonal bank. The sale of his calves would just be enough to keep the loan officer hopeful that next year's interest would be worth the risk of the bank shareholders' capital.

Then there was the weather. The wet summer had sometimes been unpleasant, but last winter had been awful. It had been all he could do to keep paths clear to get to his barns and haystacks. He had to plough through huge drifts to get to wind-bared hillsides where he could feed and bed down the cows. He had to abandon several locations because his continual manipulation of the drifts just made them grow higher and harder with each snowfall and immediate subsequent drifting event. The old Ford tractor had needed several repairs after the abuse.

He thought ahead to the call to his mother. Maybe it was time to admit defeat and do as she had recommended. Perhaps he could find work back in the Hat or in Lethbridge. The sale of land and cattle might just cover his loans and taxes and he could walk away free and clear.

Just then a couple of black calves bolted and ran kicking and jumping down the opposite knoll. Several others joined in and one old cow took a couple of jumps and threatened one of her herd-mates playfully. What should have made Mart chuckle instead caused his throat to constrict and his eyes to blur. He tried to leave behind the despairing frame of mind and urged Skip westward toward the track leading home.

Skip anticipated the oats and the companionship of his slender stable-mate. The cow-horse kept breaking into an annoying jig. Instead of reprimand, the big red horse was given his head. He broke into a tentative lope and Mart allowed it to evolve into a fast gallop. The rough ground swept past on each side of the narrow cattle trail he was following. A large ground squirrel hole had created a mound right in the path, but Skip timed his stride and flew over it without a stumble.

By the time the horse and rider reached the gate, Skip was happy to take up a steady walk and Mart found himself grinning. He recalled his first run on Uncle Seth's black mare. She was not exactly Woodbine material, but he had felt as though someone had just revealed to him the wings he never knew he had.

Mart flattered himself sometimes that he was a natural born equestrian. Whether the talent was instinctive or simply developed rapidly because of his youthful obsession was up for debate. The fact remained that he was never happier than when out on the land with a dependable mount. Would he ever find anything else that would bring him this kind of peace and joy? A short bit of reflection brought him to a conclusion. He might not throw in the towel today after all.

The ride home lacked any further reckless abandon, but it was also minus much of the self pity that had plagued the journey out. Mart grabbed a quick lunch and made a trip to the Blue Ridge Hutterite Colony to bring home a dozen bags of rolled oats. The horses were not used as much in winter, but he liked to offer them grain at least once a day when cold weather set in. He slid some of the bags into a metal-lined wooden bin and emptied four of them into a large bin next to the stalls in his shed-cum-stable. Then he made the twenty-three kilometre trip to Cardston to pick up salt blocks – a dozen blue ones for the cattle and two of the TM red ones fabricated especially for working horses. He made it to the salt and feed supplier just in time to keep the owner several minutes past closing in order to complete the transaction and load the blocks.

Mart rolled through Mountain View after hours, ignoring the school zone. He waved to the bishop of the LDS Ward who was making his way into the church from the east parking lot. A silver pickup flew past at a rate well above even the sixty kilometres per hour. Mart raised his hand two seconds too late to wave to the speeding driver. Jack Pruitt showed no sign of recognition. Was he still miffed or just in an awful hurry?

Mart stowed the salt in the old barn just as daylight began to dwindle. He made an effort to ruffle the barn cat's fur for a few seconds before heading to his mobile home for supper. After pulling off his dusty riding boots, Mart washed his hands at the kitchen sink using dish soap. The container was almost empty. He needed to do some grocery shopping and chastised himself for not having thought to go to the market in the same trip as his salt run.

Mart turned on the TV. He was just able to catch the final synopsis of the local news. He rarely made it in for the broadcasts. None of the three he got off the wind-battered antenna were news channels. He wished for satellite television sometimes, but the glitzy entertainment news program that came on next reminded him that three free channels with nothing on was better than 125 you paid for with much the same result. It would just take longer to run through them all and to figure out you should get a library card.

The program irritated him through the opening of his can of soup. He plopped the glutinous mass into a small saucepan, added water and spun the dial on the gas range to medium. He then grabbed for the remote and cursed mildly as he shut off the television and slapped the controls down on the counter. He only succeeded in getting them halfway onto the scuffed Arborite surface and the gadget slipped off onto the floor. Mart recognized the sound of the small AAA batteries scattering across the linoleum. He embarrassed himself by uttering a foul oath that exceeded the severity of the issue by several notches. He then took a deep breath and crouched to recover and reassemble the electronic device.

When he had recovered all the pieces, Mart stood. As he rose he noticed that the burner under his generic mushroom soup was not alight. The pilot must have gone out on top of the old cook stove. He turned off the gas and switched the knob on again hoping it would light this time – still no flame. He placed the saucepan on the other side and lifted the cover and burners on that part of the range. No pilot, just as he had suspected. Mart fumbled through a cabinet drawer, found the matches and struck one. He held it to the orifice where the standing pilot usually burned – no electronic burners on this outdated appliance. It was probably original to the trailer. That match and the two following burned almost to his fingertips, but the pilot would not light. He checked the one in the oven. It looked feeble, but it was still burning.

"Great! Another bill to pay." He would have to call a plumber or decide to replace the dinosaur range. He thought of going out to check that the natural gas valve had not been partially closed by some accidental bump, but opted instead to dump his soup into a bowl and slid it into the microwave. He would wait to check it until he had more light to work with tomorrow morning.

Supper was brief. His call to Medicine Hat was not. His mother answered on the second ring.

"Hi, Mom."

"Mart! I am so glad you called." Tina covered the receiver and Mart heard a muffled request for his stepfather to turn down the television.

"Am I calling at a bad time?" Mart asked.

"Heavens, no! I am not sure why I should care who Canada's next pop star should be. They all sing well, but sound pretty much the same. I think they win based on the strangeness of their hairdos and on their economical use of cloth for costuming."

Mart grinned. In spite of Tina's somewhat rebellious attitude toward the religion of her youth, she still kept many of the conservative attitudes of his Mormon neighbours.

"How have you been, son?'

"I'm OK," stated Mart. He did not think he let any of his discontent seep into the brief response, but was a little relieved when his mother called him on the scant reply.

"Are you sure, Mart?"

"Yes, I am sure – just a few things going wrong around the place. My kitchen stove is on the fritz."

"That's all?"

"Both the tractor and the truck need replacing, too." The evasion did not work. There must have been something in his voice that betrayed his need to unload.

"That's not really it, though, is it Mart?" The young rancher could hear his mother get up and walk through the room with the cordless in her hand. He heard the bedroom door click shut.

Mart felt like a haunted serial killer. It was a relief to be found out and to have to come clean. "Not really."

"Tell me what's going on. Is it the girl?"

Again Mart smiled lightly. By now his mother should know that it would be a woman, not a girl.

"Yes."

"Did she dump you?"

Mart didn't know quite how to explain it. "No. It wasn't like that."

"Did you break up with her?"

"Not that either. I'm not sure just where we stand. But what really bothers me is Kent."

"How does he fit in, or is this something else?"

"Oh, it's part of the same problem."

"What did he do?"

"It's not really his fault."

Tina hesitated on the other end of the line. "Did you do something, Mart?"

"I don't think it's my fault either. Either way I think the friendship is pretty much done."

"You mean with the girl or Kent?" Tina sounded genuinely alarmed.

"Kent."

"Oh, no! Isn't there something you can do to patch it up?"

"I think it might be too serious for that."

There was silence for several seconds. Tina Taylor was switching to advice mode. "Sometimes it's better to keep a friend than it is to be right. Even if you don't think you are at fault, you may want to consider apologizing."

"It might be too late for that, too."

"Mart, how many close friends do you have?"

Mart bridled at the question. He felt like telling her he had plenty. That would have been a lie. He knew she would know it, too.

"That doesn't affect anything."

"How many, Mart?"

"None, I guess!" Mart spat back resentfully.

Tina did not respond to the bitterness in her son's voice nor the self pity. Neither did she back down.

"Kent has been pretty much it ever since you moved there. It was always Kent this, and Kent and I that. Can you really afford to throw that away?"

"Maybe it's not me ..."

"Listen to me for a minute, Mart," Tina cut him off. "Whatever has come between you can be fixed if at least one of you can get past your hurt and pride. If not, the injury will fester and will do you more damage than it will him. Better to try and patch it up. If he rejects you, then at least you can move on knowing you have tried. It will make a difference to you and it may one day make it possible for him to come back and admit some failure on his part, too."

This time the silence was longer. Mart swung between guilt and anger. Oddly he settled on acknowledgement. She was right. He would find some way to get Kent to listen to him. He would beg if he had to. Becky was lost to him regardless. He would have to find some way to get over that.

"OK."

"Does that mean you'll try?"

"Yes."

"What caused all this?"

Mart swallowed hard. "A girl," he admitted suspecting it would cause a new flurry of interrogation.

"Same thing as happened in high school." It was a declaration rather than a question. How did she know? Mart had never said a thing about it.

"Yes. Same as back then."

"Becky?"

It was as though an electric stock prod had just made contact with his chest.

"How do you know about Becky?" Mart muttered.

"Give your Aunt Em some credit, Mart." Then she added, "You'd think you and Kent would catch on by now."

"What do you mean by that?"

"When all this is over, just remember who your best friend is really."

Mart mulled this over for a few seconds. Tina had hit the mark again.

Tina seemed to know that Mart had taken enough emotional battering. She switched to good-natured badgering about his general health, diet and common sense. Mart relaxed and started to enjoy the visit. When the call was over, Mart felt spent, but somehow better. The wound was slowly scabbing. If he could avoid continual abrasion it might heal with only an ugly scar.

CHAPTER 32 ✳ BURN

Mart's bed was lumpy and his thoughts still more uneven. He slipped in and out of a shallow sleep. He had gone to bed early, but by 11:00 he was tempted to get back up. Shortly after that he had no choice but to get out from under the covers.

All of a sudden Mart's head was ringing and his ears had quit working. He found himself half in and half out of bed. It was his upper body that had left the mattress. His legs were still up on the bed. It was dark so he could not see the smoke, but it clawed at the back of his throat. He tried to cough, but almost gagged instead. He began to see a wavering orange light through his bedroom door. He kicked the blankets from his feet and rolled onto the worn carpet. The fabric pricked his bare back. He tried to stand, but the fumes were too thick closer to the ceiling so he crawled toward the room that doubled as kitchen and dining room. It was a bad choice.

There were flames licking up the wall between the stove and sink. The window above the drain board was mostly gone as was a portion of the wall beside it. The upper cabinets were hanging from the wall, doors open and most of the dishes scattered across the floor making sharp terrain for his hands and bare knees. There was a spray of water coming from a broken pipe somewhere over there. He recoiled to get to the other exit across the hallway from the second bedroom. It was then he realized the floor was getting hot. Ignoring the lack of oxygen, he jumped up and ran. He felt a shard of glass enter his left foot, but kept moving. He grabbed the fire extinguisher from the wall beside the furnace he had shut off for the summer. He tumbled out the door and down rickety back steps he never used. He rolled onto the narrow strip of lawn before the barbed-wire fence that kept the cows out – most of the time.

Through the cracks in the poorly fitted plywood skirting of the trailer he could see flames. He stood again and limped around the end of the mobile home and to the side nearest the kitchen wall. The gas valve was open all the way as it should be to deliver his heating and cooking fuel. There were flames above it inside the wall. He pulled the pin on the fire extinguisher and hobbled in to use it. Before he did, he shut off the natural gas valve with a quick half-turn. The flames below the trailer subsided almost immediately, but did not go out completely. The fire inside was slowly spreading in spite of the water spraying from the ruptured plumbing.

Mart limped up the front door steps and opened the door. He was instantly hit by a wall of chemical-laden smoke. He ducked and coughed, allowed it to clear and entered. Lit by the fire still attempting to prevail over the effects of the water, the room seemed totally different from the one where Mart had lived for the past several years. He hardly recognized his rearranged furniture in the ghastly glow. With the extinguisher held out as if in offering before the flames, he advanced and pressed on the trigger. A white plume filled the room and choked both flame and firefighter. He emptied the red canister completely. The few remaining embers lost their battle to the fountain coming from beneath the breached counter.

The floor still felt hot so Mart gambolled unevenly back to the door. Some of the skirting had been ripped away from where the natural gas pipes emerged from the ground and ran under the black membrane that held the insulation up next to the floor. Mart could see no flames, but the metal frame of the undercarriage was glowing. He hoped no latent combustion existed that would spring from within that cushioned base. He looked at the empty canister he still held in his hand. There was another in the tractor. He should go to retrieve it. Instead he sat on the damp ground and felt gingerly around the bottom of his foot. The laceration was not large and he could just get his fingers on the blunt end of a piece of broken china. It pulled free easily and it was followed by a stream of sticky blood.

He ignored the injury and stood with the intention of heading for the barn and the tractor next to it. If he could not be certain the fire was out he would bulldoze the trailer onto the road in order to spare the barns and stop the spread to the tall, dry grass at the edges of his fields. Halfway there he looked back and slowed his lopsided flight. There was almost total darkness. He stood and watched for several seconds until he was convinced there was no more fire.

A set of headlights was coming up the gravel road at an unsafe rate. Mart had just made it back to the trailer when a pickup skidded into the yard. Another set of lights was coming from the other direction on the same road. Bill Klein and his two teenage sons stepped out of the first vehicle. Somebody from the Frost ranch would be in the next. They were Mart's nearest neighbours. Someone from each ranch had seen the fire or heard the explosion and they had come to help. They stood together looking at the devastation in the headlights. Part of the south wall was missing. The kitchen and living room windows were gone and the metal skin of the place was scorched and sagging. Awful-smelling smoke curled from the ruined hulk. Water was pouring out from under the floorboards. Bill Klein looked at Mart standing there in shock and sent his eldest son to the back of the house to find the well house and turn off the pump. The boy found a flashlight in the pickup, switched it on and slapped it against his hand a couple of times until it actually lit up.

By then there was a stream of several cars coming up the road. Bill was a tall man and he looked down at Mart. The cool night air reminded the bachelor that he was standing there in his boxers. Bill Klein peeled off his jacket and handed it over without a word. It was long enough to cover down to the hem of his underwear. That left Mr. Klein to shiver in his white tee-shirt.

The neighbours poked around until they were convinced there was nothing more to do and felt they had done what they could to be supportive. The fire truck from Cardston arrived in time for the crew to rush around and do nothing.

"Leave things as they are until the inspector can look it over," indicated the chief of the crew.

"Can I fetch some clothes from inside," Mart asked. The chief sent someone to do it for him.

Mart turned down several offers for a bed for the rest of the night. Instead he thanked everyone for coming to help and watched the red glow of their taillights recede. The fire crew was last to leave.

Mart went to his pickup. He took the keys that had been dangling from the ignition and found the one that opened Aunt Emma's door. He fumbled around until he found the valve that turned on the water. He went to the bathroom and fired up the hot water heater. In the end he did not wait for warm water, but rinsed off as best he could in cold. For the first time in eight years he would spend the night under this old roof. He selected a quilt from the linen closet. It smelled like old dust. He threw an old sheet off the worn couch and rolled up in the homemade blanket. Sleep came slowly, but it did come.

CHAPTER 33 ✴ INTERROGATION

It was seven o'clock before Mart awoke stiff and slightly disoriented. He dressed in the clothes the volunteer fireman had selected for him. He used Bill Klein's jacket and felt a pang of guilt when he realized he had made the man go home without it. He was halfway through his morning chores when a large red 4X4 pickup pulled up. The fire inspector stepped out and greeted Mart as he walked up.

"Have you been inside since the truck left last night?" he asked.

"No. They said to leave it until you got here."

"That will make it easier. Thanks. I'll hurry so you can go in and salvage what you can."

Mart nodded and watched the man start his investigation. He poked around with a small but powerful flashlight. It was only a couple of minutes before he emerged from the spot where the gas pipe went under the trailer. He glanced at Mart, but did not approach him. Instead he pulled out a cell phone and dialled on his way back to the truck. He got in and shut the door.

Mart was a bit grumpy for having missed breakfast, but went back to some small tasks around the barnyard that he had been putting off. Then he started a bit of housecleaning at Aunt Emma's. The stench emanating from his mobile home had made it clear he wouldn't be able to sleep there tonight – or perhaps ever again.

About an hour later he was surprised to hear another vehicle pull into the yard and even more so when he peered out a dusty window to see an RCMP cruiser parked next to the fire marshal's 4X4. The crisp form of Sergeant Dietrich stepped out and walked over to the fire department official. They spoke for several minutes before going over to the gas pipes. The sergeant nodded several times and then the inspector pointed at the house. The sergeant headed over to the cracked sidewalk and Mart met her at the door.

"Hello, Mr. McKinnon. Could I have a few words with you?"

Mart stepped back and allowed the policewoman to step past. He offered her a kitchen chair.

"I have nothing to offer you, I am sorry. Nobody lives here and the coffee is over there," Mart apologized indicating the smoke-damaged trailer through the side window of the kitchen.

"I should have brought you something." She smiled.

"I'll be fine once I can get into my own house."

"This is kind of becoming a habit for you, isn't it?"

Mart smiled and thought the same thing. He had hardly said two words to a policeman in the past ten years. Now it seemed like a twice-weekly occurrence.

The sergeant hesitated noticeably. "I am afraid you will have to wait a while before you can get into the mobile home."

"Doesn't he think he can find the cause of the fire?"

"Actually he found it right away."

"What was it?"

Dietrich did not answer. She pulled a notebook from her shirt pocket. The sergeant drew an elastic from around the cover and got a pen from the other pocket. "Could you answer a few questions for me that would help?"

In spite of the friendly tone, Mart's sensors went off. "Sure. I'll do what I can."

"How and when did you detect the fire?"

"I got blown from my bed at about 11:00."

"Blown?"

"There was some kind of explosion. My ears were ringing even this morning."

"What did you do then?"

Mart explained his movements through the trailer and how he got the fire out.

"So you and the neighbours extinguished the fire?"

"I had it out before they got here. They poked around a bit to be sure, but there was no more flame and the gas was off."

"Do you have insurance?"

"Yes. I have a policy in Cardston." At first he thought she was simply showing concern over his obvious financial predicament, but as Mart answered he started to get anxious.

"I need to inform you that it appears the gas lines were tampered with. That makes this a criminal investigation. If you would feel more comfortable with legal representation, we can continue this later when that can be arranged."

Mart was stupefied. Tampering? Insurance? He began to put it together. They suspected he had done something to the gas to burn the trailer and get the insurance money. But there would be none. He had not answered that question correctly. And then there were his efforts to put out the blaze. Why would he do that if it was deliberate?

"But I put it out." As soon as he said it, he knew she might think he had worked to put it out to cast suspicion off himself.

"Are you sure you don't want counsel?"

"I have insurance on the ranch – you know, public liability. The trailer is too old. The premiums became completely ridiculous five or six years ago. No insurance company wants anything to do with old mobile homes. I get nothing from the fire."

The sergeant looked directly at Mart for almost a minute. "OK. I understand that." She started on another tack. "Would there be any reason someone would want to cause you mischief or harm?"

"In Mountain View? This isn't downtown Vancouver. I can't think of anyone who would do something like that around here."

"No fights with neighbours or old grudges?"

Mart hesitated. He had just fought with Kent. Was he obligated to mention that? It only took a moment for him to decide that he would not be throwing any hint of suspicion on Kent Lindholm. That would be completely absurd.

"None that come to mind."

There must have been something in Mart's response or hesitation that twigged some part of the blond RCMP member's training. She lifted her eyes from the notebook and watched Mart for a moment. When he met her gaze and held it, she looked back to her pad and wrote.

Mart felt a strange obligation to throw her some kind of bone. "Well, there was the burglar at the Jacobsen ranch. But that was just by chance, right?"

The sergeant shrugged. "We can't really say that, can we?"

Mart thought again about Pruitt. Jack had been nearby yesterday. Mart just couldn't bring himself to suspect Jack or his daughter. What about the man in Wendell's house? Could it have been some relative of theirs? He tried to remember what Candace's husband looked like. He was built solidly like the thief had been. Boy! Had he taken a beating from an accountant? That was just plain embarrassing. He decided not to voice his speculations. But Dietrich's next question stunned him.

"What about Jack Pruitt?"

"No...not...why...why would you ask about Jack?"

Now the sergeant struggled to explain. "When we asked him about Mr. Jacobsen's accident, he wasn't exactly forthcoming."

"What does that mean?"

"He seemed to really resent the questions."

"I can understand that. He was probably worried you would accuse him of something," Mart blurted out. "What does that have to do with me?" In reality he already knew the answer.

"His daughter instantly asked if you had blamed them for spooking the horse."

Mart looked at the floor and thought for a few minutes. He looked up and confided in the peace officer. "That really bothers me. Because Mr. Jacobsen was my friend, they can only assume that I took his side in their quarrel. They'll never quit thinking I accused them, no matter what we find out later. I'll never be able to undo that damage."

"To quote my hometown minister, 'Evil breads evil'," Dietrich offered. "Often investigations bring out the worst in people. Do you think they could have had something to do with your trailer?"

Mart thought for several seconds. Jack had made his antagonism very clear. He just couldn't bring himself to shift blame onto Jack and Candace yet again. "I just can't see it."

The sergeant scratched away in her book. While she wrote, Mart thought of another possibility that seemed almost as unreasonable. There was Stimatz. The stretch between a tense confrontation and arson seemed a long one indeed.

"I just remembered that I had a bit of a confrontation with one of the bosses of Southwest Seismic a couple of days back," Mart began cautiously.

Dietrich looked relieved that Mart was coming clean. "What was it about?"

"I was asking to see if his crew had been anywhere near where Wendell, that's Mr. Jacobsen, had his accident."

"Constable Boissoneau has spoken with him. Was this before or after he did?"

"After."

"Did you accuse Mr. Stimatz of involvement?"

"No, nothing like that. I just hoped he could help you find out who was at fault."

"Do you think he thought you were accusing him or his workers?"

Mart thought about the burly man's reaction. "No. I don't think so, but he told me that he had already talked to Eric and that I should keep out of it."

"Is that all? It's actually very good advice. It is counterproductive and, in some cases illegal, to meddle in a police investigation."

Mart felt the sting of the rebuke.

Dietrich continued, "Did he say anything else to you that would make you believe he would mean you harm?"

Mart started to feel like he needed to defend his decision to even report the conflict. "Stimatz and the large Hispanic fellow who rides with him just seemed sort of threatening."

"Is there any other reason you might suspect them?"

Mart back-peddled. "I don't really suspect them. I just wanted to answer your question about possible enemies. The real reason I thought they might be concerned over me approaching them is that I think they might be employing illegal aliens from Mexico."

The sergeant looked surprised. "That is a pretty hefty accusation in itself. Did you tell Mr. Stimatz that you suspected him of that offense?"

"No."

"What made you think it is was true?"

Mart tried to come up with some rational way to explain himself. In the end he decided to downplay the idea. "I just jumped to that conclusion when I tried to figure out why they were so angry when I talked to them. It was the only thing I could think they might be hiding. I saw some of their crew out in the field. Some of them were speaking Spanish and looked like they could be Mexican."

The sergeant looked undecided for a moment and then offered this bit of information. "We looked into the background of the seismic company. Mr. Stimatz used to be full owner, but recently took on some partners. They are some recent immigrants to the US from somewhere in South America – Argentina and Columbia, I think. They may have taken on some of their relatives as employees, so they're not Mexicans."

Mart nodded. He was embarrassed. He had been caught making wild assumptions and not being very socially sensitive besides. He was coming across as the quintessential red neck.

Dietrich took several more notes and pushed Mart to identify other possible enemies. Mart could think of none. Finally it was his turn to press the sergeant for more information.

"Can I ask why you think this was not just a case of an old set of pipes giving away?"

Mart could tell the thorough policewoman was trying to decide just how much information she should share. In the end she described what the inspector had found.

"The gas line had been cut just enough to allow a small amount of gas to escape. They probably used a hacksaw to cut through part of the wall of the pipe."

Mart was momentarily distracted as he heard yet another vehicle pull into the yard. He drew his attention back to what she had said and considered it. If only a small amount of gas was escaping, that could explain why his stove would not function. There had been just enough gas flowing through the pipes to allow the old-fashioned standing pilot light of the oven to burn. The escaping natural gas had floated around beneath the trailer, but eventually some had made its way up to ignite on the small flame of the pilot. The explosion had torn free some of the skirting and blown out the wall beside the stove. Fortunately it had broken the water pipe, too. The spraying water had slowed the flames enough so that he had survived and had been able to extinguish the blaze.

Sergeant Dietrich put away her notebook and thanked Mart. She did not apologize for having questioned him as a suspect in the arson. He walked her to the door and swung it open for her to exit. Before she could do so, the tall form of Kent Lindholm barged into the small entry.

"Kent!"

Kent looked genuinely alarmed. "Bill Klein called. What is going on, Mart?"

Mart did not respond, but looked toward the partially destroyed structure across the yard.

Kent continued hurriedly, "Yes, I can see the hovel burned down. That's no surprise. The thing is a death trap!"

Mart could feel the swell of some kind of emotion rising in his chest. He couldn't quite identify it. There was some relief there – not so much that he was reassured Kent had not burned down his house, but that he had resisted naming Kent as a suspect. There was certainly the feeling of gratitude knowing that Kent had not completely washed his hands of his former best friend. And there was definitely another sentiment that Mart did not care to define.

The sergeant politely excused herself and squeezed out the door between them. They watched her head for her cruiser. Mart motioned Kent to come into the kitchen and shut the door behind him. They sat across the table and stared at one another for several tense moments. Mart decided not to mention their quarrelsome parting and concentrated on the recent conflagration.

"The natural gas exploded my cook stove. Luckily the water pipes broke and controlled the fire until I could get out. I turned off the gas and used my fire extinguisher."

"I'm not surprised those old pipes finally broke. They are as rusty as barn nails."

When Mart looked away uncomfortably, Kent asked for the rest. "Out with it! Are you injured or anything?"

"No, I'm fine. It's just that the fire marshal and the RCMP say that someone did it on purpose."

Kent looked puzzled. "Did what? You mean the fire?"

"Uh, huh."

"Somebody set fire to your house?"

"They punctured the pipe. It was a slow leak."

"Why? I don't get it. Are you an underworld boss or something?"

Mart could not help chuckling slightly at the bizarre statement.

Kent continued. "Who would do something like that?"

Mart shrugged. "Maybe it was just a random act by some nutcase."

Kent shook his head. "Don't be an idiot. Who would come all the way out here to burn down some cowboy's shack?"

The two young men sat in silence for several minutes.

"Thanks for coming, Kent," Mart said quietly.

Kent nodded, but did not respond otherwise.

Mart risked broaching the subject that was on both their minds. "I'd like another crack and explaining things. I didn't do a very good job last time. Will you give me another chance?"

Kent looked out the window and ran his fingers through his hair. It fell perfectly back into place.

"Are you going to try to fix the trailer?"

"I think it's time I moved into the house. I'll salvage what I can from over there. Most of my furniture was crap anyway."

"I could come by on Saturday if you want some help. I'm kind of tied up until then." Kent then turned to look directly at Mart. "I'd rather wait and talk things through then."

Mart nodded.

"Will you be OK here?"

Mart looked puzzled, and then gave another short nod.

Kent got up. "Be careful." There was genuine concern on the handsome features.

"Don't worry. I may be scrawny, but I'm weak and cowardly."

Kent beamed back his habitual smile. He looked relieved that Mart had kept his warped sense of humour.

CHAPTER 34 ✷ SOLITARY PATROL

Tom Wyslik called late Friday morning. Mart had his cell phone on for a change since he could not get in to the telephone in his trailer. He had asked the fire inspector to retrieve it for him.

As usual Tom wasted no time with pleasantries. "Your house burn down?"

Mart was taken a bit off guard. "Well, not completely."

"Sheila's got a roast thawing. Come over for a meal tonight."

"S-sure." Mart tried to recover from the abrupt invitation, "That would help a lot.

"Good. Do you want me to cover for you today?"

"What's that?"

"You and Wendell were scheduled to ride again. It was because Frost and his son switched for the end of July."

Mart smacked his forehead with the palm of his hand. He had not written down the trade when Jacob Frost's daughter was getting married in Idaho. Normally Wendell would have jogged his memory. The old guy never forgot things like that.

Mart looked over at his ruined home. The fire marshal had put yellow ribbon around the whole yard and had driven away with a promise to be back and finished by nightfall. His watch was inside the wreck, but he glanced at the clock on his phone. It was 9:54. There was not much he could do here until tomorrow.

"Nah, Tom. Thanks anyway. It'll be a late start, but I might as well do the ride."

"Suit yourself. I gotta ship some bulls so supper will be late anyway – around seven or eight o'clock."

"Right. I best get moving," Mart started to express his thanks and sign off, but Wyslik had disconnected.

Mart looked up and down the gravel road before ducking under the yellow tape and up the back steps. He was careful not to disturb anything, but found his boots and selected some of the least smelly clothes from his bedroom closet. He grabbed his watch from the dresser.

He let Skip out into the pasture and saddled Slim quickly. The pickup was still backed up to the stock trailer so he wound the hitch down onto the ball. With Slim saddled and inside, Mart took a look at the sky. It was one of those funny days where the cloud was high and it was bright, but not sunny. There was an intermittent northeast breeze. The cloud cover was breaking slightly over the Front Ranges of the Rockies. Mart's slicker was already tied to the saddle and his old wool sweater and denim jacket were in the cab. He would grab a sandwich from the Barn Store.

Mart got halfway into the cab of the truck and had an odd thought. It would mean sneaking back into the house. He almost wrote it off, but spoke roughly to himself, "Why the hell not?"

Mart darted up the back steps and into his bedroom closet. Behind the old black suit and a few pairs of dress slacks he never wore was a battered leather sheath. He pulled it out and dust bunnies flew in every direction. He grabbed the equally dusty stock of the old carbine and dragged it out of the scabbard. He doubted it had ever been registered. There was a nearly full box of shells on the top shelf. He took the whole thing. He slid the .30-.30 back into the oiled leather and headed out the door.

As Mart placed the gun in the cab, he wondered why he felt he needed it, but he decided to give in to his paranoia. Uncle

Seth had taught him to shoot. He had hunted deer for several years and had become quite expert with the old gun, but he had not practiced much for several years.

Mart slowed to the requisite thirty kilometres per hour going through the hamlet and swung his pickup and trailer into the market parking. He dashed in and headed back for the cooler where the prepared sandwiches lay in their vacuum-sealed plastic. He selected a salami and pepperoni specimen that looked like it might be edible cold.

At the counter Mart began digging into his jeans for his wallet. Otto just shook his head. "I imagine pickings are slim at your house. You take that one on me."

Mart was slightly embarrassed, but guessed word of his house fire had pretty much made the rounds.

Mart shuffled and looked at the floor. "I'm afraid I need some bottled water, too,"

"No problem," was Otto's reply and he fetched a six-pack of the overpriced liquid. He jammed a box of oatmeal cookies and a couple of apples in a bag and only held up his wide hand when Mart babbled an inarticulate thank-you.

Mart rolled along toward the community pasture and again raised some significant dust. This time it was the little bay that blinked back out of the open doors once they reached the Poll Haven corrals. Mart muttered his apologies to the horse and bridled him quickly. He stuffed all of the food into his hand-me-down saddlebags and looked furtively around before strapping the rifle under the off side fenders of the Eamor saddle.

The weather was turning. There was now a gusty north wind worrying the aspen trees. Some leaves were skittering around his pony's dark feet as Mart tightened the cinch and mounted. The sky was getting darker. It was a good thing this patrol would have to be a swift one.

It had not been that long since Mart had been on an unofficial ride in the southwest part of the community pasture, so he decided to concentrate his assigned ride to the southeast. He would try to get to the far end of the Middle Yearling Pasture. He warmed Slim up with a short walk and a medium trot most of the way to the Neilson Gate. He walked the small bay from there to the Stove Gate. After closing and straightening some tangled and twisted wires on that one, he clucked and Slim bounded into a lively canter. He kept to this gait through much of the New Field. Someone had left Hog's Back Gate #1 down. When Mart tried to put it up, he noticed the smooth wire loop that held the top of the gate stick in place was broken. He retrieved his fencing tool and twisted the broken wire together. This left it too short to be able to slip over the gate post so Mart had to loosen the top two barbed wires of the gate in order to make it stretch the distance. Still it was too tight for most folks to get closed again even if they managed to open it. Mart would have to get the next assigned riders to bring up some smooth wire and replace the hastily repaired loop.

Mart walked Slim from the too-tight gate to the four corners and then most of the way to the site of the old Lee Creek cabin. The weather changed yet again. The air had cooled considerably. The wind had died down to a stiff breeze with an occasional gust.

Mart had seen a few scattered herds of cattle. Four of his-own cows were in one bunch. Their calves were also close by. They were sticking to the shelter of the trees. They could sense a storm brewing. So could Slim. The horse strode along nervously and tugged at the bit.

The site of the old cabin was just barely discernable. It had been a patrol cabin back when the Poll Haven had been part of the national park. Like Polecat Chateau it had been used by scout troops and snowmobilers for many years afterward, but the Alberta authorities had been less than comfortable with the liability it posed in the form of injury to users and the risk of camping parties being the source of wildfire. The cabin had been burned purposely to avoid the potential problems.

Mart looked at the dark wall of cloud in the north. It was time to turn back. Perhaps he had left it too late. The wind was keen in his face and Slim bowed his neck and trotted energetically into it. Without dismounting or slowing the horse Mart untied the saddle strings and lifted the sweater from on top of his slicker. He removed his jacket, placed his hat over the saddle horn and shivered his way into the old wool. He had to duck quickly to avoid some low branches he could not see in the second or two his head had been covered. Mart tugged the battered Smithbilt down tight around his ears. He slipped the jacket back on and immediately felt the body warmth it conserved by cutting off the cold wind.

Mart was considering rifling the saddlebags for his leather work gloves. He glanced back to guess which one contained them. He looked up just in time to see one, then a second ATV buzzing rapidly past the junction of the trail he was on and the Mackenzie cut line. The riders appeared to be the same ones Mart had followed almost a week ago. He pulled up abruptly. He was not in the mood to confront Southwest Seismic today. Mart took stock. Perhaps they were not the same pair. But the helmets looked familiar and one of the quads had the same bulky toolbox on the rear rack. What was missing was the rug with eyes.

Suddenly Mart jolted upright. The black rug! He loosened the reins abruptly and Slim moved out at a fast trot. When Mart got to the junction, he looked down the path in the direction the two vehicles had gone. He could not see them, but he could hear the motors intermittently over the noise of the wind through the trees. He looked again at the sky to the north. He was already risking getting caught in a storm. The ATVs climbed a rise in the cut line and Mart caught another glimpse of them. He backed Slim into the shrubs as the rider at the rear stood on the footrests and scanned backward. What made these two so nervous?

The sky was black all the way to its zenith. It would no doubt be raining soon, but maybe he could chance just a few minutes' detour to see if the Argentineans were up to something. He mulled over his possibilities. He could not just follow them boldly down the wide cut line. It was overgrown, but some of the vegetation would not be high enough to screen him while sitting on horseback. If he took to the bush he would have no chance of keeping up and probably would lose them altogether.

Mart decided to wait until they got out ahead of him and then try to follow their trail. He would hope to see them before they noticed him snooping around. It would be pretty hard to pretend he was not stalking them if they spotted him.

Mart collected his sandwich and wolfed it down. He deposited the packaging back into the saddlebag and searched for his gloves. He slid them on. The right one had small holes growing near the tips of both his index and pointer fingers. With another tug on the wide brim of the battered hat, he turned Slim southwest. They rode at a steady canter. Mart stood in the stirrups occasionally to inspect the trail ahead. He alternated that activity with quick checks of the ground before him. The quad tracks looked fresh, but they were mixed with a lot of traces from other traffic.

The riders had left the gate down between the Tower and the Glenwood Saw Set fields. Mart experienced some guilt at not stopping to put it up. It was his job to make sure the gates were closed, but that would alert the riders to his presence if they returned this way.

The combination of north wind and elevation had cooled the air considerably. Mart could see his own breath and that of his horse. Mart pulled Slim back to a trot. He thought he could see an occasional snowflake in the gloom.

CHAPTER 35 ✷ PICK UP

Mart was getting increasingly anxious. He would soon reach the junction between the Mackenzie line and the other distinct former seismic cut. He was only a couple of kilometres from the US boundary and had not encountered the two riders. Perhaps they had turned off and he had not detected it. The weather had deteriorated to a great extent. Sleet pelted his jacket and there was a slushy film on the leaves he brushed past. He needed to put on his slicker, but a reduction in vigilance now would increase the risk he would be spotted. He examined the edges of the trail and almost rode right past what he was looking for.

The broken shrubs at the side of the path marked where he had found the quad trail previously. He arrested Slim's forward momentum with a slight tug and a quiet whoa. He looked around quickly, and then got off his horse, grabbing the slicker as he dismounted. He slipped it on, took another quick gander around him and crouched at the entrance to the rough new path. The slush was squashed a watery grey.

Mart cocked his head sideways and listened for any approaching motor vehicle. His hat was an impediment to listening so he removed the wide-brimmed felt. Still nothing. Melted sleet poured from the hat and onto his dampened boots. Mart could only assume that the riders would return along this same route, so he stepped back and examined the terrain. Replacing his hat, the rancher swung back into the saddle and rode uphill a short distance to the southwest. He pushed the slender bay through the bushes at the edge of the trail and along the spine of a low sinuous rise. He hoped it would take him to a point above the turnaround he had discovered before. The going was tough and made more unpleasant by the cold rivulets of water dripping from the leaves onto jeans that were exposed as his slicker was pushed back by the springy stalks of shrubs. Slim fought gamely with the thick underbrush until Mart pulled him up hastily.

Below and to the left a patch of colour caught Mart's eye. No sooner had he seen the dark blue plastic of a fender than he was startled by a low whistle from the same spot. He slipped quickly and quietly to the ground to avoid appearing above the bushes. In doing so, Mart also cut off his own sightline. Placing a gloved hand firmly against the wet brown forehead of the Arabian, Mart encouraged the animal backward.

"Back. Back, boy," Mart cooed softly.

The small horse stepped carefully back along the tangled course that had led them there. Mart watched for an opening in the vegetation and trusted the agile pony to feel his way backward. The silver of the toolbox materialized and Mart let up on the pressure he had been applying to Slim's head. Mart stood silently watching and craned his neck slightly sideways. He could see part of one quad, but no riders. He chanced another sideways step past Slim's neck and to the horse's shoulder. A chokecherry stem cracked as Slim leaned away to allow Mart some room. Mart froze and placed a calming hand on the neck of the patient animal. He cringed and watched for some sign his presence had been discovered.

It was only a matter of a few seconds before the dark clothing of one of the riders became visible in front of the wet shine of the toolbox. The man was moving furtively around the machine, but Mart could not see his face. Mart worried that his own position was visible, or perhaps the saddle could be seen above the bushes. He remained very still and hoped Slim would do the same.

Mart was slightly reassured as the dark-clothed figure moved slowly along and out of his field of vision. The rider was still searching for the source of the sound. He had not yet spotted the horseman.

"Es sólo una vaca."

Mart heard the calm statement from below. Although he did not understand the words, the fact that they had been spoken at a volume somewhat above a whisper led him to believe that the person uttering them was no longer alarmed.

Mart immediately heard another low whistle. Then there was the sound of movement coming through the forest to the southwest of his, and the quad-riders', positions. The hidden rancher did not dare shift to see what might be happening below, but the activity next to the parked ATVs increased. He thought he could hear a sharp whine occasionally above the sound of the stiff breeze through the large Douglas firs above.

One of the machines below sprang to life and chugged unevenly. Mart used the sound of the engine to cover his shift to a better position to view the tiny clearing below. He lined up a nice hole through the thinning leaves to see the front of one quad and the rear of the other. He then saw what he had been expecting. A curved black tail swayed in front of the handlebars. Then it was blocked by a human back. Gloved hands opened the silver toolbox and hefted into it a black nylon-covered object that looked much like the cheap saddlebags you could purchase at discount tack shops. The way it hung and how it was handled betrayed contents of some mass.

A second motor engaged and Mart's window was filled with a confusing flurry of activity. He assumed the men and their machines were turning to leave.

Mart followed the progress of the machines with his ears. He waited until they had dropped low enough in the hollow that he could be confident not to be seen. He led Slim around the thickest part of the patch of shrubs that had been his hiding place. He then mounted and urged Slim to push back along the ridge in the direction from which they had come.

Mart was careful to avoid openings where he might be spotted from the quad trail below. After several minutes he realized the effort was probably wasted. The ATVs were making much swifter progress than he was. Their well-worn path had allowed some speed and his way was continually blocked by shrubs and deadfall. By the time Mart had emerged cautiously onto the Mackenzie line there was no audible trace of the two four-wheeled motorcycles. Enough slush had formed in the narrow path down the cut line that he could see they had returned the way they had driven in.

A mixture of sleet and rain continued to fall. Mart's boots and the lower part of his pants were soaked through. His gloves were a soggy second skin shrunk to fit his numb digits. He realized with some consternation that the material of his slicker above and back of his left shoulder no longer shed water completely. The sky was a funereal grey from the treetops along the Lee Creek Valley in the east to the top of Hog's Back north of his position. Sofa Mountain was erased entirely by the moist curtain of the storm.

"I have definitely gotten us into a fix," stated the horseman as he leaned in the saddle to give the little bay a pat on the shoulder. "Let's get out while we can!"

CHAPTER 36 ✳ WAY OUT

The ground was slick enough by now that Mart did not let the eager equine canter. He kept to a sensible trot and slowed to a walk in spots where he remembered that fallen logs and occasional rocks hid in the overgrown path. There was no more rain. The sleet was transforming into heavy, wet flakes. Mart kept his eyes on the ground to watch for obstacles, but also to let the brim of his hat catch the snowflakes before they adhered to his eyeballs. The bare soil of the trail remained free of snow, but anywhere the vegetation insulated the partially frozen precipitation from the warm ground it was accumulating. The wind remained steady from the north and Mart shivered. Steam was rising from the wet hide of the horse and Slim appeared a deep chocolate colour rather than his normal vibrant coppery-brown. The smell of wet hair filled Mart's nostrils and a mild panic filled his head. Men and horses had perished in these early fall storms.

The young rancher cursed his impetuous decision to follow the seismic crew. Had he checked the forecast before he left, he may have decided differently. But his TV and radio where inside the soaked and burnt-out shell of his mobile home – if they still worked at all.

Mart's mind only occasionally wandered to the odd meeting he had just witnessed. He was too preoccupied with the need to get back to his truck and then out of the hills until the storm had passed. The snow was coming harder now. It was difficult to recognize anything of the path he followed. Any traces of the rubber tires that had preceded him were now completely obliterated.

Mart almost missed the intersection where the trail led off the cut line and toward the Four Corners. The snow was already up over Slim's wide hooves. They made the turn and headed northwest. The little horse's head was bowed as he pushed into the swirling flakes. Mart's hands were numb as were the toes pushing against the wet leather of his boots. Tapederos would have been nice in this weather.

The cold rancher watched closely to avoid missing the turnoff to Hog's Back Gate #1. He found it and had made it half way along the short path from the junction to the gate when Slim's head shot up. Mart knew better than to ignore the signal from the alert animal so he pulled him up short. Skip and Slim had saved him from several blunders in the past. They often detected bears, moose and oncoming vehicles several seconds before Mart could see or hear them. But this time all Mart could observe was a thickening wall of falling snow. He peered through the gloom. All he could see was a grey curtain streaked with dizzying white. Slim kept his focus on something straight ahead. Mart just plain couldn't see anything. He would have to advance. Slim took several tentative steps forward at Mart's gentle command. The wet rider wondered whether the wary pony was really alarmed by whatever was up there or if his own nervousness was simply being transferred to his mount.

Again it was Slim who was first able to focus on the object of concern. Mart quickly tugged on the reins and stared at the identical place through the tempest. It took a few moments for Mart to even determine that something real was lurking there.

Under the wide lower branches of a half-century-old spruce was an amorphous lump. The trunk of the tree broke up its form, but it seemed out of place. Mart stared hard at the ill-defined shape. He could make no sense of it. After ogling the shapeless shadow for several moments, Mart realized that whatever it might be was probably less of a threat than the snowstorm. He could barely continue to hold the reins properly. His wet hands were frigid knobs. A cold streak was running from his left shoulder down to his belt where water had penetrated the crack in his slicker. His toes were gone to him. He still needed to traverse diagonally across two sections of land and the storm was getting brutal. The intensity of the wind had increased twofold. The snow was falling as thickly as Mart had ever seen it. This storm truly had the potential to be life-threatening.

Just when Mart had decided to proceed, the shapeless incongruity beneath the boughs shifted. Snow that had accumulated at its rounded summit slid off and tumbled to a lower protuberance. The globular shape at the object's apex began to register for the shivering rancher. It was a helmet-covered head. The transparent shield at the front of the headgear turned directly toward the horse and rider who were stalled in the blizzard.

Mart stayed perfectly still. His heart almost did too. Was one of the seismic guys waiting there for him? Had they seen him? Had the cracking twig alerted them to such a degree that they were watching their back trail?

Then Mart remembered the Hog's Back Gate. Had it been down and broken when the pair had come through? That would mean the riders were already in the Poll Haven pasture before he rode in. He had repaired the wire and put the gate back up. Perhaps it was the tight gate, where before there had been none, that had alerted them to another presence. It would have confirmed any suspicions they might have had at the clearing when Slim had broken the chokecherry branch.

The reflective plastic-covered eyes seemed to be exploring the murky air. The armoured head slowly swung past where the mounted man was squinting back through the falling snow. Why had the watcher not seen him? Then Mart remembered that he and Slim had been pushing into the storm. The front of both horse and rider were completely caked in a slushy white apron that would make them nearly invisible when immobile.

Mart pulled very gently back on the soaked leather lines. Slim responded by wanting to turn away from the windblown flakes. Mart used his legs to keep the gelding straight and increased the pressure on the bit slightly. The compliant pony moved back slowly. It took only three or four of the horse's steps to completely erase the vision of the man who appeared to be lying in wait for them. Mart forced Slim to take several more backward strides. There he stopped. There were other ways out, but they were longer. If one of the crew was waiting here, was the other one already at Mart's truck and trailer?

Before today Mart would have perhaps taken the chance that these ATV riders were unlikely to mean him any real harm. But now Mart was pretty sure that the domed hut was Wendell's unsolved mystery. Mart's own discovery of the quad trail and these riders so close to that odd structure was evidence enough that the seismic crew, or at least some of them, had a connection to it. The menacing attitude of the foremen of the crew spoke volumes about their desire to hide something. And the furtive behaviour of two members of their crew, who today just happened to be riding quads near where Wendell's horse was spooked by the same kind of machines, was circumstantial evidence at least that they had been involved in the old codger's death. Perhaps their role in that incident was all they were hiding, but Mart doubted it.

Slim fidgeted. He was cold and wanted to get moving. The storm was an obvious threat, but so were the men blocking his shortest path to safety. Mart cursed and pulled the hesitant horse around to point in a direction that led away from his parked outfit and away from home. The Arabian seemed less disgruntled about the about-face once he realized that the giant snowflakes were no longer slapping him in the face.

Mart pushed the little horse as hard as he dared on the slick footing. He made directly for the Four Corners at the very centre of the Poll Haven grazing lease. At least he hoped he was heading that way. He had to continually correct his path. Eventually Slim pushed through a dense patch of shrubs and deadfall and stopped short. He would not continue when Mart squeezed with his legs and clucked. Mart climbed down stiffly. He almost fell on numb feet and slick footing. He made to step ahead of Slim only to be stopped short, too. He had walked right into tightly stretched barbed wire.

Mart grabbed the top strand with soaked gloves. He looked right and left. He had no idea whether this was the fence running east and west or the one that stretched north and south. He was completely disoriented. At first he cursed the fence for being there and then he blessed the wire that had stopped him. Had he turned the other way while stumbling along, it would have been an hour or more before he came up against another fence. Only by steering perpendicular to the blowing snow had he succeeded in staying somewhere near the centre of the pasture.

But what should he do now? If he assumed he was on the east-west line and turned left, and was in reality on the north-south fence, he'd end up heading straight south to the US border. He would die of exposure before he could determine he was wrong and turn back. If he ended up guessing correctly, he would come to the intersection of four cross-fences.

Mart tried to determine which direction was north by watching the snowflakes. They were swirling in a maddeningly intricate waltz that confused the true wind direction. He needed more open terrain, but dared not leave the fence for fear he would lose this only tangible landmark. Then he had another idea. He climbed back on his horse and Slim made as if to turn away from the sharp wire to continue on. Mart stopped him, uttered a stern 'whoa' and scrambled up until he was standing on the slick, wet seat of the saddle. He stood very still and gratefully so did Slim.

The enhanced elevation erased to a small degree the sheltering effect of the underbrush. Nearby trees continued to redirect the snow, but Mart thought he could detect a trend in the angle of the majority of the frenzied flakes. If he was right, he was facing the fence that ran north and south.

Mart slipped his butt back down onto the wet leather. He pondered only a few seconds then reached back for the sheath containing his fencing tool. His frigid, wet fingers could not extract the tool from the damp leather. He climbed down to the ground and was forced remove his soaked gloves in order to pull the implement from the reluctance of the soggy cowhide. It took ages to pull the similarly glutinous leather back onto his freezing hands. He had to use his eyes to tell if the fingers were all in the right slots. He could not feel his way into the glove.

Mart pronounced an insincere apology to the grazing lease board as he clumsily cut the wires. The first two were taut and snapped back out of the way as he cut them. The third twisted wire was baggy and Mart had to bend it back out of the way to lead his horse through. He was only mildly repentant when he scrambled stiffly onto the back of his shivering mount without repairing the breach.

Mart and Slim stayed next to the fence and crashed through low branches and tall bush that rained water and snow down on them continually. They had turned right after having crossed the ruined fence and were rewarded a short while later when they reached the junction of all four cross fences. Here the pair turned left and maintained the painful activity of bushwhacking parallel to and right next to the fence. It took what seemed like forever to reach the Wire Whip Gate. Mart could barely get the gate open and remounting was an awkward effort, but at least the path leading north-east was an obvious narrow clearing leading away from the gate. Mart felt no remorse in leaving that gate down. He felt very little else at this point. The slicker had soaked through and body heat was leaching away rapidly. He knew he was getting mildly hypothermic.

Slim perked up now that they were headed roughly toward home. They made good progress. Mart lost all sense of time and distance and was surprised when the small bay plunged recklessly through the creek at Barton Crossing.

Mart had to keep shaking his head and clapping his deadened hands to jar himself back into some form of awareness as Slim pushed doggedly on toward the Ski Cabin. The horseman hardly emerged from his stupor to celebrate when the shadowy shape of the Polecat Chateau materialized from the heavy snow.

CHAPTER 37 ✳ HOMING

THE HALF-FROZEN HORSEMAN practically fell from his mount and crawled sluggishly up the stairs leading to the door of the weathered cabin. Someone had left it ajar. He rolled in over a small drift that had formed there. He lay there in a heap. It took several minutes before Mart finally became slightly responsive to his surroundings. He identified the ancient stove at the centre of one side wall. No one had built a welcoming fire. However, someone had conformed to the convention of leaving a good supply of dry firewood cut for the next occupant. It lay inertly, begging for some animate being to draw hot, bright life from the sun's energy stored inside the wood.

Mart did not feel up to the effort. He lay motionless, staring at the cold stove and rough firewood. He was no longer shivering. He was cold right to the core of his body. The temptation to succumb was a heavy woollen blanket of lethargy. Suddenly, in a violent surge of desire to survive, the young rancher staggered to his feet, fell against the far wall and lurched over to the chill chimney. North Wind was whistling a mournful tune down that pipe.

Mart dragged at the glove on his right hand. It came free with an odd and sudden snap. He checked drunkenly to see if any fingers had broken off in the endeavour. Reaching into the pocket of the soaked jeans was like forcing a thick, unfeeling length of yarn into the elusive eye of a needle. He did not try to select the disposable lighter, but scooped everything out. Nearly a dollar's worth of change and a sopping Kleenex fell to the floor with the desired object. Mart crouched unsteadily and retrieved it maladroitly. He blessed the same caring citizen who had left the wood when he spotted a wad of newspaper on the floor next to it.

None of the wood was split, but several shattered slivers and morsels of chipped bark were scattered around the stove. He had only one chance to get this right. Mart built his fire with great care. He was rewarded when, on the second strike of the lighter, flames licked languidly up in the moist air and teased warmth from the wood. The activity of tending the hearth did as much to enliven the man as did the growing flames. Mart even had the presence of mind to shuffle to the doorway and heave the slab door closed through the accumulated snow before it.

Mart huddled in front of the fire for most of two hours. Steam surrounded him as he slowly fed fuel into the small door at the front of the battered stove. Needles of pain made him writhe as his toes and fingers came back to life. He shuddered uncontrollably and finally began to pace back and forth to revive his chilled body.

Mart became vaguely aware of fluttering in the rafters. Some birds had entered the open door before the storm and were now his unwilling cabin-mates. The firewood was almost all used up in the inefficient stove. He would have to go out for more. He was reluctant to do so, but the desire to check on his faithful pony spurred him on as much as the need to get more fuel.

Finally the rancher squeezed out the door and into the raging blizzard. Slim was nowhere to be seen. Mart stumbled and fell on the snow-covered stairs in his frenzy to locate the animal. A loud snort came from around the south side of the building. Mart stepped past the corner of the cabin to see his horse standing head down, reins buried in the snow. The dark gelding was sideways to the cabin wall, protected from the wind by the log structure. Snow the width of Mart's hand covered the saddle, neck and rump of the animal. He was shivering slightly, but did not seem terribly stressed. Mart walked over and almost swept the snow from the horse, but thought better of it. It was an insulating blanket. Mart loosened the cinch slightly, but did not remove the saddle. He slipped the bridle carefully off and thought to use his lariat to tie the horse. Instead he patted a dark cheek lovingly, left him free to find what shelter he could and went to fetch wood.

Years of recreational fire building had left the immediate area of the Polecat Chateau devoid of good fuel. Mart resorted to breaking scraggly, dry branches from the lower portion of several evergreens. Around the back of the rude edifice he was able to find a snag perched precariously upright between two live trees. With a little effort, he was able to push it down. It cracked and groaned as it fell and broken branches scattered through the snow. Mart gathered these quickly to save them from the soggy ground. The fact that the dead tree had been standing almost erect had kept portions of the wood dry. Mart scrounged for these and returned to the cabin's interior with three armloads before settling in to warm up again. He checked on Slim one more time. Even the ruckus caused by the felling of the tree had not caused the pony to shift from the protection of the cabin wall and narrow eaves.

A broken, wooden, straight-backed chair and some rusting bed springs were the only vestiges of furniture in the single room. Mart dragged a set of the latter next to the stove. He hung his slicker on the chair dangerously close to the hot metal. He hung his hat on a nail behind the smoking chimney. The chilled cowboy lay down and shivered on the narrow cables stretching from the springs on both ends of the corroded frame. He stared up into the rafters. Six beady eyes stared back. Three bluish-grey heads tilted erratically back and forth like poorly-animated cartoon characters.

The pigeons were enjoying the warmth, although they were wary of the drenched animal that had provided it. Mart stared at them. He was bone-tired, but unable to sleep. Instead he brooded over the link between Wendell's puzzle and Southwest Seismic. It was what had brought him here to hide and wait out the storm.

It was with some relief that Mart discarded his nagging suspicions about Jack Pruitt and Candace Cowan. It had become apparent also that the strange circumstances of the past few days were not the result of some accidental and tragic encounter in the woods.

The seismic crew had been concerned over Wendell's, and now his, discovery of the tiny lodge. The fact that it had been camouflaged was a clear sign that they did not want it found. The two workers were wary. The foremen were antagonistic. Mart had every reason to suspect they had intentionally attacked Jacobsen.

The missing journal had to fit in somewhere. Someone had not stopped at simply stealing the book, but had viciously attacked him in order to keep it and to escape without being identified. Had they been concerned about Wendell writing something incriminating in the diary? How would they have known he even kept a record of his daily activities? These were not your ordinary thugs. They had done enough research to suspect that Jacobsen possessed documentation of his discovery.

Then there was the big black dog. The fur at the shelter and along the path was dog hair. The rug with eyes was the same animal. But why keep him out in the woods? So they had a dog. Many people kept pets and occasionally men working outdoors took their canine friends to work with them. How could anyone object to the dog riding along with the crew?

The pigeons overhead cooed softly. Mart focused his eyes on their shadowy forms. They were disappearing as the light reflecting off the snow outside the cracked and grimy window pane faded. They were technically not native birds. They were the descendants of escaped tame rock doves. People had kept them for food and as a hobby. Some folks still played around with their homing instincts and freed their tame birds far from home with cute messages tied to their scaly legs. Some clocked their miraculous return home.

Mart sat bolt upright. Here was an outrageous idea! What if the crew was not keeping the dog in the community pasture, but only retrieving it from there? The hut was its homing loft. It had been trained to return to it. The hidden hut was only 500 metres from the United States boundary. A dog could probably carry between ten and thirty percent of its own body weight. Mart had not gotten a real good look at the animal, but it appeared to be big – at least forty-five kilograms, maybe more. There were several substances that would be pretty lucrative to move illegally across the international boundary in quantities of five to fifteen kilograms at a time, especially if you did it successfully and often. The continual presence of the seismic crew in the Poll Haven gave them that opportunity.

Mart fumbled for his cell phone. He knew there would be no service before it actually powered up and confirmed that fact. He was probably already too late anyway. The guys on the quads would have given up on him and taken the dog, the pack and whatever was inside of it out to wherever they connected with the next leg of their transportation pipeline. If it was drugs, then it would be off to Calgary or Vancouver where the market was big and the police were overwhelmed.

Mart lay back down. Perhaps the fact he had escaped would convince them it was time to shut down the operation – if his crazy speculations were even close to reality.

CHAPTER 38 ✳ RUN

THE BUMP CAME from outside. Mart's eyes flew open. He had dozed on and off and had fed most of his firewood into the greedy stove through much of the night. This time he had fallen into a deep slumber. But now he was wide awake. He listened, but heard no more noise. He rationalized it must have been his imagination – a sudden start caused by the discomfort of his wet clothes and inferior bed. He relaxed and rolled slowly onto his back. His clothing had dried in patches, but much of it was still damp. The fire had to be practically out by now and it was still almost pitch black outside. He steeled himself to yet another foray into the dark and cold for more elusive wood.

Thump! This time Mart was not startled. Slim was shifting against the outside wall. It was reassuring to know the horse was still with him. The rancher pushed himself cautiously to a sitting position. He was a bit stiff. No other harm had been done – aside from missing what had likely been a great meal at the Wyslik residence. He would have a hard time explaining that one. No matter what kind of tale he spun about yesterday and the night spent in the cabin it would probably end up an embarrassing story of lost in the woods.

He felt for his boots. Damp, but not soaked. Taking them off had been a good idea. The slicker was completely dry. So was his hat, although it seemed more floppy than before. The gloves were cold and wrinkled, but drier than the boots.

Slim snorted softly and shook on the other side of the logs. Mart smiled and started putting on his discarded footgear and coat. Then Slim snorted again, loudly this time. Probably just a passing coyote or lynx. Mart continued his slow preparations to exit in search of fuel. Then he stopped briefly and resumed his preparations with more zeal.

"Not smart to assume it's just another critter," Mart muttered to the birds stirring in the open attic.

The door pulled open with some difficulty. The drift before it had partially melted and iced over. Although there seemed to be little light emanating from the sky, the snow reflected back its pale glow. Suddenly footsteps approached the porch at a rapid gait. Mart almost ducked back inside before a dark, long face peered at him around the dovetailed ends of the logs. Slim looked comical with the load of snow forming a pointed clown's cap between his twitching ears. Mart could see against the darker silhouette of the cabin that it was now only snowing lightly.

This time the rancher hastened to push the snow off the slender horse and damp tack. In doing so, his hand caught on the exposed stock of the Winchester carbine.

"Damn!" exclaimed Mart. He had forgotten the rifle and left it out in the storm. He pulled a rim of ice from around the scabbard opening and hoped the oiled leather had kept out the majority of the moisture.

Slim tossed his head up and looked past the high platform in front of the door and toward the path leading up from the north fence line of the community pasture. Mart stopped rummaging around and listened. Nothing. He reached across the saddle to the far saddlebag. His stomach had not ceased its occasional growling since he first stirred on his Spartan bed. Otto's generosity was even more welcome this morning than it had been the previous afternoon.

Mart got no breakfast. He had not even lifted the wrinkled flap of the leather pouch before his ears caught the distant growl that had alerted the dark gelding. It was a small engine moving cautiously through the mid calf-deep snow.

It could be a rescue party. Mart sincerely doubted that. He looked up at the doorway. He was sure he had left nothing inside but his loose change. However, signs of his presence, and departure, would be obvious. The door was closed. He tightened the cinch quickly and warmed the bit superficially with his hand before slipping the stiff bridle over the horse's ice-encrusted ears. He was about to mount when he thought of his feathered friends and dashed back to push open the door. Slim had followed him to the front of the building, so Mart played Zorro and mounted by hopping from the porch. Slim sensed his urgency and spun too quickly toward the trail leading away from the growing engine noise and away from home. The pony slipped, but recovered before he actually fell. Mart was glad for the reset horseshoes. Nevertheless, he would have been happier now if he had asked for the more aggressive heel-toe variety.

Mart and Slim travelled at a cautious trot for several minutes and stopped short of the sharp turn that would lead along the wide path to the top of Poll Haven. Mart looked back down on the small clearing in front of the Ski Cabin. There was now enough light that he could make out the shape of the cabin and the white scar that was its uneven courtyard. All that was visible on that blank tableau were his tracks leading away. He waited on the impatient gelding. Slim pawed the snow at his feet. Mart ignored him and watched.

It was only a few moments before a mud-splattered machine roared into view and stopped just short of the cabin door. The rider left the motor idling and made a crouching run at the door. Another machine slid in beside the first and its operator stood and scanned ahead in the direction of Slim's hoof prints. The first man did not go up the stairs, but climbed onto the porch and slid along the wall to the open door. He looked down at the tracks leading away, jumped back down to the ground and ran to his quad. The other rider had already sped away in the direction Mart had chosen. The knobby tires cast slush and turf across the clean snow as the vehicle skidded this way and that until it could maintain traction. Mart had seen enough. He pointed Slim in the direction of the Atwood Gate and let him run.

The horse and rider maintained their reckless momentum for several minutes, then Mart pulled back and the little horse slid almost to a stop. There was no hope to outrun the machines on an open track. Slim poked through the tangled shrubs and out into the bush.

Deciduous trees and shrubs had yet to lose their leaves. The foliage had caught the heavy snowflakes and allowed them to accumulate in weighty clumps. Branches normally saddle horn-high were laden and bent to near the ground. Some small bushes were squashed almost flat. They sprang up like metal traps when the wide hooves shook them free of their wintery burden.

The noisy engines were audible by the time Mart had pushed twenty metres in. There would be no hiding from the pursuers. Tracking would be child's play. Mart could only hope that difficult terrain would put them off. He had no idea just how serious they might be about catching him. And what would be his fate should they do so?

Mart tried to ignore the sound of churning tires and breaking branches. Instead he concentrated on the rough ground at his mount's feet. The predawn gloom did little to help him guide the pony through the worst parts of the thicket.

Behind him the engines had stopped. Had they given up? He could not rely upon that type of good fortune so he goaded the game little Arabian onward and up a sharp but short incline. Slim tripped over a hidden obstacle and Mart leaned forward to determine its location.

Mart swatted at the fly that brushed past his face when he sat back up. Then he noticed a muted pop that sounded like a cat's sneeze. Flies buzzing in a snowstorm made no sense to him so he glanced quickly around. Steadied against a tree was one of Mart's pursuers. Mart looked directly back into the bore of a small calibre rifle. An odd bulge formed the leading end of the barrel and blocked the open sights. Telescopic sights hovered above the dull black barrel.

It was likely the lack of open sights at such proximity that had saved Mart. Close range and small obstructions made the use of the magnifying telescopic sights tricky. In the instant it took to realize he was being shot at, the gun spit two more times. The horseman was vaguely aware of leaves being sheared from the tree above him. He booted Slim un-gently and the pony humped up and jumped over a fallen log. They slid down the far side of the small ridge. Mart turned the horse and pushed him hard. They crashed through the bush in the hollow that ran parallel to the sharp rise. The ridge meandered slightly and Mart hoped the curved slope would hide him from the gunman.

Slim tried to slow on the roughest parts of the terrain, but Mart goaded him relentlessly. He could not think of a time he had so abused one of his animals. The horse stumbled several times, once going down on both knees. Mart's right leg took a nasty blow when he forced his mount into the space between two trees barely wide enough to accommodate them. When he finally slowed to look back, he heard the distant pulsation of a starting motor.

"They've gone back to their machines," the rancher gasped. He slid off his horse to inspect the damage. He almost fell when he tried to put weight on his banged knee. Slim was not too badly off. There were several cuts and scratches from sharp twigs, but they were high and in fleshy parts of his shoulders. Mart could see no injury to his lower legs. He patted the dark cheek and leaned his head briefly against the wide bay brow.

Mart quickly worked the banged knee. It would be fine. When Mart remounted, he drew the old .30-.30 from its case. He reached back into the saddlebag and found the cartridges.

He slipped five or six carelessly into the magazine, but thought better of levering a round into the chamber. The ground was too rough. He would end up shooting himself or his horse. He seriously doubted his ability to fire back effectively if his opponents caught up with him again, but an unloaded gun was just extra weight to carry.

The pace was slower from that point on. Mart was careful of his route and continually stopped to watch and listen. If the Southwest Seismic duo was willing to shoot, they were serious enough not to give up easily. Mart wondered how they had been able to locate him so effortlessly. The fallen snow would have hidden his tracks from the Four Corners. Besides that, these guys had come from a different entry point into the grazing lease. Anyway, the quads were not the same ones the first crew had been riding. There was no toolbox and the riders looked different. The light had been poor, but he was certain that the gunman was in green and tan camouflaged coveralls. White ones would have served better today and Mart hoped other members of the crew were not any better prepared for the wintery conditions than these two had already shown they were.

Mart had to find a way out. He was not confined to trails, but not using them made for awfully slow progress. He decided to make his way across country to the trail that led north over the toe of Poll Haven. He would try to exit by way of Little Beaverdam and Payne lakes. Perhaps some misguided fishermen would be stranded there and he could get some help. He felt for the cell phone. It was still in his pocket. He would be trying it once he reached the highest point in the trail.

CHAPTER 39 ✳ HEMMED IN

It took several hours to bushwhack to where Poll Haven began to rise out of the mixed aspen and pine forest. Mart had neither seen nor heard any further sign of pursuit. The rifle was back in the scabbard. It would stay drier there. Mart had halted at a small opening and let Slim eat a few mouthfuls of grass and drink from some of the runoff supplied by melting snow. The rider ate several of the cookies and the half-frozen apple. He drained his water bottle and refilled it from an ephemeral stream. Drinking surface water in a cow pasture was not typically a wise thing to do. However, getting sick from beaver fever was the lesser of several risks to his health at the moment.

The day remained overcast with light snow falling, but the temperature was slightly above freezing and water was running everywhere. If he read the landscape correctly, Mart was only a ten or twenty minute ride from the trail that would lead him over Poll Haven. He cast a spiteful look at the overcast sky and prayed the cloud would not impede his cell signal.

Mounted and moving again, Mart sacrificed some vigilance for speed. He was anxious to make contact with friendly humans. Slim nosed out into the open, narrow trail before Mart realized they were there. He pulled up, but found himself standing broadside in the path. He instinctively pulled the reins to get back into the bush, but Slim balked slightly at the confusing command.

Mart whispered a mild reprimand and glanced back at his mount. A wavering red dot appeared momentarily and danced between the poll and crest of the spirited horse. Mart yanked the reins sideways and Slim spun left. Pfft! A now familiar muffled report marred the silence of the forest.

The next sharp hiss was preceded by a burning sensation across Mart's right shoulder. Then Slim was flat out and heading south, down the trail away from the dancing red dot and the muted sizzle of the silenced rifle.

It was difficult to think coherently while galloping uncontrollably through the slippery slush. Clods of mud were yanked out of the surface below the sodden snow and cast randomly backward and sideways. Slim's neck was no longer curved in its proud arch, but straight out, wide nostrils drinking in the moist air, ears back and tail only slightly curved behind. Wet black mane tickled the rider's nose as he bent low over the pommel.

Mart cursed at the new leak in his slicker. Now, like the left, the right sleeve leaked at the shoulder. He could feel the liquid trickle down his arm. He shook off the idiotic annoyance. He must be in mild shock to fret about ruined clothing. The fluid was not melt-water.

Slim surged forward. He heard the approaching four-wheeler before Mart did. The agile Arabian skidded around a corner and leapt a fallen tree. His hooves clacked like a speeding train through the dry branches clawing up at the bounding duo from the downed trunk.

The sound of the motor receded and Mart realized his hunter had been forced to find another way around the timber impediment. He allowed his mount to slow only slightly and began scanning for another escape route. In the end, he kept his horse moving southward toward the tangle of Hell's Kitchen.

To Mart's dismay he detected the rapidly approaching engine noise at the same time he saw the gate was up. Slim skidded to a halt as Mart stepped from the saddle. He skidded too, right into the wire of the gate. Several new rents in his slicker were produced as he tore himself free of the barbs. He dropped the gate only wide enough to lead the gelding through and used the momentum of Slim's automatic jump into a canter to pull himself up into the seat. Mart dug in his heels and ignored the temptation to look back. The sound of the motors was close, but Mart was rewarded by the screeching sound of stretched wire as the first machine hit the carelessly dropped gate.

The minor tangle delayed the pursuing team for only a few seconds. However, the insignificant impediment gave Mart another notion. Before horse and rider could reach the abandoned saw mill boiler that was now dumped into the creek for use as a culvert, there were a couple of sharp turns. Mart quickly took down his rope. He made a small loop and dropped it over the top of a tall stump as he again pulled Slim to a sliding halt. He made two quick half-hitches around another tree and swung back up onto the wet saddle.

Slim was clawing at the muddy ground beneath the melting snow when the first ATV slid around the curve and into view. The machine's rider braked hard and prepared to swing his rifle from the strap over his shoulder, saw that the horseman was again mobile and gunned the engine. A second quad slowed to avoid collision with the first. Then the driver punched the accelerator to keep up with his comrade.

This time Mart did not miss the show. He heard the sudden muting of the first machine and the fracturing of large branches. A loud pop advertised the demise of his best lariat. He looked back to watch the rider of the first machine being slung rag-like over the crumpled handlebars. A fraction of a second later the grate of metal on metal and the dull splintering of moulded plastic rebounded from the solid tree trunks. The second rider was thrust instantly downward into the mud and slush.

Slim was rarely spooked by loud noises or unfamiliar sights. Nevertheless, the recent chase had worked the spirited pony into an excited frenzy. The crash behind him spurred him onward and Mart had to saw on the reins to bring him back to a pace that would not completely wind the animal. By the time the rider had turned south, back toward the winding path down into Hell's Kitchen, Mart had slowed to a ground-eating trot. Slim was breathing deeply, but he was far from spent.

It was surprising that the lariat trick had worked. The first rider had not seen the rope in the shadows and flat light. The second crash had disabled that rider or the quad, or he had simply stayed to offer aid to his companion. Either way, they were no longer following. Mart had been tempted to turn back and circumnavigate the accident site to get out of the pasture. However, he was uncertain both riders had been incapacitated and was leery of their sophisticated gear and aggressive tactics.

Laser sights? Silencers? This was straight out of Hollywood. These guys were not only resolute about silencing him; they were bent on doing it quickly and quietly. Southwest Seismic wanted him dead and they did not want anyone to hear the shots that did him in. They were using small calibre semi-automatics. Given the presence of two different parties on two separate trails leading into the Poll Haven lease, Mart assumed they had several likely trails covered and were moving in on him. They probably had radios to communicate with one another.

Slim was not the only one who was spooked. Mart was terrified. He had a hard time focusing on the problem or planning what to do next. He was heading south. He needed to get out of the community pasture, but that was north. He was being pushed back into the wildest part of the Poll Haven where he was less likely to get help of any kind.

Mart scanned the horizon for a rise that might allow him to use his cell phone. He patted his shirt pocket to reassure himself. It was still there. He would keep looking for a good spot to try to hit the tower on the Bird's Eye Ranch.

Mart had almost reached the junction that would either lead west to the boundary of Waterton Lakes National Park or curve east and south to the slopes of the Hog's Back. He made a decision. He would head west. If he reached the park perhaps he could get out to the Chief Mountain International Highway and flag down a motorist. Maybe park wardens would be on patrol and hear the activity of the quads illegally moving inside the park. The problem was that there was a good deal of bushwhacking to do between the west fence line of the pasture and that thin ribbon of asphalt snaking along the Belly River and Sofa wetlands. Surely he would get cell service before then and alert someone he needed help fast. He pulled out the phone and was again disappointed.

Mart's shoulder was stinging. He opened the top of his slicker and reached his left hand up and along the tattered sleeve of his jacket. The denim and sweater were sticky with blood. The bleeding seemed to have stopped.

"Just a flesh wound," Mart grinned giddily. He had always wanted to say that. Then he frowned. Frivolity at a time like this was not a good sign. He was confused and needed to shake off the shock of being hunted. He wondered how many more small bullets he could take before he was totally incapacitated. It was without humour that he visualized himself flailing in impotent resistance akin to Monty Python's dismembered knight in the Holy Grail movie. He needed to think clearly and come up with a plan.

Mart prepared to turn right at the junction. When he got there he yanked the reins and Slim stopped abruptly. There were fresh tire tracks leading west. Or were they headed east? It did not much matter. The fact was that one of his first opponents, or a new one, had arrived before him. That pretty much confirmed two things: one, that there was definitely some means of communication being used by the gunmen, and two, at least one of his latest attackers had survived to alert their friends just where he was headed.

Mart tucked Slim into the bush beside the trail. He gazed longingly west. It was almost certain that there was someone waiting for him that way. He had the feeling that his options were being limited strategically. He was being herded south. That is where his alternatives became fewer and his adversaries had the best chance of disposing of him discretely.

Perhaps he should just sit still. Mart had been thinking about who might be missing him at this point. Tina Taylor had often warned him that no one would know if he had an accident even ten steps away from the barn. His mom worried that he would lay injured for several days before anyone thought to check on him.

But this time was different. Tom Wyslik would have wondered about his absence from the roast beef supper Sheila had prepared. He would have assumed Mart had been delayed in the community pasture and would not have been too offended. Nevertheless, Mart was certain Tom would have telephoned to make sure he got home all right in the gathering storm and darkness. He may have even driven over when he got no answer. Sheila would have badgered him into it. He would have noticed the missing pickup and stock trailer if he had been to the Gwynn place.

Then there was Kent. He had offered to help Mart move his meagre belongings to Aunt Emma's house today. Would he have shown up already? Would he wait until afternoon? Either way he would know something was wrong if there was no sign of Mart having been there since Friday morning. Tom may have phoned Kent by now, too.

His friends may have called the police. No, that was unlikely. They would not have asked for help from the RCMP when the police were less well equipped to search the hills than they were themselves. They would saddle their horses, load them into trailers and scratch their way up through the wet snow and mud to start the search. They would not even be too worried at this point. It was not as if none of them had ever been trapped out in a storm before. They would expect to meet him coming out as they were going in.

That is when Mart really began to panic. His friends would be trying to rescue him from falling snow and being cold and wet. They would blunder into hostile Columbians and semi-automatic gunfire. He was terrified. Images of Tom, Reg and Kent lying dead in blood-spattered snow leapt into his already overactive mind.

CHAPTER 40 ✳ AN OFFER

Mart bumped lightly with his right leg and pushed Slim out into the trail. He could not just sit still and risk letting his friends ride into an ambush. He would call and warn them. He would turn south and hope for some other opportunity for escape to materialize out of the hopelessness he currently felt. The snow had stopped entirely. The clouds were solid, but higher.

Without warning Slim spun around and plunged straight into a steep ravine. Mart slipped half off the saddle and grabbed for the horn. He was hanging off the side as his horse ran wildly through a patch of Douglas fir and spruce. He hissed a frightened whoa. Slim slowed significantly, but could not stop entirely in the slick, slushy snow of the incline. The rancher pulled himself almost back into the seat when he was brushed completely off by the solid trunk of a seventy-year-old fir.

Mart sat gasping on the ground. He sucked air like a beached whitefish. Although unable to breathe, he searched instinctively for his hat. He had it back on his head before he could once again draw breath. Next he looked to see where his horse had gone. Slim was standing another ten metres down the slope. He had turned to stare back at his fallen rider, but his eyes were wide and wild. There was blood pouring down his right flank.

Mart ignored his aching breast and scooted down the rest of the slope on the seat of his jeans. Slim shied slightly when Mart jumped up to inspect the wound. He found a shallow gouge the length of his forearm. His horse had been grazed by a bullet. The rider had not even heard the report of the rifle.

Mart shot a quick glance up toward the trail. He was well screened down here and could hear no activity. He walked Slim around in a tight circle. The injury did not affect his ability to move. Mart could not be certain his own injuries were not more severe. It was agonizing to walk. His whole right side was badly bruised. There may be broken ribs. He felt gingerly along the right side of his chest. It hurt terribly to touch anywhere from his sternum out to the edge of his floating ribs. But what made him despair the most was what he felt in his breast pocket. There was an odd crunching sound there. Mart pulled his phone from beneath the layers of clothes. It was excruciating to reach across his bruised chest. The device was suspiciously soggy in its leatherette case. There was no response to his repeated poking of the power switch.

Mart had no time to waste toying with the obviously crushed apparatus. He threw it onto the ground in disgust, then retrieved it and shoved it into his slicker pocket. He despised litter, but mostly he did not want Southwest Seismic to know he had no phone.

An ATV pulled up quickly and stopped above Mart on the trail. The rancher stood quietly and tried to calm his frightened horse. Perhaps he should let Slim go. He might be able to more easily slip away on foot. The horse was in danger of being killed by a stray bullet. Then Mart realized they would shoot the horse if they saw him anyway. They would want to reduce Mart's mobility and be sure he remained on foot. The trusting equine would quite possibly walk right up to the gunman to be shot. No, both his and the horse's chances would be better if he remained mounted.

Slim stood very still as his owner climbed stiffly back on. Mart could hear subtle rustlings approaching from the trail above. It was time to move on. He started slowly and quietly. Moving a large animal like a horse through thick brush was not exactly prone to furtiveness. Slim was not feeling particularly stealthy either. He was still excited from the sting of the bullet and the downhill plunge. Mart gave up the hope for stealth and concentrated on a more hasty escape. The following gunman abandoned his surreptitious approach and charged down the hill.

Again Mart risked injury to himself and his horse by riding hard through very rough country. Slim charged ahead with little need for encouragement. The game pony pivoted around the boles of trees like a gymkhana star. The pain of the jostling Mart was taking almost made him slip from the saddle. Whoever had arrived from above tracked their noisy progress and dashed on foot across the slope to cut them off.

Mart did his best to parallel the trail. His pursuer remained hopeful for several minutes and continued his charge through the bushes. Eventually Slim outdistanced the gunman and Mart pointed the horse back up toward the path.

Horse and rider exploded into the trail in a shower of leaves and soggy snow. Mart looked neither left nor right, but directed the bay south-eastward. He kept Slim to a lively canter until he reached the junction with the trail leading east to the Wire Whip gate. Only a single set of ATV tracks were visible. Mart gambled that they were those of the gunman they had just lured away from his vehicle.

Mart reined in his horse. How much more of this could the little Arabian take? The horseman did not stop, but made Slim keep to a walk, all the while listening for the approach of the quad he expected to come from behind. He kept an eye on the gash in Slim's hindquarters. The blood was no longer freely flowing. The horse was not favouring the leg at all.

Mart was startled when he heard engine noise from up ahead instead of from back the way he had come. Down a lengthy slope Mart could see a pickup scratching along unsteadily in the mire. He let himself hope for just a couple of seconds before he recognized the blue Dodge 4X4 of Southwest Seismic through the muck slung along its fenders.

"I can't shake them," Mart muttered. The determination of the crew was unsettling, their efficiency was fearsome.

"Why don't they just pack up and leave?" Mart wondered aloud again. He started to push the bay back into the shrubbery. Both he and Wendell had discovered their plot. At least the crew suspected they had. In their place he would have simply disappeared. Could a few kilos of drugs every day or two really be worth murder? Then Mart remembered they had already killed Jacobsen. Perhaps that is why they were so determined to silence him as well.

"Hold on McKinnon!" a gravelly voice shouted from the open window of the cab.

Neither Slim nor Mart was in any mood to stand still. Both were hurt and significantly panic-stricken. They had pushed a few metres into the bush when they were hailed again.

"Please stop. I can help you."

Mart recognized Stimatz's voice. There was veritable pleading in it. The man was either sincere or a very good actor. Mart pulled back on the reins and the frightened horse fidgeted beneath him.

The pickup stopped where Mart had left the trail. Stimatz killed the diesel engine. Mart heard the door open.

"McKinnon?" The foreman did not leave the muddy road. "McKinnon, listen to me!" Stimatz's entreaty was met with silence. "Damn it!" he muttered.

"Say what you have to say fast. Don't come any closer."

There was hope in the stocky man's husky voice when he took up the dialogue. "This has gone too far. The old man was an accident. The boys were just trying to scare him off."

"Bullshit! They rammed his horse and left him face down in a bush. It was just plain murder."

Stimatz stammered through his next statement. "I...it was not my doing...They said he fell when they rode up to the horse."

"Look, it's too late for all that. They are shooting at me. I am not sticking around to listen to you. When that quad comes down the trail, I'll be gone."

"I can fix this. I told them you'd see reason – maybe take some cash for your troubles – lots of cash. Let me talk to them."

Mart could not see the man's face, but Stimatz sounded desperate. "I don't trust you to try. Why should I think you are any different from them?"

"They have me over a barrel, but they know I can create a lot of trouble for them. They'll listen to me."

"Why are you mixed up with this, if you're not one of them?"

"I needed the money to keep the business afloat." Here Stimatz hesitated. "They said all I needed to do was look the other way and we'd all make some good money on the side. I had no idea it would come to this."

"Why didn't they just move on when they knew they'd been found out?" Mart asked.

"They have operations like this all along this border and the one with Mexico. It's not just this thing that they are worried about. They answer to bigger fish. That's what I mean. There is big money to be had. Just agree to say nothing and I'll get them to cut you in."

Mart could hear an ATV running cautiously down the hill toward them. He clucked to Slim and lied to buy some time. "Give it your best shot, but I won't stand here in their sights while you debate it. Find me and let me know."

Slim and Mart were once more thrashing through the underbrush. And again they were headed south. Mart pushed on toward the vapour-veiled hulk of the Hog's Back. After a while he could hear one or two quads and the truck moving along the trails behind him. He emerged onto the steep track climbing the ridge. To his surprise there were no tire tracks on it. He was still ahead of them.

Mart did not relish the punishing climb to the summit. His mount showed no sign of being played out yet, but Mart knew the gelding would have to quit at some point. He would likely be forced to take a stand to spare the horse. The alternative was simply to ride the animal into the ground and then still be forced to confront the five of six armed men who he knew were chasing him.

"There just has to be some other way!" Mart cursed.

In addition to fear, anger was starting to creep along his veins. The bastards had killed the old man. They were no doubt behind the fire that destroyed his house. Now they were forcing him to punish his horse. They would catch and kill him and he did not have the stomach to stand and fight. Kent wouldn't be running like a rabbit to ground. He would have stood his ground before now. Kent – yet another reason to fight back. Mart's blond hero would have set aside his disgust with him and would soon be blundering into this little war unarmed.

Mart reached down and felt for the stock of the rifle. The cold, hard wood did little to reassure the timid horseman. Mart was uncertain he had the guts to fight and die courageously. He was even unsure he could shoot at another human being in self-defence.

The sky was getting dark again. The temperature was falling. Mart checked his Timex. The crystal was cracked and moisture had condensed on the inside. By turning it slightly sideways Mart could read the time. It was only a little past two in the afternoon. They were in for more snow.

It was as if thinking it made it happen. The north wind picked up and slushy snow tumbled from the trees at the same time as hard granules began descending like rice on a groom. They bounced off Mart's ruined slicker and made Slim tuck his nose close to his breast. To add insult to injury, an ATV made its presence known just to the rear by gunning a growling engine. Mart and Slim were again forced to leave the trail.

CHAPTER 41 ✳ THE SLOW STAMPEDE

MART QUIETLY STEPPED down from the saddle. Three or four quads had stationed themselves strategically on the trail and had pushed in along the north flanks of the narrow ridge that loomed above hunters and hunted. As far as Mart could tell, the riders had not ventured far from their machines. He silently slid the carbine from the opposite side of the saddle and waited what his mind told him was hours and his watch revealed to be little more than twenty minutes.

What were they doing?

Slim shifted slightly. The forest was instantly filled with the whine of small lead projectiles. They snapped leaves, splattered randomly into live wood in front of Mart and smacked dully into the hillside behind him.

Mart flinched and Slim skittered sideways. Both reactions were several seconds too late to have saved them. Instead good fortune had provided that service.

The hail of gunfire caused Mart to reconsider his stand. They could fire ten rounds to each of his. He remounted as quietly as he could and was treated to a farewell volley as Slim clamoured up through the woodland. Dense vegetation and lady luck were once more his allies.

Mart found a winding cattle trail and started up. He met a dozen Hereford-cross cattle coming down. Instead of driving away the beasts, the activity below had enticed them. Good weather until now had encouraged the cattle to remain scattered throughout the shared grazing lease. The stock tended to gather and drift back down toward the corrals in rough weather. They banked up against closed gates and bawled. It made roundup easier, but early storms necessitated pushing the congregated critters back if there was still grass.

It was still snowing steadily. It would be dark in a little more than an hour. The pretended seismic crew had kept Mart on the run for more than twenty-four hours now with little respite. But it was Slim who was paying the biggest price for it. He had had only a few mouthfuls of grass in that time and had been wet and ridden hard. If they could last another couple of hours, Mart needed to find a place for the little horse to rest and eat.

The cattle stalled in front of the horse and rider. They bawled and stared. Mart pushed through them, grateful that the sound of his retreat would be covered by the cacophony of their calls. He was further uplifted by what he discovered on the other side of the animals. They had churned the snow and mud into a morass. Mart directed Slim along the back-trail. He was able to do this for several hundred metres.

The storm hit with real violence when Mart was just below the crest of the ridge. He pushed Slim up along the rim toward the heaviest timber. He found what he was looking for just before the blizzard and the night squelched the remaining light.

He had discovered the abandoned wolf den three years earlier. The pups had been born and grew behind the root mass of a massive spruce that had toppled in the violent winds atop the Hog's Back. The roots stretched up, twisting in a Medusa-like halo, to a height of at least two metres. Several other smaller trees had been pushed down on top of the roots and sloping trunk. The lower end had provided refuge for the wolf family – the upper portion might well shelter larger refugees.

Mart had led his horse up the last part of the ridge. Slim was tired, but had shown no sign he would quit as long as Mart asked him to go on. The rider gently pushed the horse in under the rough asylum. It cut the wind and only a portion of the falling snow filtered between the criss-crossed branches. Mart dared not remove the saddle. There was no question of a fire. He left the shelter and ripped a mixture of dry and late summer green grass from beneath the broken canopy of the forest. He brought several loads back to the lean pony. Slim started with gusto, but lost his enthusiasm before he had completely depleted the supply of makeshift hay. He stood with head slightly lower than his withers. Mart ate the remainder of the box of cookies quickly to regenerate.

Mart gave in to fatigue, too. He was tired and his ribs ached mercilessly. Where the .22 calibre bullet had ripped his skin alternated between sting and itch. He dared not remove his slicker to investigate. The storm had transformed from wet and melting to cold and dry.

Mart sat in beneath the fallen logs and tried to watch. The wind made it impossible to use sound to any degree as a warning. Once he saw a headlight puncture the gloom below in the distance. He imagined the gunmen were frustrated with their failure. Would they remain out in the storm or retreat to return in the morning?

CHAPTER 42 ✷ CRASH THE LINE!

MART SLEPT IN fitful bouts. Slim remained motionless for much of the night. When the horse stirred, Mart fetched more grass. At least the pony would not die with an empty belly. Mart could not eat grass and was likely to meet his end hungry. The cookies were empty calories used up quickly at these below-freezing temperatures. The night was colder than the preceding one, but Mart was not quite as wet. The occasional motion while foraging for the gelding helped to fight the cold. The snow ended halfway through the night. An additional five or six centimetres had fallen.

The sky began to open up just before dawn. What little heat that was left trapped near the ground fled upward and Mart began shivering uncontrollably again. Slim was munching the latest instalment of dry grass. A snowshoe hare still in its brown summer pelage hopped past. Slim raised his head, interrupted his mastication and stared momentarily. When he returned to his meagre breakfast the hare dodged away. Mart was not even tempted to kill the animal for food. He could hardly risk the noise of a shot or the comfort of a fire.

The slow-moving cattle and the new snow had obliterated his tracks. Nevertheless it would not take Mantracker to locate him, particularly once he moved. But was the crew anywhere nearby?

Mart brushed little patches of snow from his horse and tack. He addressed the animal softly. "Maybe they've given up and headed south." But he did not hold out much hope for that.

Mart looked northward and pleaded, "Be careful, Kent!" He silently hoped Tom had left Reg at home. He was terrified his friends had already encountered the armed men.

The light came fast as the clouds in the east had almost altogether dissipated. Mart had to tighten the cinch one notch on the off side. Slim was becoming more so. Mart tugged the latigo snug and prepared to mount. Today was sink or swim. The slender horse and rider would either make it out or it would be over.

Mart looked down the slope. He suspected that was where the enemy was lying in wait if they were still here at all. He looked up toward the top of the ridge. There was nowhere to go that way either. All he would find is the weather station tower.

Mart glanced south and then back up to where he knew the silver metal of the tower often glinted back on summer days. Was there some way to communicate from there? Perhaps if he damaged the tower the lack of transmission would alert someone.

Mart shook his head. It might be days before a technician was sent to repair the thing. It was a weather station, not a communications tower. He would be dead by then and all he would get for the effort would be the word 'vandal' on his gravestone. He would be forever remembered for destruction of public property.

Mart gazed south again. There was another way to get swift attention. Rumours were rampant about what type of sophisticated surveillance gear was concealed along the 49th parallel. Mart was certain there was some remote sensing equipment along the US boundary, but suspected its volume and effectiveness was somewhat exaggerated. All that being true, it may be his only hope.

"Get out your passport, boy," was Mart's admonition to the wiry bay.

If he could reach the border, perhaps at the Whiskey Bottle Gate, he could cross illegally and hope that he was noticed. Repenting of the breach of national security in a Montana jail was preferable to innocence in death. He and Slim were going to make a run on the border!

Mart led Slim out from under the snags. He mounted and kept to a walk. He would attempt caution at least until he suspected the presence of an adversary. He tacked up the slope in an effort to reduce the grade. He angled upward and slightly south.

In less than half an hour, Mart heard the sound of rotors. The steady whop-whop of the blades was coming in from the east.

"Bless Tom Wyslik!" ejaculated the relieved horseman. The rancher had probably panicked after being unable to locate Mart for a whole day. Perhaps the criss-cross of tire tracks in the snow at the corrals and beyond had led to some suspicion.

Mart directed the Arabian into a small clearing and looked into the waxing eastern light. The reflection off the snow made him squint and cup a hand beneath the brim of his hat and against his right cheek. It took several seconds to locate the aircraft. It was flying low, but directly toward the pointed toe of Hog's Back.

It was a sleek, dark helicopter. That surprised Mart. He was used to the typical white-with-stripes or brightly coloured machines Mart associated with companies usually contracted by government agencies. Perhaps it was a government owned aircraft. He got a lump in his throat when he realized that perhaps yesterday's activities had aroused the border officials. Why he should be nervous about that, he did not know. "Homeland Security is our friend!" he muttered to reassure himself.

Mart stood in the stirrups and started to wave. It was unnecessary. The chopper was making a perfect line directly at him. The rancher hesitated and then dropped back into the saddle.

For a search and rescue mission, this team was unnervingly unerring in their trajectory. It was as if they knew exactly where to look.

Mart shivered and then encouraged Slim back under the canopy of several large evergreens. He was surprised at his own paranoia. The horse and rider waited watchfully as the pilot manoeuvred skilfully into the clearing Mart had just vacated. It lowered slowly until snow swirled in miniature tornados and skittered away beneath the trees at the edges. Mart could see only silhouettes through the reflective glass. Then the machine turned abruptly sideways. The passenger door was off.

Mart did not wait to examine the mud-splattered coveralls of the man leaning out through the doorway. He pulled Slim around sharply and put him to the slope, trying desperately to keep a sufficient amount of cover between him and the pursuing chopper. Hearing anything above the sound of the powerful engine and spinning props was almost impossible. However, Mart instinctively ducked his head at real or imagined muffled reports he took for semi-automatic gunfire.

The pilot had no trouble following the movements of the horseman in the open forest. Mart searched franticly for a denser patch. He pushed Slim carelessly and the energetic horse responded willingly. The large flying object did much to encourage the pony's flight.

There didn't appear to be any sufficient shelter on this side of the slope. Mart pointed his horse for the steeper south-facing incline hoping he would spot a thick copse just over the lip. He was near the steep and rocky cliff of the ridge, but spurred his pony over the edge and down the slope. Slim kept his feet by occasionally sliding hocks and hindquarters along the rough ground of the hillside.

While trying to avoid a shattered stump, Slim veered sideways and nearly toppled over. Mart cursed. He was going to kill his horse at this rate. The pony almost slammed into the thicket before Mart tore his eyes from the ground beneath the dancing hooves. They shot into the heavy cover and Mart pulled Slim to a halt. The helicopter shot past, skimming the treetops. Mart could track the craft by sound as it arced wide into the valley of the Glenwood Saw Set Field and came back in for another pass.

Mart was breathing heavily. He didn't know why. It was Slim who had been running. His chest was tight and he was sweating in spite of the below-zero temperature. He shouted an extremely foul oath that startled the panting horse. These thugs were not giving up. They had resources Mart had never dreamed of. Whether their access to men and machinery was due to their oil industry ties or linked to their illegal ventures Mart did not know or care. The fact was he was a ground squirrel and they were the terriers. He had been running scared and the result had been only to prolong the inevitable. He was done running!

The helicopter climbed the slope like a slow elevator. The pilot kept his armed companion facing perfectly toward the incline. Mart had tied Slim in what he hoped was the most opaque portion of the boscage.

The gunman shifted the muzzle of his rifle only minutely to compensate for the motion of the helicopter and to scan the small patch of trees for movement through his scope. Mart spied from behind a narrow but solid trunk. He could see the man search calmly and intently. Would Mart have that kind of nerve to confront his attackers? Now was time to find out. He took a deep breath and stepped out from behind the bole.

The flying gunman squeezed off one hopeful shot at the dark shape just inside the shadows. Then he flapped his hands frenziedly and shouted back at the pilot. Mart could see through the door and recognized the face of the burly Hispanic he had seen with Stimatz. The previous emotionless face showed surprise as he quickly but steadily pulled back on the stick to gain elevation. The reaction was too slow and he knew it.

Mart had seen movies where expert marksmen brought down aircraft with a single strategically-placed shot and then watched the column of smoke tower above the fiery crash. This was definitely not Hollywood and Mart had no idea where a whirlybird was most vulnerable. He had aimed directly at the gunman at first, but shifted and selected the bundle of electronics and wires that poked out just beneath the main rotor.

The small calibre bullet had whizzed past his right knee, but he had hardly flinched. He slowly expelled his breath as he squeezed evenly on the trigger of the Winchester. Uncle Seth would have been proud.

The .30-.30 saddle carbine is tough and its short barrel facilitates mobility – especially on horseback. The abbreviated barrel does not, however, allow for accuracy at great distances. The trajectory is arched and the bullet travels slowly compared to flat-shooting smaller calibres or rounds with more powder to propel the heavy piece of lead farther. This gun was the only one Mart had used to any extent. Although he had not shot for years, the one-time familiarity came back innately once the worn, smooth stock touched his cold cheek.

The small mass of the saddle rifle does little to dampen the recoil. Mart gasped as his bruised side absorbed the kick, but he kept his gaze firmly on his target. A dark round hole appeared in the fibreglass cowling just as the bird bounded out of his view as if sucked up by the inhaled breath of the gods. The black chopper banked west and south. Mart could see or hear no indication that it was severely damaged. All he had accomplished was to frighten the occupants of the aircraft. They had either been unaware he was armed or surprised he had had the guts to fire back.

Mart became aware of the echoed report of his shot. Perhaps he should have thought of that earlier. The seismic gang had been vigilant about keeping the sound of gunfire muted. They wanted to attract as little attention to his murder as possible. Mart had no such requirement for silence.

Mart returned to his horse. Slim's eyes were wide from the fright of the helicopter chase and the sound of rifle shots. The rancher leaned forward and willed his knees to quit shaking.

"Once I quit having this nervous breakdown, we're going hunting, son." Mart was embarrassed by the shaky quality of his quiet threat.

CHAPTER 43 ✳ CORPSE

The helicopter maintained its distance. It shadowed the horseman and adjusted its flight whenever its occupants caught glimpses of the cowboy moving from one thick scrap of forest to the next. Mart headed downhill and west to cut back to the trail that descended from the top of the Hog's Back. He would stick to his plan to cross the international boundary. He had little hope they would allow him to reach his goal.

When Mart emerged onto the path he was surprised to see large animal tracks. The footprints left the trail shortly after Slim began leaving his hoof prints on top of them. They were headed more or less in the direction of the thicket where the domed lodge hid. The dog's tracks were not the only ones along this trail. Knobbed tires had raced up the Mackenzie Cut Line and someone was somewhere ahead of him. Perhaps he could skirt around them in the brush?

He did not have long to wait. In spite of camouflaged jacket and pants, Mart detected the movement ahead. He booted Slim harder than necessary and the little horse sidestepped into the brambles of a rare hawthorn. Mart wasted little time bemoaning his poor luck. He tore free of the thorns and dismounted. He led Slim to a sturdy aspen and wrapped the reins carelessly around the lower branches. Then he moved slightly up the slope until he could spot a section of the path he had just left. An inefficient motor sprang to life to the south and approached rapidly. Mart sighted on a narrow portion of the pathway he could just see through the vertical trunks and lacework of branches. It would be snap shot.

Mart yanked the trigger. Uncle Seth would have been less impressed with this shot. The dark green plastic had materialized quickly and Mart had hoped it was gas tank and not a fender. A metallic clank accompanied the roar of the short muzzle. He had hit neither. The engine faltered, backfired and died. Mart thrashed back to his horse. It was a bad move. The ATV rider had un-slung his weapon and was pinging away at the sound of Mart's retreat. Mart levered another round into the chamber and jerked a hasty shot toward the repeated firing. The gunfire ceased. It gave him adequate time to get to Slim before the firing recommenced.

Mart was moving awkwardly. The ungainly angle at which he had pulled off the last shot had resulted in a lot of pain. He had not held the stock of the rifle firmly against his shoulder when he had fired. The light gun had slammed mercilessly into his upper arm and the shock rippled along his bruised side. Mart remounted clumsily and rode frantically away from the marooned gunman.

During the next hour Mart made two more attempts to run at the border. He could hear another machine moving along the cut line perpendicular to the Mackenzie cut. The rider of the first quad was away from his damaged machine and moving carefully in a semicircle to cut him off. They were not going to let him go any farther south.

Over the following two hours Mart found himself continually pushed back to the northeast until he finally re-emerged from the bush on the Mackenzie line. There were several versions of quad tracks on the trail. However, he had no way of knowing whether there were gunmen ahead of him or behind him. There was a good chance both were true. The helicopter was a constant, although somewhat distant companion. Since Mart had shown he had a rifle and would use it, the big pilot seemed to be using the aircraft more for reconnaissance than for assault.

A deep weariness was making it difficult for Mart to remain vigilant. Slim had had about enough of bushwhacking. Mart made an incautious decision and kept to the trail. He asked Slim to trot and the tractable equine complied.

They made unimpeded progress until they reached the cross fence and entered the Tower Field. Mart reached the top of a narrow rise and was forced to stop his horse. His reaction was slow. It did not matter. The blue Dodge was parked at an odd angle across the narrow path. Mart was surprised to see that the driver had been able to get this far in given the sloppy conditions. He could see nobody to congratulate on the feat. Perhaps they were undetectable inside the tinted glass of the cab. Maybe Stimatz was inside awaiting an opportunity to deliver a verdict on his proposed negotiations.

In any case Mart was done running away from the fight. He reluctantly directed Slim off the path. He was not yet so discouraged he was going to run straight into the jaws of death. He made a sweeping approach to the spot, expecting to be challenged at any moment. He was hoping to sneak past and continue his flight. The quads had backed off since their shaky exchange of fire. He could hear their motors coming up slowly behind him. They had something planned, but his mind was too dull to discern what it was.

Mart caught frequent glimpses of the pickup. There was still no movement from inside. He wondered what kind of reception Stimatz had gotten for his proposed payoff. He let Slim step cautiously out into the path just behind the vehicle. The front tires were still on relatively solid ground. The rear of the truck had skidded off an abrupt slope. Mart acknowledged his good luck and was just about to continue his flight when he noticed a dark stain in the snow behind the box. He was staring at it when a viscous drop fell from the lower portion of the closed end gate and into the blot.

Mart scanned the woods in every direction and listened closely for any nearby sounds. He clutched his rifle. It was half-cocked, ready to pull the hammer back and fire. He moved Slim to stand just off the narrow road and walked tensely to the stranded 4X4. He peaked cautiously over the muddy fender. An orange plastic tarp covered the small load. Mart took another quick look around, reached in and threw back the jumbled tarpaulin. Mart jumped back and then squinted over the side once more. Stimatz gazed back through glazed dead eyes.

There was a neat round hole in the side of the former foreman's head. He was pale, but Mart noted that his greased hair was oddly perfect. Mart made a quick inventory. The only other signs of injury were scraped and bleeding knuckles. The man had fought back before they killed him. Whatever the antagonistic seismic worker's role had been in this mess, he was now a victim of it. The offer to Mart of a cut in the profits was definitely no longer on the table.

Mart walked back to his horse. He stooped to gather the dropped reins when the first pop alerted him that he was no longer alone. Slim jumped sideways. The bullet had hit the pommel of the saddle. Mart held the rifle at his side, spun around, cocked and fired in one smooth motion. He worked the lever action and fired again. Slim had bolted down the trail ahead of him. Mart slid down a shallow embankment and levered another round into the chamber. He had only two or three bullets left. The others were safely in the saddlebags and had departed with the frightened pony.

Several more rounds were fired and sunk into the soil just in front of him or in the woods directly behind. Again Mart was saved by his opponents' use of telescopic sights at close range and through the screening branches. They had come equipped for sniping at a distance, not a running battle in the forests.

Mart could hear scrambling through the trees above and slightly behind him. He could not stay where he was. Up and into the woods ran the tired rancher. He dropped between two fallen logs and lay still.

"¡Él está allí!" one of the gunmen shouted from behind him.

"¡Apresúrese!" another voice responded on the far side of the 4X4.

Mart remained hidden. It was several minutes before he heard a twig snap. He did not wait any longer, but sat up and twisted to face the location of the sound. Mart ignored the stab of pain as he lifted the rifle. A surprised set of deep brown eyes stared back and then up came the man's silenced rifle. Mart snapped a shot and watched the fellow thrust his weapon forward and bore-first into the soft slush and mud. There was a nasal keening sound as he slumped forward. He clutched his thigh and lurched onto his face without attempting to arrest his fall. The man started to cry out and continued to wail. An occasional word in Spanish was uttered.

"¡Ayúdame! Estoy muriendo."

Mart levered another round into the chamber. He faced the path from where he assumed his second assailant would come. Time trickled past more slowly than a delay in a doctor's waiting room. The second man did not approach.

The beseeching cries of the wounded man began to wear on Mart. He vacillated between shooting him again and offering him succour. The moaning must have been even more disturbing for the other gunman. That man finally broke the stalemate and addressed Mart in a heavily-accented voice.

"Go away from there!"

Mart did not respond.

"I go to my friend."

Was he offering to let Mart go so he could help the man the rancher had shot?

"You will shoot me if I get up," Mart finally replied.

"You have a chance. If you go, I will not shoot you."

"You will let me go?" Mart stalled while he assessed the risk in accepting the offer.

"Not far. Horse is gone."

So that was it. The Columbian was giving him momentary respite, although he would soon follow or send his friends. He admired the man's honesty, or was it important to the gunman to keep the threat alive?

Mart's victim was really caterwauling now.

"I will go, but not until you move back."

"No. Go now or I come."

There was one shot left in the carbine. He hoped the remaining pursuers did not suspect he was out of ammunition. Mart cursed quietly, jumped up as quickly as he could and headed north and east paralleling the trail.

The gunman was not as truthful as Mart had hoped. A couple of desperate .22 calibre projectiles sang their high-pitched whine through the canopy just above a crouched and running rancher. Mart spun and fired his remaining round, levered out the shell and foolishly aimed and listened to the sharp click as the hammer snapped down on an empty chamber.

It was tough going. Riding had been jarring, but running over the rough ground and through the thickets was excruciating. Mart continually became short of breath and was forced to stop to allow the heaving of his sides to subside so he could endure the pain.

Mart kept his eye on the trail just visible through the thinning foliage. On each of his frequent stops he listened for approaching vehicles. He had travelled about half a kilometre when he spotted movement out in the road. He dropped onto his knees and fought a moment of nausea.

CHAPTER 44 ✳ SURPRISE!

Scarcely five minutes after determining what was approaching in the narrow, muddy road, Mart heard the cracking of twigs and short bursts of activity coming through the bush behind him. He assumed his earlier benefactor had since shed his benevolence and had again taken up the chase on foot. That hunch was confirmed seconds later when the solitary gunman stepped out into the cut line. The man scanned first eastward, then his angry face and threatening weapon swung southwest toward Mart. He did not raise his gun immediately. A malevolent sneer worthy of any movie villain spread across the dark face of the hunter. "No bullets," he stated confidently.

The next expression on the angry face was one of astonishment as Mart tilted his head sideways toward the tired bay gelding waiting patiently and nearly hidden at the edge of the path. "He had some. Just put down your gun and walk away," Mart ordered.

The man squinted and yanked up the rifle in his hands as he cried out, "You killed Esteban!"

The muffled pfft of the silenced weapon was erased by the bark of Uncle Seth's ancient saddle carbine. Mart rolled off the trail sideways. The pretend seismic worker flew violently backward. A now gun shy Slim shuffled sideways farther into the forest edge.

Mart did not bother to lift his rifle when he raised his head cautiously to survey the scene. He had taken the time to shove only one bullet into the gun. It was again empty. The Columbian's hasty appearance into the Mackenzie line had allowed Mart to take careful aim before commanding the man to put down his weapon. His shot had been true. The hastily-delivered Southwest Seismic sponsored bullet had gone wide.

Mart's adversary was laying flat on his back in the middle of the rough road. Mart ignored him momentarily and hobbled to his horse. Slim had not been hit. Mart's rifle bullets lay scattered in the slush and mud. The discarded box was limp and soggy. Before approaching the victim of his last shot, Mart wiped dry several bullets on the underside of his sweater and then reloaded the Winchester with six of them.

A furtive approach of the downed gunman revealed the rapid rise and fall of his chest. The man was still alive. Mart sensed relief and fear in equal measures.

The Columbian's eyes were wide and searched left and right before focusing on Mart's over the mud-smeared barrel of the .30-.30.

There was a ragged red hole in the front of the man's chest. A crimson stain was spreading beneath him in the snow. He gasped, "Él era mi hermano." Then he hissed in very shaky English, "He my brother." Those were his last words.

Mart stared in shock for few moments and then erupted violently, "Why? You idiot! Why couldn't you just leave me alone? Arrgh!" Mart stomped and fumed for a few seconds then stopped as he remembered that this one and his brother were not the only dangerous men in these woods.

As he shuffled back to his horse, Mart tried to erase the recent gruesome image from his head – the shockingly bright red stain spreading beneath the man in the snow, but most of all the panic and vitality fading from the eyes. Mart understood little of what really was the essence of a man. The actual biological life of a being drained with the blood, but, if it existed at all, it was through the eyes that the soul exited.

Mart dared not tarry longer. He returned to the small saddle horse who had come back to search for his human partner. "It was him or me, Slim. Him or me!" Mart rationalized his actions out loud. He climbed on and stroked the drenched hair of the horse's neck. "Thank you for coming back so it was him."

When they rode past, Slim shied away from the wide-eyed corpse that had been Mart's second fatal victim of the day. Mart mentally did the same. He tried not to dwell any further on his latest violent act. He was given little additional time for relief or remorse.

The helicopter had been hovering half a kilometre to the south. The occupants of the craft had witnessed the fall of their comrades. Anger at the loss or desperation at their failure to rid themselves of a single Alberta bumpkin spurred them into another attempt at shooting him down from the air. The machine was on top of the horse and rider before they had made a hundred metres along the trail.

Mart put Slim to a rocky, wooded hill. The canopy was sparse and Slim was frightened of the staccato sound of the rotors bouncing back off the ground and trees. Several tiny lead projectiles shredded the spiky needles of the spruces. Mart held his rifle up with one hand. The unsteady threat did little to dissuade his attackers.

Mart knew he or his horse would be hit any moment. He threw himself from the saddle and tried not to flinch as the shots fell around him. He aimed up through the skeletal branches of a solitary dead poplar. He did not try to aim for the gunman whose silhouette was thin against the high cloud. Mart pumped a single bullet into the metal belly of the aircraft. There was no change in the attitude of the pilot. He continued to position the gunman directly over Mart. Slim had plunged twenty metres up the hill.

Mart tried to breathe slowly as he took another bead on the riveted black metal. The pilot's seat should be just to the left of centre. The carbine again slammed down onto Mart's shoulder, compressing his fractured ribs. This time the whirlybird faltered, yawing dangerously toward the tall trees on the slope above Slim. Then the pilot corrected almost too quickly and the machine shot up and away from Mart.

The rancher bent over and panted. He coughed twice and was relieved that no blood was visible in the mashed snow at his feet. He remained there for a few moments catching his breath and trying to decide what to do next. He had tried to go west to the park. They had cut him off. He had then decided to go south to the international boundary, hoping Homeland Security would swoop in and take him into custody. He had gotten to within an hour's ride of the line. That was apparently not close enough for even the black helicopter to be recognized as a threat to US security. Now they had hazed him northeast. He was in the middle of nowhere and had no idea where his remaining opponents were.

Slim had never before looked this tired. He was wet with sweat and melted snow. There was mud up all four legs and on his flanks and belly. He stood on the uneven slope with his head low and kept an anxious eye on Mart. It took a lot to spook the experienced animal, but there was no doubt he was almost as nervous as his master. Mart had the depressed feeling they were both doomed. He could not even muster enough energy to rekindle the anger he had experienced earlier.

CHAPTER 45 ✵ SAVING SAVIOURS

Mart and Slim flinched simultaneously. The report of the large-calibre rifle echoed off the Hog's Back. Had the seismic imposters given up their use of silenced firearms? But the shot was too far away. It must have come from somewhere in the direction of the Four Corners. A second shot rang out. And then Mart's heart leapt as the next echo reached his ears. It was a human voice, but he could not understand the words. He cocked his head and listened intently.

"Maaaart!" It was faint and far off.

They had come for him. He could not recognize the voice, although it was sure to be one of his neighbours or fellow grazing lease members.

"Over here. I am..."

Somewhere between Mart and his saviours a small engine sprang to life. The chug-chug of the starter on a second machine followed a moment later just southwest of his location along the line. His assailants were finally giving up and pulling out. Mart almost broke another rib throwing his hands in the air in celebration. He wheezed and hugged his broken chest, but the pained smile remained on his face.

Then the grin faded. The ATV was coming at him. It was moving very fast and would be there in seconds. Mart bolted for Slim, fell, recovered and had just grasped the reins when the quad burst into view. Mart dropped the leather lines and swung his rifle toward the four-wheeler that was making a desperate charge at him. He pulled the trigger before he realized all that was in the chamber was a spent shell. By the time he had pumped it out and was ready to fire, the machine and its rider shot past in a shower of slush. Slim had spun around to face the passing motorcycle, but he did not run away.

Again Mart felt relief. His attackers were making a run for it. However, they seemed to be going out along the same path his rescuers were using to come to get him.

"Damn it!" cursed the battered cowboy. He grabbed for the reins and swung into the saddle. He hated himself for doing it, but he gave Slim both heals, and hard. The little Arabian cast clumps of mud and woodland detritus high into the air as he crouched and scratched for elusive toeholds. Soon he was flat out and skidding along the cut line, taking fallen logs like a Spruce Meadows hopeful.

Mart caught fleeting glimpses of the tracks. The springy rubber tires had banked up mud and slop where they had turned northwest onto the trail leading away from Glanders Flats and toward Four Corners. Mart bumped Slim's off side with his leg and dug the same-side rein into the wet brown neck. The little horse took the bend at a full gallop and lost his footing. Down onto one knee he stumbled. Mart almost lost his seat. He held on with the crook of his knee and a handful of wet, black mane. Slim skidded almost to a stop and scrambled back onto his feet. He took a small detour around a pair of young Douglas firs and ran back onto the trail.

After a clumsy effort, Mart scratched his way back onto the saddle, the reins and mane in one hand, the rifle in the other. He glanced at the weapon and was shocked to see that it was still at full-cock with a live round in the chamber. It was ready to fire. It was sheer luck he had not yet shot his own horse out from under him. Still flying along at an irresponsible rate, he inched his hand along the stock and slid his thumb up over the hammer.

Now came the tricky part. Mart kept pressure on the hammer and pulled the trigger to lower it to the half-cocked safety position. He kept the barrel angled away from the horse and at the ground just in case. The hammer sprang instantly back against his thumb just as Slim hopped a thin stick lying across the trail. The momentary relaxation of pressure by his thumb allowed the hammer to descend slowly, but not slowly enough to stop at the safety. It went all the way to the firing pin. Mart cringed, expecting the rifle to discharge. The gun did not fire. The hammer had hit the firing pin too softly. He yanked the hammer to its safety position halfway back, away from the firing pin. It clicked into place.

The Winchester was not the only thing that was in danger of going off half-cocked. Instead of avoiding conflict, horse and rider were chasing it. Slim and Mart had gained on the quad because its rider had been forced around some of the fallen timber. Mart had no idea what he was going to accomplish. He only knew that at least one, and maybe two, armed men were running straight at his rescuers.

The rider of the ATV made a reckless detour around two fallen trees. Slim cleared the first and then the second just as the Columbian re-entered the trail. The man's peripheral vision registered the horse and rider. He chanced a glance over his shoulder. Mart could read no surprise on the man's face. He simply turned back to the way ahead and punched the accelerator. It was poor timing. The springy wheels bounced over a tree root and when they came down the increased torque of the rapid acceleration caused the knobby treads to spin. The vehicle weaved right, then left and then left the trail altogether. Mart pulled up slightly to watch the quad shoot uphill into the vegetation of a small incline. Slim shot past the out-of-control machine. Mart did not hesitate long. He pushed the tired pony onward, hoping to reach his rescuers before another of his attackers got there.

Then it was Mart's turn to realize a threat had materialized behind him. The motorcyclist previously ahead of him had regained control and the quad was right on Slim's heels. The noise of the approaching machine spurred the little horse onward, but the ATV was gaining quickly. Mart looked back to watch the man swing his rifle under his arm on its sling.

"Stupid!" Mart spit.

The Columbian was taking no chance this time. He was driving right onto Slim's haunches where there was no risk of missing the shot.

There was no way to outrun the machine. The trail was straight and unobstructed. Mart decided to leave the path. He slowed his mount slightly to look for a safe exit. The quad was on top of them instantly. Slim heard the sound of the motor and sensed the aggressive tires almost touching his outstretched hooves.

Mart was surprised by a rough break in the little bay's stride. Had he been hit? Was he finally breaking down? Then there was another significant bump in the otherwise smooth running gait. Mart heard a loud crack and was astonished to detect a rapid reduction in the revolutions of the whining motor pursuing them. He turned his head to watch the quad's right handlebar dig into the muddy tread of the trail and its rider skid on his face off into the shrubs alongside it.

Mart was shocked. Slim had kicked the left handlebar. The machine had tipped at such a velocity that the rider had instantly been planted on the ground. Typically the little horse was so tractable you could run the entire Mountain View Elementary School grade five class between Slim's back legs and he would never even threaten to kick. Nevertheless, the little horse had just saved the both of them by doing exactly that.

Relief flooded Mart's weary mind. It was short-lived. He rounded a sharp corner. What he saw below him in an open meadow made his heart stop. The quad that had fled at the sound of the rescue party's first signal shots was coming to a halt not eighty metres from a group of three horsemen. One of the equestrians was holding a rifle in the air above his head and was hailing the man on the ATV. It was Wyslik. The smaller rider on the second buckskin had to be Reg. Kent's tall roan was nervously prancing sideways in the trail. Mart's blond friend was busy controlling his horse and was oblivious to the danger.

The Southwest Seismic man began to step off the idling machine and was pulling the sling of the rifle from over his shoulders in one smooth motion. Time slowed for Mart. He pulled back hard on the reins and hollered, "Whoa!" Slim sat down in the slush, his back feet and legs sliding in the muck and his front feet running along to compensate for the rapid deceleration. Mart left the seat too soon, throwing the rifle up over the raised bay head and slipping onto his knees and free hand. He gasped with pain as the impact of his fall transferred from his outstretched arm to his broken ribs. He fought back tears and a gasp. As soon as he had slowed, Mart knelt up, threw the rifle to his shoulder, pulled back the hammer and took aim.

There was no breeze for which Mart had to compensate, but the shot would be at least 200 metres – too far for very accurate shooting with a saddle carbine. Mart compensated by sighting the bead of the front sight and a small portion of the little metal post that supported it above the V of his rear sight. He then erased that adjustment to compensate for the downhill nature of the shot. He did all this while squeezing gently on the trigger.

The mud-spattered black helmet of the Columbian was the target. Mart felt the recoil punch back against his shoulder. He felt the wrenching of his torn and broken side. However, his focus remained on the shiny black plastic of the headgear. The man had raised his own rifle. He fired, but the small lead projectile smacked the branches of the trees to his left as he spun in the path and slowly sank to his knees.

The trio of horsemen were in the process of reacting to the threatening firearm when the bark of the .30-.30 reached their ears. Instead of aiming his own rifle, Tom threw a leg over the saddle horn and slipped from the off side of his tired buckskin. He dropped the Savage .30-06 and used his right hand to claw at Reg and drag him from his horse. Kent spurred his unruly mount off into the trees and dismounted.

Tom was lying on top of Reg, grasping frantically in the wet snow for the dropped rifle when he saw the gunman fall. Kent was on foot and halfway back to the Wysliks when he realized the ATV rider had crumpled next to his machine. He slowed and scanned the trail above for the source of his salvation. His blue eyes met the familiar brown ones still squinting over the sights of his out-of-date weapon. The gaze only lasted a second before Kent sprinted toward the quad idling in the trail. He yanked the .22 calibre rifle from the convulsing grasp of the Columbian.

"Come on, boy," Mart commanded gently, rose and limped stiffly down the hill. Slim obediently followed, his head held low and at an angle to avoid stomping on the dragging reins.

Kent had stopped covering the fallen Southwest crewman with the man's own rifle and was instead bent over him when Mart arrived. Tom and Reg had walked their horses up to the injured man as well.

"Reg, run back and bring up my horse, will you, please?" Kent's voice was gentle. "There's an old sweater in the off side saddlebag that I can use for a bandage."

Tom looked relieved that the wide-eyed boy had been given a task to soften the shock of what he had just witnessed.

Kent watched Reg tear his terrified gaze from the fallen drug-runner and stagger toward the nervous roan. Kent then turned to Mart, "What in the hell have you been up to? You sure seem to be pissing people off on a regular basis lately." His tone was stern. When he saw the physical pain and hurt expression on Mart's mud-stained visage, he repented his rough words. Impulsively he stepped over to the shorter man, grabbed his shoulders with both hands and drew him into an awkward hug.

Mart gasped as his broken ribs were compressed against those of his friend. He was released quickly, more from embarrassment than from a reaction to his pain. "I'm just a bit relieved to see you, too, Kent." He turned toward Tom. "Thanks for coming to get me, Tom,"

"I guess…You're welcome," Wyslik stammered. He was looking from Mart to the wounded man and back again, still lost given the lack of explanation.

"Here, K-Kent." Reg thrust the old sweatshirt into Kent's hands. It was a difficult transfer as the big roan pulled back and stretched the teenager's arm to its limit in order to hand the grey cloth to the rancher-turned-medic.

Kent bent over the injured man. He was forced to flip the man onto his stomach to get at the ragged hole in his shoulder. There was no exit wound. Tom instinctively bent to hold the man's face out of the snow. The Columbian was barely conscious.

"Necesito un médico. Por favor. Por favor, señor. Necesito a un medico," the man mumbled and then faded back into unconsciousness.

After they had gently propped the wounded man onto his uninjured side, Tom got on his mare and headed for high ground with his cell phone.

"Try to get Constable Boissoneau or Sergeant Dietrich," counselled Mart. "They'll know why if you mention my name," offered Mart at Tom's odd expression.

Tom shrugged and continued his search for cellular service.

"What is going on here, Mart?"

"It was the seismic crew – or part of it." Mart began. He spoke to the back of Kent's head while the blond man continued his ministrations to Mart's victim. "They chased Wendell because he had found out how they were smuggling drugs in from across the line."

"Why didn't he go to the cops?"

"I doubt he actually knew what they were up to, just enough to get the smugglers scared. When they thought I was getting wise to the operation, they targeted me."

"The fire?" Kent turned to Mart and raised a dark eyebrow.

"That and about twenty-four hours of chasing me all over hell – Hell's Kitchen."

"What's with the helicopter?"

"Damn!" ejaculated Mart looking in the direction Wyslik had ridden. "I should have told him to get the RCMP to go after the pilot. I think he must be the boss – or at least the local head man."

"Tom'll probably have wits enough to mention the chopper." Kent offered.

"They killed Stimatz. He was the real Southwest Seismic boss. The others just used his ties to the industry to get legitimate access to the border. He is up there another kilometre in the bed of his own 4X4."

"I guess you're going to have quite the interview with the police."

"They might ask to have a visit," Mart turned to see Kent's habitual grin spread across his perfect features.

CHAPTER 46 ✸ HAVEN TO HAVEN

They had waited for more than an hour in the small meadow. It had been the sergeant who had arrived with a medical crew and a Stars Air Ambulance. The skilled pilot had dropped the machine onto the trail with only a few metres of propeller clearance on either side.

The medics had dressed the gunshot wound and administered a couple of shots with hastily-prepared hypodermic needles. Kent had looked away during these last procedures. Mart smiled to think there might be a chink in the glossy armour of perfection.

The craft flew away with its new burden. The crisp RCMP member radioed for a law enforcement reception at the other end of the flight. The man was in no shape to create much of a security problem en route.

"Mr. McKinnon, are you well enough to give me just some basic information about what went on here?" she asked.

"Well you're kind of stuck here for a while, aren't you?" Mart asked.

"For an hour or so, yes. Then we'll both get a ride out."

Mart glanced at Slim. The small pony had sidled up to the youngest buckskin mare and was standing very still, eyes half closed and head low.

"No damn way!" The words spurted out before he had thought through how ungrateful they would sound.

The sergeant's expression was one of hurt surprise.

"I am sorry," Mart began in a much softer voice. He pointed to Slim. "That little horse saved my life, and I darn near had to kill him to keep ahead of those murdering bastards. I am walking out with him."

Kent interjected. "We can lead…" He did not continue. Mart's expression warned him off.

"Please. I can do it. My legs are fine and there's not much anyone can do for my ribs. I am pretty sure there are a couple broken."

"I don't think it is wise for you to ride out that far," Dietrich observed.

"I won't be riding," Mart stated.

The sergeant eyed him curiously, and then looked at the game little horse.

"We'll be with him." Kent had joined Mart's side.

Dietrich said nothing for several seconds. Then she broke into a disarming smile. "Then so will I."

After a quick radio call they headed north. Another team would fly in and collect firearms and locate the injured smugglers. Mart gave directions to Stimatz and the blue pickup.

Both Mart and the sergeant reluctantly took a turn on Tom's and Kent's horses. It had become obvious they would be thrust physically into the saddles if they didn't agree to share the walk out.

Dietrich got her report. Mart spilled out the entire story for the benefit of the RCMP member and for Kent and the Wysliks. The sergeant got word by radio that the black helicopter had been found abandoned near the Del Bonita border crossing and that the big Hispanic and his supporting gunman were missing.

"Your shot must have given the pilot a superficial wound of some type. There was a bullet hole and also some blood on the seat," Dietrich reported.

There was a white RCMP SUV next to Mart's pickup and trailer. Here is where the sergeant parted company with the ranchers. Mart had insisted that a medical examination could wait. He promised to go to emergency soon.

"I'm very relieved that you are OK," she said and placed a warm hand on Mart's shoulder. "I'll be in touch.

Tom and Reg Wyslik loaded their horses and Kent's in their outfit. Slim stepped quietly into Mart's. Kent drove Mart home. The dark rancher fell asleep shortly after they started rolling and did not awaken until Kent pulled into the Gwynn home place yard. There Kent sent Mart to the house for a shower and to bed. Mart started to argue about it. He wanted to care for his horse. Kent's expression made it clear there would be a fight. Mart reluctantly left the animal in Kent and Reg's care, but not before taking off his hat and placing a muddy forehead against the equally stained and matted fur of the slim neck. Tom helped Mart to the house and played nursemaid until the battered and weary man was wrapped in a clean quilt on top of Aunt Emma's soggy double bed. The walls of that little house seemed familiar again and Mart sighed in his contentment before succumbing to fatigue.

CHAPTER 47 ✳ MOVE

When Mart finally found his battered Timex discarded at the edge of the bathroom sink, he was embarrassed to see it was already past nine o'clock. He was even more humiliated to discover Tom had scrubbed the room clean after Mart had shed his sopping and soiled clothes all over the bathroom floor. The tough cattleman had even mopped up the mucky trail leading there from the front door.

To further his consternation, his morning chores were already done, right down to an overfeeding of the barn cat. Had Kent or Tom returned, or had some other neighbour slipped quietly in and out of the barnyard while he lazed in bed? There were people to thank who would not expect any recognition whatsoever. Mart rethought his discomfiture and decided to be a gracious recipient of the charity.

Slim was hanging over the gate next to the shabby stable. Skip was grazing a short distance away.

"Good morning, little guy," Mart cooed, looked around to make sure no one was watching, and then added, "We made it out alive. What do you think of that?" He stoked the solid jawbone of the Arabian.

Mart inspected the several superficial wounds the small horse had acquired from their reckless dashes through the brush. He paid particular attention to the nasty gash left by the bullet that had grazed his rump. Kent had applied some Dettol. The residue was obvious. Mart would continue to treat the injury over the next few days to avoid any infection. There would be a scar, but the horse seemed completely sound otherwise. Mart remembered his own bullet wound. It had been the least of his few injuries so he had forgotten to even mention it to the businesslike female cop.

The yellow tape was no longer around Mart's fire-gutted mobile home. He slipped in and got some clothes and headed for Cardston in the Toyota. He was halfway through some preliminary paperwork at the emergency room when he mentioned offhandedly the bullet wound to his shoulder. The wrinkled eyes of the receptionist flew open and he was escorted directly into the examination room. It took fifteen minutes of persuasion and a call to Sergeant Dietrich before the attending nurses and physician would simply treat him and agree to release him an hour later. Mart could tell they perceived him as a crook and a victim interchangeably before the RCMP cleared his story.

Mart was met in the hospital parking lot by the open smile of Constable Boissoneau. "How are you feeling, Mart."

"Kind of like road-kill, Eric."

"Pat sent over the report." Eric handed Mart a neatly typed set of sheets. "The sergeant." Eric clarified at Mart's quizzical look.

Mart nodded, read it through and asked for a pen to sign.

"Did you find the big guy who was in the chopper?"

Eric looked dismayed. "Not a sign of him." Then his mood lightened. "But we got three others who were involved and my colleagues in Maple Creek busted another whole operation that had been doing these illegal crossings in Saskatchewan. We have teams looking all through the farmland along the US boundary east and west of here."

"I guess that's good news."

"You will be asked to be at the trials." Boissoneau looked apologetic.

Mart simply shrugged. "Thanks for not treating me like a paranoid idiot. Tell the sergeant that, too, will you?"

"We did some more checking. These were dangerous men. The pilot and one other guy were ex-military. The others were... amateur thugs, I guess you would say – small time offenders here illegally. You were lucky to not be killed, Mart."

Mart thought back to old Wendell Jacobsen's witticism. "Nah! I had a good horse under me."

Eric did not fully understand, but grinned back.

It was late afternoon when Mart stepped into Aunt Emma's house and deposited two overfull bags of groceries. He muttered as he plugged in the old refrigerator. He should have done that before he left. Did it even still run?

There was a small white box and a note on the kitchen table. The note had his old mobile number on it and this simple message, "Remember to turn the dang thing on!!!!" Mart opened the box. In it he found a brand new cellular phone.

Tom, Reg and Sheila stopped by that evening. Tom and Reg moved the washer and dryer, the television and all of Mart's clothes over to the house. They were practically rude when they refused his help. Reg called him a gimp to his face. Sheila dusted and scrubbed while Mart kept her company and ate the plate of leftover roast beef, potatoes and gravy she had brought. She produced an entire apple pie just for him.

Tom and Reg joined them for a short time afterward. Reg seemed to really open up when Mart reluctantly filled in some of the details of his flight from the Southwest Seismic crew.

"Your little horse is pretty tough. I thought he was too small for all that."

"Slim is as tough as they come. Arabians are known for being the best endurance racers."

"Can we get an Arabian, Dad?"

Tom rubbed his knobby hand across his face. He looked at Reg with an odd smile. The man raised some of the best cattle horses in the country. He was a Quarter Horse breeder through-and-through. "I don't think so, Reg."

Sheila laughed out loud.

CHAPTER 48 ✳ CHOICE

MART SPENT THE next couple of days setting up his new residence, doing easy chores and recovering his strength. He expended a certain amount of energy, too, fending off the attentions of well-meaning and curious neighbours. The story had broken on local news broadcasts and even national all-news channels. He had just beaten the zealous news anchors to breaking the news to his mother. It took all his persuasion and her aversion to sharing a very nasty late summer cold with him to convince her to stay at home. Even Walter Taylor argued the need for a trip to Mountain View over the shoulder of his sniffling wife.

By the time the weekend had arrived, Mart's celebrity had worn thin. His neighbours were back to treating him like the dusty bachelor cowboy he had always been. Even Tina Taylor had agreed to put off her pilgrimage to the home place until Thanksgiving.

There had been one very noticeable exception to the attention the extended community had shown him. Mart had yet to hear a peep from Becky Sorenson. He had not dared inquire after her. Kent had continually been a looming presence. Finally Mart had learned she had flown to Halifax the very same evening he had spent with the birds in the Polecat Chateau. Her mother had planned a trip to visit a sister there. Becky and a cousin had gone along. Mart was unsure whether to be relieved that she was not a present complication, or reassured that she had not completely forsaken him.

There was a Friday night dance at the Cardston Legion. There were few places in that dry town where alcohol was served, but the Legion always got a liquor license for their events. It meant that the parties there got a little livelier than did your run-of-the-mill dances in the town and in the county communities.

Mart parked the faded yellow car several rows back from the doorway. He slipped in the door behind a gaggle of boisterous eighteen to twenty-year-olds. He went straight to the back of the hall where several tables were set up. Only one was unoccupied. There were several empties on it. Mart decided to sit and see who showed up. He would ask if they minded sharing the spot.

Mart was an excellent dancer. No one would ever know it. His mother had dragged him to every local Medicine Hat hoedown and musical social she could find an excuse to go to. Walter had two left feet and Tina spared her spouse the embarrassment at her son's expense. Mart could jive, waltz and two-step with the best of the crowd. His polka was exceptional. However, Mart never got up the courage to actually ask anyone to dance. When they asked him, he would agree to dance, but he always shyly hid the extent of his talent.

Mart came for the music. A local group was reeling out new country and old rock classics. There was the regular assortment of a few great dancers – mostly older couples – and some cowboys who insisted on two-stepping to everything. Many of them danced the same fast tempo to every song regardless of the real beat.

As Mart sat quietly tapping a foot he was instantaneously enveloped from behind in the odour of subtle perfume and a pair of slender arms around his shoulders. Becky's soft cheek was against his and her loose hair spilled across his neck. He gave an involuntary shudder.

Becky spun around and dropped onto the chair next to his. She grabbed both his sweaty hands and stared into his eyes from a hand's breadth away. "Marty. I heard what happened. That must have been awful!"

"Er...yeah. It was something all right."

"Are you OK? I heard you were shot."

"Uh...just kind of grazed me."

"Where, Marty?" However, she did not let him explain or show her. She slid the chair closer and wrapped her small hands around the back of his neck. She leaned her flaxen head against his dark, curly forehead. She held him there for a moment.

A perfectly polished pair of boots appeared just left of Becky's chair. Mart knew to whom they belonged and pulled back almost violently. Becky was almost pulled from where she was perched on the very edge of her chair. She tipped forward and was forced to release her grip around the back of Mart's neck.

Mart slowly lifted his eyes to look directly into the smoking blue orbs of Kent Lindholm. Kent did not speak. He just looked expectantly at Mart as if to demand an explanation.

Becky did not notice Kent. Instead she took Mart's retreat to be his habitual shyness. While Mart sat frozen in place like a doe in a spotlight, she advanced and redirected his face to hers. Her lips met his and fire raced through the cowboy's arteries.

"Mart, get up from there!" Kent ordered.

Becky almost swivelled off her chair. Her expression was one of complete surprise. "Kent?"

"Kent," echoed Mart.

Kent did not wait. He turned on his heel and walked diagonally across the half-filled dance floor.

Becky looked at Mart. "I've never seen Kent act like that."

"You shouldn't be so surprised, Becky."

"What do you mean?"

Mart did not answer that question. "I need to go." He got up and followed Kent's trajectory to the door. A middle-aged couple stopped short and glared at Mart for being the second oaf in a row to interrupt their smooth revolution of the floor.

Becky scooted along behind and slightly to the side of Mart. "What's going on? Are you two fighting?"

Mart stopped just short of the exit. "Are you kidding, Becky? You really don't know what the problem is here?"

Becky's expression was one of complete bafflement and innocence.

Mart grabbed her wrist roughly. "Then I think you better come along."

Kent was not immediately outside the door. He was just visible at the edge of the glare produced by the bare 100-watt bulb of the entry.

Mart had relaxed his grip on Becky's arm, but still trailed her along.

Kent stepped up to meet them. "Let go of her, Mart!"

Mart opened his hand and Becky stood there beside the two bristling cowboys.

"You're going to tell me that this is all innocent and accidental, aren't you?!" Kent was leaning forward, his face only centimetres from Mart's.

"Kent, you are getting this all wrong."

"Bullshit. Don't lay this on Becky."

Mart turned his attention to the beautiful blond. "Please tell him, Becky. Tell him you kissed me. Tell him about our trip to Waterton and..."

Kent's hand shot out. He grabbed Mart's shirt collar and yanked it so that Mart had to look into his eyes. The ache was back in the ribs and beneath. Mart had never seen Kent look this way. Even in bad situations the man kept his cool. Not this time. There was distain, no, hate, in the cruel twist of his mouth. His eyes were reflected almost red in the oblique light. The veins in his neck were bulging. Mart felt fear.

"Shut up! Just shut the hell up! I have told you before not to put the blame on her, you spineless, stupid bastard!"

Kent pushed Mart back, but kept his grasp on Mart's clothes. He drew back his left hand. It was made into a fist. He did not throw the punch. Instead he shoved Mart violently back. Mart's ribs crackled like cellophane wrap.

"Stop, you two! Just stop it!" Becky's eyes were closed and her hands were over her ears.

Mart recovered clumsily from the shove and the shock of Kent's verbal and very nearly physical assault. Both he and Kent stared at the red face of the young woman.

"It shouldn't be this way!" she squealed. "I spent most of high school wondering which one of you would finally have the guts to be more than just my pal." The way Becky said the last word made it sound pathetic. "I gave up on you. I found someone who knew what romance was all about. He swept me off my feet."

Becky looked from Mart to Kent and back again. Mart was still reeling from Kent's aggressive attack. Kent's face was red, but his hostile posture had relaxed slightly.

"I soon learned that candy, flowers and soft words are not all I needed. I want someone who can be my friend, too. The past couple of years all I could do was to think of you and how much I wanted to be with you."

There was a long pause. It was Mart who broke the silence. "Who?"

Becky looked at him as if she did not understand.

Mart tried again. "Which one of us?"

Kent turned his attention entirely to the beautiful young woman. "Tell him, Becky. Explain that you were just being his friend. He got it wrong."

Becky stared back at Kent. She did not immediately respond.

Kent took only a few moments to interpret the delay. He looked back at Mart. Mart could tell he felt like a fool. "I am sorry, Kent. I tried to warn..."

"Don't! You have been needling your way between us for years. Whatever you have done has just confused her. I never thought you could be so underhanded."

Mart was aghast. In spite of Becky's admission that she had feelings for Mart as well, Kent's pride was not allowing him to see her deceit – or confusion. Both.

Kent then turned on Becky. He was not threatening. Nevertheless, it was apparent he was demanding she make a declaration. "Becky. Tell him it's me – it's us."

Becky recovered quickly. "No! Don't tell me how to think! I always knew I had this decision to make. I have to choose if it will be you or Mart."

Kent's face betrayed both astonishment and suffering. For the first time in his life he was not in control of a relationship. He would be left to dangle on the same thin filament at the end of which Mart had been dancing for the past two weeks. Becky was in charge. She would dash the dreams of one or the other of the two friends or leave them both to twist in torment.

Mart had no hope for an outcome where he could truly prevail. It was unlikely Becky would choose him over Kent. Whether she did, or did not, his friend was lost to him. Years of relying on Kent to allow him to inhabit the periphery of his social life would end. The knowledge that there was always at least one person upon whom he could depend was fading in these few instants. A deep depression settled on Mart and his dark brow furrowed with the weight of it.

Kent stepped toward Becky. There was pleading in his voice. "You have to choose now, Becky."

Becky stepped back. "Don't push me. It's my life. I will take the time I need to make up my mind. It's up to me to decide."

It was then that Mart's thoughts drifted to his conversation with his mother. She had warned him that being right didn't necessarily bring success with it. Winning Becky meant losing

Kent. He could not truly win that way. But maybe there was a way to cut his losses – and Kent's.

Mart spoke softly and directed his words to Becky only. "No. I will choose."

Becky's eyes widened. She was silent.

Kent broke that silence. "Don't meddle in it, Mart! You can't make this decision for her. I won't let you try to influence her any more than you already have."

Mart continued to look only at Becky. She was the only woman he had ever really wanted. She was beautiful and she was the first to show him the kind of attention he craved. He had fallen in love with her in twelfth grade and it had never worn off. He closed his eyes and remembered his best times in school and since then. However, it was not Becky's beguiling smile that appeared and reappeared in his memories.

Mart opened his eyes and kept them directed at the object of his infatuation. But it was to Kent he directed his pronouncement. "No, I will choose." His eyes fell to the gravel at his feet. "I choose Kent." With that Mart spun on the heel of his scuffed boot and walked away through the parked cars.

CHAPTER 49 ✳ BREAKDOWN

It was difficult to find the tiny car amid all those SUVs and pickups – and through the blur created by the unmanly tears in his eyes. Mart fumbled for the keys. He dropped them twice before he opened the door, fell into the seat and shoved them into the ignition. He twisted the keys and the starter buzzed – and buzzed. The engine would not catch. Mart twisted the keys back and forth, attempting to get the motor to fire. He was desperate to escape. Several minutes of repeated futile attempts, engaging and re-engaging the starter, made no difference. The car would not start. The battery was beginning to fail.

Mart stopped trying. He stopped everything. He leaned his damp face against the steering wheel and gave himself up to despair. He had just sacrificed his dream of Becky. Had it really made any difference? Kent may feel relieved. Mart was now out of the way. He and Becky could make a life together. However, would either of the two ranchers ever feel comfortable around the other from now on? It would be unlikely they could socialize in any way when Becky was around. It was doubtful the hurt and tension would ever fade.

Mart emitted a soul-wracked sigh. He remained leaning against the cracked plastic of the wheel. Then he was startled abruptly out of his misery by a loud knock on the glass of the driver's side window. He sat bolt upright and looked through the slightly fogged glass at the face of Kent Lindholm.

Mart self-consciously wiped the tears from his eyes with his right hand as he struggled to crank down the sticky window.

Kent stared off toward the dance hall. "You really need to unload this scrap heap." He fidgeted with his own key ring and gazed off toward the mountains silhouetted against a mostly dark sky. "C'mon, I'll give you a lift."

Mart gave up trying to hide his tear-stained cheeks and stared blankly back at Kent. Kent glanced at his battered friend. Then he diplomatically gazed off over the hood of the car. He guessed at Mart's unasked question.

"She's gone home."

Mart still sat in silence.

Kent released a weary groan. Then he barked a bitter explanation. "I chose you, too, you ungrateful son-of-a-bitch. Get out of the car. I'm parked over there." He walked away. As Mart watched him go, he heard the tall rancher mutter, "Why the hell I did..?"

CHAPTER 50 ✳ GONE TO THE DOGS

THE ODD JINGLE of the phone startled Mart. He almost stomped all over the cat in his haste to get the thing out of his pocket. He silently cursed his panic. It was totally uncalled-for. It wasn't on fire, it was just ringing.

"Hello."

"Mart. For some reason I cannot fathom, a few of the old gang wants to get together to celebrate the gods' miraculous sparing of your miserable life. Billy Kratz has offered to sacrifice his house for the blow-out."

"Seriously?"

"Yes, seriously. So are you going to be difficult? Will I have to hogtie you and bring you along in the back of the truck?" said Kent.

"If you think you can."

"Don't tempt me. It really would be quite gratifying. You're not exactly on my list of favourites and it would do a lot toward my getting over it all."

Mart sighed. "When is this happening?"

"Tonight, around eight."

"OK. I'll try to be on time. I have a bit of riding I need to do. Shall I pick you up?"

"Leave your jalopy in my yard and I'll drive the rest of the way. My walking shoes are in the shop."

Mart grinned into the telephone. "Snob!"

"Stuff it!" Kent spat back. There was a short hesitation on the line. "Mart."

"What is it," Mart shot back, enjoying the old bantering.

"Becky will be there."

It was Mart's turn to contribute to the dead air.

"Mart?"

"Still here, Kent." Mart closed his eyes tightly and feigned a nonchalance he knew his friend would not take for sincerity. "Well, that would be the old gang."

There was evident relief in Kent's voice. "See you a bit before eight, then."

"I'll try to get there about then."

Mart grabbed Skip's halter and headed for the top of the pasture. Slim came right over and Skip jogged away. Mart rolled his eyes back and said, "Skip!" sharply.

The big sorrel horse stopped and turned to face the rancher. He allowed the halter to slip over his ears and plodded back to the stable on Mart's heels. Slim dashed about and arrived there before his stable mate.

Mart left Slim leaning over the gate and took Skip in to saddle him. He led the red horse out and was halfway to the trailer when Slim began to whinny. The little bay kept at it while Mart shut the end gate and latched it.

"What has gotten into you?" he asked.

Slim whinnied again in response. Mart leaned against the side of the pickup's box. He watched the dark Arabian pace at the gate. Then he reluctantly opened the trailer, led out the Quarter Horse and took him back to the barn. "You are getting off easy today, big guy."

With Skip still tied in the barn, Mart opened the gate without bothering to halter Slim. To remove all doubt the agile pony shot around Mart and directly into his stall. Mart had been letting the horse recuperate from the two days of rough riding and had used Skip for almost all his ranching chores. Slim was letting him know the vacation was over.

Mart pulled up to the Poll Haven corrals and unloaded his horse. He ran his hand softly along the ridge of flesh that was the scar on Slim's hindquarters. "Let's finish this together, then."

The ground was wet and the ruts muddy. The snow had vanished and the sunny, warm fall weather for which southern Alberta was famous had returned. Mart stopped occasionally to admire the fat cattle he encountered along the way. A warm west breeze was tickling the green and gold aspen leaves. Slim's head bobbed and his glossy black mane danced as he poured all his energy into a brisk pace.

It was just before noon when Mart pushed Slim off the trail and into the brush at Four Corners. The break in the fence was easy to find. Mart pulled the coil of smooth wire from his saddlebag and used his old hammer to pull it through the loops he had formed at the cut ends of the barbed wire. When all three strands were back up, he pointed Slim southwest to cross the Tower Field. Slim made quick work of that stretch of the Mackenzie cut line at a trot. Shortly after crossing into the Glenwood Saw Set Field, Mart started looking for the best route to take him toward the smugglers' secret bower. It took several minutes before he spotted the curved roof of the structure. Kent had started referring to it as the "Drug Mart." Mart smiled. Wendell had prophesied there would be a Poll Haven feature named after Mart should he meet his demise there. Luckily he had cheated and survived. It was Wendell Jacobsen who had really earned that honour – but more for really living there than for merely dying.

"Wait here, fella'." Mart intoned quietly as he stepped down. He retrieved a small cloth bag from his other saddlebag before going the rest of the way on foot. Mart walked cautiously around to the front of the hut. He almost sat down in the bushes as a large black object exploded from the small opening.

The dog ran past Mart and started down a slight slope to the southeast. Mart stood quietly. The animal stopped and stared back apprehensively. Mart was amazed at the size of the gaunt dog. He must have weighed fifty or sixty kilograms even in his semi-starved condition. His coat was of medium length and almost entirely black. There was a hint of dark brown on his muzzle and on his lower back legs. Mart guessed a cross between a Newfoundland and a German shepherd. The mixture of the two breeds had created a monster larger than either.

Mart did not look directly into the yellow-brown eyes. He began talking softly. "It's OK, boy. I won't hurt you. Your friends are gone. You've got to be hungry after all this time. Come have a snack." Mart reached into the bag and brought out several triangular chips of cat food. "Sorry. It's the best I could do," Mart apologized.

The rancher backed away and listened to the breeze and the birds for quite some time before the dog made a move forward. Mart ignored the animal as it walked cautiously up to the small offering, sniffed and gobbled. It backed away again.

Mart was not surprised that the dog was so timid. It would not have been a very successful smugglers' mule if it ran up to every human it saw with tongue out and tail wagging. Mart crouched and poured most of what was left in the bag out on the ground near his feet. He stepped back only a metre from the pile.

The dog looked at the food and then at Mart. It whined nervously. Again several minutes passed before the creature moved toward the reward. It did eventually take the food, but its eyes never left the stranger who was so close.

Mart could see patches of fur that had been rubbed almost to the skin where a heavy pack had been strapped. He speculated that the animal may only have known human kindness as a reward for its assigned task. It had been released to cross the border carrying its load of drugs – probably under cover of darkness. If it had ever been spotted by any sophisticated surveillance gear, it appeared as a small bear or a wolf.

Mart turned slowly to walk away. The movement elicited a low growl from the big black dog. Mart collected the bridle reins. Slim had been watching the proceedings with aroused curiousity, but was all business again once Mart was in the saddle.

Mart glanced back at the dog. "Come on, boy. You've got nowhere else to go."

It was several minutes before Slim's backward twitching ears indicated to Mart that the dog was slowly following. He chanced a look behind. The animal was trotting along twenty metres back, but did not hesitate at Mart's recognition.

The healing would begin for the dog, just as it had for Mart and Kent. Mart frowned when he thought of the discomfort he would experience at tonight's party. He hoped he could keep it together. He would likely not succeed. How would Becky treat him? How would he act when he actually had to face her? He started sweating just thinking about it.

Mart looked back at the dog. The gaunt animal had gained some ground and was trotting contentedly about five metres behind Slim's rapidly falling hooves. The dog would learn to be Mart's friend. He would learn to be Becky's again.

THE END

ACKNOWLEDGEMENTS:

M̲Y HEARTFELT THANKS to the Nelson brothers, Dan and Rick, and to Nolan Romeril for sharing their local traditional knowledge of place names, trails and legends; to Neil Leishman of the Poll Haven Community Pasture Board for providing maps and details on how the association is organized; to John Walburger for providing Poll Haven historical information by way of Roots & Branches, the Mountain View history book; to Robert A. Watt for adding to that information by sharing his Waterton Lakes National Park historical research related to the Poll Haven; to Allen Nelson for the help with Spanish translations; to James Meservy for the encouragement and suggestions; to the people of Mountain View, who still live like true neighbours and who know what the word "community" means; to my childhood friends Randy Mackenzie, Greg Neilson and Max Olsen and their families for letting me tag along and play cowboy when they could use an extra hand – or at least let me believe they could; to my mother, Iris J. Marshall, for allowing me to go when I know she worried; to my father, Charles H. Marshall, who took care of my horses while I was away at school and work; to my children for keeping the rural legacy and general interest in horses alive; and last, but certainly never the least, to my wife, Paula, for putting up with the horse foolishness and my delusions about being able to write.

Printed in Canada